The Liquid Solution

A FROG Spy Thriller

By
M.H. Sargent

ISBN: 9798857786192

Acknowledgments

Every writer needs a top-notch resource and *thank you* is not enough for Shelley Holloway at Holloway House. You are a joy to work with, and you've made each book that much better.

Table of Contents

Prologue

Eighteen Miles South of Lutete, Uganda

Joseph lay on the straw mat and closed his eyes. He was glad Hellen was beside him. It didn't matter that she was dead. She was next to him, as she had been since they'd both been fourteen years old. If he'd had any strength left, he might have tried to carry her outside so they could lie together under her favorite tree. But it was better this way. They'd lived a good, full life together. They would be together in death.

Over the last few months, every single villager had come down with a mysterious flu. In the beginning, the symptoms were quite mild. But as the weeks turned to months, the severity of the illness became considerably worse, leaving no one untouched. Insufferable headaches. Fever. A few died. Then more died. More and more succumbed every day. And not just the elderly or infirm. The youngest among them were dying at a faster pace. Hellen and Joseph had watched their daughter, son-in-law, and two grandsons, ages five and three, slip away before their eyes.

A mass grave was dug, and loved ones wrote the names of those that had passed in a memorial book. Joseph's hands had been shaking when he wrote his family's names. He was thankful for the teachings of the Christian missionaries who had lived in their village during his first eight years of life because they had taught him to read and write. It wasn't really necessary. He was a simple farmer. But unlike others that could only mark an X in the logbook, he was able to write the actual first and last names. Maybe Michael, his only son, now living in Nairobi, would read the entries in the memorial book. More than once, he had been grateful that Michael had been spared this terrible influenza. That was something positive.

Thinking back on how this had all come to pass, he simply couldn't understand why his village had been the victim of such a horrible illness. Why them? Suddenly, his eyes popped open. It was the water! Not an influenza, but the water. The water was killing them! His mind raced. It seemed impossible, but the more he thought about it, the more he knew he was right. But what had gone wrong?

The day the men in yellow trucks had arrived, the villagers had been living their lives just as their forefathers had before them—with no running water or toilets. The villagers walked more than a mile to the nearest well, carrying the oh-so-heavy pots of water back home. There was a common latrine, but the villagers didn't always use it on any regular basis. Yet they were fine. They were a hardy, healthy people.

The men in the yellow trucks proposed creating a proper water system. Like city dwellers have. It wasn't free. It hadn't been offered out of the goodness of their hearts. It had cost the villagers. Most had to take out loans. To save money, many families elected to share an outdoor water tap and a single toilet. But it was still a godsend. Or so they had thought.

Fully alert now, he knew he was correct. It was the water. The water was killing them. In a few months' time, they had all become very accustomed to the marvel of running water. It really was a miracle. Yet something told him it was the cause of this terrible illness. He rolled to his side. His small desk was just a few yards away. He needed to document his thoughts. Someone would come through the village and find not a soul alive. They needed to know what happened.

With great effort, he got to his feet. It took all his strength to get to his desk. He sat heavily in his chair and waited to catch his breath. Finally, he found a clean piece of paper, took up a pen, and started writing.

His nose started to run, so he put the pen down. It rolled off the desk. The desk had never been level. He wiped his nose with the back of his hand, astonished to find blood. Deep red blood. He needed to finish writing. He bent over to retrieve the pen and toppled from the chair.

He was dead before he hit the floor.

Chapter One

Amsterdam, the Netherlands ~ Five Months Later

Adam Patterson tapped his phone lying on the table in front of him. It immediately woke and displayed the time: 10:11 a.m. He was sitting at one of the café's four outdoor patio tables that faced the street. The only other table now occupied was taken by two older women. One wearing a plastic rain hat, although there was no call for rain. She had a pull-cart next to her. Probably going grocery shopping after her morning tea, which meant she lived nearby. He picked up his coffee cup and took a sip as he once again checked his surroundings. Just as he had been trained to do many years before.

Nothing. The quiet street remained just that—quiet. In the early morning hours, it was used as a shortcut to bypass the heavily traveled boulevard nearby. But at this time of day, it was an ordinary street again with a steady stream of vehicles, but too few to create a logjam. There were the usual scores of motorcyclists passing by and even more people on scooters. And while there were bicyclists—there were always bicyclists—not one even slowed as they cycled past the café.

His contact was supposed to arrive by bicycle. A red bicycle. That's all Adam knew. He didn't know the man's age, skin color, height, weight, nothing. Truthfully, he didn't even really know it would be a man. His only contact with the person had been via email. The contact had called himself Matthew, explaining the tie to the King James' Bible verse Matthew 24:21-22, which spoke of great tribulation—suffering to the point that "no flesh would be saved." End-of-days stuff.

It was sort of hard to believe the "no flesh would be saved" part. No flesh anywhere? Anywhere in the world? It was a pretty big world. Biblical scholars thought that Jesus had been referring

3

to what came in 70 A.D. when Romans laid siege to Jerusalem. Other scholars argue that, since Jesus did not return to earth at that time, he may have been looking far into the future. A future that could be today, considering mass destruction was readily available with NBC weapons—nuclear, biological, and chemical. All of which could wipe out everyone. Heck, the COVID-19 pandemic was just a small sample of the mayhem a biological weapon could bring about.

Normally, this guy's end-of-the-world reference would be dismissed as lunacy. But he had given Adam the exact time and location of where a suicide bomber was going to strike in Tel Aviv. That information was given to an Israeli anti-terror unit and the attack had been thwarted, saving scores of lives. That tip alone vaulted Matthew into FROG's top-tier ranking of credible sources.

Last week, Matthew had specified the time and place for today's meeting. Adam had immediately scoped out the café and found twelve tables inside, restrooms toward the back, and a back door that led to a narrow alley with a small dumpster and a single parking spot. However, the next day, Matthew changed things around, saying they should meet out front and for recognition purposes, he would be arriving on a red bicycle. Which was why Adam now dutifully sat at an outside table, at this particular café, at exactly ten in the morning.

But Matthew was now eleven minutes late. FROG protocol demanded that when a new contact was ten minutes late, the meeting was to be immediately terminated. But Adam wasn't very good at following protocol. He decided to give Matthew another four minutes.

Then and only then would he follow FROG protocol to move to his secondary position. In this case, the second floor of the public library down the street. If the table he wanted was available there, he would have a good view of the café's outside tables. Not ideal, but good enough. Provided he got the table he wanted.

The waitress, a young woman with a sleeve tattoo on her left arm, exited the café's glass entry door and hurried past, slapping the bill on the table. It annoyed him that she hadn't bothered to ask if he wanted anything more. Not that he did; it was time to leave. He stood, opened his wallet, and pulled out enough cash to cover the coffee, a scone he had swiftly devoured in a few hungry bites, and a respectable tip. He placed the cash on the table and used the saltshaker to make sure it didn't blow away.

Once again he tapped his phone. 10:14. Just then, the waitress came his way. He picked up the cash and handed it to her.

"She stand you up?"

Adam simply stared.

"The woman who was to meet you?" the waitress explained.

Adam didn't know what to say. Was the waitress conveying a message? Was Matthew a woman?

"Sorry," the waitress said. "Guess I got it wrong." She headed toward the door, then turned back and gave him a crooked grin. "Her loss. You're not too bad." A teasing grin. "For an older guy."

And with that, she was gone. Adam stared after her, eventually seeing his reflection in the glass door as it shut. He left.

Walking quickly toward the library, he couldn't help but wonder what was meant by "an older guy." What was he now? Forty-seven? Yes, forty-seven. How old was she? Twenty? At most? So, he *was* an older guy. But he didn't feel it. At least most of the time.

It was 10:36 when he got to the second floor of the library. The table he wanted along the glass front had four chairs, two facing east, two facing west. One chair was occupied by a woman. Fortunately, she was in a chair facing east, which meant he could grab a chair facing west, toward the café. Perfect. Or near perfect. In an ideal world, the table would have been unoccupied. Minutes before, he had picked up a large reference book, and now, he placed it on the table. The woman was younger than he had thought at first glance. Seventeen or eighteen, he guessed, suddenly self-conscious about his own age. She had two books opened in front of her and was busy scribbling in a notebook. She didn't even look up. Good. He wondered, if she did happen to look up, if she'd think he was old. Probably.

Adam sat down and pulled the large reference book toward himself and opened it to a random location. He glanced out the window. The café table where he had been sitting earlier remained empty. The two older women were standing now, getting ready to leave. On his phone, he quickly checked the encrypted email account he had set up specifically to correspond with Matthew.

Both of them hid their IP addresses and no email was ever sent. Since they both had access to the email account, they simply wrote messages that were saved in the draft folder. This way, they could each open the draft folder to see if there was anything new. There was nothing new now. Adam logged off.

Looking out the window, Adam saw a man walk up to the café, a loose windbreaker blowing in the breeze, a backpack slung over one shoulder, and a black cowboy hat on his head. He took a seat at the table Adam had used, shrugging off the backpack and placing it near his feet. The cowboy hat rode low on his head, the brim obscuring his face. Planned that way or happenstance? Then he abruptly got up and went inside the café.

Adam saw this and his heart skipped a beat, alarm bells going off in his head. No one leaves their backpack behind! No one! If the man had gone inside to order food or use the restroom, he would have taken the backpack with him. He wouldn't have left it right there for anyone passing by on the street to grab. Which meant the cowboy hat was planned.

Just then, a man peddled up on a red bicycle. Matthew. It had to be. Adam looked at his watch. More than forty minutes late. He willed the man to see the backpack, but the bicyclist was bent over, busy removing a metal clip that kept his pant leg from getting caught up in the bike chain. He stood and wheeled his bike onto the patio, passing the two older ladies with a friendly nod of his head as they exited. He went over to the table they vacated and leaned his bicycle on the side of the building. Then he sat down facing the street. The backpack was in view, but he showed no sign of seeing it.

No sign of the backpack guy either. So, what? In the bathroom? Having trouble making up his mind about what to order? No and no. Ten to one, the man had gone out the back, the cowboy hat discarded in the trash, maybe the windbreaker too, and he wouldn't look anything like the man who abandoned a backpack at the café. Adam thought about running up there. Getting Matthew away from there. This wasn't good. Not good at all.

But he remained frozen in his chair. Then a dark SUV pulled up in front of the café, blocking his view of the patio. He cursed silently to himself. Move! Move! It seemed to take forever before the SUV slowly pulled away. Leaving a passenger behind. A woman with waves of long blonde hair spilling over a tan jacket that she wore with a black knee-length skirt and black ankle boots. Even from this distance and not seeing her face, he deduced that she was probably a woman of means. He gleaned this from her attire, her straight posture, and the small, delicate black bag in her right hand. She could be faking it, dressing a certain way, but people usually forgot to fake good posture. Her clothes and style said she was more upscale than the neighborhood she was in, but not too out of place for anyone to look twice. Well, maybe twice, but no more than that. She stood still for a bit, then turned and faced him. Adam thought she was looking right at him. His heart raced. He was working alone. No one knew about his secondary location. So no way she was really looking at him with any intent.

She turned away just as the waitress came out. The woman said something, and the waitress gestured to a vacant table. The blonde woman took a seat. She was less than a meter from the abandoned backpack.

And then it came.

A massive explosion, rocking the library, shattering the window where he sat, and covering him in shards.

The Hague, Holland ~ Four Days Later

The middle-aged woman placed his café latte on the counter with a pleasant gaze. "You've been too busy to have my coffee? Or is someone else making it for you?" she asked in English.

"Only you," Adam said, speaking with his native Yorkshire accent. He smiled. "Only you."

He handed her his loyalty card, which she dutifully punched. Two more coffees at this coffee cart, and he would get a free one. He took out his credit card and tapped it on the card reader in front of him.

"You look tired," she said. He had known the barista for a number of years, and while he liked her well enough, he thought her remark was a bit out of place. He was a customer. Not a dear friend. Hell, he didn't even know her name.

"I'm just getting old," he replied.

She immediately frowned. "You? Never."

Tell that to the young woman with the sleeve tattoo, he thought. Dead and in a million pieces.

"Get more rest," she advised him as he put some cash in a tip jar.

He simply raised his cup in acknowledgment.

Minutes later, he entered the Peace Palace. Originally funded by Andrew Carnegie in 1903 with the idea that the world would have peace if disputes were settled in the courtroom rather than the battlefield, it was constructed to serve as the home of the Permanent Court of Arbitration, or PCA. Despite the name, there was no actual court here. Instead, the Peace Palace was home to the United Nations International Court of Justice as well as The Hague Academy of International Law where law students from all of the world came to learn international law. It also housed the world's most prestigious international law library. Here, disputes between any of the 122 contracting members—made up of countries, various organizations, and private groups—were settled by dozens of in-house attorneys.

Typical disputes that came under the PCA purview included environmental issues, territorial quarrels, arguments concerning the laws of the sea, human rights, banking, and energy. Since there was always some sort of dispute going on between member states, foreigners might be on the premises at any time for an arbitration meeting in one of the conference rooms.

Carnegie had spared no expense on the beautifully appointed building. While the iconic three-story exterior was a masterpiece in and of itself, tourists were always amazed upon entering the first floor where a stunning mosaic tile floor was complemented with flying buttresses and a soaring ceiling. The most striking artwork was on the main hall's two-story ceiling that came to a point with four separate panels that featured four goddesses— Peace, Law, Order, and Justice. The remarkable artwork collection found throughout the building, from impressive paintings to tasteful busts, could fill a museum.

Carnegie had built the Peace Palace with the firm belief that the intergovernmental arbitrary organization could avert future wars. All good and noble, but in Adam's mind, most wars were averted due to the indefatigable work of FROG operators like himself. Walking through a dimly lit corridor in the basement, it never failed to strike him as highly ironic that numerous acts of violence were planned from the basement while hundreds of lawyers on the upper floors toiled away to prevent violence. The lawyers would undoubtedly be appalled if they knew about the true nature of FROG, but the truth was that FROG was often the first line of defense for many western countries. So in their own way, they too kept the peace.

As far as the people working on the upper floors knew, FROG was the accounting firm of Froberg, Rube, Olsen and Gunst that took up otherwise unused office space in a small portion of the basement. The firm supposedly ran the numbers on the cases under arbitration, such as a contracting member's revenue loss incurred when their ships could no longer dock at a given port. In truth, the numbers were actually crunched off-site at a real accounting firm. And since the whole world was electronic, it was very seldom that someone from upstairs actually came down to the basement. If they did, they would see two beautiful mahogany doors with the brass letters reading, FROG. But the doors would never open to those who didn't belong. In fact, a pressure pad and hidden camera instantly alerted those inside of anyone within six feet of the doors. Unbeknownst to the staff upstairs, a hidden panel adjacent to the doors revealed both a numerical keypad and a retinal scanner. This was the only way to gain access.

Sliding open the wood panel, Adam looked in the retinal scanner and got a green light. Then he put in his seven-digit code on the numerical pad. He got a green light here too and opened the soundproof, acoustically sealed door, which took him from the complete silence to the usual sounds of any office—telephones ringing, printers printing, and people talking. This was the true FROG—the Foreign Reconnaissance Operational Group.

The clandestine group was started by a WWI veteran who came from a very wealthy family and didn't want the world to endure another war of any kind. He had seen his own soldiers being gassed and suffering horrific injuries and deaths. So after the war, he started a private firm that would monitor Germany without government interference in the hopes that they could prevent another war—even if it meant assassinating top players in the field. They failed miserably to prevent WWII, but they learned from their mistakes and took corrective action. They also grew by leaps and bounds and now monitored trouble spots the world over.

The name worked to a degree.

Foreign because they were working all over the globe on foreign soil.

Reconnaissance because they worked behind the scenes, gathering data.

Operational because they were proactive. They didn't wait for bad things to happen and then go after those who caused the bad thing. Instead, whenever possible, they permanently obliterated the bad actors before they could carry out their evil intentions.

Group because they were indeed a tightly banded unit.

All of this made sense of the term FROG. However, Adam had heard that the acronym stemmed from their founder—a man of short stature who had suffered multiple injuries during the war, which left him with a gait similar to that of a frog—stooped over, the arms would swing forward followed by his legs bunny-hopping forward—almost like a broad jumper.

Adam glanced at the far wall that held seven analog clocks displaying the current time in The Hague, London, Paris, Moscow, New York, San Francisco, and Canberra. He was pleased to see that he was right on time for the meeting and made his way to the nearby glass-enclosed conference room. Hal Todd, now pushing sixty years of age, was the only one there, seated at the head of the table. There were only two other seats waiting to be filled, the place settings marked with a copy of his written report about the incident, a small tablet for jotting down notes, a pen, and a glass for ice water, the pitcher in the center of the table.

Adam pulled open the conference room door and entered. "Morning."

Hal glanced up. "Good morning." He noticed Adam's drink and said, "We have a fancy new coffee maker, you know."

"The barista across the way does a good latte," Adam replied, his tone indifferent.

He studied Adam. "You okay?"

"Fine." Adam pulled out the chair and put his coffee down. "Just not sure it is a good morning as you say."

"We'll get something going soon," Hal told him.

"We're treading water."

"Patience," Hal told him. The two men went way back and generally got along, although they had also had their share of disagreements.

The door opened again and Marsha Leenhouts came in carrying a laptop. Like Hal, she was American and had worked for several years for the DIA—the US Department of Defense's intelligence arm—before being recruited to FROG. Years back, she had married a local man and started a family. Now forty-something, she held the title of president of Operational IT, which in English simply meant that all actual operational strategy was run past her before being implemented.

She had risen quickly in the FROG ranks by fixing the biggest problem with FROG—they ran completely off the grid. This meant that no other agency, police force, or country even knew of their existence. This was great for doing things their way and not answering to anyone, but it left them scrambling for fresh and accurate intel. Which was why, soon after her arrival, she built a spyware program that allowed them to electronically monitor major intel agencies including the CIA and FBI in America, MI6 and MI5 in the UK, Mossad in Israel, ASIS in Australia, and AIVD in the Netherlands.

This type of eavesdropping had paid off ten-fold over the years. In fact, the operation they were going to discuss today originated from an anonymous tip that was being ignored by AIVD, the General Intelligence and Security Service of the Netherlands. The tip was about a suicide bomber planning to strike at a café in Tel Aviv. Unbeknownst to the good citizen trying to help, relations between the intel agencies in the Netherlands and Israel had chilled a bit in recent years. Basically, someone at the top tier of AIVD felt that they gave Israel more than they got in return. And since the tip about an upcoming bombing lacked a verified source, AIVD slow-walked it.

After seeing that tip was not going anywhere after several days, Marsha had stepped in and grabbed it electronically before deleting it from their system as if it had never existed. Adam ran with the tip and started an electronic relationship with the tipster, who said his name was Matthew. Once Matthew had given the exact details of the planned bombing, FROG shared it with

Mossad, and they successfully stopped the would-be suicide bomber.

It had been shortly after that when Matthew reached out with his end-of-the-world scenario. And now, he was dead.

"Morning," Marsha said.

Adam sighed. "Please tell me you've got something."

"As usual, not near enough." She sat opposite Adam and opened her laptop. "First, as you already know, the café explosion was done with C-4. Two important points. One, Matthew gave us the heads-up that a suicide bomber was going to attack a Tel Aviv café at a given time and date. That information proved to be true, and the Israelis aren't sharing a lot about the Tel Aviv plot, but we do know the suicide bomber was packing C-4. Two, we now think the C-4 used in the café bombing here was stolen from an airbase in Germany."

"Which one?" Adam asked, astonished.

"Ramstein," she replied, referring to the home of United States Air Forces Europe and the NATO Allied Air Command. "The C-4 went missing several weeks ago, and NCIS has been scrambling to find it."

"I guess someone should tell them that it's been found," Adam said sarcastically.

"Not even," Marsha told him. "Judging from the small blast radius at the café, we think there might be as much as sixteen pounds still unaccounted for."

"Sixteen?" Hal repeated in awe. "Pounds..? Sixteen pounds..? Dear God."

"Armageddon," Adam said casually. He looked to Hal. "Not a good morning. Definitely not a good morning."

Marsha went on in her usual business-like fashion. "Since we play outside the lines, we're fighting for every scrap of information and DNA from the explosion that we can get our hands on. It's been difficult, to say the least. We're still digging, but here is what we have that is concrete."

Marsha worked the laptop and gestured to the far wall, which held a large, flatscreen television. It blinked to life, and a picture of a thirty-something man, thin, with a receding hairline looked back at them. "Meet Matthew. Or I should say, the man who called himself Matthew. His real name was William DeWine."

Hal immediately turned to Adam. "That him?"

Adam stared at the image. "I wasn't all that close, but I'd say yes." He turned to Marsha. "Nice to know who can thank for the intel. He was in some DNA database, I take it?"

"No." Marsha smiled. "We found him through the red bike, believe it or not." Adam looked puzzled and she went on. "The bike frame was pretty much intact. There was a metal tag that had been adhered to the frame. It was from the bike shop where it came from."

Hal studied the image on the screen. "And the bike shop knew who bought that particular bike?"

"They keep very good records, which has been most helpful. DeWine bought it new and took possession the morning of the bombing. Once we had that, we scrambled to get DNA confirmation and we got it."

"Excellent," Adam noted.

"We've made sure AIVD figured it out," Marsha said.

Adam understood. Since FROG didn't really exist, they could hardly follow up directly on leads, notify next of kin about a death, and so on. But once AIVD was off and running, Marsha's team would be able to electronically monitor anything and everything the agency found. Unbeknownst to them, of course. He looked at the image. "What do we know about him?"

"British," Marsha revealed. "Twenty-nine years old. Fulbright scholar. Worked for Red Arrow Capital in London's financial district as a hedge-fund manager."

"Trust-fund baby?" Adam asked.

"You're showing your distain for hedge-fund managers," Hal chided him.

"No, no trust fund," Marsha said. "He died with some accumulated wealth, but all his own earnings. He did well, and no, he had no red flags from any oversight agency."

"He was a Boy Scout," Adam remarked.

"His parents died when he was two, and he was adopted by a family of some means, but not wealthy by the strict sense of the word. He took their surname, DeWine. No siblings, biological or through the adoptive family."

"What do we have on the adoptive family?" Hal asked.

Marsha worked her laptop, and the screen changed to show a middle-aged couple with Matthew. Everyone was smiling. "Third year at university. I don't have any more recent photos of the three of them. William, or Matthew if you want, didn't do social media. I mean, nothing."

"So we can say he probably didn't know he was going to end up in bits and pieces, and it would have helped us immensely if he'd had a strong social-media presence," Adam said sardonically.

Marsha ignored Adam. "His father, Jack DeWine, is still alive, still working as an attorney specializing in real estate. His mother, Caroline, died a year ago. Heart disease. No career to speak of, but she was the co-founder of a charity promoting healthy-heart awareness."

"She have a family history of heart problems?" Hal probed. "Pretty ironic that she establishes a heart-disease charity and dies from the same disease."

Martha smiled. "I agree, and we've tagged that, but for right now, it doesn't appear to be relevant to our concerns so it's not on the front burner to dig into." She clicked to the next PowerPoint slide. An exterior photo of a glass building, the Red Arrow Capital logo front and center. "AIVD talked to some colleagues. DeWine was well liked. He had been there eight years. He took an intern job while still at university."

"So, his only job," Adam said.

"Right." The next few slides showed him with several different women. All his age, all satisfyingly attractive. "Women he was linked to, but none appear to be too serious, but we are delving deep into each one."

"Any one in particular stand out?" Adam asked. Marsha clicked back to the first picture. A rather short woman with long, dark hair. Attractive.

"This woman. Nancy Ellison. Twenty-two. Father is Robert Ellison, an earl, very wealthy and very political. Very loud about it. Believing only those that are property owners should be allowed to vote in any election. Otherwise, those on the dole will vote for socialists. Britain cannot allow any more immigrants into the country, legal or illegal, blah, blah, blah."

Adam looked to Marsha. "Her beliefs too?"

14

"All we know is she likes fast cars." Adam gave her a puzzled look. "Literally. She raced karts, that's with a K, and beat all comers, and moved on to open-wheel race cars. Last year, she earned a ride on a Formula-3 car, but there is some talk that Daddy made it happen—he's one of the team's biggest sponsors."

Again the picture changed. Now, the woman was wearing a full racing suit, with an STR Motorsports logo embossed across her chest. She was smiling for the camera.

"She any good?" Hal asked.

"Yes. Over the season, she ended up in the top three overall and now will race on the Formula-2 circuit."

Hal raised his eyebrows, suitably impressed.

"Matthew race?" Adam inquired. "He ever go to these races?"

"No and no. So let's leave his sparse social life behind and get back to what we do know." A photo of a bicycle shop now filled the screen, lots of bicycles lined up on the sidewalk. "No one at Red Arrow knew he was going to Amsterdam. Our own speculation is that he traveled to Amsterdam—alone—strictly for the meeting with Adam. We know that he arrived the day before, picking up a new red bicycle just that morning."

"Any idea why that bike shop?" Hal asked.

"Probably because it's located just a couple of miles from the café. Once the bicycle shop gave us his name, we hacked DeWine's email and found he'd made the actual purchase online days before, and arranged the pick-up date. The owner had it assembled and ready to go when he arrived."

"But Matthew was late to the meeting," Adam noted. "So, either they didn't have it ready, or he was late coming in to pick it up. Do we know which it was?"

"Neither," Masha replied. "The owner said *he* was late opening that morning. He had to take his daughter to the doctor. She wasn't feeling well, and, as we all know, you still have to rule out COVID."

Adam shook his head. He would have met Matthew on time had the shop owner's kid simply not had the sniffles. So stupid.

Marsha misinterpreted his head shake and said, "She was fine."

Adam gave her a baffled look.

Hal smiled at Adam. "I think Marsha means the man's daughter is fine."

"Right," Marsha confirmed. "She didn't have COVID, but he then took her to his mother's place for the day. He's a single parent. So, he was late opening his shop."

"So for all that, Matthew was late, very late, and he got himself blown up," Adam said with disgust. "Wonderful. Just wonderful. Who cares about a damn kid not feeling good? You ask me, the father is a fool rushing the kid to the doctor!"

~ ~ ~

His remarks had abruptly ended the meeting.

Adam realized his error and regretted his words as soon as they were out of his mouth. He sincerely apologized to Marsha. But before she could respond, there was a knock on the window behind her, and she left the room to consult with her number two. She had come back asking that they continue later. She had a lead to follow.

Hal had insisted that he and Adam go off-site for a break. The men had worked together long enough that Adam knew what Hal was doing—get him in a different setting and get his mind in a different place. They went to a nearby pub and sat at a corner table with no one nearby to overhear them. It helped that the morning crowd was gone, so the pub was fairly quiet. Hal ordered a Bloody Mary. Adam chose orange juice.

Glass in hand, Adam looked at the man who was essentially his boss—if FROG did indeed have bosses—and apologized. "I totally forgot."

Hal sipped his drink. "I gathered that."

"It was stupid."

"It was out-of-bounds," Hal chastised him. "And beyond stupid."

"I was just pissed. I mean, if Matthew or this William DeWine guy, whoever he is, if he had been on time, maybe we'd know what's going on. Now, we're floundering in the dark."

Hal didn't respond, so Adam softly asked, "He's okay, right? Her kid?"

"In remission."

Adam drank some orange juice. "You know, in a really bizarre way, when he got sick, it was good that everyone was freaking about COVID. She got him in right away, and they found the cancer."

Hal gave him a contemptuous look. "Marsha's the best there is—"

"No doubt," Adam quickly interrupted. "No doubt at all. We're lucky to have her."

"And she went through hell with her kid. So for God's sake, have some decency."

"I know, I know," Adam muttered.

~ ~ ~

More than two hours later, Marsha, Hal, and Adam were back in the conference room. Adam spoke to Marsha as soon as they reconvened. "I am so sorry. You know what an idiot I am. I was just frustrated. I didn't mean what I said."

Marsha gave him a long look. Then a hint of a smile. "I understand. And your... Well, your remarks weren't why I broke off. We found more information."

Although it wasn't necessary, Hal said, "This is an odd situation we're in, and I think we are all frustrated. We have absolutely no clue what the man was going to share, but the fact that he got blown up minutes after arriving at the café tells us he was the real deal."

No one spoke as Marsha opened her laptop and started working. In a minute, there was a new image on the screen. The café waitress with a blonde woman.

"Her!" Adam blurted out. He stood and walked closer to the TV.

Hal looked at Marsha. "Who is she?"

"The young woman is Claire Werner," Marsha replied. "Café waitress."

Adam whirled around. "The other woman?"

"Her mother."

Adam turned back to the screen, surprised. "Her *mother*? She didn't look old enough."

"She was thirty-six. Claire was nineteen, so her mother was seventeen when she was born. The mother was Arabella Werner. Mother and daughter had a falling out over a year ago. Claire moved in with some guy, got a bunch of tattoos, and her parents sort of disowned her."

"Father?" Adam asked, going back to the table and taking his seat.

"Here is where it gets interesting," Marsha said. A new image. An attractive man wearing an ankle-length dark tunic with a white collar at his throat. Smiling. "Herman Werner."

"What?" Adam asked in surprise. "A priest?"

"Church of England priest, or in this case, vicar. I found on his church's website that he prefers the term vicar so lay people don't confuse the Church of England with the Catholic Church."

Adam turned to Marsha. "Church of England? In Holland?"

"Falls under the Anglican Churches in the Netherlands." She grinned. "You really should get out more."

Adam took her ribbing in stride. "Yup. I'll get right on that."

Hal frowned. "So an Anglican vicar. Dresses like a Catholic priest, but obviously, he can marry, have kids."

Marsha nodded. "You have to remember that under Henry VIII, he couldn't get a divorce with the Catholic Church, so he started the Church of England. There are lots of similarities, including the term priest and wearing similar clothing. A vicar is a parish priest."

Adam said, "No way you knew all this crap."

"Correct. I did your homework for you." They exchanged pleasant grins and she went on. "Anyway, with Anglicans, yes, the vicar or priest can marry. Herman Werner here fully admits that as a young man he wasn't a man of faith. He turned to God, to Jesus, when his girlfriend got pregnant."

"Arabella, his future wife?" Hal inquired.

"Yes. Herman Werner was ordained as a young man. Arabella has worked in the church in various administrative jobs. She didn't need to. She came from a wealthy family."

"Not surprised," Adam said. When they both gave him a puzzled look, he added, "She looked quite posh."

Marsha looked at the screen. "The vicar here has always been very popular. Even people from his previous postings often come to him for his services. Performing a loved one's funeral, for example. Baptisms. You get the idea."

Adam sighed. "So he and his wife run a strict household and the daughter grows up, maybe rebels a bit."

"That's my thinking," Marsha offered. "Especially if she was living with a guy and not married."

"So why was mom at the café, if they were at loggerheads?"

"Her father has only spoken to the press once since the bombing. He's quite distraught. Says Claire wanted to mend fences. She reached out to her mother through her aunt, the vicar's sister-in-law." The image of a forty-something woman with wavy gray hair. "Sophie Werner. Husband, Dirk Werner, brother of Henry, died a few years ago. Complications from cystic fibrosis. And yes, he was older than his brother by a good twelve years. He left his family quite well off." She looked at Adam. "And get this. Sophie Werner was driving the SUV that dropped off Arabella."

Adam thought back to seeing the SUV parked there. "Seemed to stay there forever. I was chomping at the bit since it was blocking my view of the tables."

"Could be that Sophie was giving her sister-in-law encouragement," Marsha said.

Adam nodded. That made sense.

Hal flipped through some pages in front of him. Reading. Then he looked at Adam. "You said the woman who stood in the patio was, quote, 'seemingly lost. She just stood there, as if not sure where to go. Dressed very well, out of place for the area. Then she turned all the way around and looked toward me, in the library. If I didn't know better, I would say she actually knew I was there. The sleeve-tattoo waitress came out, something was said, and the waitress gestured to a vacant table. The nicely attired woman sat down where indicated.' Unquote."

"The aunt also talked to the press," Marsha said. "She called the bombing an unspeakable tragedy and asked that the press leave the family alone while they grieve. But, Adam, you'll like this. Sophie said that she had told her sister-in-law that she was going to wait for her on the second floor of the library."

Hal and Adam exchanged looks. Adam said, "I thought she was looking at me, but she was looking for sister-in-law…"

"That's my guess," Marsha agreed. "The aunt was walking up the stairs to the second floor when the explosion took place. I had all this information before, by the way. The reason we broke earlier was because now, I have information on a young man named Bart Werner." Hal and Adam gave puzzled looks and she went on. "Sophie's son and Claire's cousin."

"What about him?" Adam asked.

"Guess where he works?"

"The same café," Hal conjectured.

"Red Arrow Capital in London," Marsha replied.

Chapter Two

Once FROG learned that Bart Werner worked at the same firm as DeWine, all hell had broken loose as everyone's attention was focused on the thirty-one-year-old Dutchman. So far, they were still scrambling to find out if the two men even knew each other. They had been able to grab Werner's personal email, but not his or DeWine's office email since Red Arrow Capital implemented a top-flight security program. Marsha would get in, but it wasn't going to happen immediately. The personal emails of both men gave no indication that they knew each other, and, considering that the firm employed over two hundred people in their London office alone, it would certainly be understandable that they didn't.

However, was it really a coincidence that DeWine would choose to set up a meeting with Adam at the very same Amsterdam café where Bart Werner's cousin worked? Yes, it was possible, but also highly improbable. Likewise, did Bart Werner know that DeWine, a man in his own firm, had died in the explosion too? Most likely, he did, considering that authorities had interviewed some Red Arrow Capital co-workers concerning DeWine's travels to Amsterdam and subsequent death. After all, the news of a tragic death like that would spread like a wildfire throughout any office. However, there was no mention of DeWine's death in any of Werner's personal emails.

What they did find was correspondence with his mother confirming his flight to Amsterdam the next day in order to attend his late aunt and cousin's memorial service. His mother offered to pick him up at the airport, but he had replied that he would get home by train.

Which was why Adam was now sitting at the bar of a bistro in the airport's central plaza—a rather large public area that had all sorts of shops, restaurants, and convenient railway links. He was tempted to wake up his phone and scroll through the photos of Bart Werner one more time. But there was no point. Marsha had uploaded more than a dozen images, and the man's face was etched in his brain. Fortunately, they had discovered that he was quite tall—six foot three—which should make him stand out in the crowd.

Adam watched the nearby flight-information display screen constantly updating the arrivals and departures of various flights. Bart Werner's direct flight from Heathrow on British Airways had now changed from "on approach" to "landed." However, there was no need to hurry anywhere—Adam knew the plane had to taxi to the gate and Werner would have to go through passport control since England was not one of the twenty-six European country members belonging to the Schengen Area which allowed for free movement of citizens.

Finishing off his ginger ale, Adam took his time getting to the area where his target would be emerging. He essentially had two simple tasks: confirm Bart Werner's arrival in Holland, and then get close enough to pull the man's text messages from his phone. It might not reveal much, but it would be a start.

Grabbing someone's text messages without their permission was highly illegal, but FROG didn't care about that and Marsha had perfected the technique. It started by determining which cell carrier Werner used since they would have to have a phone using the same system. The Dutchman's personal email account held lots of automatic billing receipts from Vodafone, one of Britain's largest carriers. So Marsha had equipped Adam with a new Vodafone phone containing state-of-the-art firmware that would briefly allow it to steal all the text messages on Bart Werner's phone once he got in close proximity to the man.

Arriving at the waiting area, Adam scanned the faces of the growing crowd anxiously awaiting sight of their loved ones. While there were people of all ages waiting, he noticed that those under forty were the most obsessive about constantly checking their phones. How many people even bothered to look around anymore? Or were aware of their immediate surroundings? He guessed no more than 15 percent, tops. No, probably less than that. The rest were too busy looking down at their phones.

Finally, the trickle of just a few arriving travelers started to swell in number, coming their way with various sizes of luggage in tow. Adam knew these people were from several different flights arriving within minutes of each other. So he might have a long wait. Some travelers fell into the waiting arms of family members, all smiles. However, most people moved on through, knowing that no one was waiting for them.

In the distance, Adam could see a young man a bit taller than the rest, wearing an Arsenal cap and he almost laughed. Several pictures Marsha had found of Bart Werner showed him wearing the popular football club's famous red cap. He was also wearing an Arsenal red track jacket. Obviously, he was quite the fan. Adam slowly headed off at an angle so he could close in on Werner.

Adam slowed as he saw an older man, a tad stooped over, walking right next to Werner. A family member they hadn't accounted for? Werner was pulling a small, dark-green carry-on with his left hand; the old man was on Werner's right. Unlike so many others, the doddering old man had no luggage. He walked with a cane and wore a dark tweed jacket, a beret cap, and dark gloves. There was something that struct Adam as inherently odd. The gloves, perhaps? Why gloves when inside? Was the older man's hand sore from using the cane? Adam soon realized the two men weren't together. Werner was walking at a fast pace, too fast to be considerate of an elderly friend or loved one next to him.

Just then, the older man stumbled a bit and instinctively grabbed Werner's upper right arm to steady himself. Werner immediately stopped, a look of surprise on his face. He said something to the old man and tried to pull his arm from the man's grasp, but to no avail. The two remained frozen in place, passengers quickly sidestepping them without another thought.

As the old man continued to firmly hold on to Werner's arm and Adam saw immense pain on the younger man's face, he immediately knew what had just happened—the older man had used a curved blade to sever Werner's brachial artery. He himself had killed that way more than once.

Adam took off at a run, fighting through the sea of people coming toward him from the opposite direction. Finally, the older man released Werner. Although Adam couldn't see the blade, he now knew why the old man was wearing gloves. The glove on the killing hand was equipped with a retractable curved blade that, with a flick of the wrist, folded flat against the palm of the hand, out of sight. Made of a special cotton, the glove would soak up the blood nicely, leaving no trace of any gore. The perfect weapon in crowded conditions like this. And that meant the man was a professional.

As for Werner, he dropped the carry-on and reached for his throbbing right arm, which now hung useless at his side. He looked down at his right hand where blood flowed freely, dripping off his fingertips, and splattered the floor.

The old man saw Adam coming, straightened up suddenly, and took off, moving like a much younger man. He was able to quickly blend into the throng of people heading for the exit.

Adam had a split second to decide: follow the assassin or help Werner? He chose the latter.

Werner was still on his feet, but swaying mightily, his face stone white. Adam took him in his arms just as the young man collapsed. Fortunately, Werner's polyester red jacket was doing a decent job of hiding the massive amount of blood loss. Kneeling beside the Dutchman, Adam knew he had to act fast since severing the brachial artery would result in massive blood loss and could cause death in just a few minutes time. He lunged for the carry-on bag nearby and pulled it over, laying it against the injured arm to hide the accumulating blood on the floor. He didn't need an audience. Quickly unzipping the bag, he found a long-sleeve T-shirt right on top and used it as a crude tourniquet, tying it off as tightly as he could. Better that Werner lose the use of his arm than lose his life.

A few people now looked on, but not one person asked if they could help. Welcome to today's world, Adam thought.

Adam leaned close to Werner. "I was to meet DeWine at your cousin's café," he said in English, his voice low. Bart Werner's face immediately changed. Complete recognition. "The man that did this to you made sure DeWine was silenced. Understand?"

Werner started to speak and Adam leaned close. Nothing.

Adam pulled back. "You understand what's going on? DeWine was blown up. Nod if you understand what I'm saying."

24

The young man was completely terrified, but he nodded. Good. Urgently, Adam said, "What was DeWine going to tell me?" Nothing. While Adam would swear that Werner wanted to share, he was bleeding out so rapidly that either his brain wasn't functioning normally or he simply didn't have the energy to speak. Or both.

"Please help me," Adam implored him. "What was he going to say?"

"Hey, there!" a voice called out in Dutch. "Is that blood?"

Adam now saw that his tourniquet had failed—blood was seeping out from under the carry-on and onto the white concourse floor. Damn. He looked up to see a man about his age staring down at them. "Yes, yes it is. Call for an ambulance. Please."

The stranger just stared.

Angry, Adam said, "You want to help, call 112!"

"What happened?" the man asked.

"Call for help!" Adam shouted.

The man reached for his phone. Adam turned back to Werner. "What was DeWine going to say?"

Werner mumbled something and Adam leaned close. But he couldn't make it out. "What was DeWine going to tell me? C'mon!"

Bart Werner struggled to speak. Finally came the faint reply in English: "The joker."

"The joker?" Adam asked, baffled.

A slight nod. Then Werner took his last breath.

Damn!

The blood was attracting attention from the crowd. Not wasting a precious moment, Adam felt the dead man's pockets and found an iPhone in the jacket's zippered right pocket. He grabbed it, and, looking at Werner's lifeless face, said in Dutch, "I'm calling her now. Don't worry. Paramedics are on the way."

He made a show of waking the phone for his audience. Password protected of course, but he feigned dialing and put the phone to his face. "Yeah, yeah, we called for help."

As the onlookers gawked at the blood, he quickly walked away unnoticed.

FROG Headquarters, The Hague

With over a hundred trains a day making the thirty-minute trip between the Schiphol Airport and The Hague, Adam was back at FROG Headquarters less than an hour after Bart Werner had been killed.

As soon as he had walked in, he handed Werner's phone to Marsha.

"We've already scrubbed footage of the incident," she told him. "You are there, but you're seen as a good guy, trying to help a fallen traveler."

"I *am* a good guy," Adam replied bitterly.

She gave him a puzzled look. "That's what I said."

The truth was, FROG had access to the real-time airport security footage for many international airports. Usually, they pulled video when they were looking for a specific individual, but it was also useful when they wanted to alter footage to fit their own agenda. In this case, when Adam had jumped on a train bound for The Hague just as the doors were closing, he had immediately contacted Marsha. Her number two had then started collecting airport video footage and editing it to suit their needs before putting it back on their servers. By the time Adam's train arrived at The Hague, the scene would show authorities only what FROG wanted them to see. It wasn't quite fair to law enforcement, but FROG operated by their own rules.

Although Adam would eventually look at the edited version of events just out of curiosity, he was more anxious to see what they had on the assassin.

Amsterdam, the Netherlands

For three days in a row, Lars had essentially failed to do what the kidnappers wanted. Or in this case, the cat-nappers. They had stolen Milo, his only true companion for over ten years now. Clearly, the kidnappers had no clue about his job. He couldn't do what they were demanding even if he wanted to. And even if he could do what they wanted—whoever "they" were—he would surely end up in prison, which meant he would never see Milo again anyway.

Tonight had started like every other night. He had arrived on time to start his usual graveyard shift. Parking his car in the usual spot, he had gotten out and opened the rear passenger door to retrieve his thermos and lunchbox when he heard a man say, "Milo is anxious to get home." Whirling around, he had found a man just a few feet away casually smoking a cigarette.

Lars had stared at the stranger, then gathered his items and locked his car. His heart hammering in his chest, he angrily said, "What you people have asked me to do is impossible."

"You want a dead cat?"

Lars faced the stranger, angry. "Everything is securely locked! I don't have access to anything! Nor would I even know where to find it even if I had access!"

"No, no, no," the man had said, exhaling smoke. "People work around the clock sometimes, we know that. Not everything is locked when people are working there."

"So what? I'm not alone in there! I can't go anywhere I want!" Lars had argued.

Then the man patted Lars's cheek a few times. It was demeaning. "Think, Lars, think. Pull the fire alarm. Everyone hurries out, you do what you have to, and Milo comes home, yeah?"

The man had stood so close that Lars could smell his cigarette breath. Lars knew the man was insane—pulling the fire alarm would not work. But instead of arguing, he'd simply remained silent.

Then the man held out a small piece of paper, which Lars had reluctantly taken. It just had a phone number. The man had said, "Get what we need," then turned and walked away, tossing the remnants of his burning cigarette. He looked back. "Soon, Lars, soon. Milo is waiting."

Lars hurried to the side entrance of the building and nervously punched in his code. The steel door unlocked and he quickly entered. He stayed right there until he heard the reassuring sound of the heavy door automatically locking in place behind him. Only then did he start to breathe again. He was going to be okay.

But a split second later, he was shaking like a leaf.

Looking through the glass half of the closed door of the breakroom, Gretchen Black studied the man sitting alone at the table. He held a steaming cup of tea with both hands, but his eyes were vacant.

"He's been with us sixteen years," said Max Becker, standing next to her at the door. "No marks against him."

"He's basically a janitor?"

"Sanitation Custodian," Max corrected her.

She gave a small laugh. "Really?"

"Really. In truth, we're a specialty lab, obviously there are a lot of dos and don'ts, things you don't want anyone going near, that sort of thing."

"He good?"

"Excellent. I'll give you an example. In one of our smaller laboratories, he was mopping the floor and found a soiled Band-Aid. Most people would dispose of it. But he didn't throw it out. He took a plastic bag, bagged it, wrote the date and time and where he found it, and left it on the worktable right there."

Gretchen gave him a skeptical look. "And that was good?"

"The Band-Aid was one of several that were logged into evidence. It had dropped to the floor in one area, gotten picked up on the bottom of a shoe of someone else, and fell off where he found it."

"By then it was contaminated."

Max nodded. "Yes, of course, but the technician knew they were missing one. So, yes, accidents happen, but with him acting the way he did, he helped the lab techs retrace what happened to the missing Band-Aid."

"Personal life?"

"Fifty-nine years old. Lives with his elderly mother."

"Single?" Gretchen asked.

"As far as I know."

Gretchen sighed. "And his cat has been stolen."

"That's what he's saying, for blackmail purposes. He won't say any more than that, and he'll only talk to you—the police." Gretchen looked at him with a raised eyebrow. Max smiled. "He'll never know the difference, and, truthfully, the police wouldn't listen to him."

"Hmm," she said under her breath.

"Besides, if something is going on that concerns this lab, I want to know about it. And you guys are better than the police."

Gretchen gave another sigh. Max was a senior executive at the lab, and he had called her directly since they had worked together in the past. He didn't know about FROG obviously and had pegged her as a working stiff in the intelligence division of AIVD. Which was just fine with her. And ironically, it was where she had started her career. Max had woken her up just after one in the morning, asking her to come to the SkyLark Lab right away to interview a man who might be being blackmailed to get evidence out of the lab. She had reluctantly left her warm bed, dressed, and gone to her bedroom safe, selecting a picture ID that listed her as a police detective.

Max looked at her. "Ready?"

She nodded, and he opened the door for her. She noticed that Lars physically jumped when the door opened, clearly nervous. Smiling, she said, "Mr. Vervloet, my name is Greta Drott. I'm a police officer..."

Lars didn't move a muscle. He sat frozen in his seat.

Keeping the smile on her face, she showed him her ID. He didn't look at it, so she placed it in front of him. "I'm a detective."

Finally, Lars looked at the ID.

"Can I sit down?"

Lars didn't reply, but she took a seat near him, pocketing her ID.

"Coffee?" Max asked. "Tea?"

Gretchen smiled. "Coffee, please. Black."

Max started a Krups coffee maker. Silence as the three waited for the coffee. Max brought it over and said, "I'll be down the hall."

"Thanks," Gretchen said.

Max left and Gretchen sipped her coffee, studying the man. "You okay?"

"Milo's probably already dead anyway."

"Your cat?"

"Yes," Lars replied.

She pulled out a small notebook and pen. "Let's start from the top. How do you know Milo was taken?"

Lars gave a surprised look. "They showed me a picture of him!"

"Doesn't mean it's a recent picture," Gretchen gently countered.

"You don't understand!" Lars retorted, quite frustrated. "Milo went missing sometime Monday night, when I was here. Working. When I got home, he didn't greet me. He's more like a dog than a cat. Always happy to see me." Lars looked away, embarrassed.

Gretchen waited, but he didn't go on. She gently said, "So you got home Tuesday morning, and Milo didn't greet you... And your mother resides with you?"

Another surprised look. He looked away again. "For the last year. She played bridge that night. Down the hall. She feels terrible. Said he must have dashed out when she came home and she didn't see him."

"And the picture?" Gretchen prodded him.

"Came the night after he disappeared. Tuesday night, about nine. I was having my breakfast." He glanced at her. "I sleep days."

"I understand. So, they contacted you, how?"

"A text with a picture of Milo sitting on top of the morning newspaper." Lars smiled. "Milo loves paper. He'll sit on any paper."

"And you're sure it was Tuesday's newspaper?"

"Of course! See for yourself!" he said defensively, digging a phone out of his pocket. He scrolled for a minute until he found the text and handed the phone to Gretchen. Milo was a black and white tuxedo, staring at the camera. She enlarged the image with her fingers and could clearly see Tuesday's date on the newspaper.

"See? See?" Lars asked. "There's a term for that. So you know they really have your loved one and they are okay. I forget..."

"Proof of life," Gretchen said.

"Yes!" Lars said, excitedly. "That's it!" He pointed to the phone. "That's what that is! Proof of life!"

"I agree," she replied. "You have more texts?"

"No. No, that was it." He gripped the tea mug. "Mother feels awful. But near as I can tell, they broke in when she was playing bridge." He looked at her. "Milo never wants to go out. Ever."

Gretchen noticed the text was sent from a blocked number. A burner phone, no doubt. She jotted that in her notebook, then forwarded the photo to her own phone and put her info into his contact list. Returning the phone to him, she explained, "I gave you my name and number. It's in your phone, okay?" He nodded numbly and she asked, "So, how do you know what they want if there were no more text messages?"

"They were waiting for me! Waiting for me when I got here! Just after eleven-thirty."

"That night? Tuesday night?"

"Yes!"

"You say, they?" Gretchen prodded.

Lars frowned. "Well, a man. Not the same man as tonight— the first time, it was a younger man. Maybe thirty. Tall. Tonight, more my age, my height."

Gretchen scribbled in her notepad. "Just the two times?"

"Yes. They speak English, not Dutch."

Interesting, Gretchen thought. "And what did the younger man say? The first man? Tuesday night?"

"My English is not all that good, but I understood," Lars told her.

Gretchen added that detail in the notebook. "What did he say?"

Lars looked up at her tentatively. "He said that the lab had something that belonged to them. It was mistakenly taken as evidence from that restaurant bombing." He studied her. "The restaurant in Oud West?"

"The café, yes."

Lars went on. "I have to get it and give it to them. Then I get Milo back."

"What, exactly? What evidence?"

Lars ignored her questions, angry now. "It's just so stupid! Everything here is under lock and key! I sanitize the area. The floors, any workspace left free of material. Sometimes, there are laptops or a notebook left out. I only clean where there is nothing related to anyone's work." He gestured toward the breakroom. "Like here. I clean this. Every speck of it. And the fridge, these people, they don't keep it clean it all. I never remove any food, but

I clean the refrigerator shelves. The microwave. Clean the floor, this table, the chairs."

"Okay," Gretchen said.

"The autopsy room, the storage room. You know, where they store bodies before and after autopsy? And the bathrooms. All those areas are my responsibility," Lars said proudly. "Oh, and the trash. I take out all the trash."

Gretchen didn't really need the details of his job, but she smiled dutifully anyway. "You've got a big job."

"Exactly!"

"I need to know what he wants you to take," Gretchen said softly.

But Lars was on a roll, burning with indignation. "I told him! I said I don't know where they keep any evidence. And hell, even if I did, I wouldn't have access to it! Everything is locked tight around here!"

"Right," Gretchen said. "The evidence he wants?"

Lars stared down at the table. "He said Milo dies if I don't get it."

"I'm sorry," she said with genuine empathy. He was wound tight, and she needed him at ease. After a brief pause, she asked, "And nothing more until today? Tonight?"

Lars now had tears in his eyes. "The second man, he said he knows there are times when people work all night. He said when that happens, not everything will be locked. So I'm to pull a fire alarm and then find it."

He shook his head. "The man made it sound so simple. But it's not! Look around here. Everything is safely stored! Hell, there are cameras! I can't get my hands on anything. It's a joke." He sighed. "Mother keeps blaming herself..." He gave her a miserable look. "I can't tell her the truth. I just can't."

Chapter Three

FROG Headquarters, The Hague

"So what did you do to me?"

Two looked up as Adam entered the spacious office she shared with Marsha who had gone home. While Adam could be gruff, Two found him to be likeable. She called up the video footage on her computer and hit play.

Adam stepped close, leaning over her shoulder. It started rolling with his back to the camera as he sat at the bar of the airport restaurant. As planned of course. Never face a camera if you can avoid it. Then he stood up and moved off, obese by anyone's definition. He also had a goatee.

"Geez," he said.

"There is a lot of footage of you. We didn't have a lot of options," Two told him. Her real name was Nora Stern. She was twenty-seven years-old and Austrian by birth. She had served as Marsha's number two for six years now, hence the nickname. "We added ninety pounds, in case you are wondering." When he didn't reply, she added, "You have to admit, that guy doesn't look like you."

"No, no," Adam agreed. "Ninety pounds. Geez."

Like every field operator at FROG, Adam had to undergo a full 3-D body-imaging scan on an annual basis just for situations like this. While you hoped it would never be needed, sometimes, it was. In this case, his entire body was altered with a massive weight gain. While the goatee wouldn't matter—if the police were looking for him, seeing him clean shaven would hardly matter. But losing nearly a hundred pounds? Not so easily done.

"God, I look ugly," Adam muttered.

"Right, so we didn't have to do too much."

It took him a beat, and then he gave her an annoyed look. "Cute."

Two smiled, pleased with herself.

Adam continued to watch and saw his obese-self catch Bart Werner and ease him to the floor. But instead of immediately unzipping Werner's carry-on and finding the long-sleeve T-shirt for a makeshift tourniquet, in the video, he first found the wound. Only then did it show his actual movements— pulling the carry-on alongside Werner's arm in order to hide the blood on the floor, unzipping the case and finding the T-shirt. "I won't even ask how you did that."

"Looks good, though."

Adam agreed. "I'd buy it."

"You immediately knew what to do, almost like a doctor, and we were afraid that would generate some questions."

"Okay, you got me. How did you do that?" Adam couldn't help but ask. "I never hunted around for his wound."

"I took some of the footage of you talking to him, took your hand movements and, with a cut and paste, made it so you are looking for the wound. Then it was the real images of you dealing with it."

"So nothing of me talking to him?"

"A bit," Two said. She enhanced the video, and you could see him talking to Werner. "Can't read your lips. We hid that."

Adam had to admit that her work was top-notch. He watched as obese Adam found Werner's phone, stood, and moved off, his backside now huge. "Geez," he said under his breath.

"Yeah, you carry your weight on your rear end too. Sorry."

"Don't be sorry. You do good work, Two." She beamed. "Am I still on the train coming here?"

"No, Cologne."

Adam grinned. "Maybe they've got a good weight-loss clinic there."

Less than hour later, Adam, Hal, and Two were in the conference room, this time with Two working a laptop instead of Marsha. It was just past six in the morning, and Adam had to settle for a FROG coffee instead of dashing across the street. Not quite as good as the nearby barista made, but it actually was better now that they had the new coffee maker.

"Nothing at all?" Hal asked Two, clearly astonished.

"Nothing," Two replied.

"I don't believe it," Hal replied bitterly. "To do what he did, he's a professional."

"Either he is new to us, or he is very well disguised," Two explained. "The partial glimpses we have are not enough—facial recognition is drawing a blank."

Hal looked at Adam. "Age?"

Adam shook his head. "No way of knowing. First sight, he looked older, shuffling along using a cane. But obviously, it was all an act. The cane, stumbling, it was all done for one reason—"

"To grab Werner's arm," Hal interrupted.

"Exactly. Once the deed was done, he suddenly took off like a young gazelle."

Hal turned back to Two. "Last known location?"

Two frowned. "Lost him in the shuffle." When he frowned, she quickly added, "We're still on it. We'll find him."

Just then, there was a soft tap on the glass wall of the conference room. They all turned. The door opened and Gretchen stuck her head in. "Good time?" she asked.

"Come, come," Hal said, waving her in.

Gretchen hesitated briefly, then came in with a nod of acknowledgment to Adam. She looked at Two. "I emailed you a couple of photos. Should be in your inbox."

Two quickly turned her attention to her computer as Gretchen took a seat next to her.

Hal said to Adam, "Gretchen responded to a call just a few hours ago that pertains to this case."

Adam looked at her. She looked great, and he felt uneasy. The last time he had seen her, they had been working well together on an op, and it felt like they were on the road to something personal. Before it could get to that point, he had been assigned a job in Africa and used the break to push her away, ignoring her texts and emails. She had gotten the message loud and clear and had gone silent. "Do tell."

"Max Becker, VP at SkyLark Labs, called me very early this morning," Gretchen explained. "He needed some help with an employee who has been compromised. Ideally, he wanted someone who could pose as police to the employee, but at the same time, keep things under wraps."

"Why you?" Adam asked.

She looked him in the eye. "We worked on something together a while back. He thinks I'm AIVD."

"Good for us," Two chimed in.

"SkyLark is handling the café explosion—autopsies as well as the collection and processing of all evidence," Hal added. He looked to Gretchen. "Go ahead."

Gretchen continued. "Max said that a janitor who has a solid history at the facility is being blackmailed into stealing a single piece of evidence from the café bombing."

"What evidence?" Adam asked.

"A black cowboy hat," she replied. "Found in the rear dumpster."

Astonished, Adam said, "Cowboy hat is our bomber. No doubt!" He turned to Hal. "Read my report. I theorized he got rid of the hat. And maybe his windbreaker. Goes out the back, dumps the hat, maybe the jacket, and poof! He looks nothing like the guy who left the backpack!"

Two looked at him, puzzled. "If he put the hat in the dumpster, he must've known it might end up as evidence."

"I agree," said Gretchen. "This was a well-organized attack, but you suddenly want your hat back?"

"Maybe they didn't expect the hat to be part of the evidence collection," Adam replied.

"How far was it?" Hal asked. "The rear dumpster where it was found?"

Adam tilted his head back, closing his eyes. Finally, he said, "Out the back exit, twelve paces straight, eight paces to the left."

Hal knew this was the way Adam's brain worked—whatever he had experienced, no matter how long ago, he could recreate it in his mind with great precision. Just then, Marsha silently entered the conference room, a laptop held against her chest and a coffee cup in hand.

Adam shook his head. "So the question is, why did forensics take it?"

"Take what?" Marsha asked.

"Black cowboy hat," Hal said. "Employee at SkyLark Lab is being blackmailed to get it. So the question is, if the hat was dumped there, alley off the back of the café, how did forensics know to look for it?"

Marsha scowled. "From a witness."

"A real witness?" Adam asked with surprise. "Or a FROG witness? I talked about it in my report."

"No, a real witness." She put her coffee down, sat down and opened the laptop. She looked at Adam. "Glad you read all the eyewitness reports."

Adam was about to argue, but he knew there was no point and kept quiet.

Marsha found what she was looking for. "Okay, the investigators had already ID'd the backpack as the bomb source with C-4. So they heavily canvassed the area, including asking nearby businesses about seeing anyone with a backpack. They got lucky. A woman from a clothing store down the street said she was headed up there to pick up some coconut pancakes. A guy, quoting now, 'In a black cowboy hat, a backpack over his shoulder, walked very fast past her. She remembered thinking the cowboy hat was silly. This isn't the Wild West. But she pegged him as an American tourist.' Unquote."

"Why didn't she get caught up in the explosion?" Gretchen asked.

"Got a call from her manager with a computer problem so she went back without getting the food."

"Lucky for her," Two muttered. She frowned. "Still, you'd think if you're the bomber, you'd ditch your hat further away than the back alley."

"A better question is, how'd he know it was picked up by forensics?" Marsha asked. "The bomber."

"Good point," Hal said.

"He had a spotter," Adam offered. "Or maybe he himself saw it collected." When Hal frowned, he added, "You know how many people must have been watching everything? It's human nature. Go to a disaster site and see what's going on."

"The area would have been barricaded off," Hal argued.

"With security tape, yes," Adam argued. "We're not talking about picking up a paperclip and bagging it. This was a cowboy hat. Pretty big. You would see it."

"Okay," Hal agreed.

"Not to change the subject, but I found something on our airport assassin," Marsha said. "Last night, I couldn't sleep. I kept thinking I missed something on the guy."

"He went into a men's restroom and came out in a disguise that we haven't been able to trace," Two explained.

"Yes and no," Marsha responded, quickly working her computer. "It's my fault. I just didn't wait long enough. I got impatient. Expand it to who went in and out by forty minutes on each end and you have this." She turned to the large screen at the end of the room.

A man pushing what looked to be an older man slumped in a wheelchair, a plaid throw over the disabled man's legs. His head was down, his chin on his chest, and he was wearing a beret.

"Time stamp is twenty-oh-nine," Marsha said. "That's when they go into the bathroom."

Two suddenly understood. "Way before we were looking."

"Exactly."

The footage now fast-forwarded, all kinds of men entering and exiting the restroom. Finally, it slowed.

Marsha said, "This is thirty-nine minutes later."

They saw the man they had pegged as the assassin entering the restroom.

"See that?" Marsha said. "Nearly forty minutes after the man in the wheelchair goes in and still hasn't come out. Forty-minutes!"

"The assassin comes out in the wheelchair," Adam surmised.

"Can't validate that yet, but I'm pretty certain," Marsha said. "But again, a very long wait. Twenty-eight minutes later. That's why I say they were patient."

"Where'd the assassin go?" Adam asked.

"Right back here." A disability van. "Go back in time, and we first find them in the short-term parking area. Handicap section, of course." The van was parked pretty far away from the camera, but they watched as its rear doors opened and a mesh metal ramp then folded down, parallel to the ground. What looked like an older man sat slumped in the wheelchair, the plaid throw over his legs, was pushed out onto the ramp and the ramp was lowered to the ground.

They watched as the tape sped up, jumping from camera feed to camera feed as they followed the man in the wheelchair until he disappeared inside the restroom. Then it was back to the assassin entering the restroom. Marsha explained, "So nearly forty minutes after the disabled man goes in, our assassin enters—"

"They were incredibly patient," Adam remarked.

"Like I said," Marsha agreed. "Putting the two of them up, side by side now..."

What appeared to be identical images showed a disabled man being pushed in a wheelchair. In each photo, the disabled man was slumped in his seat, chin on his chest and wearing the dark beret. But in the first one, the man sat noticeably higher in the seat.

"First guy is taller," Gretchen noticed.

"Yeah, I agree, but truthfully, I would have never looked twice," Hal said.

"Exactly," Marsha agreed. "So you tend to think there wasn't a switch. But here's the kicker—look at this guy coming out of the bathroom."

A younger man wearing a blue New York Yankees baseball cap and a mid-thigh-length leather jacket exited the restroom. He looks toward the camera, and Marsha froze on his face.

"He's not our assassin if that is what you're thinking," Adam remarked. "No way. Too young."

"I agree, he's not our hitman," Marsha said. "Just trust me on this, not one man entered wearing a blue baseball cap or this type of leather jacket—see how long it is? We have one guy in a baseball cap, but it is solid white. That guy is heavy-set, and we have him enter and exit. There were three other men in leather jackets, all waist-length. No leather jacket with this kind of length, okay?"

"Okay..." Hal said, following along.

Marsha quickly worked the computer.

"So, what?" Gretchen asked. "The Yankees fan is the first man in the wheelchair?"

"Yes, I'm certain of it," Marsha continued. "And why? Quite simply because this guy comes out, but never goes in."

"How soon?" Adam asked. "How soon does our Yankees fan come out after the assassin goes in?"

"Six minutes and twelve seconds."

Adam looked at her. "More than enough time. Yankees Man and his friend wait in the disabled stall. Assassin comes in, the Yankees Man gets out of the wheelchair, they have the baseball cap and leather jacket under the throw blanket, and he walks out. The assassin gets in the wheelchair."

"That's the way I see it," Marsha confirmed. "Here are the two men, side by side."

Yankees Man was on the left, exiting the restroom, the assassin pasted in on the right, entering.

"Big height difference," Gretchen said.

"About six inches," Marsha said.

"Which is why he sits up taller in the wheelchair."

"Exactly," Marsha agreed. "They are good, but yeah, this was an oversight."

"Anything more on the assassin's face?" Adam asked.

"Yep, watch this. This is almost to the exit."

They watched as the disabled man was wheeled toward the automatic sliding doors. His chin still at his chest.

"Watch... A woman coming in, she trips..."

The video slowed, and they watched in slow motion as a woman lost her footing and ended up falling just feet away from the assassin. Startled, the man in the wheelchair quickly looked up. This image was now frozen on the screen.

"A bit blurred, but we'll dump it in facial recognition," Marsha said. "After this, I traced them right back to the same van."

"What about the man pushing the wheelchair?" Hal asked.

"I need to play with that today. First glance, I have to say we don't have a lot. He seems pretty savvy about where the cameras are. Didn't even flinch when the woman fell. But we'll get cracking on it."

"And the tall man in the Yankees cap?" Gretchen asked. "He go to the van?"

Marsha shook her head. "He went out a street exit. We eventually lose him."

Adam smiled at Marsha. "Excellent work. Really excellent." He turned back to the screen, studying the image of the disabled man. "The assassin had two accomplices so this was well thought out."

"They knew Bart Werner would be coming in, what flight, and they planned it," Hal remarked. He looked at Marsha and Two. "We need the names of everyone who got off flights at that time who had to go through passport control."

"Easier than that," Adam said. "He would be on the same flight. No chance of missing Werner on this end if you're on the same flight. Keep it clean and simple. That's what I would do anyway." He turned to Marsha. "You can get passenger names, but he's top-notch. You'll come up empty."

"How'd he get his weapon through airport security?" Two asked.

"Ceramic," Adam quickly replied.

Two nodded. She looked at Marsha. "What about the license plate on the handicap van?"

"Just a partial," Marsha replied. "I dumped it into the system."

"Can you go back to the Yankee guy?" Gretchen suddenly asked.

It took a minute, but then the image of the younger man appeared. Facing the camera.

"Perfect," Gretchen announced. "That's just perfect."

London, England

Once inside the building, Adam didn't look around for the lift. He took the stairs, two at a time to the fourth floor. He was a bit winded once he got there, even though he was in pretty good shape. Good for an older man, at any rate.

In the corridor, it took him a minute to figure out the numerical scheme. He was looking for flat number 404. He walked past it twice, on purpose. No hallway cameras. Good. And amazingly, he found only one wireless doorbell camera, and it was on the door of the last apartment. Thank heavens. He had come to despise the stupid things. They really weren't good for his line of work. Doubling back, he stood in front of the door at flat 404. Finally, he knocked.

This was the part he dreaded most—having no idea who or what was behind the door. Marsha had found Bart Werner's rented flat, but other than the owner's name, there was no way to know if Bart had a roommate, live-in girlfriend, live-in boyfriend, or lived alone. Even though Adam had ID that said he was London police, it would be best not to go down that road.

He knocked again. Still nothing. He looked around. The corridor remained empty. His raps on the door had not brought any unwanted attention from a nosy neighbor. Using his lockpick, he had the door open in less than half a minute. He quickly entered, softly closing the door behind him, all the while holding his breath, half expecting the chirp of an alarm. Looking on either side of the door, he was relieved there was no alarm. Silent or otherwise.

He pocketed his pick and glanced at his watch. Five minutes. No more than five minutes. His first order of business was to make sure he was alone so he made quick work of going room to room. The flat consisted of a tidy living area with a fifty-inch plasma TV, a small kitchen, a single bedroom with a bathroom, and a tiny office area. Fortunately, the flat was empty.

He focused on the office, which was furnished with a desk, chair, and mahogany two-drawer filing cabinet. No computer. So, what? A laptop? That he took with him? No charger plug left on the desk. He stood to the side and bent over, peering at the desk from that height. And he saw it. The clear imprint of where a laptop had been, a thin layer of dust surrounding the footprint. Werner must have taken it with him for his return home.

Adam jimmied open the filing-cabinet drawers and found nothing but typical household bills, bank and credit-card statements, and a thick file on river cruises. Nothing in the desk drawers except empty pads of paper, scotch tape, scissors, and a stapler.

Back in the living room, he looked around. Two paintings stood out. Not inexpensive prints, but real paintings. He carefully looked behind each one. Nothing. No safe. Rummaging through the kitchen, he discovered that Bart Werner probably never cooked. There were no pots and pans. Several unmatched plates and small bowls. Hardly anything in the refrigerator unless you counted the two six packs of Amstel beer as food. The freezer held several frozen pot pies.

Next, he scoured the bedroom. Bart Werner had been very neat for a bachelor—the bed was made. Adam opened the drawer of the single nightstand and found a small bottle of Excedrin Migraine and an unopened package of condoms. The bathroom held no medications whatsoever. Toothpaste, an electronic toothbrush, shaving items, cologne, and a bottle of contact lens solution. No signs of a woman sharing the space.

Adam glanced at his watch. His time had expired several minutes ago. He ran his hand through his hair. This was their only chance, and he had found nothing. He went back into the bedroom and looked under the bed. Several trainers. He pulled them out and ran his hand inside. Nothing. He put them back and stood. Time to go. Then he decided to look one last place.

He lifted the mattress and found a rather thick 16 x 20 piece of cardboard. He pulled it out, surprised to find it heavier than it looked and realized why—there were two pieces, neatly tied at both ends. He laid it on the bed and untied one end, flipping the top cardboard over so the two pieces were side by side. Both sides were filled with some sort of diagram. There were all kinds of squares, filled with writing and lines linking the various squares, much like a family tree. The penmanship was small and very neat, but he was looking at it from the wrong angle. He pivoted the whole thing so it was now vertical. At the top of the chart were two words: The Joker.

That was all he needed to see. Quickly refolding the two cardboard pieces, he took the time to tie them together. He too could be neat and tidy. Tucking them under one arm, he went to the front door. There was no peephole, so he pressed an ear to the door. He couldn't hear a sound, so he slowly opened the door. The corridor was still empty. He stepped into the hall, quietly closed the door behind him, and headed back toward the stairs.

Opening the door to the stairwell, he heard voices and abruptly stopped in his tracks. They were a flight or so below. Going up or down? A man's voice. "You should make a habit of taking the stairs every chance you get. It's good for you."

"Bullshit," came another voice. Definitely grumpy. "Notice the manager isn't bothering with this shit."

"He's got an extra few stone on him too."

The voices were getting louder; they were coming up.

"Swear to God, I don't know what the hell you're good for, Constable."

Police. Damn.

"I'm good for keeping you in shape, Sergeant," came the reply with a laugh.

Adam silently retreated, making sure the heavy stairwell door shut with only the faintest click. He walked quickly back down the corridor, keeping his head pivoted away from the single doorbell camera and turned the corner to find the small alcove for the lift. He pressed the call button, his heart hammering. It seemed to take forever, but finally, the lift doors opened with a soft chime. No one inside. He stepped in and pressed the first-floor button and then the close button. Again, it seemed to take forever, but finally, the doors slowly closed.

Amsterdam, the Netherlands

At just past nine in the morning, Amsterdam was awake and bustling, and, to keep pace, Gretchen was drinking yet another cup of coffee as she drove through the city streets. Over the last several hours, she had been thoroughly filled in on everything FROG had so far.

Gretchen's phone instructed her to turn left in a quarter mile, and she looked over her shoulder before changing lanes. It was almost laughable that SkyLark Labs didn't even have the evidence Lars Vervloet needed to exchange it for his cat. Just an hour ago Max Becker had told her that SkyLark Labs had never had it—it had been shuffled off to another lab that they often used when they had too much going on. And the café bombing had overwhelmed them. Max had told her that they knew the hat may or may not have been worn by the bomber, but a thorough check of it could be done at the university level.

In other words, it's not worth his staff's time. Which was why Gretchen was now following her GPS directions to Goshart Labs where it would be her job to get the exact specs of the hat so they could get a duplicate and make a swap—one hat for one cat. Two had laughingly dubbed the operation "Cat in the Hat Part II." The plan called for them to put a tiny tracker inside the duplicate hat, have Lars make the swap, and the hat would lead them to the actual bomber.

Stuck in traffic, Gretchen's mind drifted to Adam. To her, he looked a bit fatigued, but that was certainly understandable considering the all-nighter. She thought he was especially kind to Marsha and wondered what that was about. It couldn't be personal. Or at least she didn't think so. Marsha was happily married to a law professor and had two children. She tried to remember what had happened with one of the kids. Cancer of some sort. But doing okay.

Following her phone's directions, Gretchen pulled up to the secure entrance of Goshart Labs where she showed the guard her police ID and was promptly waved through. Inside, it had taken just a minute before a young man, maybe thirty, came to retrieve her from reception. He introduced himself as Finn Gelens.

The lab area was fairly big, with different techs working on whatever it was they worked on. Finn took her to his work area, which consisted of two identical extra-long tables, one holding an iMac twenty-seven-inch computer. The other, the cowboy hat. He turned to her and got right down to business. "No prints, but I did find blood."

"Blood?"

Chapter Four

Amsterdam, the Netherlands

"That's substantial."

Finn had just used luminol to show her the blood spot on the left crease of the black hat. Completely invisible to the naked eye otherwise. He concurred. "Yes, it's sixteen millimeters in size. Certainly not insignificant."

"Any idea how it got there?" Gretchen asked. "When you first said you found blood, I thought it would be on the brim."

"We might never know, but I have a theory," the lab tech said nervously, as if he had overstepped his authority.

"Go ahead," she said.

"Okay," he replied, clearly pleased. He slipped on a pair of disposable nitrile gloves. "I'm the bomber. I don't know it, but I've cut the tip of my middle finger on my right hand. I'm bleeding." With his right hand, he picked up the hat and placed it on his head. He took it off and held the hat outstretched toward her. "Where are my fingers?"

Gretchen saw that his middle finger was on the center dent of the left crease, just below the crown. Perfectly overlaid on the blood spot. "Geez."

"Yep," he said. He put the cowboy hat back on the table. "Taking it on or off with blood on the pad of his middle finger."

"DNA?"

"We don't do that here."

"Let me guess. SkyLark."

He smiled. "You'll have to ask them."

She stared at the hat, as if willing it to talk. "Question... Would there be skin cells on the inside of the hat? On the head band? Where his forehead touches?"

"I checked, but nothing. Instead, I found some fabric pieces not belonging to the hat itself. Specifically, a micro fleece."

"Micro fleece?" she repeated.

"Probably from a moisture-wicking skull cap."

Gretchen was confused. "Which is… what, exactly?"

Finn quickly typed on his computer and then pivoted the monitor toward her, which showed a young man modeling a thin, tight-fitting beanie cap. "Athletes like these. Keeps you cool in the summer; you don't have sweat coming down your face. And motorcyclists swear by them—they wear them under their helmet. They're quite popular."

She pointed to the image. "So the hat owner, he wears something like that under his hat?"

"Obviously, I'm just guessing, but it could be because he knew the hat would serve its purpose as a bit of a disguise, and if he discarded it, he wouldn't want it coming back on him."

"Okay, that works I guess." She mulled it over. "But then he cut himself, and he leaves a ton of DNA behind." What she didn't say out loud was that this could explain why the guy was so desperate to get it back that he was now blackmailing Lars Vervloet .

"Could be diabetic," Finn offered. "Pricked his finger for a test strip. Didn't realize he was still bleeding."

Gretchen sighed. They could continue speculating, but at the end of the day, it didn't really matter. What mattered was seeing if the blood could be linked to anyone in the system. She said, "I'm going to need everything you can give me on the hat. Everything."

FROG Headquarters, The Hague

Due to the fact that the cardboard found in Bart Werner's apartment was too large for the overhead bin on a commercial flight and there was no way it was going to be put in the cargo hold, Adam had flown back to The Hague using FROG's account with NetJets. He had ended up on an Embraer Phenom 300 with only one other passenger, an older gentleman who didn't even glance at Adam. If the solitary flight attendant thought it was odd that he didn't have any luggage and only the cardboard for a carry-on, she hid it well, simply asking him if he wanted her to store it for him up front. He had declined the offer, instead asking for a latte and a late breakfast.

When Adam arrived at the FROG offices, Hal, Marsha, and Two were anxiously waiting to see the organizational chart for themselves. They moved into the conference room where Adam had carefully untied the two cardboard panels and laid them on the table. Two had immediately left, returning with a professional Canon digital camera, explaining that she planned to photograph it so she could put it in the computer, which would allow them to edit the chart as they saw fit.

"Excellent," Marsha said to Two.

Two took off her shoes, got up on the table in her stocking feet, and started taking pictures of the diagram. The others simply stared at it, trying to decipher it. Hal pointed to one section. "Some of these are just initials, not full names."

"Move your hand," Two said to Hal, who quickly withdrew his hand, allowing Two to keep shooting.

"Some have a first or last name," Adam said. "Might be able to match them to Red Arrow employees."

"Done," Two announced as she handed the camera to Marsha. Hal gave her a hand getting off the table.

"How long?" Adam asked Two.

"I don't know," she said with a grin. "It's not like I've done this before." She took the camera and left the room just as Gretchen entered carrying a laptop and a large paper shopping bag.

Gretchen handed Marsha the laptop. "All yours. And if at all possible, I promised to get it back to them in a couple days."

"Shouldn't be a problem," Marsha said agreeably, leaving the room with the computer.

Adam gave Gretchen a puzzled look. She said, "Werner's. It was in his carry-on."

"Police had it?"

"Airport police had returned the bag to the family. Very early this morning." She looked to Hal. "I only saw his mother. I asked her about the name you gave me, William DeWine. It didn't mean anything to her. She's pretty torn up."

"She mind giving you the laptop?" Hal asked.

Gretchen shook her head. "She hadn't even opened the carry-on. She couldn't bear to. She just wanted to know what happened, how her son could be killed, things like that." She grimaced. "I didn't have any answers."

"No one does," Hal told her sympathetically.

Gretchen stepped up to the table to see the cardboard diagram. "What is this?"

"It was under Werner's mattress," Adam related.

Gretchen leaned over to look closely. She quickly pointed to the top entry on the chart, asking, "The Joker? What's that about? The Joker?"

Adam filled her in on what they knew. "First we heard the term was when Bart Werner uttered his dying words." When she frowned, he went on. "I asked him what DeWine was going to tell me. That's what he said. The Joker."

"Do we know what it means?" Gretchen asked. "What he was referring to?"

"No clue," Adam said, shaking his head.

"Well, we need to find out." Gretchen reached into the large paper bag and pulled out a tan cowboy hat. "This is the exact size and make of the assassin's cowboy hat. It's made by Cantilever, a popular European hat maker."

Adam was about to say something and she waved him off, explaining, "It's not black, I know. They didn't have black, but I got this from the only Cantilever shop in the city, and they're trying to find one." She took off the leather hatband and showed it to them. "Comes with this. All leather with these metal tokens repeatedly woven into the leather."

Adam reached for the hatband, studying it. "What am I looking at?"

"The four suits in a deck of cards. A spade, club, diamond, and heart."

"Okay. So?" Adam remarked, handing the leather hatband to Hal.

"With one metal piece that is a bit bigger. The Joker."

Amsterdam, the Netherlands

Throughout the day, Gretchen had sent Lars Vervloet a total of four text messages, asking for a quick meeting. Each and every one was ignored. Two had checked Lars's phone number and told her, "It's turned off."

"You got his address," Adam had reminded Gretchen.

Hal shook his head. "We need his cooperation, not anger."

"He wants his bloody cat, doesn't he?" Adam retorted.

"He works all night and sleeps during the day," Gretchen reminded Adam. Finally, just after two in the afternoon, Lars responded. He suggested they meet at a hole-in-the-wall Indonesian eatery near his home. Marsha promptly did her homework, announcing that the place was renowned for serving the best iced ginger coffee around. There were only six indoor tables, two outdoor tables, and it looked like most customers preferred take-out.

In the hopes that the people who were blackmailing Lars would have him under surveillance, Hal and Adam were nearby, watching: Adam in a parked Range Rover; Hal at a city park just opposite the eatery where there were several outdoor chess tables available to the public. He was an avid player and immediately started playing, giving him the perfect cover. All three were connected with invisible two-way radio earpieces.

As planned, Gretchen had arrived twelve minutes early, and as soon as she walked in, she realized she was absolutely starving. She was the only customer present, and the proprietor, an older man, smiled from behind the glass case that held various breads and exotic-looking cakes. An older woman sat on a stool behind a cash register. Probably his wife.

Glancing at the selections posted on the wall, Gretchen ordered a hot tofu pudding with sweet ginger. Once she had paid for the treat and taken a seat at a table by the window, she heard Adam's annoying voice in her ear. "Sounds god-awful."

She was very tempted to tell him to piss off, but she refrained. Best to ignore him. She had her phone on the table and looked through it, mostly because that was typical of anyone alone these days. In other words, it was a prop. Minutes later, the older woman brought her the tofu dish and Gretchen thanked her. She took her spoon and dug in. "Delicious," she quietly announced.

"Yeah, yeah, yeah," Adam remarked in her earpiece.

She looked up just in time to see Lars across the street, waiting for the light to change.

"At the northeast corner," she quietly announced. "Yellow jacket."

"Got him," Adam confirmed.

The light changed and Lars joined several others crossing the street. "Approaching now," Gretchen said.

"Yep," Hal said quietly. She could hear the faint clink of a moving chess piece.

Lars entered and saw her, but showed no sign of knowing her. He ordered a coffee from the old man, paid the woman, and came over to her table. Still standing, he stared at her large cup. "What's that?"

"Sweet tofu pudding."

He made a face and sat down. He leaned forward, quite anxious. "Well?"

Gretchen woke her phone and found the image. She rotated it and showed it to him. "He look familiar?"

"Who is he?" Lars asked.

"Please, just look."

Lars took the phone and squinted at the image. "It's not a very good photo."

"I know," Gretchen agreed. It was the grainy image of the man in the wheelchair, looking up as the woman fell near him. "You recognize him?"

Lars shook his head and slid the phone back to her. "Who is he?" he repeated.

Gretchen didn't reply. Instead, she worked the phone, called up another image, and handed him the phone. "How about this one? You see him before? You can enlarge it."

Lars took the phone and did as she suggested, enlarging the image. Suddenly, his eyes grew large. He clearly recognized the man. "How'd you find him?"

"Who is he?"

"I told you! I don't know his name!" Lars angrily declared.

Gretchen noticed the older couple looking at them. She quietly told him, "Easy. We don't need a scene, okay?" Lars realized his error and sat back. Gretchen smiled at him for the sake of the eatery owners. "Help me out. Tell me how you know him."

"He was the younger man. Waiting for me at work that night. He showed me a picture of Milo on his phone and told me to get the hat."

"Okay... Good."

Irritated, Lars said, "Who is he?"

"We honestly don't know." Lars was about to erupt, but she waved him quiet. "I'm telling the truth. We think this man, whoever he is, is linked to another crime. That's all I can say."

Lars looked disgusted. "How does this help me get Milo?"

Even though Adam and Hal knew the order of the images she was going to show the witness, she wanted to leave no doubt that they knew he had identified the younger man from the airport. She asked, "Was this man wearing a Yankees hat like this? When you saw him?"

"No," Lars said testily, folding his arms across his chest. "I want Milo home."

"I know you do. So we're going to take the advice you were given." He looked confused and she smiled. "You're going to pull the fire alarm."

He looked astonished. "What?"

"Yep," she said with a confident smile. "Tonight."

Now he looked horrified. "Are you insane? I'll be fired!"

She quickly glanced at the eatery proprietors, then turned back to him and said in a quiet voice, "Shh. Keep your voice down."

Lars leaned back again, subconsciously creating space between them. "I don't know..."

"Max Becker agreed to the plan."

Lars was clearly surprised. "Mr. Becker?"

"That's right. It's tonight or not for several days at best," Gretchen patiently explained. "So we're doing it tonight."

Lars simply stared. Obviously quite unsure.

She smiled, keeping up the pretense that they were having an amicable discussion. "According to Max Becker, tonight there will be nine techs working late. We think the people that have Milo are watching. Maybe just watching the parking lot so they have a general idea of how many people are inside." Nothing. Was he even listening? "Lars, you remember? You were told people work late, if you pull the fire alarm, you can get the hat. They'll run out, not securing everything. Remember?"

"He won't fire me? Mr. Becker? You're sure?"

"I promise," Gretchen reassured him. "It's all set. In fact, he will have the evidence ready. You will pull the alarm, he'll give you the evidence, and you'll simply walk out with it. But a few minutes after the other staff members. In case they are watching. Okay?"

"Then... then what?" Lars nervously asked.

"Then you call the number they gave you and tell them it's done. You have the cowboy hat."

Lars raised his coffee cup to his mouth, but his hand was shaking so hard he had to put it down.

Gretchen told Lars to give her a five-minute head start, then he should go home and get ready for work. Leaving the eatery, she headed south. Hal's position in the park was closest to Lars's building, and he needed to follow from the front. In other words, once Lars was headed his way, he had to get ahead of him and, using the reflections of storefront windows, keep an eye on him to see if he had surveillance.

"Checkmate," Gretchen heard Hal say over her earpiece. She could hear an argument, a man with a thick Polish accent. She couldn't make out the words. Then the scraping of a chair. "Sorry, mate. Doctor's appointment."

"You're screwing up their winner-take-all system," Adam teased.

"They'll just have to get over it," Hal replied. He was walking fast and starting to sound a bit winded. "I'm out front. Looks like he's going straight home."

"Roger that," Adam said. A moment of silence, then: "Status, Gretchen?"

"At the end of the first block now," she said.

"Roger that." Dead air, then, "Try to burn off those 900 calories you just ingested."

"Let's go head-to-head on a fitness test," Gretchen retorted.

Adam laughed, and she was pleased. In just the one day, she had seen Two trade barbs with him and realized she should do the same. Yes, he had lots of seniority compared to her, and yes, she had thought they were about to embark on a passionate relationship, but she had to ignore all that. Treat him like he's her big brother—with lots of ribbing. And since he knew she was in top physical shape, call him out on his snide remarks.

Gretchen slowed, looking down at her phone. This was a ruse to be able to look around without being obvious. In fact, to anyone watching, it would appear that she was slowly turning in a circle to get the best angle of light on her phone. There were only two people on the street, neither of interest.

She kept walking. The plan was to loop around a couple blocks and end up approaching Lars's building from the opposite direction of Hal. Adam was to conduct a wider circle pattern around the area in the Range Rover.

"Hey, guys, can I step in?" It was Two, back at the FROG Headquarters, jumping onto their radio communication system.

"Go, Two," Hal immediately said.

"Okay," she replied. "For whatever it might worth, I'm confident that Yankees Hat is six-four to six-five."

"That's something," Gretchen said. At least it would rule out a lot of people. Hal simply grunted.

"I think this is bullshit," Adam groused. "They aren't watching this guy. They're hoping he comes through. That's all."

"And if he doesn't?" Hal asked. "Come through?"

"Bomb the lab," Adam said nonchalantly. "At least that's what I'd do if they had evidence I didn't want coming to light. They know how to do bombs. They've proven that."

"I was thinking you grab his mother," Hal offered.

"But will he want her back?" Adam countered. "He wants the cat, but the mother? Might be a tough call."

Everyone was quiet for several minutes. Then Adam said, "Status check."

"Still behind me," Hal said. "No one even close by."

"Nothing here," Gretchen related. Fortunately, at this time of day, the neighborhood was fairly quiet. Gretchen had to contend with scooters zipping past, but virtually no foot traffic. "End of the second block," she told them. "Heading east now... Repeat, heading east now."

She turned the corner, thinking she didn't want to have to agree with Adam, but this probably was a waste of time. This particular street was quite nice, with a series of three-story walk-ups on her right and cars parked side-by-side facing one of the city's many canals. She wondered what it cost to live here.

Ahead of her, a red Mini Cooper started to back out, and Gretchen had to wonder if such a coveted parking spot would be available whenever the driver returned home. If not going far, it was undoubtedly wiser to leave the car and use a bicycle. No doubt parking was a premium on a street like this.

As the Mini Cooper fully backed onto the street, revealing the vehicle next to it, Gretchen stopped dead in her tracks.

Up ahead was a white handicap van.

Chapter Five

Amsterdam, the Netherlands

Hal slowed and kneeled down to tie his shoe. An old trick, but effective. Looking over his shoulder, he saw Lars enter his building. He rose and said, "Okay, he's back to the nest."

"Anything?" Adam grumbled. "Or was this a waste of time?"

"Guys?" Gretchen cut in, a bit frantic. "Two, I've got a handicap van here. GM Express. I need the partial. Repeat, I need the partial on the handicap van."

"Shit! You've got it?" Adam asked with excitement.

"Last two are lima, echo," Two calmly relayed from their base in The Hague. "Repeat, lima, echo." She paused. "Although first letter could be an I, India. We're scanning using both."

"It's India," Gretchen calmly stated. She then proceeded to read off the full handicap plate including the registration date, which was still good.

"Status," Hal said urgently. "Anyone nearby?"

Again, Gretchen used the ruse of looking at her phone to slowly spin around. The street was dead. "Negative." But she suddenly felt extremely vulnerable. After all, the walk-up flats had windows overlooking the street and canal. Right where she was standing.

"Okay," Two said. "A 2015 GM Express Mobility van with that plate was stolen three nights ago in Lisse."

Lars was utterly exhausted. The Indonesian coffee hadn't even tasted good today. He hit the call button for the elevator. He and his mother lived on the top floor, so no way he was walking up six flights. The lift came and the doors opened. He stepped in and hit the button for his floor when another man in a bright blue sweatshirt and New York Yankees baseball cap quickly followed him into the lift. It took Lars a minute to realize he had seen the man before. In the dark parking lot of his workplace. And then on the lady cop's phone.

"Ah, we meet again," the man said in English.

All Lars could think was that the man was taller than he remembered. The elevator doors shut and the lift started to rise. Suddenly, the man hit the red emergency-stop switch and the lift immediately shuttered to a stop.

"Find Lars! Make sure he is okay!" Adam shouted in their ears. "Knock on his door if you have to!"

Hal knew what to do and he didn't need Adam telling him. He ran for the apartment building entrance, his mind racing.

Two's voice now said, "Flat number six-zero-nine. Repeat, flat number six-zero-nine."

Inside, Hal lost precious time trying to find the elevator. He hurried over and found an elderly woman waiting, leaning on a three-prong cane. She was looking at the numerical display above the closed doors. He hit the call button impatiently.

"I think it's broken," she told him, looking at the numbers up above.

Hal followed her look. The floor-indicator light was alternatively blinking between the two and three. Two and three. Damn! He turned to the woman. "Stairs! Where are the stairs?"

She pointed using her cane. He went running.

In the elevator, the cab light for the three-button kept flashing on and off in rapid fashion. Lars had never seen anything like it. Of course, he had never been stopped mid-floor before either.

"Who was she?" the tall man asked.

"W-who..?" Lars stuttered nervously.

"Don't even try to lie."

"She's just this woman—"

"Not attracted to the likes of you," the tall man said with derision. He stepped close, and suddenly the tip of a switchblade knife was under Lars's chin. Lars could feel the tip bite into his flesh. "The truth please."

Lars closed his eyes. "She... She used to work there."

"Where?"

"SkyLark…" he mumbled, fear gripping him.

"She a tech?" The knife dug in deeper and Lars held his breath. He was going to die. Right here. In the elevator. "Answer me. She a tech?"

Hal raced up the stairs, updating the others as he went. "Elevator is stuck between two floors." On level two, he found the elevator alcove and saw the same display as below, the floor-indicator light bouncing between the two and the three. He tried to pry the doors open with his bare hands. That was a joke. "Can't open the door."

"Go up to his flat," Adam said calmly. "Wait there."

"Interrupting," Two said over the radio. "Want me to call in the stolen vehicle or not?"

"Question is, is it abandoned or about to be used again?" Gretchen replied. If the Dutch police recovered the van, they might be able to get prints. Right now, FROG had nothing. An image of the tall man was about it.

"Stand down for now," Hal instructed, his voice labored as he hurried up the stairs.

"Agree," Adam said. "No way it's parked that close to the janitor's flat by chance. We wait. Gretchen, you okay?"

"Affirmative," she replied.

Inside the elevator, Lars continued to feel the knife tip under his chin. Finally, he said, "Is Milo alive?"

"Who is she?" the man spat out.

Lars wasn't good at lying. Which should be a good thing. But right now, it wasn't a good thing at all. "You killed my cat." He didn't know what else to say. He'd be dead if he said the attractive woman was a cop.

"Milo's alive, asshole!" the man said with disgust.

For some reason, Lars believed the man. Milo was alive!

"Tell me! Who is the woman!?"

Lars's mind scrambled. Finally, he confessed. "Administration."

"I don't believe you," the man immediately replied.

"She worked for Mr. Becker." Lars didn't know where the lie came from, but in odd way, it felt right. The knife eased a bit. Maybe the man knew the name Becker?

The man studied him. Finally, he said, "Why did you meet her?"

"To find out where it might be... The hat."

"You asked that? The cowboy hat? You asked that?" The tone was angry and the knife dug in, quite hard.

Lars could feel a trickle of blood drip down his throat. Instead of making him fearful, it suddenly emboldened him. "Leave me alone!" He pushed the man back, and it actually worked.

The man acquiesced and stayed a foot away, but it was clear who was in charge. And it wasn't Lars.

Using the back of his hand, Lars wiped away the blood on his neck. But seeing the blood just made him angrier. He looked up at the man. "Milo better be alive. Tonight, I will pull the alarm. I know where to find the hat, and I will get it." He stabbed the red emergency button, and the kill switch unlocked, allowing the elevator to slowly resume its assent, giving him courage. He stared at the man. "My cat isn't alive, you don't get the hat. Understand?"

The tall man unexpectedly laughed. He calmly pivoted and hit the button for the fourth floor. A minute later, the lift came to a rest and the doors opened. The tall man peeked out, but there was no one waiting. He hit the button to keep the doors open and stepped close to Lars, meticulously cleaning the bloody blade tip with Lars's sweater. "Tonight," the man whispered. "After that, Milo dies."

Then with a flick of a wrist, the knife retracted, and he was gone.

By the time he made it to the top floor, completely out of breath, Hal headed for the elevator. He was relieved to see the floor-indicator lights showing that the lift was coming up. Taking a few quick steps down the corridor in order to get a lay of the land, he saw the door for 609 nearby. Satisfied, he went back to the elevator and leaned against a wall to wait. It really had been a while since he had been in the field, and, judging by how winded he was, there was no doubt that he belonged in the office.

Just then the elevator pinged, and Hal pushed himself off the wall, standing up straight. The doors opened and Lars step off. Upon seeing Hal, the Dutchman jumped a mile—obviously quite spooked. Hal gave him a reassuring smile, showing that he was no threat. He could see a long smear of dried blood on Lars's throat. Lars hurried off, and Hal stepped into the elevator. Obviously, Lars had been assaulted when the elevator had been stalled between floors. But by who? And why? The doors slowly started to close and Hal hit the hold-open button and stepped out again, peeking around the open door. Lars was entering his flat, the door shutting behind him. Good. The man was home safe.

With her phone in hand, Gretchen had taken a seat on the front steps of a nearby apartment building as if waiting for a ride. From this vantage point, the van was only about twenty yards away, and she could easily monitor the entire street. Glancing to her right, her heart skipped a beat as she saw the tall man coming her way with a long, loping stride and wearing the New York Yankees baseball cap. "Got Yankees Man," she relayed. "Repeat, Yankees Man approaching."

"Sit tight," Adam said. "I'm one block over."

~ ~ ~

It wasn't usually Marsha's job to do anything for a FROG operation other than keep things running smoothly from their headquarters in The Hague. But with other operators scattered across the globe and Hal, Gretchen, and Adam tied up for the afternoon, someone had to meet Max Becker at SkyLark Labs and give him the tracker. It came down to either her or Two, and since Two was already monitoring the comms of Adam, Gretchen, and Hal, she opted to do it herself. She dreaded the traffic, knowing it would take a good hour to get to Amsterdam and another full hour to get home. On the other hand, it would be a nice distraction to be out of the office for a bit.

Becker had told her to use a VIP parking space out front when she arrived, and she was grateful for the close parking. She wanted to make this a quick turn around and beat the traffic home. Her cell phone chimed and she glanced at the display. It was a text from Two. "Arrived safe and sound, I see." With a happy emoji face.

She replied with a thumbs-up, grabbed her purse, and headed for the entrance. Inside the large lobby, she gave her cover name to the security officer on duty. She had chosen the name of a woman who also worked undercover at AIVD, since she had to be from the same government agency as Gretchen. If Becker or the security guard or anyone else tried to find the real woman, they would hit multiple roadblocks. If nothing else, AIVD protected their assets quite well.

The security guard checked her name off a list and picked up the phone—speaking to someone on the other end in hushed tones. A man of about sixty soon approached and introduced himself as Max Becker. He escorted her to his personal office on the ground floor where he used an RFID card to unlock the door. Considering his status at the company, she had expected a nicely appointed spacious office with large windows. Instead, it was a small, bleak office cluttered with books of all kinds, many of them stacked on the floor. The only window was quite small and overlooked the parking lot.

He gestured to the books. "Writing a rather complex book on DNA sequencing of viral infections, and my research tends to accumulate here quite rapidly."

She gave a polite smile, noticing that Becker had cleared off his desk and the two cowboy hats sat there. One was the real hat, which Becker had picked up himself from Goshart Labs earlier that day. The other had just been sent by courier from the hat shop—fortunately the boutique had just gotten in a black cowboy hat, complete with the joker hat band, in the correct size.

Now it was up to Becker to do his best to have the duplicate hat ready by late that night. This meant holding it over a vaporizer as it spewed hot steam, softening the now-stiff fur-base felt so it would be more malleable, allowing him to shape it so it was a clone of the real thing. Then he would have to add any stains that the original might have and finally coat the brim and crown with a vacuum metal composition that used zinc and gold to pick up fingerprints off fabric, since the original hat had a noticeable dusting of the fingerprint powder. If the owner thought he was getting his hat back in pristine condition, he would soon learn otherwise.

"You're doing this yourself?" Marsha asked.

Becker looked at her. "Yes. It's best this way. Besides, it is sort of fun to go back to my tech days. Be hands on instead of pushing paper and writing every spare minute. But when you think about it, this is all rather silly."

"Sir?" Marsha asked, baffled.

He smirked. "If they think by blackmailing my employee, they get the evidence back, all good and fine, but don't they realize reports are already done? DNA reports on the blood samples have been sent out, fingerprint analysis is done? All that will still be on record, with or without the actual hat."

Marsha had thought the same thing herself. But she had a hypothesis. "My guess is that they are thinking that with no physical evidence on hand, it could be argued that whatever you have forensically can't be used in court."

"Rubbish," he said dismissively with the wave of a hand.

"Anything on the DNA?" she asked.

"Not in the system. But if you guys find him, we can link him to the hat."

"What about prints?"

"Same," Becker said. "He's not in the system."

"And you went far and wide, right? Interpol? You went everywhere?"

He looked a bit annoyed. "He's not in the system."

"Right," Marsha said, suddenly grateful she only had to deal with FROG personnel, not people like Becker. She removed a tiny plastic bag from her purse. "Here it is."

Becker took the bag and held it up to the light. "Amazing, so incredibly small."

"You'll have to use tweezers, but the blue tab on the back comes off. Then it will stick to any surface. It's already live and working. A colleague correctly tabbed me here when I pulled in." What she didn't say, since he didn't need to know, was that it would stay active for another seventy-two hours. They just had to hope that would be enough time.

~ ~ ~

"Sitrep," Adam said.

"Sitting there," Gretchen replied. "Yankees Man got in the van, but he hasn't started it yet."

"Damn! I'm double parked," he groused. "I can't stay here forever."

Hal chimed in. "I'm now down at the end. Just pick me up when you come through."

"Copy that," Adam replied.

Gretchen had no doubt that the three of them could take the man. However, they wanted to tail him in the hope that he would lead them to all involved, including the assassin of Bart Werner. Finally, she heard the engine start. "Okay, vehicle is running. Standby…" She studied the dark screen of her phone, keeping her head down. She didn't want to tip him off that she was interested in the vehicle. She heard the annoyingly loud warning beep as the van backed up, and she couldn't help but look up. Anyone would. She immediately looked down at her phone again, telling the others, "He's leaving. Repeat, Yankees Man is leaving."

"Okay," Adam responded. "I don't want to turn in until he is pretty far down. Moving in on your mark."

"Roger," Gretchen said. It didn't take long before she saw he was at the end of the one-way street, the left blinker on. Then the van turned. "Clear to pick me up. He's gone."

The Range Rover quickly approached, barely stopping to allow Gretchen to jump in the front seat.

"He's stuck at a light," Hal said. He came trotting toward them and got in the back seat. At the end of the road, Adam stopped for only a nano second and then floored it, going left across oncoming vehicular traffic. An angry motorist gave Adam the finger, but the job was done—the handicap van was only two cars ahead of them.

After a few miles, the road narrowed to one lane in each direction with curbs protecting the wide center area laid with standard-gauge tracks for the city's electric trams. Overhead were the crisscrossing electrical lines. There was also the usual collection of pedestrians and scores of bicyclists, all vying for the same space along the sidewalk.

Hal sat forward, leaning between the front seats. "When I lived here, I sometimes thought I should run for mayor simply to synchronize the lights. It used to drive me nuts."

"He takes us to the assassin, I'm finishing the man off," Adam announced.

"We need these guys alive," Hal reminded them.

~ ~ ~

Stretched out on the van's sofa, she desperately wanted a drink of water. However, since the day's first light, her mouth dry as cotton, she hadn't taken a swallow from the offered bottle of water. She now knew it was poisoned. With what, she didn't know. But she knew it gave her an awful bellyache and then suddenly made her sleepy. Unbelievably sleepy. So instead of drinking the water, she had faked it. The last four times, she had taken a small amount in her mouth, simply to satisfy him, and as soon as he turned away, she had turned over and buried her face in the small pillow, silently spitting it out. Then she would lie there, barely moving. And wondering if just the minuscule amount in her mouth would be enough to knock her out.

Moments ago, she had awakened with a start at the sound of the doors unlocking. She hadn't realized he had left, but he must have. Finally, all of her senses were coming back to her, the sleepy haze lifting, and now her heart was racing. Minutes ago, it had taken all the courage she had to remain motionless on the sofa when he came back to check on her, as he always did. She pretended to be asleep. Once again, he nudged her shoulder, calling out her name. "Amber? Amber? You awake?"

She told herself not to flinch. He wasn't going to hurt her. If he had wanted to hurt her, he would have done so long before now. He was just keeping her drugged. So she pretended to be asleep. She stayed that way for what seemed like forever. He was right there. Looking at her, she knew. She tried to stay relaxed even though her heart felt like it was going to leap out of her chest. She kept her eyes closed, willing him to leave her.

"Amber? You thirsty?"

She didn't move. She was lying on her back, her hands folded over her heart. She imagined she might look like the picture of pure innocence. A fifteen-year-old girl napping on a sofa. Except for the fact that her wrists were bound together with a thin, but strong rope.

"Amber, c'mon!" He nudged her, much harder. "Just take a swallow so you stay hydrated, okay?"

Now a violent shake. She moaned, her eyes fluttering open. She saw the same bright blue sweatshirt he always wore and the same stainless-steel water bottle in his hand. It's all she needed to see, and, pretending a drug-induced haze, she closed her eyes again. He didn't say a word, but he did check the rope. It was tied securely. No way she was getting her hands free. She knew that all too well.

Satisfied, he grunted, and she heard him go up front, get behind the wheel, and start the van. They'd only gone a very short distance when the van stopped. Traffic? Or a stop light? Maybe both. She couldn't see from the sofa. The van inched forward, and then they were moving at a good speed.

Her heart in her throat, she knew it was now or never. She rolled to the floor and crawled forward, very slowly. Then she knew she had to just do it. She got to her feet, staggering a bit since her hands were bound together and her balance was off. The van abruptly stopped, throwing her to the passenger-side wall. She let out a startled cry, and he looked over his shoulder and saw her.

Without hesitation, Amber dashed forward. She wedged her torso between the front seats and was somehow able to grab the stainless-steel water bottle from the cupholder. He tried to grab her, but she was able a step back, albeit a bit off balance, staying just out of his reach. It took her a minute, but she got the top off the water bottle and lunged forward again. Steadying herself against the passenger seat, she held the water bottle between her bound hands and drenched his face.

He yelled in anger, inadvertently pulling the steering wheel to the right. She raised the bottle like a cricket bat and brought it down on his head. Hard. Seemingly unfazed, he reached around to grab her and got ahold of her shirt. She tried to pull away, but he was too strong. With no other choice, she bent over and bit his wrist, hard, tasting blood.

He hollered in pain. And let go.

Gretchen noticed it first, pointing ahead. "Hey! Is the van was trying to pull over?" They were now at a virtual stop at yet another light, and although there was no room to move a vehicle off the road, the van was now angled to the right. "He's trying to get over!"

"What the hell?" Hal mumbled, still leaning between the front seats for a clear view.

Just then, the handicap van rocked forward, stopping hard.

He had simply been dazed, so Amber had hit him on the head again with all her might, and the van lurched to the right. She was thrown forward and almost lost her grip on the water bottle. But she didn't. She straightened and hit him once more, just for good measure. He slumped in the driver's seat, the van gently rolling until it stopped at the curb.

She hurried to the side door and tried to open it, but it was locked. She immediately realized that with the vehicle running and in gear, the doors would remain locked. The van had to be in park. In order for her to do that, she would need to be in the driver's seat. Obviously, that wasn't an option.

Her heart raced. She was trapped!

From the Range Rover, the FROG team saw the light turn green. Traffic ahead moved. But not the van. With no room to maneuver around it, irritated drivers blasted their horns.

Amber suddenly remembered. Julie had told her that there were a couple of emergency switches. Just for situations like this, when the driver gets in an accident and the disabled person has to get out. She wracked her brain, looking along the sides of the van. Where was it? She didn't see anything. Then she remembered— one switch was on the steering column! Somewhere on the steering column. She went back to the front seat and, with her hands tied together, leaned over the man's shoulder, squirming to get close to the steering column. She was halfway over his seat and still she couldn't reach past the steering wheel. The man was so tall, the seat was positioned as far back as it would it go. Of all the rotten luck!

"We can grab him," Adam pointed out as he stared at the stopped vehicle. "No one has gotten out. He's there. I say we grab him."

"Wait," Hal cautioned. "We want him to go to home base. We grab him now, we might have nothing."

"Yes, if they were moving we'd have that chance! They've stopped!" Adam argued. "Maybe he's broken down. Maybe he's out of gas, I don't know. But look around! We're in the heart of the city with people everywhere. He makes a run for it, we lose him."

The din of honking horns grew worse, grating on everyone's nerves.

Amber wiggled and wiggled and eventually reached the steering column. The man hadn't flinched. She had successfully knocked him out. She frantically felt for the button. Where was it? It seemed to take forever, but she finally felt a raised knob and anxiously pressed it, hard.

She heard a loud warning beep and looked over her shoulder. The rear doors were slowly opening. It worked! Thank God! She was mesmerized by the welcome sight. She knew once the doors were open, the power lift would slowly start to fold down. She would be free! Actually free! Finally!

She pushed herself off the man's shoulder, surprised when he suddenly seized her wrists. Her heart racing, she twisted violently against his grip. Fortunately, he wasn't at full strength and she was able to break free.

"Look!" Gretchen yelled, pointing to the van.

The rear double doors were swinging open, followed by the lift gradually moving into place. Scores of pedestrians stopped to watch. Some using their phones to record the strange spectacle. The lift was now parallel to the street below.

Suddenly, a girl appeared from the interior of the van, running fast but quite awkwardly with her hands clasped together in front of her. She dashed across the stationary lift and sprang off the end, her long red hair flying behind her, her arms raised above her head, her hands perfectly aligned with one another—as if she was imitating an Olympic diver holding some sort of strange artistic form. She landed awkwardly on the street and rolled, instantly hidden from view by the car directly behind the van.

With that, Gretchen was out the door, shouting, "I'll stay with her!"

She took off at a run.

Chapter Six

Amsterdam, the Netherlands

They were now in the dank basement of a three-story walk-up.

Minutes earlier, when Adam had realized that Yankees Man was ditching the handicap van at a very fast walk, he jumped out of the Range Rover, shouting at Hal to take the wheel. The immediate area was in complete mayhem, frustrated drivers honking their horns, pedestrians and bicyclists stopping to watch the whole thing unfold. Many people were busy taking pictures of Gretchen as she helped get the young redhead away from the area. She had to shout "Police!" several times in order to break through the crowd. Adam had no idea where they had gone.

He had been too busy trying to keep up with the tall man without bringing attention to himself. But in short order, when Yankees Man realized that Adam was in pursuit, he had taken off at a dead run, and the race was on.

After running through various streets, the man had dashed into an apartment building and ran downstairs. They had ended up in the basement that was used as a common storage area, littered with old bicycles, unwanted furniture, and various odds and ends. Further along, the basement area dead ended at a communal laundry room with two washing machines and one dryer. Fortunately, neither was in use. Hopefully, no one would be coming down to use them any time soon. The last thing he needed was to be the star on someone's video that would be posted all over social media.

Now squared off about twelve feet from each other, Adam expected the man to rush him—put up a fight. And depending upon how skilled the man was, Adam could be in for a very tough battle. However, the man simply stood against a large furnace, staring at him and breathing hard from their race through the streets.

"I get it," the man said in English. "You're some sort of vigilante out to save the world. I get it."

Adam simply stared. Lars had been right—the man wasn't Dutch. He was American, speaking with a New York accent.

The man continued. "I know what you're thinking, but I swear, I didn't hurt her. I'm not that kind of person."

Adam waited for more denials, but they weren't forthcoming. So Adam asked, "What's your name?"

The man glared. "Are you listening? I didn't hurt her. I swear!" he insisted, clearly frustrated.

"Maybe. Maybe not. What's your name?" Adam asked.

The man shook his head, repeating himself. "I didn't hurt her, I swear."

"Your name?" Adam asked again.

"She bit me! Look!" He pushed up his right sleeve to expose his wrist for Adam to see, but Adam was too far away to see much. "She bit me!"

"You were hurting her," Adam calmly told him.

"No! It wasn't like that! I swear! I never hurt her! I drugged her, yes! I had to, to keep her quiet. That's it, I swear!"

"That's good to know." His tone was sarcastic.

"She was just there, you know?" the man argued. "It wasn't my fault!"

Adam nodded thoughtfully. "Okay, I'll play along... Who is she?"

"I don't know, I swear. Amber. I mean, she said her name is Amber."

"From Lisse?" Adam asked. The man seemed surprised and Adam went on. "You like young teens, that it?"

"No! Look, I got the van. I stole it. I'll admit that. But she was already in there. I'm telling you, I didn't know!"

"You didn't see her?" Adam was skeptical.

"It was night!" He now put a hand just above his waist, no doubt suffering from the abdominal pain of a side stitch from running hard. "There's a sofa in there. She had a blanket over her. I didn't see her. I just needed the van!"

"To get the killer away from Schiphol Airport."

The man's face instantly changed—a mask came down. He knew he was now in uncharted waters.

Adam continued, pressing his advantage. "The assassin was on Bart Werner's flight, and once they landed and made it through passport control, he did as he was hired to do and killed the young man."

The man straightened up. Maybe this would come down to hand-to-hand combat after all.

To tamp that down, Adam said, "All of AIVD is looking for you. You do know AIVD, right? Kind of like your FBI and CIA rolled into one?"

The man shook his head. "I was told to kill her, okay? Kill her!" he argued. "I didn't. I couldn't. I mean, she's just some kid. I'm not a killer."

"You helped a killer get away from the airport. Same thing in my book." Nothing from the man. "Who is he?"

The man stared at Adam, frozen.

"Who killed Bart Werner?"

Still nothing.

"Who is The Joker?" Adam asked.

Now the man's face showed fear. Pure fear.

"Tell me the plan," Adam went on. "You killed a lot of innocent people at that café to keep it quiet, so tell me now."

"That wasn't me!"

"No, it wasn't. You're too tall," Adam calmly replied. "But you want The Joker cowboy hat. So, you're in this as deep as it goes."

Yankees Man stared at him. Every revelation from Adam was throwing him for a curve. "Please…"

"You tell me, you won't serve time here," Adam promised him. "You can go home. We'll let the Americans sort it out."

The man seemed to consider the offer. Finally, he shook his head. "She bit me," he repeated. This time, he folded back the cuff of his sweatshirt. Adam thought it was to show the bite mark again. But there was something attached to the inside of the garment. Perhaps a button. The man put the cuff of the sweatshirt to his mouth.

Adam instantly realized what was happening and sprang forward. "No!"

He landed on the man, and they fell to the floor, the Yankees hat flying through the air. But the button or whatever it was, was already in the man's mouth. He bit down on it, and Adam fought with all his strength to open the man's mouth and dig it out. However, the man continued to clamp down hard, and all Adam managed to do was open the man's lips, thereby coating his fingers with white foam.

The man convulsed once, his face slowly went slack, and the deed was done.

He was dead.

~ ~ ~

"You live here?"

"My mother did," Gretchen said. She had grabbed the door key from under the mat, reminding herself not to put it back. It should have been removed long ago. She went into the kitchen, opened the drawer where her mother had kept miscellaneous junk, and found the six-inch gardening shears used to trim the front hedge.

The girl was in the living room, looking around. The sheer curtains were pulled across the wide window, a diffused light spilling across the old carpet. When Gretchen walked back in, the girl asked, "She's dead, huh?"

"Afraid so." She took the girl's wrists and cut off the rope.

"Thanks," the girl said, rubbing her wrists. She continued to look around.

Although Gretchen planned to sell the place, she had cousins living in Gibraltar who wanted to come help her sort through the memorabilia before listing the house. And that was fine with Gretchen. She really hadn't wanted to tackle the house—and the memories—all on her own.

The girl turned back to her. "Why are we here? If you're police, we should be at a police station."

Great, Gretchen thought. Just great. The kid wasn't stupid. Finally, she said, "You ever hear of AIVD?"

The girl shook her head. Gretchen said, "Government security service."

Studying her, the girl said, "Like a secret agency? James Bond?"

Gretchen smiled. "Sort of, I guess."

"Why didn't you take me there? There must be an office. We're in Amsterdam, right?"

"Right."

Suddenly the girl's face changed. "I was here once. A long time ago. My mom was sick, and my dad and I brought her up here to see a doctor." She looked away. "Stupid doctor couldn't do anything to help so we went home."

"I'm sorry."

"You know what the doctor said?" It wasn't really a question. The girl didn't seem to be expecting a reply; she was staring at her feet.

This wasn't the conversation Gretchen wanted to have with the kid, but she had to gain the girl's trust. She remembered Hal's axiom, be patient. Gretchen quietly asked, "What did he say? The doctor?"

She looked up at Gretchen in surprise, as if she didn't remember her own question. "It was a woman. She said because my grandmother had breast cancer and died, and Mom had breast cancer and she was going to die, that I was going to get it." Gretchen was clearly surprised, and it showed on her face. The girl went on. "Yeah. Crazy, huh? She said, at some point, I was going to get it too, and I would only live a long life if I did that surgery, you know?"

"A mastectomy?" Gretchen guessed. "A double mastectomy?"

The girl nodded.

Gretchen said, "What did your parents say about that?"

She looked at Gretchen. "My father wasn't there. He was in a bar. Drinking. It was just me and Mom at the doctor's office." Gretchen gave an encouraging smile, and the girl continued. "Mom said we needed a nice treat, so we found this little restaurant and had some pie. Apple pie with lots of ice cream."

Gretchen smiled. "Sounds good to me."

The girl grew serious. "Mom said not to do that surgery. She said I should, you know, self-check. She said that woman doctor? That was just her opinion. But there are all kinds of new medicines being discovered. Plus, I might not even get it, you know?"

"Good advice if you ask me," Gretchen said.

"Got any food?" the girl suddenly asked.

~ ~ ~

Shortly after the Yankees Man died, Adam had given Hal his location and then turned on one of the washing machines, selecting the hot water tab. Nearby was a box with a little bit of dry detergent left at the bottom, and he used that to wash his hands thoroughly as the tub filled. The water became too hot, and he had to switch the cycle to a warm wash before he was finally satisfied and stopped the wash cycle, shaking his hands dry before rubbing them across his chest. After that, he started looking around for what he needed. He found it in the dryer—a clean load of clothes. He found a small cloth and realized it was a baby's shirt. Sewn across the chest was a pink elephant. He used his pocketknife to cut up the shirt. He needed only a small section. He put the remainder of the torn garment in a nearby trash can.

Hurrying over to the stairs, he saw and heard nothing. With the coast clear, he went over to the body and cut into the man's forearm. Since the man was dead, he didn't bleed, but Adam cut again and got more than enough of the man's flesh to provide DNA. Using the blade so he wouldn't contaminate the specimen, he placed a small amount on the clean cloth, then wrapped it up tightly. Finally, he wiped the blade on the dead man's jeans.

Realizing he couldn't have the man's blood on the blade, he hurried to the stairs. Still quiet. He went back to the washing machine, switched it back to a hot-water wash, and ran the blade under the hot water. When the water ran clear, he turned off the machine, dried the knife, and dropped it into his pocket.

He heard a noise and stuffed the cloth in his jeans pocket. To his relief, it was Hal carrying a small device, no larger than a large cell phone. "Got DNA," Adam told him. With that, he took a watch position at the bottom of the stairs.

Hal immediately got to work. He had only used the mobile device once before and in that case, he had lots of time. Right now, he felt under the gun. They were in a public place, and at any point, someone could come downstairs to use the laundry.

He quickly pulled the biometric fingerprint scanner from its protective sleeve and pressed the power button. It immediately came to life, and he clicked on the icon for the left hand. Then he firmly imprinted each of the five digits on the biometric screen. They got a hit. He looked at the scanner. "American. Prints on file, but no link to criminal activity." He glanced over at Adam. "You get pictures?"

"No, better do it. We're clear," Adam replied.

Hal took out his phone and shot several pictures. They had photographs, fingerprints, and DNA.

Game, set and match.

FROG Headquarters, The Hague

Hal, Gretchen, and Adam arrived back at FROG by five that afternoon, and by then, Two had procured what she could of the dead American, a man named Mac Thornburg Senton. Convening in the conference room and working off a laptop, Two gestured toward the screen. A man wearing a business suit was smiling back at them.

"Mac Thornburg Senton. Thirty-eight," Two said. "Graduated from Harvard and went straight to Wall Street, working for Goldman Sachs. Hedge-fund manager there for twelve years."

"Prints come from the SEC?" Adam asked, referring to the Security and Exchange Commission, which required equity firms to submit employee fingerprints to the FBI for criminal background checks.

"Exactly," Two replied. "And before you ask, nothing on him in terms of police records. As far as I can tell, he was squeaky clean."

Gretchen gestured to the screen. "That a picture of him working there? Goldman Sachs?"

"No. Believe it or not, it's from his days at Red Arrow Capital." Everyone stared at Two, clearly surprised. "I know. Amazing, huh?"

"So he worked for Red Arrow in New York?" Hal slowly asked.

"Only for a year. Then he transferred."

"To their London office," Gretchen surmised.

"Yes and no. First, to Dubai. One year there, then off to London. He was there just seven months, and then he simply vanished."

"Vanished?" Hal repeated.

"That's my word," Two clarified. "Officially, Red Arrow says he retired." The screen changed to show a letter on Red Arrow letterhead. It was five sentences long. "His retirement announcement. Short and sweet. Dated ninety-two days ago."

Hal squinted at the screen. "What's it say?"

"Boilerplate company retirement announcement from their media-relations department. Thanking him for his hard work, wishing him luck in his future endeavors, yada, yada, yada."

"Any sign that the company wanted him out? He under investigation, maybe? Gretchen asked. "That would explain his early retirement."

"Nothing that I can find. But I've only had his name for an hour or so."

"He has to show up somewhere," Adam argued.

"Nothing so far," Two told them. "As far as I can tell, he went completely off the grid. And look, I've got his full name, I've got his Social Security number, his date of birth. I've got him. But I'm coming up with zilch."

"Nothing at all?" Hal asked.

"No taxes paid anywhere, so if there is income, it's under the table. No active bank accounts or credit cards. He's not in any cellphone company database, no utility company, nothing. Not even time spent in any hospital or jail. No airplane travel since he retired. Nothing on social media. But I've only had time to look here in Holland, the UK since he worked there, and America. The computers are looking now throughout Europe and Dubai. After that, we'll try Russia and Asia." She sighed. "I need more time. I mean who knows, maybe he'll show up in New Zealand or Australia, but right now, I'm not finding him. That's why I say he vanished."

She put up the picture of the smiling Mac Senton again. Hal leaned back in his chair, his hands laced behind his head, staring at the ceiling. "So, we have William DeMint, calling himself Matthew, who got blown up at an Amsterdam café, working for Red Arrow. We have Bart Werner, who got sliced up as soon as he set foot in Holland, working for Red Arrow. And now, we have American Mac Senton dying in Holland after chewing on a cyanide drop-dead pill, *retired* from Red Arrow."

Adam gave a heavy sigh. "They all knew each other. They had to."

"Right," Two said. "I found this. Taken four days before he vanished."

Hal eagerly sat forward. The screen changed to show a picture of Nancy Ellison, the short, attractive race-car driver that DeMint had been linked to. She was wearing her racing gear and DeMint was on one side of her with Senton on the other side, wearing his blue New York Yankees baseball cap. All three were smiling happily.

Adam pointed at the image. "We need everything we can get on the woman. And turn her inside out."

~ ~ ~

Marsha was back at FROG a little after two in the morning. The operation wouldn't begin for another couple of hours, but she wanted time to catch up on things. Her husband, Nathan, had gotten up with her, and while she was showering, he'd made her a sandwich to take with her. Hours later, he would make sure the kids got off to school. She honestly didn't know what she would do without him. As a spouse of a FROG employee, he knew that his wife worked for an off-the-record intelligence firm, but nothing more than that. And he was terrific about her sometimes-strange hours. The children simply believed she worked for attorneys at the Peace Palace.

Once at FROG, Marsha read a note from Two, who had left to go home just a few hours before having said she had done all she could for the time being. Two had left their state-of-the-art computer systems still searching for any information on Mac Thornburg Senton and also an English woman named Nancy Ellison. Two also reminded Marsha that their three operators had to be wheels-up before three that morning.

Marsha had quickly gotten up to speed on what had transpired earlier that day, and she thought it had all worked out amazingly well, all things considered. First, that the girl Amber hadn't been injured in her jump from the elevated handicap ramp. It turns out, she was a gymnast in school and she knew to roll with her fall, just as she did in tumbling. Once Gretchen helped her to her feet, she'd easily kept pace as Gretchen guided her away from the scene and prying eyes. They had jumped on a tram and made it to the flat belonging to Gretchen's late mother. The perfect place to debrief the girl.

As for Hal and Adam, luck had held for them; they'd been able to leave the apartment building unseen. They had just gotten in the Range Rover when Gretchen had contacted them, explaining where she was and that she needed food. Lots of food. The girl was starving. The men agreed to pick up Chinese food.

Gretchen had wisely set up her phone to covertly videotape the four of them sitting around the dining-room table, inhaling the food. Prompted by Gretchen to tell them how she had come to be in the stolen van, Amber had nonchalantly told them that every night for the better part of a year now she slept most of the night in the handicap van. The vehicle belonged to her schoolfriend's father, and he never went anywhere at night.

"You homeless?" Adam had asked.

Amber had blushed. "No. I just like it there, that's all."

Adam stared at her, then pointed his chopsticks at her. "Good place to hang out with your boyfriend."

"What? No," she responded, almost offended. "No way."

"Okay, then I have to ask—who is hurting you?" Amber had given him a deer-on-the-headlights look, but Adam pushed. "Your father? Brother? Some family member, I imagine. Someone at your family home, anyway."

The girl had looked horrified, and Gretchen had wanted to kill him.

"No! No one!" Amber insisted.

Adam nonchalantly continued eating as if he hadn't heard her.

After several minutes, the tears came and Amber confessed. "Mom always said he was a mean drunk. Some people, they drink and get sleepy, or happy, more relaxed."

"But not your father," Gretchen said. In their earlier talks, Gretchen had learned that after Amber's mother passed away, it had just been the two of them. Her father hadn't remarried.

Amber had rolled her eyes the way teenagers do, passing it off as no big deal. "When he couldn't hit Mom anymore, he started hitting me. So I stay away." She gave Adam a penetrating look. "Happy?"

Adam seemed surprised by the question. "Hardly. He's weak, and, truthfully, I hate weak people. Man or woman."

This threw Amber. She clearly didn't know what to say, and everyone continued with their meal in silence. Finally, Gretchen turned to Amber, curious. "Doesn't he wonder where you are?"

"He gets off work around four. Goes to a pub or two." She gave a feeble smile. "Or three. Comes home. By then, I'm gone."

"In the van?" Gretchen prompted.

"Yeah. He comes home, and sometimes, he makes it to his bedroom. But usually, he… he falls down in the living room."

"Out cold," Adam surmised.

"Yeah." No one spoke for a few minutes, then Amber revealed more. "I put a webcam in the living room. And his bedroom. I use the app on my phone to see if it's safe, and I go home. Before it gets light. Mostly, I need the toilet. I can't wake up Julie's family, and there isn't one in the van.

"Sometimes, I do my homework then. I don't have a laptop. Just a desktop, so I can't drag that to and from the van. Anyway, if my homework is done, sometimes, I sleep. Then I shower and leave for school." She grinned. "I can see on the cameras once he wakes up? He checks stuff. He can tell I was home. I think he just thinks I'm always in my room sleeping when he gets home."

"He doesn't peek in, when he comes home late?" Gretchen asked.

"I keep the door locked at night and go in and out the window."

Gretchen had been impressed. "Smart."

Once Gretchen had texted Two the girl's full name—Amber Frist—and her home address in Lisse, Two had found that the girl had not been reported missing. The van had been reported stolen, but there had been no mention about anyone being kidnapped.

When Gretchen had asked Amber why her schoolfriend hadn't told anyone, the redhead had sighed. "I dunno. I mean, her parents would be mad. And then my dad would find out, and that wouldn't be good, you know?"

The whole episode was depressing to say the least.

Investigating the family, Two had learned that the mother had died two years before, and a copy of the death certificate confirmed cancer. Amber had been telling the truth. The father had been arrested once for assaulting his wife, but she had declined to press charges at the time and that was that. There had been no calls to the house for domestic disturbance since then.

It was Two who had made sure that social services in Lisse had the resources in place to immediately help the teen. From what she found, Amber would have plenty of support. But in order for her to get it, they needed Amber to show up at a police station and tell them everything that had happened to her—the abuse at home, why she had been sleeping in the van, the tall man keeping her drugged, and then her escape.

The police wouldn't need to confirm her escape—video footage of the girl diving off the handicap ramp had instantly gone viral, the police asking for assistance in identifying the girl and locating her. While there had been no formal identification, there were some Facebook posts from kids in Lisse saying that it looked like their schoolmate Amber Frist.

Meanwhile, the police had secured the handicap van, and soon thereafter they got calls about an unidentified dead man in an apartment basement. Someone had taken a picture of the dead man—clearly showing the dried white foam around his mouth—and put it on social media. Needless to say, it had spread like wildfire.

Gretchen had walked Amber to the front steps of the closest police station, making sure the teenager knew that she shouldn't mention AIVD. Amber had agreed and Gretchen had given the girl a quick hug goodbye and sent her on her way. Amber had looked back once, then disappeared inside the police station.

Wondering if there was anything new on Amber Frist, Marsha surreptitiously logged on to the Dutch National Police system. This allowed FROG to monitor the entire police force since it operated as one national police agency divided into twenty-five different geographic regions. Once in, she drilled down to the city of Lisse. And it was right there. Front and center. She read it, yet she couldn't believe it. She printed the report that would go in their hardcopy workbook.

Marsha looked at the clock and realized time had gotten away from her. She quickly grabbed a fresh cup of coffee and went to the FROG lounge. From the glass door she could see inside the comfortable room where the other three were currently sleeping under the dim lights, resting up for what promised to be a long night. She wondered if Gretchen had been the first one in the room and had thereby snagged the leather sofa, having grabbed a pillow and a blanket from the closet. Or if the men had been chivalrous. Adam had taken one of the four recliners, a fleece blanket over him. Hal had done the same.

The lounge was constructed with soundproof walls to allow anyone inside to have peace and quiet as they recharged their batteries. As if feeling Marsha's penetrating look, Gretchen stirred, stretching her arms lazily. She slowly sat up and grabbed her shoes off the floor, put them on, and stood. Wearing the blanket around her shoulders like a shawl, she emerged from the lounge.

She stopped short, surprised to find Marsha standing there. She immediately knew something was up and quietly closed the door behind her. "Lars, right? He's bailed? He hasn't shown up for work?"

"He's there," Marsha assured her. "You guys are still on schedule."

Gretchen was clearly relieved and looked at the clock. "Coffee."

"One sec," Marsha said, grateful that it was just the two of them. They didn't need any caustic comments from Adam. "It's the girl. Amber. She was taken home."

"Right." Gretchen knew it was only a thirty-five-minute car ride, tops. The Amsterdam police would have driven her home.

Marsha went on, the police report fresh in her mind. "Two social workers from Child Protection Services met them there. The plan was to allow her to grab whatever she needed, clothes, school stuff, get her to a foster home. But that just enraged her father. He went ballistic. First, that she had run away. And then that social workers were there."

Gretchen could see it clearly now. "But the police were with her?"

"Two cops. But her father... He..." Marsha struggled to finish her sentence.

Gretchen glared at her. Impatient. "What? Tell me."

"He hauled off and hit her... Again and again before anyone could react," Marsha said. "He's a big guy, I guess... It took both cops and a social worker to pull him off, and by then..."

Gretchen shook her head. "No... Please, no..."

"She was declared dead at the scene."

Gretchen continued to shake her head.

Marsha quickly added, "He's been arrested. Police body cams show the whole thing. He won't see the outside ever again."

"Coffee," Gretchen mumbled, quickly brushing past Marsha before her emotions got the better of her.

Amsterdam, the Netherlands

"You ask what's going on?"

"I tried," the SkyLark Labs tech said.

Max Becker sighed as he glanced at his watch. In less than an hour, Lars was supposed to pull the fire alarm. Whatever was going on, he needed to fix it. Now.

"I haven't seen him too often," the tech offered. "But he always seemed okay. Very polite. Asking if it was all right for him to clean while we were working. Was it okay to do the floor? Could he empty the trash? Just polite. Didn't want to get in our way."

"Right," Max said dismissively. "I'll take care of it."

The tech took his cue and left. Max glanced at the cowboy hat that now sat on a nearby chair. To his eye, it was identical to the real thing that had been analyzed by forensics. He had been able to pull out the interior satin lining just enough to paste the tiny tracking device to the inside of the hat. After tucking the satin lining back where it belonged, he doubted anyone would ever be able to tell it had been tampered with.

He left his ground floor office, making sure the door locked shut behind him. Walking quickly across the quiet industrial carpet, he got to the men's restroom and gently pushed open the door. Just as the tech had described, Lars was sitting on the floor, his back against the wall, his knees drawn up to his chest, silently weeping. The janitorial mop and bucket set was nearby. He had no doubt come inside to clean and then, what? Suddenly fallen apart? It made no sense.

Max stepped inside. "Lars?"

Lars didn't look up, but he did swallow down a sob. He wiped his nose with the back of his hand, took a deep breath, and looked up. His eyes were red, his face wet from tears. Seeing Max staring down at him, he bowed his head.

Heaven help us, Max thought. Even though he was wearing a pair of his all-time favorite dress slacks, he sat on the bathroom floor next to the janitor. He wished his wife were here. She could tell him what to do. What to say. He tentatively reached out and patted Lars on the knee. "You'll do fine."

Lars tried to say something but faltered.

"Police will be there every step of the way, believe me. You have nothing to fear."

Suddenly Lars turned, shifting his position so he faced Max. "Why me? Why me?"

Max wasn't sure what the correct answer was, so he gave a small shrug, as if to say, who knows?

"Why not a scientist? They work with evidence all day long—they would know where to find something. I'm a sanitation custodian. Why me?"

"I don't know," Max replied honestly.

"I've seen both men, you know," Lars said, the emotional upheaval subsiding. "I would recognize them. So why let me see them? Because they know they're going to kill me."

"No, no. No, Lars. No," Max reassured him. "They want the hat, that's all."

With that, Max pulled his cell phone from his pocket. He fiddled with it and then handed it to Max. "She's not well. She's on a lot of different medications. For her heart. Her blood pressure. She's not well!"

Max hesitated, then took the phone. It took him a bit to decipher the image. An older woman, probably well into her seventies, sitting in a large, overstuffed chair, each arm on an armrest. No smile, but a resolute expression on her face, which made her look quite dignified. As if she were wealthy and had certain expectations. Oddly, there was a cat in her lap. But the cat's head hung down well off her thigh on her right side, appearing either very relaxed despite the peculiar pose or...

"Look at the next one," Lars urged him.

Max scrolled to the next image. This picture was of a man, clearly dead, the eyes open and a white paste around the right side of his mouth. Max looked to Lars, completely baffled.

"That guy was at my flat today! In the elevator with me! I promised I'd have it. I thought it would be all right." When Max didn't say anything, Lars got angry, waving a hand at the phone. "Did you see Milo!? Did you see?"

Max now remembered the cat's name and went back to the first image. He enlarged it and could now see the cat's throat had been cut. Hence, the reason the cat's head dangled off the woman's lap.

"They have Mother," Lars said, choking back a sob. "Milo's dead and they just... they just put him on her lap like that! Her heart!" Again, he motioned to the phone. "Go the next one, go past the dead man."

Max did as he was instructed. It was the image of a note typed in a bold, large font:

An eye for an eye. One dead man, one dead cat. Guess who is next?

Chapter Seven

FROG Headquarters, The Hague

No more than thirty minutes earlier, Hal had grabbed Two's ergonomic desk chair and positioned it close to Marsha's desk so he could see her large monitors. The screen on the right displayed the red blinking light of the tracker. Stretching stiffly, he found himself wondering what all the fuss was about with such ridiculously expensive chairs. They certainly weren't designed for comfort, that's for sure. Marsha and Two's spacious office had just the two desk chairs, and he had been too lazy to grab a nice leather chair from the conference room. So he continued to twist and stretch his aching back.

Suddenly there was a loud beep from behind him. He whirled around to see the image of a man on Two's monitor. Facial recognition software had found a hit, using the image of the man from the wheelchair at the Amsterdam airport. Next to him was the face of another man, the image taken from an angle and somewhat blurry. Between the two faces, a text flashed: 88.3% similarity.

Marsha was now looking over his shoulder. "Pretty high considering the other image is indistinct." She used the mouse to click on something and a name appeared. *Goran Petrovic.*

"The assassin?" Hal asked in astonishment, staring at the screen. "I thought he was a ghost. No known image. Name came from prints, but even that has been considered iffy."

Goran Petrovic had been pegged as the killer of more than thirty people over his two-decade career. Quite a few were simply wealthy people that some family member probably wanted out of the way. Others were government figures of all stripes in America, Europe, Russia, and Asia. He didn't take out only those on one side of the political aisle or the other—he simply killed who he was paid to kill. And since he had been careful to use disguises most of the time, even with the growing proliferation of security cameras everywhere, there had been no known photo of the man.

"Since when does someone have a photo?" Hal asked irritably.

She reached past him to click on another tab. "We missed it. Interpol came up with this image after the assassination of Putin's right-hand man, Ivan Ivanoff, some years back. Always thought that was a silly name... What were his parents thinking...? Ivan Ivanoff. Ivan times two?"

"I've tended to think he wasn't real, this Goran Petrovic. Just a made-up name for any high-profile murder that officials can't solve," Hal mused.

Marsha studied the screen. "The second image was taken from a surveillance camera down the street from the murder. It was speculation that the image might be Goran Petrovic. Just a guess, really."

"Until now," Hal said.

"Until now."

Amsterdam, the Netherlands

They had argued incessantly about which fast-food restaurant to go to, with Adam saying it would be smart to get pizza since it was fine eaten cold and more than likely they were going to be stuck in the car for some time. Gretchen preferred Subway—it was healthier. With neither giving an inch, they finally settled the matter by flipping a coin and Gretchen won. So they now ate their sandwiches inside the Range Rover which Adam had parked on a quiet street a couple of miles from the SkyLark Lab.

"You have to just forget it," Adam told her with his mouth full.

She turned and gave him a nasty look, but he was too busy opening a bag of chips to notice. She replied briskly, "I'm fine."

"Look, I liked the girl too. But this wasn't our fault."

"I know," she bristled.

"You ask me, an asshole father like that, her fate was sealed when she disappeared. He thought she had run away and as time went on, his anger and alcohol just fed his grievances."

Gretchen didn't say anything, but her blood pressure was going up quickly. She didn't need his two-cents worth. She certainly hadn't *asked* for it.

Adam went on. "You think about it, what else could we have done? We made sure Child Services was aware, right? We could hardly keep her. Take her to FROG."

"Please, stop," Gretchen said. "Just stop."

"Actually, I blame social services. You know full well that the man comes home blasted, and you take her back there? No! Stupid! Go early in the morning when he might be sober. Or, hell, go after he's gone to work. Let her get her things and it's done and—"

"Stop!" she suddenly shouted.

Adam actually jumped in surprise.

She glared at him, her eyes well-adjusted to the dark cab. "Just stop."

Now uncomfortable and needing something to do, he tapped the iPad sitting on the console between them. It came to life. The red dot hadn't moved.

Just then, Gretchen's phone rang. She checked the screen. "Max Becker," she announced.

"Speaker." When she didn't acknowledge the request, he added, "Please."

Holding it in her hand, she did as he asked, and said hello.

"Hello. Max Becker, here. We have a problem."

She and Adam exchanged looks. "What's that?"

"He's, well, he's just fallen apart."

Gretchen could see Adam was going to jump in and take over the call, but she waved him off with a stern look. "In what way? We're less than ten minutes from the time to pull the fire alarm."

"I know, I know," Max said. "I've tried my best, but, well..."

"Where is he? Is he there? At the lab?"

"Yes, yes. I found him sobbing on the bathroom floor, but I was able to get him to the lunchroom. I just stepped outside so I could talk to you."

Again, Adam was chomping at the bit, but she waved him off and said, "What happened?"

"The cat's dead. Its throat was cut."

Looking at Adam, Gretchen asked, "How'd they tell him? Text?"

"Yes.."

"A text message? Saying that?"

"A picture," Max clarified. "But there's more…"

Gretchen braced herself. "Tell me."

"It's his mother. They have his mother," Max explained.

"Are you sure? Absolutely sure?" Gretchen asked.

"Afraid so," Max replied. "They put the dead cat on her lap and sent the picture. So it's clear they have her."

"Let me talk to him."

"Wait, there's more…"

"What?" Gretchen asked crisply.

"The next text had a picture of a dead man. I've now seen it on the lunchroom TV. From the local news. He had kidnapped a young girl, kept her in a handicap van. Lars says that he's one of the men who want the cowboy hat and—"

"Back up a minute," Gretchen said. "This text picture that was sent, it is the same photo everyone else in world has seen, right? Same you saw on TV, right?"

"Well, yes, I suppose," Max replied.

"Okay. So, is that it?"

"Yes. Wait, no! No. There was one more text. So first, the dead cat in his mother's lap, then the dead kidnapper, and then a photo of a typed note… Hold on… You ready? I can read it to you."

"Go."

"It says, 'An eye for an eye. One dead man, one dead cat. Guess who is next?'"

Gretchen sighed. "Put him on."

"He's really upset…"

"Put him on!" Gretchen demanded.

"Hold on…"

Adam reached over and tapped the mute button of her phone. "This changes nothing. He gives them the hat, we trace that, and hopefully his mother is released."

Before Gretchen could reply, she heard a tentative voice. "Hello..?"

She took off the mute button and said, "Hi, Lars. This is Greta, from the police. Mr. Becker told me what happened, and I'm so sorry..."

"They'll kill her," he interrupted in a despondent voice.

"No, no, they—" Gretchen began.

"They will!" Lars insisted. "They cut Milo's throat! Did you see? Did you look? They'll do that to Mother!"

~ ~ ~

Max Becker knew there were exactly nine people inside the building, including himself and Lars. He needed to make sure all nine got out safely. In the back of his office, he had found a large, wadded-up blue plastic bag from De Bijenkorf, a popular high-end Dutch department store. He had no memory of the bag, nor what he had originally used it for, but it suited his needs now. He put the cowboy hat in the bag and left his office, once again making sure the door locked behind him. He headed back to the lunchroom with the blue bag in hand.

It had seemed to him that Lars had a better handle on his emotions after talking to the policewoman. Entering the lunchroom, he was surprised to find Lars wiping down the counter that held the microwave oven and the coffee maker. He turned and seemed surprised to see Max standing there. "Might as well do my job."

"Yes," Max said. "Yes, very good." He put the blue bag on the table, and Lars slowly approached.

"That's it?"

"Yes."

Lars put aside the wet cloth he was using and tentatively opened the bag. He glanced up, surprised. "It looks dirty."

"Dusted for fingerprints."

Max glanced at his watch. "We're past due. You ready?"

"Yes," Lars replied.

Max told him, "No one should be in this area. They're all upstairs."

"I know," Lars said.

"You need to be the last out. A good five minutes after everyone, okay?"

Lars nodded. They had discussed this before. If the kidnappers were watching, it had to look like all the regular personnel had promptly evacuated, allowing Lars to take advantage of their quick exit, allowing him time to find the hat. He looked to Max. "Thank you, sir. Your support has been very generous."

Greatly embarrassed, Max said, "I'm going now."

~ ~ ~

Mavis was simply at her wit's end. She wanted to scream—for help and out of frustration—but she couldn't since she was gagged. And even though she had tried and tried to free herself, it was no use. Using nylon hose, the man had firmly tied her arms to the chair's armrests and her calves to the chair legs, leaving no wiggle room at all. Worse, she had her son's dead cat on her lap. No matter how hard she tried, moving her hips every which way she could, she couldn't get Milo's remains off of her lap.

She couldn't help but wonder if she was going to die in the chair. With her son's dead cat in her lap.

The whole thing was rather absurd. The man had come to her door several hours ago asking if she was the lady who was missing a cat. He said he'd seen her note by the elevator. Her heart sang with joy as the man described Milo to a T. He explained that the cat had dashed into his flat and he had tried and tried to grab it, but with no luck. Could she please come look? The cat didn't seem all that friendly, and he was afraid to pick it up. Right there, Mavis should have known better. Milo was the sweetest cat alive. He'd go up to anyone and rub against them, expecting some friendly pets in return.

Yet, she had hurried out the door, going with the man and thinking of how thrilled Lars was going to be. He hadn't been the same since Milo had gone missing. Her signs at the elevator alcove of each floor had yielded nothing. Nothing at all. The man had unlocked the door and they had entered what had to be a double-size flat. Each room was enormous and so fancy! She felt she had somehow been transported to eighteenth-century France. The furnishings were top-of-the-line. The paintings absolutely gorgeous, although she had no idea who the artists might be. They just seemed, well, unaffordable.

"Have a seat," he had told her, gesturing to an elegant Louis XV armchair. When she hesitated, he'd smiled. "It's perfectly fine. Please."

And so she'd sat down. The big chair was certainly comfortable, but just as she'd settled in, the man stepped behind her and dug his fingers into her neck, the pain excruciating! The next thing she knew, she was waking up. She found that she was gagged, with her arms and legs tied to the chair.

Her heart racing, she'd tried to get her bearings, and then the man emerged from somewhere, holding Milo. He had explained that Lars had something the man wanted. To make sure Lars complied, Milo was going to stay on her lap for a photograph. He put the skittish cat on her lap, and she desperately wanted to speak to Milo and pet him, reassure him it would be all right, but of course, she couldn't. The man held Milo by the scruff of the neck, and suddenly a long knife appeared in his other hand.

She could only stare as blood drained from the cat's sliced neck, spilling onto the plush carpet below. She wanted to cry out, but couldn't. Why? Why had the man killed her son's cat? And why did he have to kill him so viciously?

The man had looked her right in the eyes as he slowly lowered the dead cat to her lap. He then told her to smile for the photo. Unwilling to do so, she'd put on the vilest expression she could muster. The man was evil. Pure evil.

She prayed that Lars would give the man what he wanted and all this would be over. She tilted her head back and closed her eyes. What she really wanted—besides having Milo off her lap— was the toilet. She was on diuretics for her heart, and she urgently needed to relieve her bladder.

~ ~ ~

The shrill fire alarm sounded like a police-car siren, but with alternating frequencies. Over this crazy pandemonium, the woman's words kept echoing in his mind. "Lars, you're in control. You, and only you, have the evidence they want. Do what they say, and we'll be able to get your mother back safe and sound."

The policewoman asked a zillion questions about his mother, her daily routines that he had never given much thought to. "It's not any help unless you're absolutely sure of your answers, okay?" she had told him. "And it's perfectly understandable if you're unsure, okay? Just say so." He had done his best, and he now believed that he had answered each question accurately. Then the woman advised him about the drop—the police would be close by, but unseen, and he was to hand over the evidence as instructed, and then they would move in. The woman ended the conversation promising him one more time that they would get his mother home safe and sound. He wanted to believe her.

FROG Headquarters, The Hague

"Found it!" Marsha called out from her office.

Hal came rushing in. On Marsha's left monitor was the image of a man, his back to the camera. "When? When was this?"

"Four hours ago. Just minutes after Lars left for work."

The idea had come from Adam, and Hal was grateful for the reminder that many people used doorbell security cameras. When Gretchen had quizzed Lars about his mother's daily routine, she had asked if anyone on their floor had such a device. He said the woman across the hall and gave her name. Working her magic, Marsha went into the Vivex cloud server, by far the most popular manufacturer of small-business and home-surveillance systems. With the neighbor's name, Marsha easily grabbed the woman's account. Vivex really needed better security.

From there, Marsha simply looked at the surveillance. She soon found that Lars had been correct—the woman's doorbell camera automatically recorded audio and visual when motion was detected nearby, including activity outside Lars's door. Marsha knew that such devices had come under fire from many critics who said that you shouldn't be able to tape a conversation of people passing by your door. But Marsha loved the technology.

"Turn it up," Hal said.

Marsha boosted the audio to its maximum. Visually, the man's back was to the camera. All they could say for sure was that he was wearing a black wool jacket and he had dark hair. "I've seen your note... by the elevator?" the man said clearly. "I think your cat went into my flat."

"Oh my God!" Mavis exclaimed. "You found Milo? Oh, dear heavens!"

"I'm staying at the Airbnb? On the second floor?"

They could see the older lady shake her head. "I don't know it."

"Well, your cat ran in and he doesn't want me coming near. Can you come please? Perhaps he'll come to you."

"Yes, yes, of course," Mavis said. She shut the door momentarily, then stepped out, locking the door behind her. An instant later, both of them disappeared from view.

After viewing the doorbell video, it had taken Marsha all of thirteen minutes to pinpoint the flat being rented through Airbnb.

Amsterdam, the Netherlands

"He's there. He's got the bag, we're a go," Adam said using night-vision binoculars. His cell phone was resting on the wide console between the seats, with the speaker on. "I repeat, we're a go. Can you confirm?"

"Yes, I got it here. We're actively running," Marsha replied referring to the tracking device she could see on her computer.

After Gretchen had left, calling for an Uber ride, Adam had canvased the area, driving with the headlights off and using a thermal digital riflescope to look for heat signatures. He made several sweeps, and all he saw was a stray dog. No people at all, and the few cars that were parked in the area were not giving off heat either. They had been parked for a while.

Confident the kidnappers were not in the immediate area, he repositioned the Range Rover so he had a perfect line of sight to the parking lot. He had seen the first firetruck arrive within minutes of the fire alarm being activated. Eight people were accounted for outside, and, by using the binoculars, Adam could see each face. Lars had been the last one out.

It would probably be some time before the firefighters would declare the lab safe and allow employees back inside. Max Becker had said there was little doubt that everyone would go back inside as soon as they could. Except for Lars. He was to go straight to his car and leave the area. There was a shopping mall two miles away where Gretchen had told him to park and contact the kidnappers.

As far as Adam was concerned, all was good. Lars was out, he had the evidence in hand, and the tracker was live.

~ ~ ~

Gretchen knew she shouldn't let Adam get under her skin. But for some reason, he seemed to have a knack for it. This time, it came when he had vehemently chastised her for telling Lars that they would get his mother back. For all they knew, the mother was dead. And that was when she'd gathered the other half of a sandwich she had been saving and said, "I'll see what I can find. Later." And with that, she hopped out of the Range Rover and walked away at a fast clip. If she had expected Adam to follow after her or plead with her to come back, she would have been greatly disappointed. But she hadn't expected it.

Once a good distance away, she opened her Uber app and summoned a ride. Only then did she call Hal, telling him of her plan. At first, he balked, but then he agreed. It really didn't take two people to follow the tracking device—Adam could easily handle it with Marsha's help from their end.

"Look, there's no backup for you," Hal had told her.

"I know."

There had been nothing more to say. Arriving at Lars's apartment building, she had gone up the stairs and found the Airbnb flat on the second floor. Fortunately, this time of night, no one was around. It was eerily silent. Removing a lock-pick kit from her pocket, she went to work, and in less than a minute, she heard the click of the single-cylinder deadbolt sliding back. She quickly pulled her Glock from her holster and used her other hand to silently, and ever so slowly, push open the door.

~ ~ ~

Lars parked in the deserted shopping-mall car park as he had been instructed and turned off the car's engine. Now it was a waiting game. He picked up his cell phone with shaking hands and made sure it was on. And of course, it was. Again, the woman's reassurance echoed in his head. "Lars, you're in control. You, and only you, have the evidence they want." He told himself she was absolutely correct. He was in control.

FROG Headquarters, The Hague

Marsha noted Lars's location. Once again, Hal sat in Two's chair, watching her large monitors. "He's there," she said.

"Signal?" Hal asked.

"Five by five. We're fine," she replied.

Hal glanced at his watch. It was just after four in the morning. They were behind schedule. Which didn't matter, except that it was easier to work in the shadows. He didn't want Lars doing what the kidnappers instructed in daylight. Mostly because it would be easier to get a jump on the bad guys if they were operating in the dark.

As if reading his mind, Marsha said, "You know what concerns me?" This time, she turned in her chair to face him. "Whoever is doing this, they are in that flat."

Hal shook his head. He had already considered this. "Look, it's what all our operators do." When Marsha just stared at him, he added, "Work solo."

"I know. It's just…" Her voice trailed off.

"She's one of our best. Let her do what she's trained to do, okay?"

Marsha nodded and turned back to her monitor. What she didn't know was that Hal was just as worried. He knew full well that if the Airbnb flat held multiple bad guys, Gretchen could end up in a world of hurt.

Amsterdam, the Netherlands

Like Hal, Gretchen had noted the time. For her, four in the morning was perfect. It was the time of day when the human body naturally ran out of gas and wanted to rest. Studies showed that students pulling an all-nighter cramming for an exam often lost their edge just after three in the morning. Even the best of the military sentries holding watch duties weren't quite on their toes between three and five in the morning, especially if they hadn't slept well before their watch duty.

She cursed her luck that she didn't have night-vision goggles. But this op had been decided on the fly, so once inside the flat, she had to wait by the front door, waiting patiently for her eyes to adjust. All her senses heightened. She heard the ticking of a rather loud clock somewhere to her right. But there was nothing else.

Finally, she could see well enough to start clearing the flat. As Marsha had reminded her minutes before entering the building, for all they knew, the man who had talked about this flat as a ruse and Lars's mother were somewhere else entirely. It was a good point, but there was only one way to find out. Hopefully, she wouldn't run into an irate Airbnb renter with a cricket bat in hand.

~ ~ ~

"You don't tell me shit, understand?" the man irritably told Lars in English.

"I'm not leaving the hat where you say," Lars said. "I have it. You don't. You have my mother. We simply exchange items, and we're both happy." Lars was pleasantly surprised by his calm demeanor. Inside, he was terrified. But the woman cop was right—he held all the cards.

There was a long pause on the other end of the line, and finally, the man said, "Okay, okay."

Feeling empowered, Lars sat up straighter in the car seat and said, "Tell you what. We will meet at the—"

"No!" the man thundered. "I'll trade you, yes. But we do this where I say. Not you."

Lars decided not to push his luck. "Fine. But you need to understand, first I need to see Mother. Then and only then will I give you the stupid hat."

Chapter Eight

Amsterdam, the Netherlands

The address meant nothing to Lars. He had promptly put it in his phone and was surprised to learn that it was in the Westpoort borough, an industrial area with very few residences. Part of him was hoping that he would be directed to the Red Light District where prostitutes sat half-naked before large windows, showing off exactly what a customer would be getting for their money. The area was very popular with tourists, and even at this hour, there would people milling about which might help ensure a safe exchange.

He pushed the button on the phone for map guidance to start and made sure the speaker volume was set on high. Then he started the car.

~ ~ ~

"Adam, he's getting on the A5 motorway. Heading west," Marsha announced. "Repeat, heading west on the A5."

"Got it," he replied.

Marsha could see Adam's location from his cell phone tracker. "You're about two miles behind."

"There is some traffic, but not a lot out here," he replied. "I'll keep my head down and let you guide me."

"Copy that."

~ ~ ~

Her heart in her throat, Gretchen kept going, moving through the flat with her gun in hand. She had cleared the kitchen, dining room, two bedrooms, and a small office. As far as she could tell, the closed door up ahead was the last room to clear—most likely the master bedroom. She silently opened the door, ready for anything.

But there was nothing. Only a large bed with enough pillows to fill her entire flat. She quickly cleared the dressing room, closet, large bathroom, and the space under the bed. Nothing. Only then did she head back to the very large main room to check on the old woman she had seen as soon as she had started her reconnaissance. Even though she had desperately wanted to see if the woman was alive, she was working solo and had no choice but to clear each room first. Stepping into the room, she looked around and found a light switch.

What she hadn't been able to see in the dark was plainly evident now—Mavis Vervloet had been gagged, bound to the chair, and now sat awkwardly slumped with her chin on her chest. The remains of the cat lay on the woman's lap. The lights didn't rouse the woman, and Gretchen feared the worst, instantly aware that if the woman was dead, she'd never hear the end of it from Adam. Putting her hand on Mavis's neck, Gretchen nearly jumped a mile when Mavis suddenly snored. Flooded with relief, Gretchen smiled to herself, wondering what kind of snore the woman could produce when she wasn't gagged.

Gretchen positioned herself directly in front of the woman. "Mrs. Vervloet." Nothing. She shook Mavis's shoulder and in a louder voice repeated herself. "Mrs. Vervloet."

The woman instantly came awake, startled and immediately fearful.

"Police, ma'am, police." She smiled for the woman. "It's okay now." She took off the woman's gag.

Lars's mother just looked at her, as if trying to comprehend the incomprehensible. She didn't say a word, just stared at Gretchen. Then, as if remembering, she slowly looked down at her lap. Gretchen quickly realized and very gently, very respectfully, picked up the dead cat and put it on the floor.

"Let me get you free, and I'll get you some water," Gretchen told her. She pulled a small switchblade knife from her boot and went to work on the nylon hose bindings. "You're safe, okay?"

Mavis still didn't speak. Once her arms were free, she rubbed her forearms as if warding off the cold. Gretchen released the bonds holding the woman's legs to the chair. "It's over now. You're safe." Finally, it dawned on Gretchen. "Are you hurt, ma'am? Are you in pain?"

Mavis shook head, giving Gretchen the first confirmation that the old woman heard and understood her. Gretchen smiled. "Good, I'm glad."

The woman studied Gretchen for some time before asking, "You live here?"

"No, ma'am. No." The woman didn't say anything more, so Gretchen asked, "You sure you're not hurt?"

Suddenly, the tears came, streaming down the old woman's face. "I'm so sorry..."

Surprised, Gretchen took the old woman's hands in hers. "No apologizes," she told her. "No apologizes. None, okay? You've been through a great ordeal."

"You don't understand," Mavis said. "I peed on the chair. Twice. I just couldn't help it..."

Gretchen took the sobbing woman in her arms.

FROG Headquarters, The Hague

Marsha and Hal exchanged looks. Finally, some good news. Gretchen was on speaker. "She's pretty stiff. Pretty uncomfortable. But I think okay."

"Where is she now?" Hal asked.

"In the bathroom. She, eh, she urinated in a chair. She has a bad heart and is on diuretics. Being tied to the chair for that long..." Gretchen didn't finish her thought. "She should probably go to the hospital, be checked out."

"Can you get her to her own flat? I'll call it in," Marsha said. "We don't want your current location on any record."

"Affirmative, but we need S&G." She was referring to people who were very well paid to sterilize a location and go. No questions asked.

"Right," Marsha agreed. "The chair and the cat."

"Won't be a simple in and out," Gretchen said. "They cut the cat's throat, there's a ton of blood for such a small animal."

"Got it," Marsha said, writing herself a note. FROG had a list of reliable firms worldwide that would quickly do the task. In this case, the firm selected would presume that AIVD had called for their services. "Shouldn't be an issue. The Airbnb shows these guys booked it for the next several days. We have plenty of time."

"Anything on Lars?" Gretchen asked.

"Adam has eyes on him," Hal told her. "He is now in an industrial area, parked in his car, but he hasn't gotten out. He hasn't dropped the hat."

"What's the hold up?"

"No clue."

"I'll call him."

Amsterdam, the Netherlands

"She's not anywhere near here, is she?" Lars asked.

"Put it in the bin," the voice on the other end of the phone told him.

"I need proof-of-life," Lars insisted.

"Do you see it? The bin? Put it in the bin!"

Lars looked out the passenger window. The outdoor trashcan was twenty feet away, on the walkway to the large industrial building nearby. It had a covered dome lid that allowed for trash to be deposited from all four sides. The lid could be easily removed to allow for the emptying of the bin. The man had instructed him to take off the dome lid, put the cowboy hat inside, and put the lid back in place. Then once he drove away, he would he be told where his mother was.

"She's dead, just like Milo, right?"

"No," the man said. "Do as I say, and you get to see her."

Lars's phone buzzed with an incoming call and he fumbled to see the screen. It was the woman cop. He hit the decline button.

"Proof-of-life." With that, Lars ended the call, his heart racing.

FROG Headquarters, The Hague

Looking at her monitor, Marsha could see that the cowboy hat remained stationary, somewhere in an industrial park area. It hadn't moved for some time. Since Lars would have to exit the same way he had entered, Adam had kept vigil several blocks over, waiting for Lars to leave after dropping off the hat. With Marsha guiding him, Adam could then follow whoever picked it up. But as time went on and Lars didn't answer Gretchen phone calls, Adam had inserted his cell phone earbud and left his vehicle to see what was what.

He had gone in on foot, wearing his night-vision goggles and carrying his backpack over one shoulder that held his gear. He hadn't encountered anyone and had taken up his position on a grassy slope opposite the parking lot where Lars had parked his car. Beyond the car park was a large stand-alone building. Stretched out flat on the ground, he kept alternating between the night-vision goggles and the thermal digital riflescope to monitor the area. He clearly saw the heat signature from Lars's car and Lars sitting in the car, but that had been it.

Sweeping with the thermal scope again, he suddenly got a heat signature from the side of the stand-alone building opposite him. At first, he thought it might be heat from a metal heating grate, but then it moved, indicating that a person was standing against the corner of the building. "Got a solitary spotter," he quietly said.

"Location from you?" Hal asked.

"Hold on..." Adam looked at the scope-finder range. "Two hundred forty-three meters, due west."

"Lars still in his car?" Hal asked.

Adam adjusted the scope to Lars sitting in his car. "Still in his car, affirmative."

Amsterdam, the Netherlands

"How you feeling?" Gretchen asked Mavis who was now back in her own home. She had emerged from the bathroom where she had taken a shower and now wore flannel pajama bottoms and a mismatched flannel top. Sheepskin slippers covered her feet.

"Better since I took my pill," the old woman remarked. She had been quite concerned that she had missed the prescribed time of her diuretic.

Gretchen smiled. "And better for taking that nice hot shower." She didn't mention anything about getting out of her soiled clothes, stained with both her own urine and Milo's dried blood. "We can get you to the hospital."

"No, no," Mavis said with the wave her had. "I'm fine. Just needed my pill." Suddenly distraught, she asked, "Where's Lars? Is he coming home now?"

~ ~ ~

Lars had ignored the constant calls from the woman cop. He knew that the police were somewhere nearby, at least that is what he had been told, although he couldn't see anyone. And he knew they wanted him to leave the evidence. But if he did that and the kidnapper didn't tell him where his mother could be found, what leverage did he have then? None. Absolutely none.

His phone buzzed again. He looked at the screen and did a double take. Was the image real, or some sort of fake? With somewhat shaky fingers, he enlarged it. The frame that filled his screen was of the woman cop and his mother, both smiling for a posed selfie. Could this be? Could it really be?

The phone chirped. A video. Showing his mother, from the shoulders up. He hit the play button. "I'm home, Lars. Milo… I'm so sorry, he…" She couldn't finish her sentence.

Now he saw the woman cop. "I found your mother, unharmed…"

"Tell him what happened to the chair…" his mother said off screen.

Then his mother was on screen again. "Lars, I'm so ashamed. They tied me to a chair. I was there for so long and you know my bladder these days, what with the medication I'm on. I couldn't help it. I ruined the most beautiful chair in the whole world! I feel just awful about it."

Now the woman cop looked at him. "We're in your home. I'll show you."

The video rotated, displaying his flat. It moved to the kitchen, his kitchen, the cop saying, "You left a coffee cup, unrinsed in the sink." The video showed a close-up of the dirty coffee cup. "I'm sure you recognize it."

"It's not like him to do that. He's out of sorts, no doubt," his mother said off camera.

Lars couldn't believe it. The camera flashed on his mother, now standing and seen from head to toe. She was wearing her flannel pajamas. She had been wearing clothes in the kidnapper's photo. She was really home. And safe.

He stopped the video mid-stream and dialed the cop. She immediately picked up. "Lars, it's over."

"Can I speak to Mother, please?"

A scuffling sound. Then his mother. "Lars, dear? Are you okay?"

"I'm fine."

"Can you come home? It's been the most awful day. Just awful."

~ ~ ~

"He's getting out of the car," Adam told Marsha and Hal. Gretchen had given them a heads-up on what to expect after she had finally gotten through to Lars. The cowboy hat was to be deposited in the trash bin.

Wearing the night-vision goggles, Adam watched as Lars crossed in front of his car and went over to a nearby trash can. He picked up something near the base of the rubbish bin, and Adam realized it was a candy wrapper. The idiot couldn't help but pick up trash. Insane.

He watched as Lars then lifted off the dome lid and deposited the candy wrapper and then the cowboy hat inside the bin. He replaced the lid, making sure it was secure.

"Cowboy hat is in the rubbish bin," Adam said. "Repeat, hat is in the rubbish bin."

Adam watched as Lars got in his car, started it, and slowly drove off.

"Lars is in his vehicle, leaving the drop site, repeat, Lars is leaving the drop site," he told them.

Adam pulled on the night-vision goggles and looked toward the building. The heat scope still registered the man, unmoving. Why wasn't he coming for the cowboy hat? Lars was long gone. Thinking that perhaps someone else was going to pick up the evidence, he looked through the night-vision goggles again, scanning the area. But the surrounding area showed nothing but an empty landscape.

"Sitrep," Hal said.

Adam pulled down the goggles. "Nothing to report. The man I have on site, still two hundred plus meters away, hasn't moved yet."

"Maybe someone else is there," Marsha suggested.

"Negative. It's quiet."

"Be patient," Hal said. "He'll grab it."

"Possible he has spotted you?" Marsha asked.

Adam had already considered this. "If he's got my toys, yes, it's possible." But there was nothing to be done. Just lie low and hope for the best.

And then it came, a huge explosion, the light so bright that Adam instinctively buried his face in the grass, covering his head with both arms.

Manama, Bahrain ~ Two Weeks Later

Looking around, Gretchen was surprised that there were so many women in the stands actively cheering. To her way of thinking, the deafening sound of the open-wheel Formula Two race was something only diehard male fans would enjoy. Add the constant roar from the enthusiastic crowd to the incessant whine of the engines, and the whole atmosphere just gave her a headache. Adam had given her a pair of ear plugs as they had taken their open-air seats, and she was extremely grateful.

Even though Gretchen certainly understood the importance of role playing, the truth was that Nancy Ellison would never know they had attended the race. That said, Gretchen did find herself rooting for car number 4 as it sped over the road course. This was Ellison's first season in a Formula Two car after finishing in the top three at the end of last year's F3 beginner series, allowing her to move up to the next level. The competition would be stiffer now and she had to do well here to move up to Formula One.

Ellison had made it clear on her various social media accounts that she was going to achieve her ultimate goal of racing Formula One race cars. As the only woman racing formula cars at any level, she enjoyed a huge following. It didn't hurt that she was attractive. However, it wasn't all accolades. She also had her fair share of detractors who said her wealthy father had bought her a ride with STR Motorsports since he sponsored the race team. To Gretchen's way of thinking, this was ignoring the fact that Ellison had already proven herself on the F3 circuit. As to whether Ellison would have been chosen by STR Motorsports without her father's pocketbook, Gretchen would let others decide. Either way, she believed the twenty-two-year-old had already accomplished a great deal.

She and Adam had flown to Bahrain earlier that day with one objective—find out what Nancy Ellison knew about Mac Senton, the New York Yankees man, Bart Werner, and William DeWine—the three men who had worked for Red Arrow Capital and were now dead. It was probably a long shot, but they had nothing else at this point.

Just two weeks earlier, they had held great hope that the cowboy hat would be picked up by whoever had set off the café bomb and that would break the case wide open. However, whoever it was that had blackmailed Lars for the hat had simply blown it to bits to cover their tracks. As Hal had wryly commented the next day, "Well, I guess there is a little less stolen C-4 out there now, anyway."

They now knew that the assassin who had killed Bart Werner was Goran Petrovic, but even that meant little. They did have Werner's organizational chart that listed The Joker at the top and either initials or perhaps partial names listed in some spaces on the chart, but so far, that had given them nothing to go on. Perhaps they weren't actual people, but nicknames Werner had given the players behind the scenes. It was impossible to know. It obviously meant something to Werner, but whatever that was, he took it with him to his grave. His laptop held nothing of interest, although there was one email from Mac Senton, but it was related to a shared client. As for that client, he had passed away in a small plane crash two years ago and nothing could be found on the dead man. "No skeletons," according to Marsha. When Adam balked that everyone has skeletons, she had shaken her head. "Not this guy. Sorry."

All other UK Red Arrow Capital clients had been run through the computer, but they came up with nothing. A deeper dive on William DeWine, aka, Matthew, gave them nothing. The same for American Mac Senton. Hence, the trip to Bahrain for the F2 Grand Prix race. In discussions about how best to approach Ellison, Adam had presumed he'd talk to the race-car driver on his own, but Hal had insisted that Gretchen join him—Nancy Ellison might respond better to a woman.

Adam now leaned close and shouted, "Let's go."

Gretchen was surprised they were leaving early, but it was fine with her.

FROG Headquarters, The Hague

"C'mon," Two whined. "Let's go."

Marsha didn't respond, and Two abruptly left the conference room. Two's anxiety—about something she had discovered and insisted that they meet in the conference room to discuss—had her in knots. Marsha, on the other hand, was in her own world, having brought her laptop into the room so she could continue her deep dive on Robert Ellison, Nancy's father who apparently bankrolled his daughter's formula race-car passion.

A minute later, Marsha looked up and saw Hal outside the glass wall, talking on his cell phone. Their eyes met and he held up a finger. He was now over fifteen minutes late to the meeting he had agreed to an hour before. Just then, Two hurried in carrying a sausage broodje that she had heated in the microwave oven. The hot sandwich smelled good, and Marsha realized she was hungry. Hal came in, pocketing his phone.

Two was immediately chagrined. "I'm starving." There was an unspoken rule of no eating in the conference room. Marsha never understood that. It should be no liquids considering the danger of spilling a drink on a laptop.

"So I see," Hal said, taking his customary seat at the head of the table. As usual, each of them had a pad of paper and pen in front of them for any note taking.

"Sorry," Two said, putting the sandwich aside.

He waved her off. "Eat."

Two didn't need to be told twice. She took a huge bite of her sandwich.

Hal went on, explaining, "Adam just called. They went to the race but didn't wait for it to end. He wanted a lay of the land at the hotel. She's got an entourage of sorts, and they want to get her alone, obviously." Hal now looked at her expectantly. "Okay, let's hear it."

Caught off guard with a full mouth, Two quickly swallowed. "Here's what I found." She tapped a few keys on her laptop and presented the same photo of Mac Senton they had seen before—the dead American wearing a business suit and smiling at them.

Two wiped her mouth with the back of her hand. "New York Yankees man, what do we know? Not much, right? Mac

Thornburg Senton. He's American, worked at Goldman Sachs in New York, then Dubai, then Red Arrow Capital in London. He went to ground and ended up stealing a handicap van in Lisse so he could help Bart Werner's assassin escape from the airport after the hit. Then he showed up in the van with the teen girl, got cornered by Adam and ate cyanide, right?"

No one said anything, and Two moved on to the next photo. It showed a smiling woman in a hospital bed, holding a newborn baby. Mac Senton was right there too, a loving arm around the woman, facing the camera with a big grin.

"He's married," Marsha said, surprised.

"No. Never married," Two explained. "But he was the father of the baby. A girl named Mia. This was seven years ago."

"You talk to the woman?"

Two shook her head. "I'm having a hard time reaching her. I have now left a message with her sister who lives in California, hoping to get to her. Nothing yet."

Hal waved at the image. "So, what? I mean, I want to know *why* he disappeared from the face of the earth, where he was, and most importantly, what the hell he was doing working for The Joker. Totally irrelevant that he fathered a kid, totally irrelevant."

"No," Two said firmly. "No, the kid is important."

The screen now showed a toddler lying on a hospital bed and hooked up to a number of tubes and machines. "She was pretty sick, right off the bat. Poor respiratory function. They even did some sort of surgery."

Hal sighed. "Okay…"

"When he vanished, he already had a good sum of money. From his days at Goldman Sachs, working in Dubai, and at Red Arrow in London. Those funds were put in a trust. For the girl. She has cystic fibrosis." They looked at her. "And if the kid dies? That money goes to an American cystic fibrosis foundation that is working to fix the genetic mutation that causes the disease.

"The kid's mother? Her name is Elizabeth Thomas. She was active on social media some years back. But she's tapered off. She's married now, obviously to someone else, and has another child, completely healthy and five years old. She deleted some old posts, but as you guys know, nothing you delete is ever really deleted. This one is a typical rant."

Again the screen changed. It was a social media post that read, "Tragic? What's tragic is that Mac lied to me. I'm a carrier. He's a carrier. But when I found out I was pregnant, I asked him. He said no. He's fine."

Two looked at them. "Cystic fibrosis is an inherited disorder. A baby needs to inherit a copy of the bad gene from each parent."

Marsha understood where she was going. "So Mac Senton was a carrier, yet he lied about it?"

"That's what she says. But I don't think so. Look."

The screen showed a middle-aged man leaning on a handicap walker, wearing an oxygen nasal cannula, the tube snaking down to a small tank on the seat of the walker.

"This is Dirk Werner," Two said. She looked at them. "Bart Werner's father. He died years back from respiratory failure—"

"Stemming from cystic fibrosis," Marsha said, finishing the thought.

"Exactly," Two responded.

Hal leaned back in his chair. "No offense, Two. You do great work. But this—"

"Hold on, hold on," Two interrupted impatiently. "Let me finish." She realized she might have overreached, but Hal gave her a go-ahead nod.

Two took a deep breath. "Okay…" She worked her laptop and now a different picture of Dirk and a pre-teen Bart Werner appeared. In this photo, they were seated close together at a restaurant table, smiling for the camera. "That trust fund that Mac left for his kid? Bart Werner is the executor of the trust."

"They knew each other. We knew that, so I guess it's fair to say he trusted Werner," Hal said.

"No. Mac Senton trusted Bart Werner because they were half-brothers."

Chapter Nine

FROG Headquarters, The Hague

Marsha shook her head. "None of this makes sense. If they were half-brothers and Mac Senton appointed Bart Werner as the executor of his will, he wouldn't want the guy murdered as soon as he landed in Amsterdam. There's no way."

"Exactly!" Two said excitedly.

"We're missing something," Hal said.

"I have a theory," Two said.

"Give me a minute. I'm texting Gretchen and Adam. We need to see if the race-car driver can confirm this."

Marsha caught Two's eye and mouthed the words, good job, and Two beamed.

Hal looked up. "Okay."

"Here's what I'm thinking," Two said. "Once his kid was born with cystic fibrosis, Mac realized he had to have been adopted. I think he did one of those ancestry DNA tests."

"And he found his father," Marsha offered, playing along.

"Exactly."

"But the guy was dead," Hal reminded them.

"Right. But he finds out Dirk Werner has a biological child. Bart Werner," Two said.

"So, he approached Bart," Marsha theorized. "They learn they are indeed half-brothers."

"Okay, I'll buy that," Hal said. "But one brother helped kill the other. This is some twisted Cain and Abel stuff."

"No!" Two said, abruptly pushing back her chair and starting to pace. "No... Let's just presume a few things here if you will..."

"We work on *facts,*" Hal rebuked her. "Not presumptions."

"And half the time, our *presumptions* are confirmed to be *facts*," Marsha reminded him. "But to get to the fact, we need the presumption to point us in the right direction."

Hal sighed and looked to Two. "Fine, but don't leave out the fact that we do know he played a part in his half-brother's killing. That's a *fact*."

"Not if he didn't know it was going to happen," Two argued. Hal frowned and Two quickly went on. "They discover they are half-brothers, and guess what? Bart Werner knows something bad is going down. Something much worse than COVID is coming. He confides in Mac. So William DeWine, aka Matthew, comes here and—"

"Wait. Why?" Hal interrupted. Two stopped pacing and looked at him. "Why didn't Mac come here to meet Adam? Why was it DeWine?"

Two simply stared. This had obviously not been factored into her working theory. "I don't know." She resumed pacing, then stopped and pointed at him. "But I will. I will."

Marsha now jumped in. "If you're right, this whole thing, this plot that is going to bring down the world, it has to start with someone Bart knew. Either socially, or through his work."

Two picked up the idea. "So maybe the link is Robert Ellison—we know both Bart and Mac befriend his daughter who races cars—"

"Except I've searched Red Arrow clients," Marsha countered. "Ellison isn't there."

"Could be in a trust," Two said. "He's super rich. He has a trust. Or several trusts not in his name."

Marsha made a note to check on that.

Hal looked at Two. "So Mac doesn't know his half-brother is about to be offed. He got the van. He was in the men's room for the bait and switch. Why exactly?"

"Because he's working undercover," Two told him. They both stared at her. "Doing what he's told, he gets the van and all that. But no way Mac knew Bart was about to be killed. He would have never been a part of that. No way."

"And you're basing that on the idea that he won't go along with Bart being killed because the guy is his brother?" Hal challenged. "You don't know that."

"No," Two insisted. "I'm basing it on his actions with teen, Amber. He picked up the handicap van not realizing she was in there. He told Adam he was supposed to kill her and when you look at the café bombing, not only was DeWine killed, but lots of others were killed, then you have the murder of Bart Werner, right there in front of a zillion people at the airport, so these guys play for keeps. They didn't want her alive. But he defied them. He couldn't release her or they'd find out, right? She's a teen. She'd go right back on Facebook or whatever. So he tries to buy time by drugging her and not hurting her. When she got away, he ran too. But Adam caught up with him and he realized it was over."

"If he's a good guy, then why not just turn himself in?" Hal argued. "He could have told Adam what was going on and we'd be all over it. Instead, he killed himself?"

Two frowned, realizing their boss was correct. There was a gaping hole in her working theory.

Manama, Bahrain

To Gretchen, Nancy Ellison seemed stiff as a board, the tension palpable. She finally said, "I heard, yes. I reached out to his mother. I've never met her, but I have the home address, so I wrote a note."

"Any idea on who killed him?" Adam asked.

"What? No! He was a gentle soul."

Gretchen thought maybe the woman was hiding something. Such a quick denial.

Adam and Gretchen had been waiting for Nancy Ellison when she arrived that evening at the Al Areen Palace and Spa, after taking a respectable fifth place in the race. The luxury hotel was popular with racing-circuit drivers since it was located just fifteen minutes from the Bahrain International track. It turned out that, on this night, her only entourage was her business manager, Garth Henderson, who hadn't been impressed with their Interpol credentials, even going so far as to tell them that whatever they wanted would have to wait.

Adam had taken a step forward and gotten right in the man's face. "We talk to her *now*. Either here or the closest police station. Her choice. Understand?"

Not surprisingly, the four of them had gone to Nancy Ellison's large suite and taken their seats in the well-appointed living room. Nancy politely offered drinks from the bar, but everyone declined.

She got herself a beer and drank from the bottle. Gretchen carried a thin file folder which she placed on the coffee table. Adam had announced that he was going to record the conversation and Nancy was fine with that. What she didn't know was that his phone app would not only record the interview, but also beam it live to FROG Headquarters. Meanwhile, Gretchen would monitor her cell phone for any text messages from FROG since Two, Marsha, and Hal were monitoring the conversation and might pass on information they needed.

"We have a dinner meeting with a sponsor in less than ninety minutes," Garth Henderson said, making a point of looking at his watch. He was probably close to sixty years old and carried himself with a conceited air.

Adam glared at the man. "We're here until we say we're done, understand?"

"She needs to shower and—"

"And you're wasting our time, so kindly shut up if you want to remain in the room," Adam countered, his withering look enough to quiet the man.

Gretchen gave Nancy a reassuring look. "How did you meet Bart Werner?"

Nancy looked at Henderson and said, "It was a dinner like I have to go to tonight." She turned to Gretchen. "This isn't Formula One. We bleed money, and we need a ton of support. That means sponsors." She gave Garth Henderson a nasty look. "I do a lot of these dog-and-pony shows."

"They are not dog and—" Garth started.

"Quiet," Adam firmly said, and Garth closed his mouth.

"Go on," Gretchen said to Nancy. "Was Werner a sponsor?"

Nancy laughed. She reached for her beer and took a long pull. "He had a client that wanted him along. A widow of, I don't know, maybe fifty? Older. She liked to have him on her arm, if you get my meaning. It was a joke."

"Who was the woman?"

Nancy looked at Garth. He said, "Victoria Tenney. Very wealthy, and yes, she's an important sponsor."

"Victoria Tenney," Adam repeated, just in case his team back at the office hadn't picked it up. "Brit?"

"Yes," Nancy replied. "Bart sat next to me, and we hit it off, I suppose."

"You dated." It wasn't a question. Gretchen made it a statement.

Nancy looked surprised. "No. No, it wasn't like that. I mean, we got along that night. We're close in age. I mean everyone else at the table was a lot older."

"Present company included, I suppose," Garth said bitterly, giving Nancy a contemptuous look.

"What was the relationship?" Gretchen probed.

Nancy sighed. "We were friends. I travel a lot, so I guess it's more like we were text friends, you know? When he understood our need for sponsors, he tried to help. He'd talk to some of his wealthy clients. He brought them out to a couple of races."

"Did it work?" Adam asked. "They sponsor you?"

"I don't think so, no," she replied, glancing at Henderson for clarification.

Henderson shook his head. "No."

"But your father helps, right?" Gretchen asked.

She rolled her eyes, betraying her young age. "You're reading the crap out there. My father has helped STR Motorsports, but you know why? The woman he's dating now? I mean, it changes monthly, but that woman, her son wants to be a crew chief. He's now a Jack Man with STR."

Gretchen gave her a puzzled look.

"Jacking up the car for tire changes." She rolled her eyes. "His mother wants to buy him the crew chief job."

"With your father's money," Adam suggested.

"STR Motorsports was my ride before Dad met the idiot woman. I mean, that's how they met. STR had a party, he was there with me, and she was there to support her son. So yeah, he's given STR money, but to please her, not help me. In fact, I wish he hadn't. I swear, I've told him to do something else with his money. He's hurting, not helping, for God's sake."

Her anger was deep, and it was obvious she was telling the truth.

"Okay," Gretchen said. "So no romance with Bart Werner. But he introduced you to his brother, Mac."

Nancy gave a startled look.

"He was the romance," Gretchen went on. "Not Bart, but Mac." It was a stretch, but Gretchen knew how to read women.

Nancy licked her lips, glanced nervously at Henderson, and then gave Gretchen a nod.

Henderson was obviously surprised. "Who is this? This Mac person?"

Adam stood and looked at Henderson. "Give us a few minutes, okay?"

"What?" He retorted. "No."

"A few minutes. Now."

Nancy looked at him. "Please go. I'll be on time for dinner, I promise."

Henderson finally stood, giving all of them nasty looks. Adam escorted him out the door. When he came back, he said, "Mac Senton? Bart introduced you, obviously."

"Bart and me, we were friends. He told me that an American was asking him to do a DNA test. The guy was a New Yorker and was certain they were brothers."

"Bart didn't want to do it?" Gretchen asked. "Take the test?"

"He thought it would hurt his mother."

"But you encouraged him to do it," Gretchen said.

"I kind of told him he had to."

"Because of the cystic fibrosis."

Again, Nancy gave them a surprised look. "Yeah."

"And then what? They became buddies?" Adam asked. "Mac and Bart?"

"No, not exactly. I mean, Mac moved to London, got a job at Bart's company. And I guess it worked. They got to be friends. I mean they had a ton in common. Not just their jobs, you know? They both loved to play chess. They both were really good and would have all kinds of matches." She smiled at the memory. "They'd bet on the games, keep track of who was winning the most. Bart was always ahead, but not by much. It was funny to hear them trash-talk chess moves, you know? They were both super competitive."

"And you and Mac became close," Gretchen suggested.

Another eyeroll. "Until he dumped me."

"What happened?"

"Said he wanted to be closer to Mia." When they gave her a blank look, she said, "His daughter."

"He cut it off cold-turkey?" Gretchen asked.

She sighed. "Bart told me he thought he'd be back soon, a couple months, maybe. But he stays in touch, on his terms, of course. Uses a different number."

"Mac?" Gretchen asked, surprised.

"He texts me, no phone calls. I guess, you know, he doesn't want Mia's mother—his ex—to know. But crap, she's married. It's so stupid. So we texted. Daily. And then lately, nothing. He just won't respond at all... Just ignores me."

Adam asked, "How'd you know it was Mac? You said it wasn't his number."

She tearfully read from the phone. "*Hi there, polesitter.*" She glanced at them. "That was his nickname for me, you know? No one knows that. No one. It's Mac." She gave a sheepish smile. "He always says I'm the best of the best."

"Hence the term, polesitter," Gretchen said, getting it.

"Go on," Adam said.

She continued to read. "Sorry for dropping out. I thought this would be easy. It's been tougher than I figured. I have to do what they say."

"Who? Who is they?" Adam anxiously queried.

"I don't know," she said.

"Are there more?" Gretchen asked.

"That was the first one. Then several days later, he said, "*If I goof up, they will kill Mia, and I know they mean it.*" She looked at Gretchen with tears in her eyes. "It gets worse."

"We need to hear it. Keep reading, please..."

Nancy scrolled through the messages on her phone. "They took out Bart and that was just cruel. I'm trying to stay ahead of them. This was a mistake. I'm so sorry. I love you, and I love Mia. Hold on to that, okay?" She turned to Gretchen again. "You asked if I know who killed Bart. I don't, I swear. But Mac does... I mean, don't you think? 'They took Bart out?'"

"He didn't talk about who 'they' were?" Gretchen asked.

Nancy shook her head. "I keep trying him. Probably eighty times a day, I call, I text... There's no voicemail set up, and he, I don't know, he's just stopped talking to me."

"How long has it been?"

"Sixteen days."

Gretchen looked to Adam who nodded. Turning to Nancy, she took a breath and said, "First of all, he didn't break up with you. As you can tell from those texts, something was terribly wrong, And from what you read to us, he loved you very much. And I'm so sorry to be the one to tell you this, but Mac is dead."

The woman was clearly shocked. "No... No, there's no way..."

Gretchen opened the file and pulled out the picture of Mac dead on the basement floor, white spots around his opened mouth. Before showing it to Nancy, she gave the woman a soft look and said, "I need you to take a breath. This is going to be hard to see." She slid the photo across the table to Nancy who reluctantly picked it up.

She immediately recoiled at the sight. "I don't understand... What's happened..?"

Gretchen said matter-of-factly, "The traces of white around his mouth are from a cyanide pill." When Nancy just stared, Gretchen added, "He took his own life."

"No, no..." She started to cry. "Please..."

"He died sixteen days ago... That's why the texts stopped. I'm sorry."

The photo dropped from her hands, and she grabbed a nearby pillow, hugging it tightly and rocking back and forth. Finally, she looked at them again. "In New York? He died in New York? Mia is in New York."

"Amsterdam."

She immediately ceased rocking, taken aback. "Bart was killed in Amsterdam."

"And we want to arrest whoever did it, but we don't know who they are," Adam said. "That's why we need your help."

"I don't know, I told you," she blurted out in frustration. She started rocking again, doubled over, holding the pillow. Staring at the floor, she said, "They were going to kill Mia. That's why, right?" She stopped rocking and looked at them. "He did it to save Mia?"

Gretchen and Adam exchanged puzzled looks.

"I'm not following—" Gretchen started.

"That's what he meant!" Nancy suddenly grabbed her phone and started scrolling. She stopped and seemed to be frantically reading something. Finally, she looked at Gretchen again, her hands now trembling. "He was trying to tell me, and I just didn't get it… I didn't understand…"

Gretchen gently took the phone out of her hands and read the text out loud. "I tried to do the right thing, but it's gone so bad. I was stupid, and I'm sorry. They know my link to Bart. They can grab my money. They took out a hundred thousand, US, and put it back, just to show me the power they have. If I make the wrong move, if I go to the police, the FBI, Mia dies and there will be no money for research. There is no way out now. I'm so sorry."

Nancy started rocking again. "That's what he was saying, right? He had no choice but to die?"

Gretchen looked to Adam. "The last text here says, *Sending a key. Sorry, but there is no one else I trust.*"

FROG Headquarters, The Hague ~ 20 Hours Later

After learning that Mac Senton had sent a key to Nancy Ellison's home mailbox, Adam had asked for her mailbox key and immediately left for London. She lived in a high-rise luxury apartment building very close to Hyde Park. No doubt paid for by her father. Inside the lobby, Adam found a wall of mailboxes near the elevators, just as Nancy had described. She hadn't been home for a couple of weeks, and her mailbox contained the usual junk mail that seems to cling to any person with a mailing address, dead or alive. There were also various catalogs, several snail-mail bills, and one letter with no return address but postmarked Amsterdam. Squeezing the envelope, Adam realized there was no way it contained a key. He impatiently ripped it open to find a single paper ticket for something called Baggage Storage located at the Amsterdam Schipol Airport.

While he was on a flight back to Amsterdam, Marsha found that the Baggage Storage was located in the basement between Arrivals 1 and 2. Apparently, it was widely popular with travelers who didn't want to cart all their luggage from place to place. While there are other lockers on the main floor, the basement storage catered to those storing especially large suitcases and allowed items to be left for up to thirty days.

Once Adam had Mac's luggage in hand, he had been sorely tempted to open it right there and sort through the contents. But he had refrained after Hal reminded him that they had to x-ray it first. No point in opening it and being blown to smithereens. That thought quickly sobered him.

Back at FROG Headquarters late that afternoon, the bag was x-rayed, deemed safe, and opened. It contained lots of clothes, two pairs of shoes, and some toiletries. Two quickly decided they were all Mac's personal belongings, based on the size of the clothes. The prize was a padded envelope found wedged between some clothes.

Marsha opened the envelope and placed all the contents on the conference room table. There were six color photos, all of the same man, looking to be about thirty-five years old, and, according to Two, a total hunk. In the first photo, he was wearing a black cowboy hat and leaning against a red Maserati sports car. In all the others, he still had the cowboy hat, but now he was on horseback. In one photo, he was roping a calf. There was nothing written on the back sides of the photos to tell them who the man was.

"Cowboy hat," Gretchen said. "Could be our bomber."

Marsha handed a photo to Adam. "You're the only one who saw him."

Adam studied several photographs very closely. He shook his head. "The hat worked—his face was obscure. I honestly can't say for sure."

The next item was a legal-size paper showing the same organizational chart that Adam had found at Bart Werner's London apartment. However, this one had more information. The chart itself was now labeled *Trojan Steed.* And where the previous chart had The Joker as the top person, this chart had an actual name: Clyde Redfield.

"So, what?" Gretchen said. "A steed is a horse. So this is a trojan horse of some kind?"

"Who knows?" Hal replied. "But at least we know who The Joker is." The new chart also had a few more initials and partial names filled in than the previous chart. The last item from the envelope was a handwritten note: *Please make sure this gets to Elizabeth Thomas. Her address is below. She is not responding to earlier correspondence and it is vital that she sees this. Love, Mac.*

Adam turned to Marsha. "This is the woman that had his kid, right? With cystic fibrosis? And they've had a falling out."

Two immediately answered, "She's employed by Goldman Sachs in New York. I've poked around a bit, but we never gave her a priority."

"Do more poking," Hal told her. "She's top priority now."

The next morning, they were back at it. Marsha started the meeting by saying, "The programs we ran overnight came up empty. Haven't got anything on partial names or the initials. So we might strike out on that. Also nothing on Trojan Steed. It drew a blank. But there is plenty of material on Clyde Redfield."

"He started Red Arrow Capital," Adam said.

"Right," Marsha said. "There is a ton of stuff on him, Q&A interviews, all that. There is one interesting thing that may be linked to whatever is going on—he founded an organization called Sustainable Growth Syndicate—a global group that advocates for population control. They're adamant that we can't sustain our current world-population levels. He has actually funded smaller organizations that go so far as to demand forced human sterilization. *Forced sterilization.*"

"On others," Gretchen scoffed. "Not for the landed gentry, like him. But for the poor and downtrodden."

Marsha nodded. "It's along those lines, yes. Basically, it is backed by the U.N. So there is that issue. Also, I found inside the British medical system that he had an operation for liver cancer over a year ago. Private hospital. That's not public knowledge."

"Glad to know everyone's medical records are so tightly sealed in my beloved homeland," Adam said sarcastically.

Marsha smiled.

Gretchen said, "So we have William DeWine, aka 'Matthew,' Bart Werner, and Mac Senton who all worked for Red Arrow Capital, and Clyde Redfield who founded the company."

Everyone started talking at once and Hal slapped the table. "Let's stick to the facts as we know them. I don't want speculation." He looked to Marsha and Two. "What else do we have? Concrete."

Marsha worked her laptop. "Here are all the photos from the packet." On the screen, a slide show began of the man. "Remember, there was no name on the backs of the photos, but we found him. His name is Ethan Redfield, he's the son of Clyde Redfield. A vice president at the company. Clyde's only living son. An older son died in Iraq, Special Forces, some years back. Ethan is forty-one and spends a lot of time on a family-owned cattle ranch in Wyoming."

"Do you have anything of him without the hat?" Gretchen asked.

"Sure," Marsha said. "Putting them up."

On the large screen there were now several photos of Ethan Redfield at social events. In two different ones, he was wearing a tuxedo. Two was correct—he was very attractive.

"All Red Arrow events," Two said. "This is how we identified him, by the way. We were looking at his father and saw these on the Red Arrow website. They identified the son. It's definitely him."

"There's one more thing," Marsha volunteered. She glanced at Hal. "Not a fact, but I think we need to consider it. Just a sec…"

The screen changed to show a photo of what looked like a Catholic priest standing with a woman on either side of him—one woman was about his age, the other much younger. He was wearing a black robe with a white collar at the throat and a bright green preaching scarf. "Remember these guys?" Marsha asked. "We have Herman Werner, his wife, Arabella, and their daughter, Claire. Arabella and Claire, the tattoo waitress to use Adam's description, died in the café blast."

Now the screen showed a close up of the organizational chart. One box was filled in with the initials H.W. Next to it in another box was the name Vic with a question mark in red. In both cases, the name and initials were underlined twice in red.

Gretchen immediately said, "H.W. is Herman Werner and Vic is, what? Short for Victoria? We just learned about Victoria Tenney, the woman who sponsors race cars."

"No clue," Marsha said. "I'm just tossing it into the mix. We have lots of initials, we're not finding anything, but Herman Werner is Bart's uncle, so maybe he's part of this. That's all."

"The two underlines in red?" Adam asked.

"No idea," Marsha said. "But those are the only initials or names underlined like that on the chart."

"Oh, no," Two suddenly muttered staring at her computer. "Oh dear God…"

Marsha looked at her. "What? What's wrong?"

Two didn't respond at first. Finally, she looked up. "Nancy Ellison. She just had a horrific crash." Two typed on her computer. "I set up for alerts on her. This just came in from the Daily Mail."

Now the conference room TV screen displayed the still image of a Formula car with the video prompt arrow overlaid on top. Two clicked on it and the car took off, the only car on the track. It took a sharp curve and then came into a straight-away swerving to stay in the middle of the track.

"Daily Mail says this was a practice run," Two explained. "They are now in Budapest. They get several practice runs to familiarize themselves with the track." The car flashed past the camera.

"That's her," Gretchen confirmed. "The number-4 car."

The race car negotiated an S curve and suddenly went wobbly, somehow unable to get back on course, veering left and right, clearly out of control.

"Ah, geez," Gretchen mumbled.

The race car appeared to be leaning left, heading straight toward a wall. The impact was violent and gruesome, the car splitting in two, and then exploding in a huge fireball.

"Oh God," Gretchen said.

The camera stayed on the fiery scene, the remains of the car engulfed in flames. Firefighters were quick on the scene, spraying the car with white foam. It wasn't uncommon to see drivers emerge from such a conflagration since they wore fire-retardant suits. But there was no movement, no signs of life from the wreckage at all. Finally, the short video froze on the massive fire.

The room was silent for some time.

"We watched her," Adam said. "She was good. Better than good. No way that was driver error."

Two was busy on her computer. "Got video of her crew chief. Hold on…"

The fiery image of the crash was replaced with a close-up of a middle-aged man. He looked ashen. The video began. "She kept saying, 'It's squirrelly, something's off, I'm fighting for everything right now. It's too squirrelly, something's wrong, something's wrong.'" He ran a hand through his hair, clearly distraught. "I said, bring it in. Let's take a look… She said okay, coming in, but then…"

Again the video abruptly stopped.

"Nancy Ellison was just murdered," Gretchen said.

Chapter Ten

The Hague, Holland

The following morning Adam sat in the back of a pub located just a block away from the Peace Palace, nursing an orange juice and making handwritten notes in a spiral notebook. It was close to ten in the morning, and he had been sitting alone at a back corner table for several hours now. While he could have been doing this work at their office, he liked being in a pub where life went on as it always did. Witnessing the everyday routine of the customers and staff was oddly comforting—these people had no idea that there was a diabolical plan currently in motion that would wipe out much of civilization. They were simply living their lives. As they should.

Meanwhile, he was writing down the issues plaguing his team in the hopes that something would pop and they could finally get a step ahead of the bad guys. If nothing else, it would be nice to stop the pointless deaths. The list of the dead read like *The Twelve Days of Christmas* with five dead café patrons, three dead Red Arrow Capital employees, one dead kidnapped teen, one deceased race-car driver, and a slain cat sprawled on an old woman's lap.

He didn't think he had ever been a part of a case that had gone so far sideways so quickly.

"Hey."

Adam looked up to find Gretchen standing there. He was surprised, but happily surprised that she had come. Looking at her fresh face, he thought she looked quite well-rested, unlike himself. He gestured to the empty chair across from him and she sat down. A waitress came by and Gretchen ordered a coffee and a full meal. She gave him a sheepish smile. "Couldn't eat last night."

He nodded.

The waitress promptly returned with a carafe in hand and filled Gretchen's mug. Gretchen looked at Adam. "It was

Henderson, Nancy Ellison's business manager. It had to be. Not meaning to, I'm not saying that."

Adam handed over his notebook. "Number three."

Gretchen took the notebook and read it out loud. "Henderson, because no one else knew 'Interpol' was there and I kicked him out."

Adam looked at her. "He was pissed off. He bitched to someone about it."

Gretchen gave him back the notebook. "Who?"

"No clue. I asked Two and Marsha to grab his phone calls. We taped our interview and they can look at the time I kicked him out, so anything after that."

Gretchen agreed. "Has to be someone who could tamper with her car. She said it was all over the place."

"I agree."

Gretchen studied him for a bit. "You can't blame yourself, you know."

"I don't," he quickly replied, his tone defensive.

She looked at him and said gently, "If he talked to someone and that led to her death, it would have happened anyway. It wasn't because he got kicked out. And we had to get him out of the room. If you hadn't done it, I would have. We needed to be one-on-one with her."

"I know," Adam said, resigned. "She didn't deserve to die."

"No, she didn't," Gretchen said, taking a sip of her coffee. "You get some sleep?"

"Enough." She gave him a doubtful look. "Okay, no. My mind won't turn off, that's the problem."

Gretchen gestured to the notebook. "Tell me your thoughts."

As much as Adam was a loner, there was something about Gretchen that made him want to share. But only with her. Not with anyone else. When they'd worked together before on cases, his desire to include Gretchen angered him, and he found himself purposely annoying her so she couldn't get too close. Last night, while tossing and turning, he finally understood that she was an asset—a yin to his yang, or however that worked. She complemented him. And instead of pushing her away, he should welcome her thoughts.

"First, no particular order here, just random questions," he told her.

She took a sip of coffee. "Go."

"Why Amsterdam? The three Red Arrow guys worked in London. Why not somewhere in the UK? Somewhere closer to home?"

"Easy, to keep themselves under the radar. Maybe they knew they were being watched. Or suspected it. Maybe that's why Matthew bought a bicycle. If someone is following you, make it a bit harder by jumping on a bike, getting lost in the shuffle."

"But he didn't lose anyone. The bomber was there before Matthew. They knew where he was going," Adam pointed out.

"Someone leaked it then. Maybe Bart Werner, maybe Mac, maybe it was an email that got hacked. But the point is, he didn't know that. He thought he'd make it hard for someone on foot or a car to follow. He just didn't know that it didn't matter. They knew his destination without tailing him."

Adam jotted that in his notebook. He liked her thinking. "Why *that* café?" She was about to speak and he quickly added, "Don't say because Bart Werner's cousin worked there and all that."

"But that is a valid reason. Bart gives him the layout, he knows there is an outdoor patio. Not very big, so it's easy to meet someone you don't know. Remember, Matthew changed it from inside the café to outside. He said he'd be on a red bike, making him stand out even more." Gretchen took a sip of coffee and looked at him over the rim of the mug. "Better question is, is the waitress's father, the vicar, tied in to this? And that's why that café? If so, it's a pretty big jump that he would be involved without Bart Werner getting him involved."

Adam hadn't considered this. "You mean, they reached out to the vicar to see if he could help?"

Gretchen shrugged. "Why not?"

Adam followed her logic. "That crosses off another question I had." He glanced at his notebook. "I'm asking myself, why go to AIVD? You're in the UK Why not go to Scotland Yard or MI6 with your tip?" He looked at her. "So Bart Werner knows something, all three men do, he reaches out to his uncle for help. So they tip off AIVD."

Gretchen thought for a minute and then said, "Or they tip us off because whatever is going on, whatever is planned, is here. Right here. Or at least originated here."

Adam wrote this down. He looked at her and said, "I had a whole different line-of-thought with the vicar, by the way."

"Okay, go," Gretchen said.

"I'm thinking every person on that chart is up to no-good. I'm thinking he's working with The Joker, that's why he's on the chart, right?"

"Maybe, *if* the initials are for him," Gretchen agreed.

"Let's say they are. But guess what? The vicar has had a change of heart... He wants out. He tells his nephew who tells Mac Senton and Matthew. But what if the bad guys don't want him jumping ship? So the bombing, killing off not only his snitch, Matthew, but his wife and daughter, it is all a warning shot across the bow."

Gretchen sat back in her chair, clearly taken back. "Oh, boy... I don't know... I mean..."

"We need to find him. Talk to him," Adam said, scribbling in his notebook. When he looked up, he saw Gretchen was staring at her now empty coffee mug, running her index finger over the rim over and over again. "Gretch?" She glanced up. "Talk to me."

She gave him a sheepish smile. "I'm old-fashioned. Vicars, pastors, ministers...? They're the good guys."

Before Adam could remind her about the countless number of boys abused by Catholic priests, his phone buzzed with a message. Then Gretchen's phone buzzed. And the waitress brought Gretchen her breakfast.

Amsterdam, the Netherlands

Hans Wolter was lying so still, his breath so shallow, that Vicar Werner almost thought he was too late. On the other side of the bed was Hans's daughter, Justine. Their eyes met as she wiped away a tear. Dipping his fingertips in the holy oil, he touched Hans's forehead and in a firm, but soothing voice, gave a short prayer. As he ended the prayer, Hans suddenly opened his eyes and gave a feeble attempt to swat the vicar's hand away.

The vicar smiled at his long-time friend and parishioner. "Ah, still with us and feisty as ever I see. "

"What was that? What are you doing?"

"Prayer of healing, my dear friend."

"Healing! Rubbish! We all know that won't do a damn thing." Hans turned to his daughter, plenty angry. "This your doing, I take it? I don't want this nonsense, for God's sake!"

Caught off-guard, all Justine could say was, "Please don't take the Lord's name in vain, Daddy."

Hans waved his hand. "I'd like to speak to the vicar alone, please."

Hurt, Justine glanced at Werner who gave her a small smile. He hadn't seen this coming either. With that, Justine quietly left, closing the bedroom door behind her.

"I need to sit up," Hans said.

A strong man, the vicar easily lifted Hans up, placing more pillows behind him. "Good?" he asked.

"Actually, what's good is that she is so worried about me," Hans said. "I needed to see you... How are you?"

The vicar gave a weak smile. "I have faith in God."

Hans waved the thought away. "Rubbish, man. You lost your lovely wife and your daughter. Good to have faith. Fine. Better to have a living family, no?"

The vicar had to fight back the tears. If nothing else, he could count on Hans to give it to him straight. Finally, he said quietly, "I barely make it through each day. The nights are impossible."

Hans nodded, as if satisfied with the honest answer. "I suppose you could say the same for me." Hans motioned to the bedside table that held a glass of water. Werner quickly picked it up and helped Hans to drink. After a few minutes, Hans continued. "I should have never involved you... It was... well, it's unforgivable."

"It is only right to help others, in any way we can. Righteous, even."

"Righteous?" Another wave of the hand. "Your nephew is dead. And his two friends. Their blood is on my hands, Vicar."

"What are you talking about?" the vicar asked, confused. "What friends?"

Hans ignored the question. "Tell me, were you going to meet there too?" When the vicar frowned, Hans said impatiently, "The café? You were to be there too?"

"What? No. No, that was Arabella. Claire wanted to talk to her. I was hoping… well, eventually that Claire would want to talk to me."

Hans seemed to think on this. "You didn't put them up to it? Arabella or Claire?"

"Put them up to what…?"

"Meeting DeWine!" Hans said with irritation.

Vicar Werner frowned. "I don't know what you're talking about."

Hans studied him for some time. "You really don't, do you? A man named William DeWine. He was at the café. One of the dead."

Vicar Werner gave him a blank look.

"You didn't read about those killed? Media made a fuss about it. Some older ladies that have tea there most mornings. Claire, who has worked there since she was fifteen—"

"Stop," the vicar interrupted, emotionally distraught.

"Arabella, wife of an Anglican priest—"

"Stop!"

"An Englishman named DeWine," Hans continued. "You read about him? *He* was the target. *He* is why Arabella and Claire are dead."

Werner simply stared at his parishioner, not comprehending. He had always believed that the bombing was horrifically bad luck. Bad luck that it was *that* café. Bad luck that Claire was working that day. And awfully bad luck that Arabella and Claire were there together, talking for the first time in ages in order to mend fences.

"Check online. Any newspaper. You read bios about each one, each bomb victim, and you see that DeWine worked at Bart's company."

The vicar felt his knees go weak and looked around. A comfortable chair was a few feet away, and he found himself collapsing in it.

"I thought you could fill in the missing pieces," Hans said. "I thought you orchestrated it. Have DeWine go to the café, pass something on to Claire."

The vicar felt his heart race. He had come to terms with the bombing. It was a horrible tragedy. Nothing to do with him. Or Hans. Or the choices they had made.

Hans continued. "Claire worked there for years and, what? DeWine was at same café by chance? A coincidence? I don't think so. Maybe Bart told him to go there." When the vicar didn't reply, his face now drained of color, Hans asked, "Did you talk to your nephew? About Mr. DeWine?"

The vicar didn't reply. He was struggling to wrap his head around what Hans was telling him.

"Vicar!" Hans said, annoyed. "Did your nephew tell you about DeWine? That he was coming here? Maybe bringing in material we need?"

Werner finally looked at his friend. "He's dead. Bart died at the airport. Some lunatic attacked him—"

"Answer me. Did Bart tell you about DeWine?"

Werner shook his head. "I never heard the name…"

Hans paused to give this some thought. "It wasn't happenstance. Couldn't be. DeWine was targeted. Why he went there, to your daughter's café, I'm not sure. But he was assassinated to use the term. They were collateral damage, I'm sure of it. Arabella and Claire."

The vicar was overwhelmed. He couldn't respond. He had no words. The old man was wrong. He had to be wrong. Arabella's and Claire's deaths were due to a senseless, random attack. They had to be. Bart too. He was in the wrong place at the wrong time too. The idea that the tragic deaths were not random? Could this be true? And if so, how could he not have seen it? How could he have been so blind?

"You must not let them die in vain," Hans told him. "Listen to me, Vicar. Are you listening?"

The vicar numbly looked at Hans.

"The secretary desk… go…" When Werner didn't move, Hans motioned across the room. "Now! Go!"

With great effort, Werner pulled himself out of the chair and went over to the well-polished oak secretary desk that stood a good seven feet in height with two glass cabinet doors above a fitted slanted piece that held a brass key. He had seen these antique desks before and knew that slant dropped down to serve as a writing surface.

"Turn the key," Hans said. "Open it."

The vicar did as he was told, pulling down the writing top to reveal scores of drawers, all fitted with brass inlays. It really was a beautiful piece.

"Vicar?" Hans called out, which started a coughing fit.

Werner quickly went over to his friend. He gave the old man some water, which seemed to help. Hans silently offered his hand. Werner grasped it and said, "You're wrong about Arabella and Claire. You're wrong."

"Listen to me. Pull out the first four drawers. There is a panel there. It's a false back," the old man said in a raspy voice. "Open the panel by pushing the bottom left corner. Inside, you will see it... It is up to you... You must fix this."

"No, listen. It was happenstance with Arabella and Claire—"

"Quiet, and do as I say..." the old man argued, his hand squeezing Werner's hand with surprising force. His face suddenly softened. "I shouldn't have bothered you to begin with, but that is water under the bridge, as they say. And I'm sorry. I'm deeply sorry. Too many have already died. I didn't see that. I am so, so sorry. This must be remedied. I beg of you... Please."

Hans released the vicar's hand, and the priest reluctantly went back to the secretary desk. He did as he was instructed and pulled out the first four drawers, carefully setting them on the writing desk. He then pressed on the panel. It sprung open, revealing a business envelope. There was no writing on it, nor was it sealed. He opened the envelope and saw a neatly folded paper inside. Removing the paper, he discovered that it was old, perhaps a piece of dated parchment paper. Very carefully, he unfolded it. Whatever was written on the parchment was done with a steady hand, but the words were gibberish as far as Werner was concerned. Staring at the meaningless words, he asked, "What is this?"

When Hans didn't reply, he turned around and saw that the old man was now slumped to the side, his eyes closed.

FROG Headquarters, The Hague

"Help yourself," Two offered, standing in the back of the conference room, plate and fork in hand, eating a heated slice of groninger koek—a popular Dutch rye gingerbread.

"I'm starving, thank you," Gretchen said, the wonderful aroma of the ginger, cinnamon, and nutmeg filling her nostrils. She chose a thick slice since she and Adam had abruptly left the pub without her taking one bite of food. "Where'd you get this?"

"Albert," Two mumbled, eating quickly. "He works in catering upstairs. They had all this food for an arbitration meeting between Malaysia and someone, I can't remember who. But I guess there's some bad blood, because they nearly came to blows before the whole thing even started, and everyone stormed out." She grinned. "Their loss, our win."

Gretchen laughed and took a bite. "Hmm."

"I know, right?" Two said, pleased.

Marsha, Hal, and Adam came into the conference room. Hal peered closely at the platter. "That gingerbread?"

Speaking with her mouth half-full, Gretchen said, "Delicious."

Marsha grinned at Two. "Your boyfriend get you this?"

"He's not my boyfriend," Two protested. She brought her empty plate to the table and took her seat, her laptop open and ready to go.

Hal helped himself to a slice and glanced at Adam. "Eat. Sugar helps the brain work you know."

Adam didn't say a word, but even he couldn't resist, grabbing a slice too.

"So much for the no-food rule," Marsha said sarcastically, taking a seat and opening her laptop. "Both Two and I have some things of interest. I'll go first." She worked her computer, and the image of an attractive middle-aged woman appeared on the large screen. "This is Victoria Tenney. We learned about her when Adam and Gretchen questioned Nancy Ellison. Listen to the audio from that evening… the first voice is Nancy Ellison. She is talking about how she met Bart Werner."

"He had a client that wanted him along. A widow of, I don't know, maybe fifty? Older. She liked to have him on her arm, if you get my meaning. It was a joke."

"Who was the woman?" they heard Gretchen ask.

"The man you'll hear is Garth Henderson, Nancy Ellison's manager," Marsha quickly explained.

"Victoria Tenney. Very wealthy and yes, she's an important sponsor."

The audio stopped and Adam said, "So she is important how?"

Marsha said, "You asked to see if Henderson made any calls once you kicked him out of the room. He called one person..."

"Her?" Gretchen asked with disbelief, looking at the screen.

Marsha said, "Yes, Victoria Tenney."

"Who is she?" Hal asked.

"The sister of Clyde Redfield," Marsha said, much to everyone's surprise. "And yes, it was family money that started Red Arrow Capital, so let's just say she is a multi-multi-millionaire in her own right."

"So she funds race cars and Nancy Ellison's manager calls her minutes after Adam and I show up," Gretchen said. "And the very next competition after that phone call, Nancy Ellison's car has issues and she dies. That's not a coincidence. No way."

Marsha went on. "And here's a tidbit—when her brother started the Sustainable Growth Syndicate, she was a spokesperson for them. That was some years ago, and she doesn't seem to be front and center with the syndicate right now, but it seems fair to say she believes in curbing world population."

"Great, another nutcase," Adam grumbled.

"Don't forget we have this." She worked the laptop. The screen now held a close-up of part of the Joker family tree. It showed the initials H.W., underlined twice in red, then the word Vic next to it, likewise underlined but with a question mark. "Red Arrow Capital deals in hedge funds. Maybe this is just a chart of the investors. And her name was abbreviated and with a question mark because she is a family member. Maybe she funds lots of things. Race cars, hedge funds, who knows."

"Start with the vicar," Hal advised. "I don't think it's going to be easy to talk to this Victoria Tenney character."

"I'll get over to him and try to get some answers," Adam said.

"Agreed," Hal said. "But Gretchen goes too." Anticipating push back, Hal looked directly at Adam. "Her touch with Nancy Ellison gave us lots of information. You can be a bull in a China shop, and he is a man of the cloth." He looked at Gretchen. "Be respectful."

Gretchen nodded.

"Two found something we also need to discuss," Marsha said.

Two worked her laptop, and the large screen showed a picture of Ethan Redfield on horseback, a black cowboy hat on his head. "As you know, this is Ethan Redfield, son of Clyde Redfield, founder of Red Arrow Capital. Now we can add nephew to Victoria Tenney. He's an executive vice president at the firm. I was able to find speeches he gave at various Red Arrow events, and I matched his voice to the voice of the man who came to Lars Vervloet's home saying he found the cat, Milo."

"Certainty?" Adam asked.

"Speaker Identification, meaning the two speakers are the same person, is eight-six percent."

Marsha jumped in. "Which is *very* high, considering one voice was taken from the audio of a doorbell several feet away. And his back was to the tiny microphone."

"So if Ethan Redfield was blackmailing Lars for the cowboy hat, I think it's safe to say he is our bomber," Gretchen said.

"No proof of him being the actual café bomber, but yeah, it's starting to look that way," Marsha agreed.

"I need that picture in print," Gretchen said. "I can take it to Lars and his mother. She should confirm that he was the one who took her to the luxury apartment, tied her up, and killed Milo. Lars might confirm Redfield is the guy who approached him in the office parking lot."

"No," Hal firmly argued. "Cancel that."

"What? Why?" Gretchen asked in surprise. "It might give us confirmation of where Ethan Redfield was at a given date and time."

"We do all that, then the janitor and his mother are going to want to know who he is, have we arrested him, all that," Hal explained. "We are muddying waters when we don't need to." He sighed. "Find the damn vicar and let's get some answers."

Chapter Eleven

Amsterdam, the Netherlands

Having entered the church from the street, they stood just inside the nave waiting for their eyes to adjust to the dim light. An older woman, probably hearing the heavy entrance door squeak open, shuffled out to meet them. She was a bit stooped over, reading glasses swaying from a chain around her neck.

Gretchen smiled warmly. "Good morning. We're looking for Vicar Werner."

The old woman immediately turned and looked toward the front of the church. As her eyes adjusted, Gretchen could see a solitary person sitting in the very first pew. The elderly woman turned back to them. "It's a difficult time. Perhaps I can help?"

With that, Gretchen pulled her AIVD ID. The woman put on her reading glasses and peered at the identification. She then took a step back, pulling her glasses down. "Is this to do with Claire's café?"

"We need to talk to him," Gretchen said softly.

The old woman again glanced toward the sanctuary. "He lost a dear friend today. If you could perhaps wait?"

Adam stepped forward. "We can't. Sorry." He swiftly headed down the nave's center aisle, and Gretchen could only give the old woman a perfunctory smile as she quickly followed. She caught up with Adam studying the vicar who had his elbows on his knees, his hands clasped together, and his head bowed. It was impossible to know if he was praying or contemplating a problem with his bowels. Gretchen thought that the vicar must have heard their footsteps, especially her low-heel boots clacking on the concrete floor, but he remained frozen. Adam turned to her, and she signaled for him to take the initiative. Bad cop to her good cop. Gretchen woke her cell phone and hit the recorder app.

"Sir?" Adam said quietly. Nothing. "Vicar? We need a word please." Still nothing. Adam looked quite annoyed and in a loud voice said, "Sir, we need to talk to you about the murders of your nephew Bart, your daughter Claire and your wife."

This worked. The man swiftly pivoted in his seat and looked up at them.

Gretchen stepped forward and flashed her ID. "We're with AIVD." She thought the man looked older than his pictures, and she wondered if the family deaths had taken their toll.

Adam, always impatient, sat next to the vicar and pulled a sheet of paper from his pocket. He carefully unfolded the chart and showed it to him. "Your nephew did this. We need your help filling in the blanks."

The vicar slowly took the chart.

Adam pointed to a section. "That's you, Herman Werner, right?"

The vicar looked closely where Adam pointed. "It's Hans."

"Hans?"

The vicar looked at Adam. "Hans Wolter. You know him?"

"No sir, I don't."

The vicar faced the sanctuary. "He died this morning." The vicar let his hands fall to his knees still holding the chart. "You can expect it. Like this morning, I was fully expecting it, and somehow, it is still a shock." He turned to Adam. "He had been ill for some time."

"I'm sorry," Adam said. He took the chart from the priest and pointed to the H.W. on the chart. "So that's Hans Wolker." The vicar nodded. Adam pointed to another entry. "See this? Vic?" he asked. "Could that be you? An abbreviation for you, the vicar?"

Herman Werner leaned over to see the writing. "Hans thought Victoria was involved. He was convinced."

"Victoria Tenney?" Adam asked. It was nice to have confirmation on what they had already deduced on their own.

The vicar nodded, seemingly lost in his own world.

"There are two red underlines with Hans and Victoria," Adam said. "What does that mean?"

The vicar took the chart again, peered at it briefly, and handed it back. "Original investors, perhaps. I don't know. Hans was, anyway. One of the first investors. Victoria Tenney has an open pocketbook and puts money wherever. But Hans said she was a part of this."

Adam waited. Nothing more was forthcoming so he asked, "Part of what, sir?"

The vicar shook his head. "I'm not sure. An investment group of some sort."

Adam pointed at the heading on the chart. "An investment called Trojan Steed?"

The vicar didn't respond. Suddenly he turned to Gretchen. "He said something this morning... That Bart was assassinated... "

When Adam didn't respond, Gretchen said, "Yes, sir, I'm afraid so."

The vicar stared at her. "Hans said his friend too. Bart's friend. A man named DeWine? Is that true?"

Gretchen glanced at Adam and answered the vicar. "Two men he worked with have died, yes. William DeWine and an American, Mac Senton."

"Senton? Mac Senton?" the vicar repeated, greatly alarmed.

"You know him?" Adam asked. Nothing. Adam went on. "Mac Senton. Tell us about him. You know him."

Still nothing. The vicar stared at his lap. Finally, Adam gently touched the vicar on the arm. "Sir? You know Mac Senton? He worked where Bart did."

The vicar turned his head in surprise. In a harsh tone he said, "They were more than co-workers. Mac Senton was Bart's half-brother." He shook his head and sighed. "I never even met him." Distraught, he looked to Gretchen. "He was killed you say? Why? I don't understand."

"Mac Senton was working on the inside, trying to help," Gretchen explained. "Just like William DeWine was helping, just like Bart was helping."

"They killed him?" the vicar asked, clearly distraught. "Like they killed Bart?"

"He took his own life," Gretchen said softly. "These people were going to hurt his child and he felt he had no choice."

The vicar shuddered and sat in silence for some time.

"Tell me about Hans Wolter," Adam finally asked. "What can you tell us?"

The vicar sat back against the pew. "Oh, where to start? A good, good man. He pulled me out of a cesspool, helped me find

God." A smile now, remembering. "Oh, he could cuss like a devil. Speak harshly. Never of others, but just his manner. You met him, he wouldn't strike you as a follower of Christ." A faint smile appeared. "Just today, he told me in no uncertain terms to stop..." His voice trailed off.

"Stop what?" Adam asked.

"Prayer for the sick." Another smile. "I used a sacramental oil. I think that is what bothered him. Said it was rubbish." He looked at Adam, suddenly concerned. "He believed. He was a righteous man, don't get me wrong."

"And he invested in this Trojan Steed fund?" Adam prompted gently.

"Hans said it was the devil's work. Whatever was going on, he wanted no part of it. He tried to get his money out, but they wouldn't let him. He said he'd take them to court... Clyde laughed at that and said it would cost him more in attorney fees than the investment. Promised Hans would get a good return, but Hans said it would be tainted money. The work of the devil..."

They waited for him to go on, but apparently, he was done.

"Sir?" Gretchen asked. "Why was this fund evil? I'm not following."

"He told Bart to look into it," the vicar replied. "Get the British government involved. Get someone involved. Stop it."

"Okay..." Gretchen replied. "But an investment in what exactly..? Stocks? Bonds? Property? Futures? What?"

"I don't know. Hans had known Clyde Redfield for some years. Made good money with him, and he didn't need to do it. Hans, I mean." Another smile, remembering. "He paid for our new roof ten years back." The vicar grew solemn, then said, "He was a good man. A kind man."

After some silence, Gretchen quietly asked, "Did you know that Bart and maybe Hans, they called Clyde Redfield The Joker in that chart?"

"Hans did that, yes. That was his word for the man." The vicar looked at her. "I've never seen those Batman movies. I don't believe they lift the soul. But Hans said Clyde was a criminal mastermind. A psychopath."

"So he called him The Joker."

The vicar looked up sharply at Gretchen. "Clyde Redfield advocated for population control. Our population is exploding and going to kill us all."

"Do you know specifically what he meant? How to control the world's population?"

The vicar gave a wave of his hand. "I only know he wants half the world wiped out. At least that's what Hans told me. That's why he called him The Joker."

Adam tried again, pointing to the chart. "No idea what these initials are? You gave us Victoria Tenney and your friend, Hans. Any others?"

The vicar peered at the chart again. "I don't know, but maybe they are the investors. The ones wanting less population."

Adam and Gretchen exchanged looks. This made sense.

"Hans say what the money was going to be used for?" Gretchen asked. "Or invested in? What specifically he was so worried about?"

The vicar shook his head. "He said he was sorry." He looked at Gretchen. "This morning. He said he was sorry for involving me. He reached out to me, asked that I get him a meeting with Bart. The two of them, they met quite a bit. All I know is Hans warned him to be careful of The Joker. He thought maybe Bart could learn things from the woman."

"Victoria Tenney?"

The vicar nodded. "I told Bart that God chooses us for different challenges, and if Hans is worried there was something amiss with this fund, or the group putting it together, whatever it was, then he had an obligation to do what he could." A tear suddenly rolled down the vicar's cheek. "I don't know how Bart was handling it, but for some reason, he brought in the man named DeWine, and Hans said they killed DeWine." He looked at Gretchen. "And you agree."

"Unfortunately, yes."

"Why the café? Why did this man, this DeWine man, go there?"

"We don't know for sure."

"Is Hans right? If DeWine hadn't been there, Claire and Arabella would still be alive?"

The Hague, Holland

It was very peaceful here. As it should be, Gretchen thought. Sitting in her parked car near the front entrance, she imagined the ancient brick house would have many stories to tell if it could talk. Certainly, the nearby chapel would have some words. She volunteered to be here since she knew the place—it was the funeral home that she had used when her mother had passed away. She still remembered the first question she was asked when she sat down with the funeral director. "Do you have funeral insurance?"

Funny, but only now did she notice the large swath of green grass to the west making the area very pleasing. A green spot in the middle of the city. She watched as a black hearse pulled around to the back.

The front door opened, and a tall woman with short blonde hair exited. Two had spun her wheels trying to track down the woman. Now she had landed in their laps. Gretchen got out of the car. It was time for some answers.

~ ~ ~

Exiting the mortuary and walking down the brick pathway toward the quiet street, Elizabeth Thomas suddenly stopped. There was nowhere to go, really. She had used her Uber app to summon a ride, so she had to stay put and wait for it, even though her instincts were to walk off all her swirling emotions. She stood on the path, tilted her head back, and closed her eyes. And willed herself not to cry.

She didn't know what she had been thinking. Other than being a selfish bitch, she very much wanted the death certificate in hand. The money would make a huge difference, and she felt that she had earned every penny. And yet now, she felt as if nothing mattered anymore.

It was his face, she realized. He looked... Well, alive. And handsome as ever. She could almost picture that crooked smile that had captured her heart so many years before. "I'm innocent," he had said with a twinkle in his eye. "And I'm an open book. Ask me anything."

At that time, Elizabeth was in her sixth year as a fraud investigator with Goldman Sachs. It was an internal arm of the company, conducting due diligence when their own employees might have stepped over the line. Often correcting something before the feds even knew about it. The case involved Mac Senton, along with two other employees, who were being scrutinized for possible insider trading. "Also, I'm available for dinner tonight. I can't pay the bill since that would look like bribery, so we'll have to go Dutch. Once you clear this up, I'll make up for it by taking you wherever you want."

She hadn't been impressed that day. He was arrogant. It took over a month to clear up the matter, and she discovered that, as he had claimed, he was innocent of any wrongdoing. And then, she surprised herself by telling him that she wanted to go to San Francisco for dinner—specifically, she wanted to eat at the luxurious penthouse restaurant atop the Mark Hopkins Hotel which featured extraordinary city views. Mac hadn't missed a beat. He had simply asked, "Saturday night?"

Where had they gone so wrong? Well, Mia of course. Not that Mia was wrong. She wasn't, naturally. But all that came from her birth. When Elizabeth learned that she was pregnant, she was thrilled. She knew that even if Mac freaked out about the pregnancy and didn't want to support her in any way, she wanted this child. It was past time. And when she sat down and told him the news, he was ecstatic. Like a little kid being told they were going to spend the weekend at Disneyland. Then she explained about the gene factor she carried. He assured her there was no cystic fibrosis anywhere in the family.

How long had she hated him? How could such love flip to such pure hatred? She had been convinced he had purposely lied. It didn't matter how many times he swore he had told her the truth. And yet, she never gave him the benefit of the doubt. Why was that?

Weeks ago, she received a FedEx letter at the office from a mailing center in Lisse, Holland. It contained a brand-new pink Lancôme lipstick. Tied to the lipstick was a tiny card that read, *"I will always love you and love what we had. Saw this today at a mall and couldn't resist purchasing it. Enjoy."* The purpose of the delivery was not the lipstick, however. It was a handwritten letter explaining everything that he had learned about his biological father—a man who had been temporarily relocated by his Dutch firm to set up a satellite office in Bridgewater, Connecticut, the town Mac had been born in. The man had stayed for more than six months and no doubt had had an affair with Mac's married mother. There was a black and white photo of the man, and Elizabeth could immediately see the family resemblance.

Mac explained that he had had no idea of his true lineage. He went on to say that he would always financially support Mia and should something happen to him, all of his assets would be going to Mia. If Mia were to pass away—she had already endured her share of close calls—he'd like that money to go to cystic fibrosis research. He also said that he had gotten caught up in a very big mess, and he was going to do what he could to make sure people weren't hurt. But should things go sideways, he carried her card in his wallet, naming her as his emergency contact.

Hence the call from the US Consulate General's office in The Hague, telling her that Mac Senton had died. It was not required that she show up in person, but she had wanted to. Much to her husband's consternation. Minutes ago, she learned that she would not be going home with the death certificate—it had been issued in Dutch. She would need an International Death Certificate in English. She paid the fee for the translation and knew it was marked "urgent," but in all likelihood, she would be returning home without it. Sort of ironic, really.

It was at that point that a very nice older gentleman wearing a dark suit and white gloves, introduced himself and told her that a viewing was available—if she so chose. She took him up on the offer and was now completely undone. To see Mac like that. Laid out on what looked like a bed with soft, silk sheets. She had made the mistake of touching his face. His flesh had been ice cold. Of course, it was cold. He was dead. Again, what had she been thinking?

She asked for a few minutes alone, and the older man departed with a slight, respectful bow, closing the door behind him. Looking at Mac, she told him she was sorry. Sorry for all the anger and the blame. Sorry that she had been so bitter for so long. And then she cried, uncontrollably and unashamed.

Feeling the warmth of the sun on her face, she let the tears fall once more.

"Excuse me, Mrs. Thomas?" a voice called out in English.

Elizabeth turned, quickly wiping away her tears.

A woman younger than herself flipped open some sort of ID. "Greta Drott, AIVD," the woman said. When Elizabeth showed no reaction, the woman quickly added in English, "Dutch General Intelligence and Security Service." She gave a reassuring smile. "I'd like to ask you some questions about Mac Senton."

For a flicker of an instant, Elizabeth wondered what the hell Mac had gotten himself into. Upon learning that he had died under mysterious circumstances, she had gone online looking for any clue about what had happened. She found numerous articles about a tall American wearing a New York Yankees hat who had kidnapped a Dutch teen. The video of the redheaded girl leaping from the back of a handicap van, her hands tied together. Mac quickly pegged as a pedophile. Mac poisoning himself rather than be taken into custody.

When her husband saw the same news articles, he completely lost it, saying that they must keep all this from Mia. Elizabeth pointed out that Mia was just seven years old, so she certainly wasn't surfing the internet, seeking information about her biological father—a man she barely knew. However, Elizabeth knew that someday, when she was older, Mia would ask about him. What happened between Mac and the kidnapped teen would be accessible. But for now, she was too young to know all this, which was a blessing.

Elizabeth glared at the policewoman. "He wasn't a pedophile."

"No, no he wasn't," the woman immediately agreed. "He got in with some very bad people, and they told him to kill her, kill the girl."

Elizabeth just stared, completely flabbergasted.

The Dutch woman went on. "He couldn't do it. He *wouldn't* do it. Mac saved her life, although the newspapers will never tell you that."

A four-door Volkswagen Polo pulled up. Dark blue, as the driver had specified, and with an Uber sign on the dashboard and an Uber sticker on the rear passenger window. The Dutch woman saw the car and said, "I can take you where you need to go. But we really need to talk."

Elizabeth remained frozen, unsure what to do. Then she remembered the last line of Mac's letter. *"No matter what, trust no one."* She quickly went to the waiting car.

"Mrs. Thomas, please!"

Elizabeth jumped in the back seat, slamming the door before the policewoman could stop her. "Go!" she implored the driver.

FROG Headquarters, The Hague

"What the hell?" Hal said, his anger boiling over. "Another damn piece to a jigsaw puzzle no one can solve." Hal and Adam were in Marsha's office.

The good news was that it had taken Marsha just minutes to decipher the language on the parchment paper—it was Middle Dutch, a hodgepodge of similar West Germanic dialects used in written and oral communications around 1200 A.D. Compared to today's Dutch, it looked like a vastly different language. Which explained why the pastor had been baffled by the paper and happily passed it along to them.

Marsha had scanned the document, then dumped it into a translator software. The bad news was that as Hal had correctly groused, the text left them completely baffled. The English translation was now staring at them from Marsha's left monitor in a large font.

> He favors an MLB squad and will assist
> For once funds are in hand and
> A place for gold that they refine
> So the end games begin, lives to be lost
> Save those who have a solution ready to sell
> For they will prosper in all the world
> ET call home, due diligence is key

"First, the second line about gold to refine, that's from the Bible," Marsha said. "It's from the book of Job and actually says, *"Surely there is a mine for silver, and a place for gold that they refine."*

"You know the Bible that well?" Adam queried.

"I ran it through a program that looks for any key terms that are published or known," she replied with a grin.

"Let's start from the top," Hal suggested with irritation. "Who is *he*? *He* favors… Who is he?"

"Has to be Mac Senton," Adam said.

Hal turned and snapped, "And he's going to assist how? He's dead and just gave us a few more names in the chart. Big wow."

Adam ignored him. "Mac Senton wore a Yankees baseball cap." He tapped Marsha on the shoulder. "What's the name of that league? The one for professional American baseball players?"

"You mean Major League Baseball?" Hal quickly asked.

"Very good," Adam replied, surprised.

"You seem to forget that I'm American." Hal looked back at the screen. "I should have seen that. MLB. And he probably favored the Yankees."

Marsha wrote on a pad. "Okay, 'he' is Mac Senton. He was assisting Bart Werner, and in turn, Hans Wolter."

Adam went on. "Funds are needed for whatever this op is, that much makes sense. Next line is the Biblical line about refining gold… End games we get. Gets back to what Matthew was contending, end of the world, lots of people die from a plague or whatever. We get that."

"Except for those who have a solution ready to sell," Hal mused, looking at the text.

"In other words, someone is going to profit," Marsha said.

"And now we go to ET call home crap. This is nuts," Hal grumbled.

"I agree," Marsha said. "Doesn't fit."

"Why talk in riddles?" Hal complained. "This is insane. The document was well hidden, physically hidden from prying eyes, in a language no one speaks, so what the hell? Spell it out for God's sake."

Adam tapped Marsha on the shoulder again. "Mac Senton's girlfriend, the one who had his kid? She's at Goldman Sachs, right?"

"Yes," Marsha replied. "Why? What are you thinking?"

"Due diligence is a term for investments, right? Do your homework?"

"An audit!" Marsha said. "She's an investigator at Goldman Sachs. She probably does due diligence, I'll bet you!"

"What's her name?" Adam asked.

Marsha typed on the computer. She turned to Adam. "Elizabeth Thomas."

"ET call home," Adam said.

"Gretchen's talking to her now," Hal said.

Schilderswijk District, The Hague

"This isn't right," Elizabeth anxiously told the driver. "We're off course. I'm staying at the Marriott. The Marriott Hotel?" She caught his dark eyes looking at her in the rearview mirror, but he didn't speak to her. "I'm sorry, I only speak English... Do you speak English?"

Still nothing. She knew something was wrong, very wrong, because it had taken her nineteen minutes to get from the Marriott to the mortuary. She knew it was exactly nineteen minutes because she had an appointment at the funeral home and the hotel concierge told her to allow thirty minutes. She had used Uber and gotten to the funeral home in exactly nineteen minutes. Even with some stop-and-go traffic.

Glancing at her watch, she saw that she had now been in the car for nearly forty minutes. Looking out the window, she realized they were now in a poor neighborhood, the buildings deteriorated, many spray-painted with graffiti. Those on the street were young men with dark skin. Standing around, idle.

"Please. We are off course," Elizabeth said. "I'm going to the Marriott."

The car slowed for a red light. Screw it, she thought. Get out and start over. They had just passed a small restaurant with a sign in Dutch and English that read, *Vietnamese Food—Excellent.* That would work for her. Get away from the nonspeaking driver. Get to a safe place with people around. She reached for the door latch, and suddenly all the doors instantly locked. Her heart beating wildly, she looked at the driver through the rearview mirror. "Please. Let me out, now," she said in a firm voice.

"No," the man growled. "We close to hotel now."

Bullshit, she thought. She didn't have any idea where she was, but this hellish place was far from the Marriott.

FROG Headquarters, The Hague

"Where are you?" Adam anxiously inquired, the land line in the office on speaker.

"In Schilderswijk," Gretchen replied, her voice a bit raspy coming through the car's Bluetooth system. "She's staying at the Marriott. We know that much. So she either has business in a sketchy part of town or she is being taken somewhere against her will. And don't ask me which it is because I don't know."

"That's not an area anyone goes to unless they live there," Hal said. "Lots of Muslims, mostly Moroccans and Turkish."

Marsha said, "Gretch, I'm tracking you now... I've got you east on Hoefkade Street..."

"Yep," she said.

"Hang tight," Hal said. "Adam and I are heading out. We think the American woman may be the key to whatever is going on."

Schilderswijk District, The Hague

Elizabeth stiffened as the car pulled up in front of a dark-green closed warehouse door. Again, she frantically tried to open the door, but to no avail. She slid across the back seat, trying the other door. She was locked in.

"Let me out, dammit! You can't do this!" she hollered.

The warehouse door slowly began to roll up, and the driver anxiously inched the vehicle forward. Once the door was raised just high enough, the driver stepped on the gas and the car darted inside, the roofline clearing the bottom of the door by mere inches. Maybe twenty feet inside, the driver stopped the car. She tried to look around, but it was too dark to see much of anything, the only light coming from the raised door behind them. There was a screeching noise, and she quickly turned to see a man rolling down the metal door.

An instant later, it was pitch black.

Chapter Twelve

Schilderswijk District, The Hague

Elizabeth Thomas's heart was hammering in her chest, her mind terrorized as she floundered underwater, desperately trying to get to the surface. She didn't want to die! She tried to kick her legs and move her arms but found she couldn't move. She started to panic, thinking she was going to drown.

"Ah, you are awake," a male voice said, his English heavily accented.

It slowly dawned on Elizabeth that she wasn't underwater. She wasn't drowning. She tried to see who was talking to her, but everything was black. She felt something brush across her face, and suddenly she was looking at a very bright light. She squeezed her eyes shut and turned her head away from the harsh glare.

"Sorry about the chloroform, but you were a bit of a handful."

Chloroform? What the hell? She slowly opened her eyes and looked around. Nearby, she saw a silhouette of a man holding a dark hood in his hand. The hood at least explained why she hadn't been able to see. She tried to move again and discovered that her arms and legs were tied to the chair she was sitting on.

Her first instinct was to demand accountability—who was this man and what did he want? But she knew from her years of interviewing employees under investigation that the hardest ones to break were those who gave her nothing. Just a simple yes or no, never anything more than that. Those who anxiously talked often ended up inadvertently divulging something she could use against them. She didn't want to give this man anything—she would make his job difficult and keep silent.

~ ~ ~

Gretchen saw the Range Rover pull up behind her, the headlights flashing once. She tapped the brakes twice. All clear. Both Hal and Adam got out the vehicle wearing black tactical gear

147

including black backpacks and multiple weapons. To the average person, they looked like members of Holland's Royal Netherlands Marechaussee, the country's elite police tactical unit. Which was the idea, of course. They were the good guys, not the bad guys, so no need to call the police, the police were already here. Hal opened the front passenger door and tossed her a Kevlar vest as he climbed in. Adam surveyed the quiet neighborhood before swiftly hopping into the back seat.

Hal opened a box and handed out their radio communication devices. She inserted her earpiece. Adam asked, "Green metal door to the left, correct?"

"That's it," Gretchen replied.

"How sure are we?"

"A hundred percent. I hung back when the Uber driver pulled onto the short driveway and waited. He drove inside and the door came down."

"Marsha pulled up a Google image," Hal said. "Looks like a big metal rectangle with the roll-up door at the street and one side door."

"That's why I parked here. There's been nothing. She's in there."

"Give me ten," Adam said and slipped out the car.

~ ~ ~

Adam darted around the south side of the building. He was thinking two things—be sure there is only the one side door and don't approach off the street, where a watchman would most likely be canvassing.

"Systems check," he whispered as he got to the end of the building. He was using a hands-free voice-activated microphone to communicate with Gretchen and Hal.

"Five-by-five," Gretchen said.

"Five-by-five," he responded. "No southside door, no back door. Heading to the north door."

Still at the back of the building, he nearly stepped on several cigarette butts and a crushed cigarette box. No doubt a spotter stood here from time to time. Looking around, he saw that there was a pathway past some other nearby warehouses. But it didn't look like anyone would be watching this place from any buildings nearby—they were all windowless, corrugated-metal warehouses.

Adam squatted down and looked at the cigarette box. It had the Cleopatra logo, the most popular cigarette brand in Egypt. So was the watcher Egyptian perhaps? Interesting.

He left the debris untouched and peered around the north corner. Just then, the door opened and Adam quickly pulled his head back. He could hear the door shut and carefully peeked around the edge of the building. A man was relieving himself on a small bush a few feet from the door. He wore black pants and a black hoodie. No sign of a gun, but Adam guessed he had one. Once the man zipped up, he removed a pack of cigarettes from his breast pocket.

~ ~ ~

A part of Elizabeth wanted to laugh. What the hell had she been thinking telling herself not to give the man an inch? Give curt yes or no answers if she answered at all? In just four minutes of questioning, she had been struck furiously three different times. Two violent punches against her left cheek, the second one so vicious she lost part of a back molar and fiercely bit her tongue, a steady stream of blood now flowing down her chin. The last blow was a vicious slap against the back of her head. Slowly regaining her senses after that blow, she saw the man held what looked like a small sack on a leather tassel. He tossed the sack in the air and caught it as if it was a baseball. She could hear something rattle each time he caught it.

As if reading her mind, he said, "Lead." He came close and she stiffened in fear. Through her blurred vision, she saw him open the pouch and spill a few lead balls into the palm of his hand.

Elizabeth estimated that they were about double the size of a child's marble. That's what he was hitting her with? God, it hurt. She just wanted it to end.

The man carefully put them back in the sack and sinched the top. "I can do this as long as you want. Understand?"

She looked up at him. "I honestly don't know what he was doing," her voice sounding as if she had a mouthful of cotton. "He didn't tell me, I swear. We hardly ever talked."

"See? Not so hard, eh?" The man's face suddenly changed. "What was in the FedEx package?"

"The FedEx—?" She started to say, surprised. But she had barely got the words out when the man swung the sack, this time hitting her on her left ankle. She screamed in agony and doubled over in pain.

The man grabbed a fistful of her hair and yanked her head back. He glared down at her, his face contorted in rage. "We know you got it. What did he send you?"

~ ~ ~

"What is the meaning of this?" Adam asked in Dutch.

The man whirled around, clearly astonished. To Adam's thinking, the man was so incredibly stupid, he hadn't a clue that he was already compromised, even though Adam was still a good twenty feet away. Startled, the man began to reach for a weapon at his waistband, but Adam just kept approaching, his hands cupped in front of him, as if holding a special offering. The non-threatening posture made the man in front of him hesitate.

"Look!" Adam said, offering up his two hands filled with cigarette butts and the crushed cigarette box. "I ask you, are these yours?"

Curious, the man leaned forward to look at Adam's hands. With that, Adam tossed the cigarette butts in the man's face, following up with a vicious punch in the throat, crushing the man's windpipe. The man dropped to the ground, making a horrendous wheezing sound as he clutched his throat, his eyes wide in panic. Adam rolled the man, removing his semiautomatic from his waistband and setting it aside. Next, he pulled the hoodie up and over the man's head, wrenching each hand away from the throat in order to completely free the garment.

Adam knew that, most likely, the man was going to die, but he wasn't one to take chances, so he took a pair of flexicuffs from his belt and bound the man's hands behind his back. Next, he inspected the gun, cleared the chamber, then pocketed it. He checked to make sure the man didn't have an extra gun at an ankle and found none. Not that the man could reach it, but he could have a friend arriving shortly.

He pulled the hoodie on, covering his police uniform, and quietly he said, "One tango down at north door. Repeat, single tango down, north door. Going in now."

"Copy," Gretchen said in his ear.

~ ~ ~

The man continued to stand over her. Her entire leg was on fire, throbbing with excruciating pain. Desperate to please her interrogator and end the abuse, Elizabeth said, "The letter talked about Mia... Our daughter." It felt like her injured tongue was twice its normal size, and she thought her speech sounded slurred. She prayed he could understand her. "She's sick..." The word came out sounding like "slick."

A creaking sound, and the man turned. She caught a glimpse of another light spreading across the warehouse floor. It was the Uber driver.

The man torturing her squinted, the bright light trained on her hampering his own view. "Get the cutters," he said. The door shut and the additional light was snuffed out.

Her heart thundered in her chest. Cutters? What the hell?

The man turned his attention back to her. "What did he tell you about the fund?"

Elizabeth shook her head. "What fund—?"

The man raised the sack over his head.

"No! Please!" Elizabeth cried out. "I don't know of any—"

Suddenly there was a single hissing CLAP sound and the man cried out, dropping the sack as fresh blood sprayed across her shirt. The man whirled around, cupping his shot hand and there was another CLAP. The man fell to the floor, hollering in pain.

CLAP... CLAP, CLAP, CLAP.

Elizabeth looked down at her tormentor, just a few feet away lying on his back, blood from both knees and both elbows, both hands. Suddenly the warehouse went dark. It took her some time to realize that the bright light was aimed at the floor, not her. The Uber driver slowly came forward, and she frantically pulled on her restraints, desperate to escape. He pulled down his hood, and with the ambient light from the spotlight, she slowly realized that he wasn't the driver.

The gravely wounded man on the ground tried to move, and the man with a gun stepped close. "Next one is in your head. I honestly don't care." The gunman turned back to her. In a quiet voice he asked, "Who else is in here, Elizabeth?"

Fearful, she shook her head. "I don't think anyone."

"Are you sure? Think. Who else is here?"

"The guy that handled the roll-up door," Gretchen said through his earpiece.

Adam said, "The guy that rolled down the door when you drove in..?"

"I don't know," she stammered, her words slurred.

The gunman patted down the injured man for weapons and found none. He then grabbed the wounded man by the collar of his shirt and dragged him off.

In the dark corner of the southeast end of the warehouse, Adam dropped the man on the floor. The man started to say something, so Adam kicked him in the head, and just like that, the man fell silent. As far as Adam could tell, the warehouse—one large rectangle—was completely empty aside from the car, Elizabeth Thomas sitting in a chair, and the light.

Adam squatted down, listening to the sounds of the building. He knew that while the suppressor on his Baretta had tamped down the sound of the gunfire, the metal walls of the warehouse conversely jacked up the sound. Add to that the man's screams, and anyone inside had heard plenty.

He had planned to do a quick recon of the building as soon as he entered, but he immediately realized that Elizabeth was in danger, so he had acted. Stupid, really, but it wasn't the first time he had acted solely on gut instinct.

With his eyes adjusting to the single source of light shining on the floor, he saw the four-door sedan more clearly. The Uber car. No one in the driver's seat, no one waiting. Adjacent to the roll-up door, he saw a glass-enclosed area. An office, perhaps? Then he saw it out of the corner of his eye—a shadow moving right to left, darting behind the car.

Adam instinctively moved several yards away from the man on the floor and dropped to the ground, his eyes focused under the car. He saw the feet slowly creeping forward. He took aim and fired two shots. CLAP, CLAP. The man went down with one long horrific scream. Unfortunately for Adam, the man's head was blocked by the car's front tire. Damn.

Moving silently, Adam circled around. The man was curled up in the fetal position, clutching his bullet-ridden feet. His Uzi was on the ground, just under the car. CLAP. A headshot.

Finally able to do a recon, Adam silently approached the small, glass-enclosed area. A makeshift office with a desk and chair. A file cabinet. No one here. He checked a small bathroom. Empty. It took him six minutes to clear the warehouse. After which he announced, "We're clear. Repeat, we're clear, over."

Gretchen was quick on the mark. "Roger, clear." He could hear relief in her voice, and it gave him comfort.

"Bring the tango to the north door inside here, and we'll need the fingerprint kit."

"Roger that," Hal said.

Adam approached Elizabeth, who was bleeding heavily from her mouth. Funny how he hadn't even noticed that before. "And the first-aid kit," he added.

Surrey, England ~ Three Days Later

Adam was once again doing a complete perimeter check. He didn't have to do it. He honestly didn't think they were in jeopardy. But he needed to do something, and staring at the four walls wasn't helping. Surveying the quiet countryside, he had to admit the four-bedroom country home was ideal for their needs.

First, it didn't have neighbors anywhere close by, which gave them complete privacy. Secondly, it sat on a bit of a rise off a private lane, which gave them a 360-degree view to see anyone approaching, either on foot or by car. Lastly, the old home was single story, so Elizabeth had easy access to the entire place on her crutches. Doctors had instructed her to keep the surgically repaired ankle elevated as much as possible, which she did only on a hit and miss basis. And that was usually when her ankle screamed in pain so much that she was forced to park herself on an overstuffed chair in the great room with her leg on a couple of pillows on top of the ottoman. Due to the temporary dental crown and the stitches in her tongue, she was living on yogurt, puddings, and smoothies.

The spacious floor plan combined the very large great room with a refurbished state-of-the-art kitchen. There was no dining room—that had been eliminated to enlarge the kitchen. Instead, a very long country table sat against the kitchen's far brick wall, featuring a long bench with back cushions against the wall and chairs opposite to easily seating twelve comfortably. In addition to the bedrooms, there was also a decent-sized office located off the laundry area and mud room, but Two announced that it was too dark and cramped and promptly set up her laptop on the far end of the long kitchen table, her back against the brick wall and the scanner/printer on the floor by her feet.

The decision to relocate to England had been three-fold. One, they wanted to be closer to the "epicenter" as Hal called it. More and more evidence was pointing to the Redfield family's involvement—this included Clyde, his son Ethan, the would-be American cowboy, and Clyde's sister, Victoria Tenney. Plus, it looked like whatever was going on was concentrated at the Red Arrow Capital's London firm, where "Matthew," aka William DeWine, Bart Werner, and Mac Senton had all been employed. Two, they had no idea why Elizabeth Thomas had been kidnapped and tortured for information she swore she didn't have, but they feared that if she returned to her life in New York she could be kidnapped again. And since her family and office knew she was in Holland, it would be best to place her somewhere else. Three, if the bad guys' evil plot involved the Trojan Steed fund, they wanted the ability to pick Elizabeth's brain about that since she investigated hedge-fund trickery for a living.

Fortunately, Elizabeth had immediately agreed to help. However, she had the dilemma of what to tell her husband. Marsha had come up with a plausible excuse—her company, Goldman Sachs, wanted her to quietly investigate an ex-employee, now living in Germany. So quiet, that her secretary wouldn't even know about it. This gave her cover with her husband, and should he inadvertently reveal to others that she was in Germany, that wouldn't even be close to the truth, helping to keep her true location under wraps. She also kept him in the dark about her injuries, knowing that if he knew the truth—which had been explained to the Dutch doctors as being the result of a car accident—he would immediately drop everything to tend to her. Which ironically, was the last thing she wanted as well. With him in the dark, the FROG gold standard of deception was upheld— you can't disclose what you don't know.

Meanwhile, Marsha had worked from the vicar's hypothesis that the chart's partial names and initials referenced investors in the Steed fund. It was a slow process, but she had matched more than 80 percent of the incomplete names or initials to individuals who openly advocated for stringent population-control measures. Some were well-known wealthy industrialists, some were celebrities, and a few were leadership members at the United Nations. However, knowing the names of most of those invested in the fund didn't get them any closer to understanding the diabolical plan.

Making his way through the knee-high grass in his newly acquired Wellington boots, Adam thought back on how things had unfolded in the warehouse just days before. The man he had disabled outside the north door had been brought inside, quite dead. Adam hadn't been surprised, nor did he much care. Before leaving, he had simply cut off the flexicuffs and pocketed them. No need for the police to see that the man had been restrained. An autopsy would reveal cause of death and that would leave them with enough to puzzle about. Hal had quickly processed the fingerprints of both deceased men, using a portable reader, but had come up empty.

When Hal moved on to the last man, surprisingly still alive, he'd taken one look at all the bullet wounds and asked Adam sarcastically, "Any joint you missed?"

"A few."

The wounded man had glared at them, but with both knees, elbows, and hands shot, he was powerless to fight them off. Hal cleaned the blood off the man's fingertips with a wet wipe and scanned his prints. He'd instantly hit pay dirt, reading from the scanner, "Goran Petrovic."

"Interesting," Adam had said. The good news was that, since Interpol had the assassin's prints on file, there was no doubt the man would spend the rest of his days in prison.

"Need some assistance," Gretchen had interrupted.

When Adam and Hal had turned their attention to Gretchen, she'd already slipped an air splint on Elizabeth's lower leg, the flexible plastic boot providing uniform pressure to the injury. There was nothing to be done about her mouth wound except to let her bite on absorbent gauze pads.

Hal looked at Adam. "We'll take her, you do what you need to. Just make it quick."

Gretchen had given Adam her car keys so she and Hal could use the more spacious Range Rover to transport Elizabeth to the hospital.

Stepping over a fallen tree limb, Adam wondered if he was growing soft—too soft to continue in this line of work as he recalled looking down at the assassin after administering some morphine to ease the man's pain. "We know you took out Bart Werner," he'd said.

When Petrovic shook his head, Adam added. "Facial recognition. You looked up from the wheelchair when that woman fell in front of you."

Petrovic's face had changed in an instant. He knew Adam was telling the truth, not hunting around for information.

Adam went on. "You didn't need to kill Bart Werner. He didn't know shit, it turns out."

Petrovic just stared at him.

"I've used the hook blade many times myself," Adam told him. "I just don't understand—why not wait? I mean, it was a risk. In the airport, all those people. Too many witnesses."

Petrovic looked smug. "They don't know what they don't know."

"I knew."

Petrovic smirked. "But you chose to try to save him."

"Yes," Adam said.

"If you really have used the hook blade, you would have known it was too late," Petrovic said with a superior tone.

"I had to try."

Petrovic smiled. "You are stupid then."

"No, just optimistic that you didn't quite penetrate far enough. He had the jacket on."

"I don't miss. Ever."

"Neither do I," Adam told him. "Who is paying you?"

Petrovic shook his head. "It doesn't work that way."

Adam knew this, of course. A top assassin took a job without any knowledge of who actually hired him. Funds were wired, instructions given, but no other information was exchanged. Adam had then taken another tack. "Nancy Ellison just loved to race cars."

Petrovic's eyes widened with surprise.

"How did you do that one?" Nothing from the assassin. "Impressive, at any rate. Sabotaging a race car like that."

Finally, Petrovic smiled just a bit. "Grease."

Adam had frowned. "Grease?"

"Grease the pig... Find a weak link. Pay him well to get access to the car."

Adam had then gestured to the empty chair. "Elizabeth Thomas is like Bart Werner. Doesn't know anything."

Petrovic simply stared, all smugness gone. "Finish the job."

"What was that about a fund?" Adam asked.

"From one killer to another, finish it."

Adam thought it over. "Tell me about the fund."

"Be honorable," he hissed, obviously still in some pain.

"Tell me about the fund and I will."

"Your word? I tell you, you finish this."

"You have my word," Adam had promised.

At that point, Petrovic had acquiesced, admitting that he had no details about whatever the fund was per se; he was simply to question her about who she may have talked to about it. Once she told him all she knew, he was to kill her, of course.

Adam had asked a few more questions, but it seemed likely that Petrovic was telling the truth. So he started to leave.

"Hey! Finish the job!" Petrovic had frantically called after him.

Adam slowly walked away.

"I told you the truth!" Petrovic yelled, his breathing labored. "Do it! Finish me!"

Adam kept walking.

"Bastard! You gave your word!"

"I lied," Adam had calmly told him and exited using the north door. Only once in Gretchen's car and miles away from the warehouse had he called Marsha and told her to call the police about shots fired at the warehouse.

Returning to the house, Adam found Elizabeth sitting in a chair with its back to the kitchen table. Gretchen was hovering over her, using her cell phone flashlight to look inside Elizabeth's wide-open mouth. Two was at the opposite end of the table focusing on her laptop. Adam stopped dead in his tracks. "What's going on?"

Gretchen straightened up. "Going to remove the two stitches."

Elizabeth looked at him. "I can't stand it anymore."

At the hospital, emergency-room doctors had discovered tooth fragments in her deeply sliced tongue. The wound had been cleaned out, requiring two stitches in order to ensure proper healing. The stitches were due to be removed in a few more days, but Adam knew that mouth injuries could be the most annoying. However, he didn't think they should tend to it themselves. "Walk-in urgent centers come to mind."

"Thank you!" Two agreed.

Gretchen gave him a nasty look. "Someone told me we're supposed to be keeping a low profile."

"I have scissors and tweezers in my bag," Elizabeth said. Using her crutches she left the room before Gretchen could change her mind.

Adam turned to Two. "Got her pinned down?"

"All I can go by is social media, but I'd say the chances are good she's at her country estate." Before he could ask, she added, "The one out here. Twenty minutes door-to-door."

Gretchen frowned. "So, what? We go ring her bell and say what exactly? Hello, Mrs. Tenney. Did you arrange to kill a Formula race-car driver? And the Steed fund, what exactly is that for?"

"She's having a fundraiser there in a couple of days," Two said studying her computer.

"Really?" Adam asked.

"Black tie," Two added.

Elizabeth returned with a large black tote bag over her shoulder. Propping her crutches against the table, she pulled out another chair and sat down, digging through the bag. She started placing items on the kitchen table. Wallet. Sunglasses. Makeup bag. Reading glasses. She kept digging through the contents until, in sheer frustration, she just tipped the bag on end and emptied everything on the table. A lipstick rolled toward Two. Rummaging around the items, Elizabeth picked out a small plastic case. "Here!" she triumphantly announced. "Traveling sewing kit. Includes tweezers and small scissors. We should be good to go."

"Lancôme," Two said, picking up the lipstick. "Nice."

Elizabeth rolled her eyes. "From Mac. Used to be my favorite color and brand. Key words, used to be."

Adam looked at her. "When? When did he give you this?"

"It's meaningless."

"When?" Adam growled.

"It was in the FedEx package he sent."

Elizabeth saw his reaction and immediately said, "I'm not stupid! I checked. It's what it is—lipstick. That's all."

Two removed the cap and twisted the base. A bright red shade of lipstick appeared.

"See?" Elizabeth argued.

Two pulled the waxy lipstick off and kept twisting the lipstick base until a USB drive slowly appeared.

"Oh my God," Elizabeth quietly uttered.

Chapter Thirteen

FROG Headquarters, The Hague

"Great call, Marsha. Great, great call," Hal marveled.

Marsha appreciated his words, but she was just relieved that her gut instincts had been proven right. The day before, after Two had discovered that the lipstick Mac had sent Elizabeth contained a hidden flash drive, everyone had presumed it would yield a great secret message. Yet the drive only contained photographs of Mac, Elizabeth, and Mia. A huge disappointment, to say the least.

For Marsha, the entire FedEx letter never made sense. Mac could have called or emailed Elizabeth to explain what he had learned about his biological father and the cystic-fibrosis link. To her way of thinking, the real reason to send the FedEx package was to send her the flash drive. And the real reason to disguise it as her favorite lipstick was to keep the contents secret should the FedEx package fall into the wrong hands. Moreover, the fact that the assassin knew about the FedEx shipment and had tortured Elizabeth about it, told her the flash drive held something more than family photos.

But it wasn't until she suddenly woke up at four the next morning that she had the answer—Mac had hidden a text message in one or more of the photos. This wasn't the first time that she had woken up with the answer to an ongoing problem. Anxious to get to the office to find out, she had inadvertently awakened Nathan by showering so early. Like many times before, her husband had taken it in stride, going to the kitchen and preparing her a cheese, ham, and thinly sliced pickle sandwich, which he handed to her as she hurried out the door.

At the office, she didn't even take the time to brew herself a cup of coffee. Instead, she once again opened the digital file, but this time, she used an extraction program that allowed her to control the shadows and highlights of an image while also altering the hues and saturation. The first four photos yielded nothing. She started to think she had been wrong. But the fifth photo revealed hidden text:

Sorry, but I'm passing the baton to you. I know the danger this places you in, but there is much at stake...

It took some time, but in each of the following images she found more text. She dumped each text into Notepad, and when placed in chronological order, the message was clear as day. And at the same time, as opaque as mud.

"Please tell me there is more," Hal said, studying the text message which was now fully displayed on her left monitor.

"Afraid not. I need some coffee," she announced, scooting her chair back. "And some food. You set us up to discuss all this, right?"

Hal stuck his head outside her office door and glanced at the far wall where analog clocks displayed the current time in various countries. England was one hour behind Holland. "You've got six minutes."

Surrey, England

Over the last hour, Two had worn herself out lugging heavy catering equipment from the three vans out back to the estate's vast kitchen and the various staging rooms. So far, she had hauled in four heavy coffee urns, ten cases of wine, plastic crates filled with wine and cocktail glasses, various chafing dishes filled with prepared exotic entrees, insulated food-delivery bags with cold dishes, and now, she was carrying a huge cast-iron pot filled with mulligatawny soup. Normally, the heavier items, such as the cast-iron pot, would be transported on a wheeled cart. However, the estate manager had insisted they park all the vans in back where the ground was deeply rutted, leaving them no option but to walk everything in by hand.

A good forty yards on the other side of their vans was a huge barn where some horses watched their activity from inside their stalls. Horses nearby meant that they not only had to avoid twisting an ankle by stepping in a rut, but they also had to avoid any horse droppings. No one wanted to be responsible for carting horse dung into the manor.

As Two now entered the huge kitchen, Malcolm, the head chef, saw her struggling with the load and quickly took it off her hands. She would have liked to have said thank you, but she was too winded to utter the words. Instead, with her hands on her knees, she tried to catch her breath. She felt like she had just completed a marathon.

When she finally managed to stand upright, pushing her glasses back up her nose, Malcolm caught her eye. "Glad you could help us out today." He motioned to a red insulated bag in the corner. "Help yourself. That one is for us." She didn't move simply because she wasn't sure she could make it across the room. Unbeknownst to him, this was the first time in her young life that she had done any sort of manual labor. The most she had ever done was carry a new server from one room to another inside FROG Headquarters.

Thin by nature, she always presumed she was fit. However, she now knew she had zero strength. She promised herself that she would join a gym as soon as they returned to The Hague. Her stamina was frightfully awful. The chef smiled. "Worst is over. I promise. Take a break. Please."

Two went over to the red cooler bag. She unzipped it and chose a pink lemonade. Popping the lid, she promptly guzzled half in one long gulp.

"Better?" Malcolm asked with a grin.

She let out an embarrassing loud burp, quickly covering her mouth with her hand, her face turning beat red.

"You just belch?" Adam said in her ear, startling her so much that she physically jumped and nearly spilled the remainder of her lemonade.

Malcolm noticed and frowned. "You okay?"

"Yeah, yeah," Two said. She held up the drink. "Thanks."

"We're two people down, so I should be thanking you."

"We practiced me jumping in with remarks," Adam reminded her. "Get used to it."

"Right."

The chef actually grinned. "Glad you agree."

"Sorry, I just…"

"You're a tad nervous. No worries. You're fine. Finish your drink, get something to eat, and then you can unpack the appetizer plates. We'll dish up in the butler's pantry."

~ ~ ~

Gretchen poked Adam in the ribs. Hard. "Stop torturing her!"
"Hey," Adam complained, rubbing his side.
"Stop it. I mean it."
Adam grimaced. "We have one chance. One. And Two is it."
Elizabeth laughed. "One and Two. Very good."
Both Gretchen and Adam gave her an exasperated look, and she quickly turned her attention back to the screen where they could see everything Two was seeing through a tiny camera attached to the frame of her glasses. The glasses were a prop. Two normally didn't wear glasses of any kind. For audio communication, she wore a small earpiece, which allowed both parties to hear each other. They saw that she was currently grabbing a banana from the red cooler bag.

The fact that FROG had an operative working undercover at Victoria Tenney's estate had come about because they had no other option. It was that simple. While Marsha had uncovered Mac's messages hidden in the digital photographs, it left them with more questions than answers. Marsha had forwarded the full message to Two, who cast it to the TV at their safe house in anticipation of a conference call to discuss their next move. The message had read:

Sorry, but I'm passing the baton to you. I know the danger this places you in, but there is much at stake...
A new hedge fund called Trojan Steed by Red Arrow is new twist on the old idea...
Wealthy people make money by hatching a plot that they already have a solution for, ready to sell.
Think of the USA canceling pipeline so oil now goes via rail. Who owns the railroad?
Warren Buffet.
Will send more info as I get it. Working with two others on this.
We do know in a very short time it will cause massive deaths, worldwide.
You know how to peel the onion of a hedge fund.

Top known players are Clyde Redfield, son Ethan Redfield, and Victoria Tenney.
Remember, no matter what, trust no one.
More to follow.

Hal had initiated the call at the appointed time, and for the last half hour or so, they'd been trying to decipher the meaning in the message. Gretchen said, "It talks about a solution ready to sell. For a problem that maybe they purposely create—that's very similar to the parchment-paper message written in Middle Dutch."

"Yeah, we caught that too," Hal said. "And as we all noticed, Trojan Steed is probably a trojan horse. But what that means exactly, who knows?"

Elizabeth agreed. "I imagine to outsiders, it will look like a miscellaneous collection of companies, properties, whatever. It will look harmless, but there will be a purpose for each acquisition, even cash on hand. Once they've got all the pieces in place, all bets are off. Something will happen, and those assets in the hedge fund will come to life."

There was some silence as everyone continued to re-read Mac's hidden message. Finally, Adam looked at Elizabeth. "When did you get the FedEx package? The lipstick?"

Elizabeth was clearly unnerved and said, "I don't know. A long time ago, I guess."

"A week? A month? A year? What?"

Flustered, she said, "A month, maybe."

"Nothing after that?"

She shook her head. "I know I should have talked to him. About him finding out about his biological father. But..." She seemed to fight back tears. "I think I was still hanging on to my anger... You have a sick child, you want to blame someone. I blamed him."

Adam didn't care about her emotions. He motioned to the screen. "He says more to follow, but you got nothing more?"

She shook her head and wiped away a tear.

"You sure?" he challenged.

"He called and called. I ignored him. I just couldn't... I couldn't talk to him."

"Nothing by snail mail, FedEx?"

"No."

Gretchen spoke up. "Which is why he turned to Nancy Ellison to pass on the information."

Adam nodded thoughtfully. "He says 'working with others.' Present tense. That matches that this was sent a month ago, when Bart Warner and DeWine were still alive and well."

After some more discussion, they found themselves stalled on their next move. Marsha admitted that her attempts to piggyback onto the computers of Clyde Redfield, his son Ethan, and Victoria Tenney via numerous phishing emails had failed. Either the three family members were very computer savvy and knew better than to open an unrequested link, even when it was disguised as coming from their personal cell-phone carrier or Red Arrow Capital, or they all had top-of-the-line firewalls on their devices. Marsha was convinced it was the latter.

That's when Two reminded them that, according to her social media posts, Victoria Tenney was having some sort of gala fundraiser at her manor in two days' time, which was conveniently close to their safe house. Two eagerly suggested that this was the perfect opportunity to get inside the manor, get ahold of her laptop, and insert malware that would allow them to access all her files, emails, and web searches in real time.

This set off much speculation about how they might do that. Two did some digging on the catering company Victoria Tenney mentioned and a plan came together: get hired by the catering company, and they could waltz right in. Two and Marsha got bios on the catering staff and found two young women who worked for the company and shared a flat. They became the target, with the idea that if they were two workers down, the company might be forced to hire an outsider. More digging found the young women had Uber Eats accounts, which were used a lot. That very night, Adam accepted their food from the Uber Eats driver right at their front door. A quick tampering of the food, and the women would have no choice but to stick very close to a toilet for a few days.

At first, the plan had been for Gretchen to play the role of a caterer and infiltrate Victoria Tenney's office. However, days before, Gretchen had developed a seasonal allergy that had her constantly sneezing and blowing her nose. There was simply no way a catering firm would hire her in that condition. Next up to do the task was Adam, but there was a huge problem—the catering company was owned by Malcolm Finch, the head chef, and he only hired women. Preferably young women.

It had been Elizabeth who suggested that Two do the job. Of course, Elizabeth had no idea that Two had never been trained for field work—she was a computer analyst, plain and simple. Not a field operative.

However, there really was no other alternative. Which was why the day after Malcolm Finch learned that two of his employees were out with food poisoning, Two had conveniently shown up at his office, a stellar résumé in hand, and was promptly hired. Adam and Gretchen had prepared her as best they could on such short notice. They repeatedly told her they were fifteen minutes away by car and they would be seeing and hearing everything she did and could talk her through any rough spots.

Inside the zippered pocket of her cargo pants, she had two items: a tiny listening device that they hoped she could place in Victoria Tenney's office and a thumb drive that she would use to load malware onto Tenney's laptop, which would allow them access to the entire device. Providing that she could get away from her catering duties long enough to find the office, do the deed, and not be discovered. The only thing in their favor was that Marsha had found a remodeling permit from several years back that included a layout of much of the 11,000 square-foot manor, which Two had committed to memory.

~ ~ ~

Two was not in a good mood. Not because she had been on her feet for hours carrying trays of food and drink as she made her way through the expansive ballroom filled with haughty guests. Not because some of the guests acted like she was a waitress, telling her what appetizer they would like. The most offensive was a woman of about forty, wearing tons of jewelry, a sheer top that left little to the imagination concerning her bustline, and sheer bell-bottom pants with such a wide flair at the ankles that Two was amazed she didn't trip over her own long pants. She kept telling Two to find some "better vegan foods."

No, the reason she was in a sour mood was because the flash drive was in her shoe. Her right shoe, to be exact. She couldn't feel the tiny listening device that was in her left shoe. The plan had been that the devices would remain in her cargo-pants pocket until they were put into use. Now she couldn't help but worry that both would be damaged by the time she needed them.

The reason the devices were now in her shoes was that just before guests were due to arrive, Malcolm had told her to get changed. She gave him a puzzled look. She had taken the job with the understanding that she could wear what she wanted, the only caveat being that she had to wear solid-black comfortable shoes. Trainers were fine, provided they had no colors or logos. A white Nike slash was not permissible. Gretchen had gone shopping and found a pair of black trainers.

Seeing her confusion, another girl took Two to the vans where all the servers—there were nine of them—were choosing clothes in their size from a generous selection of freshly dry-cleaned garments still in their plastic bags. It turned out all the slacks were the same—tight-fitting, black stretch pants. The tops were starched white button-down blouses with black piping on the collar and cuffs.

She nearly panicked when she realized she was going to have to take off her cargo pants and leave the electronic devices behind. Fortunately, Gretchen walked her through the situation, asking if the black pants had pockets. No. She then said to put the devices in the arch of her shoe. Two didn't like the idea—you didn't put important electronic devices in your shoe. But she had no choice. She had done as Gretchen had suggested, putting one in each shoe, and then went back to the large kitchen where she was given a white apron with the company logo over the left breast which she dutifully put on.

Two found herself alone as she now entered the ample banquet room just off the ballroom which they were using as a serving room. No doubt, more food was about to come from the kitchen, and other servers would join her waiting to pick up more trays of appetizers or wine, champagne, and mimosas. She quickly whispered, "Marsha, you on?"

It seemed to take forever, but it was really only about six seconds before Marsha was in her ear. "I'm here."

"What the hell?" Two hissed. "Tell me I'm not damaging everything."

A brief hesitation. "They still in your arch?"

"Yeah, they're in my arch. I mean I can't feel the bug, it's small. But I can feel the thumb drive. I'm walking, you know. You can see me walking, right?" She looked over a shoulder. The coast was still clear. "I'm probably breaking it!"

"Trust me, both can handle a nuclear bomb," Marsha assured her. "You're fine. If one moves to the ball of your foot, take a break and complain about your bunions. Then re-arrange things."

"I don't have bunions," Two refuted in disgust.

"You do now," Adam said. "Use any excuse you need."

"Oh," Two said with comprehension. She saw a server coming from the kitchen. "Right. Out."

FROG Headquarters, The Hague

"A nuclear bomb?" Hal asked.

"She's worried, but trust me, the flash drive is inside a hard plastic case. They're made to withstand stuff. It's fine," Marsha told him. "Water is the biggest worry and she knows that as well as anyone—she's not going to place her feet in a bucket of water."

"There is foot perspiration though."

She gave him a startled look. She hadn't thought of that.

Hal quickly realized his error and said, "But so what if the plastic has some sweat on it, right?"

She nodded, though she wasn't quite sure. "Right." She turned her attention back to the architectural plans for the manor.

Marsha and Hal were in the conference room, the large screen in front of them displaying in real time what Two was looking at. She was in the kitchen looking at Malcolm. Two other chefs were scurrying around, but she seemed to have his attention.

Marsha quickly hit the button to unmute the TV, and they heard Malcolm say, "Sure, take five."

"I passed on my other breaks. I'm due fifteen."

He gave her a surprised look.

"And I'm taking the fifteen owed. You said earlier that would be fine."

He hesitated and then said, "Fifteen. No more. Supper is in thirty-five minutes."

With that, Two turned on her heel and left.

Marsha looked at Hal who smiled. "She's tough."

"She knows she needs at least fifteen minutes."

"Hell, given the size of the manor, it may take fifteen minutes to find the woman's damn office."

Marsha's cell phone rang, and she could see it was Gretchen. She answered, putting it on speaker. "Set your timer. She's got her fifteen."

It was Adam who said, "Already done… Hey, good call telling Two it could withstand a nuke. I think you calmed her a lot."

"And good call about the bunions," Gretchen said.

Marsha kept her focus on what Two was seeing in real time and the house plans. She said, "Okay, we're going live in a few seconds. I have the lead. Everyone else has to remain quiet unless it is vital…"

"Yep," Adam said. "You got the lead."

Hal had berated Adam when he had chirped in when Two had been drinking the lemonade. Hal had put the rules in place. Marsha had the lead for two reasons—she was closest to Two, so it should be her voice guiding her number two, and secondly, if there was a problem downloading the malware, Marsha was the only practical person to help out.

Marsha went on. "In three, two, and… Hey, Two. Good job getting the full fifteen. You okay?"

"Dandy." Two sounded out of breath.

Two turned and started walking down a long corridor, about six feet in width. Alcoves left and right held various kinds of artwork, including paintings, small statues, and colorful vases, a spotlight in each alcove highlighting the pieces.

"You see this stuff?" Two asked quietly. "Amazing."

"You're way out of bounds," Marsha said. "No speaking."

A firm reminder that Two was now a long way from the party, and if she was spotted, she would have a lot of explaining to do. The party was essentially contained in the north wing of the manor. According to the house plans, the office was in the southeast wing and had large windows that overlooked an expansive grass area, sometimes filled with horses.

Two glanced behind her, but the corridor was empty. Facing forward again, the hallway widened by a good ten feet. Marsha glanced at the plans. "Door is about five feet away. Right side."

Marsha felt her heart beating rapidly. She could only imagine how fast Two's heart was beating.

Marsha's phone chirped. A text. *She seem okay to you?* Marsha knew this was Adam, not Gretchen. Hal picked up her phone and replied, *She's tight, just like you get when it's crunch time. Chill.*

Surrey, England

Two stopped in front of the closed door and looked back down the corridor in the direction she had come. Empty. She looked the other direction, where a large archway drew the eye to what she knew was the library beyond. The door appeared to be a heavy mahogany. She put her hand on the bronze door lever and very slowly pushed it down. The door was unlocked. This in itself was huge. She slowly pushed it open, only to hear its hinges let out a loud, groaning creak. She froze. It was quiet. Praying no one would hear, she opened it just enough to squeeze through. The door creaked again, but not quite as loudly. With her heart hammering in her chest, she peeked inside. A very large room with huge windows giving ample light. Just as the drawings had indicated. She stepped inside and quickly closed the door behind her, which yielded another irritating squeak.

To her left, against a wall, was a massive fireplace and several plush, comfortable-looking chairs. Nearby was a mahogany hutch used as an office bar with quite a selection of bottles. All very nice, but Two's main focus was straight ahead—a very large desk and a massive leather chair. All she could see on the desk was a stack of papers on the far-right side and an antique-looking small desk lamp on the opposite corner. No desktop computer and definitely no laptop. Damn.

She looked left toward the seating area around the fireplace. Clearly no computer there. When Two turned back toward the desk, she saw sudden movement to her right and jumped a mile. It took her a beat to realize it was her own reflection—in a large mirror. There was something beyond her reflection, something moving, and she whirled around. Another room off the office with a window. A large leafy green tree was very close to the window and the smaller branches were blowing in the wind. She turned back to the mirror and saw it—the swaying tree branches was the movement she'd seen.

Two quietly stepped into the other room. A sectional sofa with a coffee table took up most of the space, the sofa facing a large-screen TV mounted on the wall. An intimate, small room. No desk here. No sign of the laptop.

She went back into the large office and simply stood there, a feeling of defeat washing over her. All this work, and the laptop could be anywhere. In a million other rooms. Thinking it would be sitting in the office had been a stupid assumption.

"Could be in a desk drawer. Start looking," Marsha instructed her.

Two quickly went around to the front of the desk, and Adam suddenly chimed in, reprimanding her, "Stay low, below the windows! We have no idea who might be outside and can see you!"

Fearful, Two immediately squatted down below the windows. There were three drawers on the left side. She opened the top drawer, just four inches in height. It contained some loose papers, a thick Post-it pad, a wallet-size checkbook, and an old-style flip cell phone. The next drawer was deeper and held a neat stack of manila folders. Each filled with papers, but she didn't bother to snoop. She needed a computer, not papers. The last drawer was locked. She pivoted around and saw it. An attaché computer case resting against the inside of the desk's interior knee space. She quickly unzipped it. An Apple laptop.

"Great," Marsha said. "First, let's put the bug under the desk. The desk chair on wheels?" Afraid to open her mouth, Two looked directly at the chair's casters. Marsha said, "Okay, put the bug in far enough back that she won't feel it if she sits down and grabs the desk to pull herself forward."

Two sat down and quickly unlaced her left shoe. She had a flash of panic when she didn't see the tiny bug. But she felt around the insole and found it. Her hands were shaking nervously as she peeled off the blue backing. Then she pushed the wheeled chair out of the way and crawled under the desk and secured it to the underside of the desk.

"Excellent," Marsha told her.

Just then she heard a noise and froze.

"Eight minutes gone, you're on schedule," Marsha announced. "You got this."

"Stay on the floor," Adam chimed in.

Another sound. Somewhere close. Two held her breath.

Adam was lecturing. "Do the computer work from the floor. We can't risk someone seeing you—"

"Shh!!" she hissed.

A creaking sound. It was the door! She scooted under the desk, pulling the chair in behind her. Then she saw her left shoe.

Sitting there, in plain sight.

Chapter Fourteen

Surrey, England

Two lunged forward and grabbed her shoe as she heard a man say, "You should grease the hinges." British accent.

Then a woman's voice, "I'll get right on it." She had an attitude, whoever she was. Tenney?

"Don't be cheeky." A scolding tone. Her father?

Two's heart pounded in her chest as she silently scooted all the way to the back of the desk's knee well, hugging her knees tight against her chest, the shoe still in one hand. She was grateful that the large desk afforded spacious legroom and most importantly, that the front panel went all the way to the floor. She was confident she was well hidden.

"C'mere," the woman said.

"No, look—" the man said, his tone serious.

"You smell so good…"

"I want—"

"It may have been some time now, but I know what you *want*. Believe me, I know." She laughed.

There were murmurs from both that could easily be heard, and it didn't take much imagination to visualize that something sexual was going on.

"Oh dear God," Adam muttered with annoyance.

A part of Two wanted to burst out laughing, and she quickly turned her head and bit her upper arm to keep herself quiet. How could she go from completely terrified to almost giddy with hysterics at the flip of a switch? Then she wondered how Adam could hear the two lovers as clearly as she? Then it dawned on her—the listening device was just above her head. Obviously, it was working just fine.

Something creaked above her, and she imagined that the two were going at it on top of the desk. She thought of Adam's warning about the windows. Would they really have sex in front of the windows? With a hundred guests on the property? A few perhaps strolling the grounds, drinks in hand? Whatever they were doing, it seemed to go on forever, but it probably wasn't even a full minute. Finally, the man said, "Stop, please."

"You always smell so good, I swear I can't help myself," the woman giggled.

"Stop… Please, I want to talk." The tone was serious.

"We'll talk later…"

Although Two couldn't see the couple, she figured the woman had to be Victoria Tenney. It was her office, after all. No way it was some party guests looking for some privacy.

"Stop! I mean it!" the man was clearly angry.

"Ouch!" Surprise in her voice. "Damn you."

"We need to talk. I have to understand—"

"I've told you a thousand times! I swear, I don't know what happened. You ever hear the saying, shit happens? Well, guess what? It does."

"Oh, come on. Be reasonable. To this degree? No way," the man argued.

"Well, I'm telling you, I don't know. So, what? Why are you here? For money. It's always money."

"I have to investigate this," the man said. "That means taking time off from my job. You know this."

"I talked to Morgan—" the woman started.

"What?" the man was angry. "You talked to *my* boss?"

"He agrees with me. You know why?"

"Yeah, he doesn't want to be anywhere near this. Afraid of how it looks. Me? I want the truth, plain and simple."

"No…"

"I also want to do a proper burial."

"For all of them?" the woman scoffed. "Are you out of your head?"

"Let me do what I need to do," the man said in a softer tone. "Please."

There was silence for some time. Finally, the woman said. "I'll transfer the funds." This had to be Victoria, for sure.

"I want a check. Today. Right now."

"Dear God, you're impossible."

"Write this last check, and I promise, you won't hear from me again."

Another creak of the desk. Two saw the top desk drawer slide open and there was noise as something was taken from it. Two closed her eyes, recalling the drawer's contents. Some loose papers, a thick Post-it pad, a flip phone, and a wallet-size checkbook.

"Thank you..." the man said.

"It's not like I don't care. I just think bad things happen. And I'm tired of you going on and on about it."

"Do you know what happened?" he asked.

"What is that supposed to mean?" she asked bitterly.

"Do you?" he persisted.

"No, I don't, okay? And I get it. Whatever it was, you don't want it coming back to your company. I get that—"

"That's not it at all and you know it! That's you and Morgan. Not me!"

"Where's a damn pen?" she asked. Two could see a hand rummaging around in the open drawer.

"Here," the man said.

A pause, and she said, "A Montblanc? How regal of you." Silence, and then she went on. "A hundred and fifty, and we're done. Understand me? We're done."

"Agreed," he said.

Two waited. Something was tossed in the drawer, and then it was shut. The checkbook, no doubt.

"Go," the woman said. "I don't want to be seen together."

"Really?" the man scoffed.

"Turn right, go through the library, and make another right. I will follow later."

Another creak of the door. Then nothing for some time. Two was sorely tempted to move, but as if reading her mind, Adam said, "Stay put, Two... Stay put..." She remained frozen. Waiting.

There was noise, and the chair suddenly rolled back, frightening the heck out of her. She half-expected to see Victoria Tenney's face peering down at her. Instead, the woman sat, her nicely shaped legs, in sheer stockings, coming toward her. Two tried to make herself smaller and was again thankful for the deep knee well. The top left drawer opened. Two heard a loud beep. The flip phone being turned on?

"One hundred and fifty thousand," the woman said in a brisk tone. "I want it back in my account by the end of the week." A long pause, then, "No, no. Nothing like that. He's harmless enough... Right."

A snap sound. Closing the flip phone. The phone was put back in the drawer and the drawer slid shut. Two remained frozen. Completely frozen. The woman stood. The chair was promptly rolled back under the desk, and Two found herself unable to breathe. It seemed to take forever, but finally, she heard the door once again squeak loudly. Then there was silence. Nothing but silence.

~ ~ ~

Adam, Gretchen, and Elizabeth stared at the flatscreen. Elizabeth remained in the overstuffed chair, her broken leg on the ottoman in front of her. Adam and Gretchen stood, just feet from the TV screen, Adam holding the cell phone in his open palm.

They watched, but there wasn't much to see. Two seemed to be looking at the floor, focused on the bottom part of the chair.

Gretchen reached over and hit the mute button on the phone. She didn't want to share her thoughts over an open line with Hal and Marsha, which Two could obviously hear quite well. When Adam gave her a puzzled look, she said, "Good call on telling her to stay put."

"I'll say," Elizabeth agreed.

"You thinking what I'm thinking? Victoria isn't really gone?" Gretchen asked.

"Why wouldn't she be—?" Elizabeth started.

"Quiet, please," Adam snapped at her. She promptly shut her mouth. He looked at Gretchen. "She opened and shut the door, and now she is waiting in that TV room?"

"Oh my God," Elizabeth said.

"Quiet!" Adam shouted.

Gretchen shook her head. "Who knows? Maybe she saw something when she sat down in the chair. My other thought is, does she have cameras inside the office?"

"Shit," Adam said. "Let's not voice that." He looked at his watch. "We're out of time." He hit the mute button and said,

"Two, we're silent on this end. Looks like the office is empty. Roll the chair, very, very slowly away just enough to peek around the desk. Do not stand up. Repeat, do not stand up."

They watched as Two quickly put on her shoe. Then the chair moved ever so slowly. She looked around the office. It certainly appeared to be empty.

Adam and Gretchen exchanged looks. Adam said, "Listen, Two. Great job, okay? You've got no time for the computer. We got the bug, and it's already paying dividends. Let's get you out of there and back on duty."

FROG Headquarters, The Hague

Hal and Marsha were on the same page as Adam. There was no time to download the malware at this point. Only by luck was Two still in play. Hal had sent a text to Gretchen's phone telling Adam to go ahead and walk Two through leaving the office. There was no need for Marsha to be the lead since the computer was now out of play, and Adam had taken over anyway.

"Do me a favor," Adam said over the speaker phone. "Don't stand up. Remember the window. Crawl away from the desk until you're almost to the door, okay?"

They watched as Two started to crawl past the desk. Then she abruptly stopped. She turned back and scurried to the desk.

"Two..? What are you doing..? You've got to get out of there," Adam instructed.

Surrey, England

Two stared at the computer case then quickly took the laptop out of the case, cradled it in her arm as if it were a rugby ball, and started to crawl away.

"Two?" Adam thundered in her ear. "Two? What the hell?"

"Leave me alone, or I swear to God I'll yank out this stupid earpiece!" she hissed. She kept hobbling away from the desk on her knees using one hand and was now even with the other room. She glanced in that direction and didn't see anything. She looked behind her and decided she was far enough from the windows. She placed the computer on the floor and stood up. She took off her apron, laid it on the floor, placed the laptop on it and wrapped it up.

"Two—" Adam started.

"I'm going out," Two stated. She picked up the concealed computer, holding it tight against her chest. "Don't yell in my ear. This is *my* choice, *my* risk."

And with that, she opened the office door, another loud creak.

~ ~ ~

"What happens if—" Elizabeth started.

Adam turned and angrily pointed his finger at her. She got the idea and promptly shut her mouth. Turning his attention back to the screen, he saw that Two was back in the long corridor, heading back the way she had come. By the luck of the gods, no one was around. Once again, Two looked at the beautiful art pieces in the lighted niches. Something was up ahead. A woman was approaching. Damn.

~ ~ ~

As Two got closer, she realized the woman was old. At least sixty, probably. She walked a bit stooped over, holding a six-inch China appetizer plate in one hand at an angle. She saw Two coming and stopped in her tracks, suddenly swaying unsteadily.

"You okay, ma'am?" Two asked, genuinely concerned.

"The loo?" the woman muttered with an air of superiority.

Two gazed at the plate containing some partially eaten spears of asparagus and a generous dollop of hollandaise sauce. She reached for it. "I'll take that ma'am, if you're done."

The woman seemed surprised to find that she was holding something in her hand and promptly thrust it at Two. "The loo!"

"I'm not sure, actually," Two stammered. She pointed up ahead. "I think this way, okay? Need to turn around."

The woman slowly turned herself around and they started down the corridor together. With no one else in sight, Two let the woman get a few steps ahead and swiftly moved the computer to her left arm, holding it on her forearm like a tray. Then she turned the plate over, purposely smearing the uneaten food across the apron, the asparagus falling on the floor. She used the back of the plate to spread the hollandaise sauce even more. Satisfied at the mess, Two hugged the apron-wrapped computer tight to her chest

, holding the empty plate in her right hand. In a few long steps, she caught up with the woman and gently took her by the upper arm with her free hand. Two kept waiting for Adam to chirp in, but he didn't say a word. She had to wonder if the thing was even working. He never kept his mouth shut.

The old woman leaned on her a bit and then gave Two a conspiratorial wink. "Champagne doesn't always agree with me."

Suddenly, the woman stopped short. She froze in place. A startled look on her face.

"Ma'am?" Two inquired.

The woman didn't respond. Finally, she said, "I think I just leaked."

Two didn't know what to say to that. Finally, she managed to say, "Can you walk a bit further? We're almost there."

With a determined resolve, the woman straightened her spine a bit and stumbled on. Still nothing from Adam. Even about the bladder leakage. No doubt now that the earpiece was malfunctioning. It had to be.

It seemed to take forever before they were back near the large ballroom, the serving room off to their right. Just then, Malcolm came through carrying a large chaffing dish. He put it down, saw Two and the woman, and immediately came over.

"Where have you been? Your break is long over! Supper is on," he told her.

"She wandered off," Two whispered. "Needs the loo."

"Oh, for God's sake," he muttered. Then he noticed the hollandaise-smudged plate in her hand.

"She spilled it on me," Two quickly explained in a hushed voice. "My apron. I'm sorry…"

He reached for the apron, but Two promptly turned away. With some care, she lifted the apron a bit so he could see the hollandaise stain on both the apron and her blouse. "Be nice. She's a guest and it was accident."

"Total waste of the best hollandaise in Europe," he said with complete disgust. "Get changed. There are plenty of shirts just for this sort of thing. Put the soiled things in the laundry bag."

Two nodded, then said, "Can you take her to the loo, then?"

She was gone before he could reply.

~ ~ ~

Once Two made it outside to the vans, computer in hand, Adam chimed in, and with a heavy sigh, said, "Okay. Nice. Very nice."

Two jumped a mile. She really thought the microphone was dead. She didn't respond, although her heart was now back to beating at full throttle. She hurried over to the last of the three catering vans and opened the rear door as he added, "Go ahead and put it in the laundry bag. Keep it wrapped in the dirty apron. I'll get it from there."

"*I* will," Gretchen argued. "A woman won't be noticed as much a man."

After a minute of silence, Adam asked, "You can hear us, right, Two?"

Two glanced around. The area was completely quiet. The only living creature anywhere near was a solitary horse, watching from its stall. "Excellent job, Two. Just excellent," she muttered sarcastically, clearly annoyed.

"I said good job," Adam replied defensively.

They watched as Two carefully put the computer in a large red nylon bag stamped *laundry*. She added her own blouse and selected a clean blouse in her size, ripping off the plastic dry-cleaning bag. Buttoning up the blouse, she said, "No one opens the computer. I mean it. Don't touch it."

Marsha agreed. "It will no doubt have password protection, so she is right. Don't touch it. Just take it back to the safe house, and I'll be in touch."

As Two shut the van's door, Adam said, "Look down. Look at the plate." Two did as she was told and he added, "Okay, got it."

There had still been no one around, so Two said, "It's the last van. You can see that, can't you?"

"You can never have too much intel, Two. Never." There was silence, and then he asked incredulously, "Did that woman pee in her pants?"

~ ~ ~

Late that evening, Hal and Marsha had flown in on a NetJets plane and joined the others at the Surrey safe house. It had been Marsha's idea. Actually, she insisted on coming. She wanted a complete copy of the laptop so that both she and Two could divide up the spoils and get working. Yes, they could have done the job with an electronic transfer, but Marsha explained that it could take days. Literally, days. They didn't have days.

Within minutes upon arriving at the house, Marsha had set up a hard-drive duplicator dock on the kitchen table. Although she only needed one empty drive, she had brought three just in case. She would have made a good Boy Scout. Always prepared.

While Gretchen kept the coffee and hot food coming, Marsha and Two rolled up their sleeves and went to work. After Marsha had duplicated the laptop's hard drive, she had one immediate goal—make sure that they would always be able to get into Tenney's email and Red Arrow accounts even after Tenney discovered that her laptop was missing and changed her login credentials on those accounts.

In both cases it had been quite easy—they noted Victoria Tenney's security questions and answers and then added another cell phone number to the account with the hope that if either organization sent a SMS text message for authentication purposes, they might get lucky by picking it up on their end. Marsha knew perfectly well that the average person rarely looked at their account settings, and they were hoping that Tenney would be the same and not notice another number associated with either account.

Next, having logged in to Red Arrow Capital using Victoria's credentials, Marsha started poking around. With Elizabeth sitting beside her, they estimated that Tenney's holdings alone made her worth nearly two billion dollars. Marsha then tried to find what she could on the Trojan Steed hedge fund. But there was nothing. No hedge fund with a name even close to Trojan Steed. She couldn't help but think that Mac had made a mistake, but Hal theorized that the Redfield family changed the name once they were aware that Mac, William DeWine, and Bart Werner were watching. Now it was simply operating under a new name.

"But which one? Do you know how many hedge funds this company has? This is a joke," Two complained, fatigue from her long day and night catching up with her.

"Wait," Elizabeth said. "Check for something called due diligence."

Marsha quickly found the tab. "Got it."

Elizabeth pointed at the screen. "It's there! Second from the bottom."

"Yep," Marsha clicked on the icon, and it came up with a new login box. She used Victoria's credentials, but it came up with an invalid password alert. She tried again. No luck.

"You sure you got it right?" Hal asked Marsha. "No typos?"

Marsha gave him a scathing look.

Hal raised his hands in surrender. "Let's leave it for now. Everyone's wiped out."

"No," Marsha retorted. "We do this now. Right now. We're inside. We finish this."

"Surely—" Hal started.

Marsha cut him off. "For all we know, Victoria is going to her office right this minute to get her computer. Once she reports it lost, we could be locked out forever."

"You have her credentials—" Hal started.

"Which knowing how highly strung these guys are, might soon vanish. We're hoping not. We're hoping she simply updates her account with a new password, which we'll see. But who knows."

"So what do you do?" Elizabeth softly inquired.

"Find a backdoor," Marsha impatiently said.

It took some time, but she finally found a way back into the site posing as an admin user. Her hands flew across the keyboard, and she said, "Okay, okay. Looks like Trojan Steed is a locked account. We have several users. Clyde Redfield, Ethan Redfield, Victoria Tenney, and Oliver G."

"Hold on, hold on," Two said, working her own computer. "I got an email in her account from an Oliver G at Red Arrow tech support."

"Get the name of someone else in the department," Marsha said.

"What are you thinking?" Elizabeth asked.

"I'm the administrator. I'm going to let someone else in that account. Someone on computer support staff so if anyone sees it, they won't think twice."

"Okay," Two said. "Got another email from a Taylor B. at tech support."

"No last name?" Marsha asked.

"Not that I can see."

"Okay, here we go…" After several minutes, she said, "Taylor B. is now added to the limited users on the Trojan Steed account. Giving him a password…" After a beat, "Okay, going back into the due-diligence file and pulling up the account… Logging in as Taylor B… with the password…"

"Let's print everything we can," Adam said.

"I don't believe it!" she said in anger. "It's demanding verification!"

"Probably a two-step verification account," Two said.

Suddenly, there were repetitive chirps from the computer.

"It's timing me out!" Marsha said, alarmed. "This sucker is timing me out!"

"How much—?"

"Less than thirty seconds! Damn!" Marsha said, stabbing the keyboard. The chirps ended.

Two said, "That guy now has an email and text with a verification code."

"Fine. We can play by their rules." Marsha looked at Two. "You set up a Gmail account." She looked over her shoulder. "Someone, anyone, I need a phone number. Not any of ours."

"Got a burner," Gretchen said. She went to the kitchen and found it buried under some paper napkins. When Marsha was ready, Gretchen read off the number.

A few minutes later, Two looked at Gretchen. "That number again?"

Gretchen read off the phone number, and an instant later, the phone pinged. She read off the six digits.

Two nodded. "Okay guys, we got an email for Taylor."

"Give it to me," Marsha said.

"Okay," Two said. "TB not disease, one word, capital T, capital B at Gmail."

Marsha glanced up at her. "You kidding?"

"I think you're close to exhaustion," Hal told her.

"Do you know how many people use Gmail? You want to sit here all night playing the game of names already taken?" Two groused.

Again, he raised his hands in surrender.

"And to think no one ever thought of that one. Amazing, really," Marsha said sarcastically.

"It popped in my head when I started with TB," Two said defensively.

Marsha smiled while shaking her head. After typing it in, she was all business again. She glanced at Two and Gretchen. "It will time us out again. Looks like we have thirty seconds or less... Ready?"

Both Two and Gretchen nodded.

"Okay, logging in one more time," Marsha said. "Wants the verification code, and we're on the clock!" The incessant chirps started again.

The burner phone pinged. "Got it!" Gretchen said.

Two said, "Me too... I have 8-0-4-7-5-4."

"Yep," Gretchen said.

"Repeat," Marsha instructed as the chirps continued.

Gretchen methodically read off the number and Marsha typed it in. A moment later, she said triumphantly, "We're in!" But then another box covered the screen. "Big surprise. These idiots want me to create a separate password just for this account." She wrote something on a pad of paper and then typed it in. She shook her head. "Now I get to log in one more time."

"With the new password?" Adam asked.

"Yep." She typed again and finally sat back. "We're now officially in. Steed is now open for business!"

"Good job!" Elizabeth said, leaning forward to get a look at the screen.

"How big is it??" Two asked.

"Not too big, fourteen MB," Marsha replied. She studied the screen. "We've got 178 files here. Looks like I can copy, how about that?"

"Love it!" Two said triumphantly.

"Okay, I'm sending the files now..."

Within a minute, all the Trojan Steed documents landed in the new Gmail account. From there, Two forwarded them to their FROG server using encryption software. Meanwhile, Marsha printed the fund's seventy-eight-page Initial Offering Memorandum. She had wanted to print another copy so that Hal could look it over on the plane ride home, but they had run out of paper, so she had left the only hardcopy on the kitchen table for Elizabeth to sort through.

London, England

Oliver Gamble was in such a deep sleep that the persistent beeps on his phone became his rhythmic rows on the River Thames. In the dream, he was once again a sophomore at Oxford where he took great pride in being a crucial member of the Pembroke College intercollegiate eight-man rowing team. It was that year that they narrowly missed being crowned "Head of the River" after competing in the Summer Eights four-day regatta. The dream continued, but now the coxswain was urging encouragement with beeps instead of his usual blustery shouts. They pushed hard coming down the stretch and crossing the finish line, but once again, it hadn't been enough. The bitter disappointment in his dream was as real as it had been on that actual day years ago.

Even though the race was over, the chirps continued, floating across the flat water. Finally, the incessant chirps brought Oliver out of his dream and into the waking world. With a start, he realized that the beeps were from his phone, and he quickly fumbled for the device sitting on the nightstand.

He squinted at the display. The words Verify Now flashed repeatedly in red letters. He stabbed at the small screen and the chirps finally ended. A new screen popped up. "New Authorized User Closed Face Steed."

Closed Face was his own term for a one-time user to have limited access. Almost always a tech support person. Quite common and usually not a big concern. But in this case, it was devastating—the case file was Steed, the fund that Ethan Redfield seemed obsessed with. In fact, Ethan had personally told him that no one else was ever to have access to the file while it was pending in due diligence. Oliver had been at Red Arrow long enough to know this wasn't normal. But he also knew not to question any of the Redfields. Not if he wanted to keep his job.

"If I want anyone else in, you'll be the first to know. No other users unless I okay it, understand?" Oliver had dutifully nodded yes only to have Ethan point a finger at him for emphasis. "If anyone, *anyone*, logs in other than the four people we have now, you tell me. Immediately. Day or night. Understand me?"

Oliver had clearly understood and set up the fund so that technically it was listed, should some government agency bureaucrat want to poke around, but it would be protected with a bulletproof cyber shield. Even if you had the usual password attributed to one of the four accounts—his or one of three Redfield family members—this file demanded an entirely different password. If you didn't have the right authorization, the clock started ticking. Since he had implemented the stopwatch, no one had gotten in. Then again, no one had tried. Until now. He stabbed at another tab to see the identity of the username.

It was Taylor B.

What the..?

He instantly sat up and looked at Taylor, sleeping soundly beside him. His phone hadn't awakened her. He glanced at his phone again. Yes, Taylor B. was accessing the Steed file. In real time. Yet she was asleep next to him. What the hell was going on?

Suddenly in a cold sweat, all Oliver could think was the two other people who had gotten in before he had implemented the tight security measures. William DeWine and Bart Werner. And both times, he had dutifully presented Ethan with the proof of intrusion.

And both times, the unauthorized user had violently died a short time later.

Chapter Fifteen

FROG Headquarters, The Hague

Marsha and Hal had gotten back to The Hague just before six in the morning. Both had gone to their respective homes to get some sleep. And both were back in the office in by midafternoon. Hal saw Marsha arrive and went to her office. "You get some sleep?"

"Amazingly, yes," she replied. "You?"

"Some."

Marsha logged on to her computer and started checking on things. She realized Hal was still hovering behind her, so she asked, "Something I need to know?"

Just then, a loud beep sounded from her computer. She anxiously clicked on it. "Getting noise…"

"Noise?" Hal repeated.

Marsha's phone rang, and she answered hitting the speaker button. "You on this?"

"It's the door," Two said through the speaker. "That door squeaks like crazy, remember?"

"Right," Marsha said. "Let's keep this line open and just listen."

"Elizabeth is outside," Two said. "But Gretchen, Adam, and I are here."

"Hal's here on this end," Marsha said.

Hal pulled Two's chair close to the desk. Marsha gestured to her office door, and Hal leaped up and shut it. As he sat down, they could hear a rummaging sound and then a woman's voice. "No, no, no…" More rummaging. "Damn it! Damn it all to hell!"

Nothing for a few minutes. Ambient noise, but no more words. Finally, some sort of buzzing sound.

After several minutes, they heard a knock—perhaps on the door? And another voice, a woman. "Ma'am?" She sounded far away.

"You clean in here?" Victoria asked abruptly. "Today?"

"No, ma'am. If you'd like—"

"No, I would *not* like!" Victoria told her. "My laptop is missing."

The other woman said tentatively, "Perhaps in your bedroom, ma'am?"

"The carrying case is here! See! This is here, the computer is not!"

They could only presume Victoria was showing her the empty laptop carrycase. This meant that she probably never used the laptop without having the case nearby.

"Who else is here this morning?" Victoria asked.

"My sister and niece. You know them. They've worked here periodically when we need—"

"Yes, yes. Have they been in here? This office?"

"No, ma'am. No." The voice sounded mortified. The woman quickly went on. "We've been working together. The kitchen, ballroom, and bathrooms have been the priority. No one has been down here."

Silence, and then Victoria issued her an order. "Please leave and shut the door."

"Ma'am," came the quiet reply. The squeak of the door, no doubt being closed. Then it was silent.

A very faint beep.

"She's turning on her burner," Two explained.

Just then, they heard Victoria speaking. "Adrian deposit the money?"

Marsha and Hal exchanged looks.

"Well, guess what? The asshole stole my computer." Silence, then, impatient, "When? Between sometime yesterday afternoon and now. That's when." More silence, then she erupted in anger. "I know there were a zillion people here, but no one came down here. It was tucked under my desk, you'd have to come in, come all the way around my desk to even see it. No, no, this was Adrian. I brought him in here, I wrote the check, and now, my laptop is gone! It's him, I know it is! Yes, fine, look..."

It remained silent for some time, and Two took the opportunity to say, "Guess I'm off the hook, anyway."

"Quiet," Adam chided her.

Victoria said, "Right… So he's at his London flat. That makes your job easier. I'll tell Ethan to get my money back. Your job is to find him and get my computer back. Then take him out." More silence before she erupted again. "Yeah, I know what I said, but the bastard took my computer! Take care of him! And get my computer back!"

With that, she must have hung up the phone. They could hear the slamming of a drawer. After that, it was quiet for some time. Finally, they heard the door open and shut. They waited a full three minutes but there were no more sounds.

London, England

Oliver Gamble had been at his desk at Red Arrow Capital since four that morning. He was hardly the only employee in that early. In fact, since hedge-fund managers work the phones calling clients all over the world, there were usually a few people in the office at any given hour, day or night.

Before leaving, he had woken up Taylor and told her what was going on. She was both angry and frightened. She knew her life was in danger, and she had insisted on going with him to the office. However, he had told her to stay put. He knew what to do and if anything, her simply being there at such an early hour could raise alarm bells. He was often called in at all hours, so he would be okay. He told her not to leave the flat—for any reason. There was plenty of food, just stay put. At seven a.m., she should call in sick.

She had argued that it wouldn't take that long to remove her name from the list of authorized Steed users, so she should plan to show up for work as usual. However, Oliver explained that it was not just a matter of erasing her entry login from Steed. He would need to clean up all traces of the hack, and that would take time. He didn't need to remind her that if he failed, she was as good as dead.

In the end, she gave in. They agreed on an all-clear code. Once he was positive the break-in couldn't be traced to her, he would text her yesterday's Manchester United final score. If he gave her the wrong score, she was to run for hills. Taylor insisted that she would stay and fight, but as Oliver pointed out, unless they could find the real hacker, which would be nearly impossible, no one would believe her. Taylor finally agreed she'd leave for Barcelona. It was the only place she could think to go. She had spent a semester there as an undergraduate.

It had taken mere minutes for Oliver to remove all traces of Taylor as a user on the Steed file. From there, it took him some time to retrace what had happened—a very clever hacker had gotten inside by breaching a fault at the backdoor and posing as an Admin user. Once they were in, all they had to do was add Taylor to Steed's authorized-user list. He had to admit, the hacker was good—he had long thought all of their backdoors were airtight, but he now saw a tiny flaw. It was not something most hackers would be savvy enough to exploit. This guy had. Oliver patched it so it wouldn't happen again and set up an alarm to alert him should the hacker try again.

Next, he got into Taylor's email account. There were already nearly forty new emails waiting for her. Some were from staff members seeking further assistance. A few from other tech people seeking her guidance on an issue. Nothing out of the norm.

Then he saw it. Another email under her name—this one was TBnotdisease@Gmail.com. It took him a minute to realize it was her initials and then the words "not disease." He clicked on it. There was only one email in the inbox, having arrived at 2:57 a.m. There was no subject line. He opened it. There was no message in the body of the email, but there was an attachment. With great trepidation, he opened it. A zip file. He opened this and found it contained every single file from the Steed account.

Oliver went back to see who sent it. The same Gmail account. Very clever. Nothing to point at who did this. He now deleted the email from both the inbox and the sent box. He went into the Trash file and deleted everything there. But there was one more step. At Red Arrow, all deleted emails went into the main storage vault for sixty-five days. This was just a good safety backup and had proven invaluable on more than one occasion. Inside the vault, he found the sent and received email with the Steed files among all her previously accumulated trash. He selected the Steed file email to be removed. A pop-up warned him that the email would be permanently deleted and could not be restored. He hit the delete button.

Finally, he went back to Taylor's account with Red Arrow and took down the Gmail account under her name, leaving only her work email.

Oliver sat back and wondered if he had missed something. He couldn't think of anything. Glancing at the wall clock, he reached for his phone.

He needed Freddy's help.

Surrey, England

"I found him!" Two shouted with great excitement, sitting at her usual spot at the far end of the kitchen table. "I found him!"

Elizabeth, who was sitting at the opposite end of the long table, reading through the various Steed documents, looked up at Two over her reading glasses, with a puzzled look.

Gretchen closed the refrigerator door, popped open a yogurt, and began stirring it with a spoon. "Found who?"

"His full name is Charles Adrian Weatherspoon," Two replied.

Gretchen shrugged. The name meant nothing.

"Adrian! The guy Victoria Tenney put on her hit list!"

"You said Charles," Elizabeth pointed out.

"But he goes by his middle name, Adrian," Two said.

The front door opened, and they turned as Adam came in with several bags of groceries. He and Gretchen had flipped a coin to see who would go to the grocery store and stop at an office-supply store to pick up ink for the printer and more paper. He had lost.

Two eagerly looked at him. "I found Adrian, the man Victoria is going to kill."

With zero emotion, Adam put all the items on the kitchen table.

"Did you hear me?" Two asked impatiently. "I found the man she's going to kill!"

"Actually, she instructed *someone else* to kill him," Adam said matter of fact. "Her hands will be clean."

"I'm serious!" Two complained.

"I am too," Adam countered. "Very serious. Details matter."

Gretchen gave Adam an annoyed look and started putting the groceries away.

Adam turned his attention to Two. "Talk to me. Who is this guy? I thought we only had a first name, no surname."

"Right. So I went through her emails. Found an Adrian Weatherspoon in her contact list. Found some social media stuff. Pictures of him and Victoria on Instagram. Not too recent. In Kenya, Serbia, Florida, Wyoming. Either they broke up, or he hasn't posted stuff with the two of them, but they're a couple. Or were, anyway."

"Anything besides social media?" Gretchen asked.

Two read from her screen. "He's a chemical engineer. Whatever that is. He was born and raised in Liverpool, now lives in Dubai, but has a flat in London."

"Which fits with Victoria's conversation earlier today," Gretchen remarked. "Whoever she was talking to pinned him down in London."

Two went on. "Forty-three years old. Not married. Not sure on kids. Works for a company called Al Friqet Industries in Dubai. They do clean water, wastewater, and sewer stuff. They say clean water is quote, 'essential to life,' unquote."

"Wait, wait, wait…" Elizabeth said eagerly. "I think I saw them." After flipping through some papers, she pulled one out. Reading it, she said, "Yeah. Al Friqet Industries… Good grief…"

"What?" Adam asked.

"Steed is getting a pretty good stake in it. It's publicly traded, and they're in for nearly four percent right now."

"That's a lot?" Gretchen asked.

"You kidding? It's huge," Elizabeth told her. "Publicly trades on the New York stock exchange. Five percent or more, Steed has to file with the SEC. Right now, they're staying under the radar."

"So it's important to them," Adam said. "We need to find out why."

"Maybe Adrian told Victoria something about the company," Gretchen offered. "They were or are still lovers. Victoria gets insider information, some other company is going to buy them out, something like that, so they buy up a bunch of stock."

Elizabeth made a face. "Maybe…"

"Guys!" Two complained. "Hello? We have to do something!"

Adam frowned. "Such as?"

"Such as warn him that he's about to be killed!"

"It doesn't work that way."

Two just stared. "We let an innocent man die?"

"Listen—" Adam began.

"No, you listen!" Two argued. "This is on me! Me! I grabbed the computer. And because I did that, she thinks this Adrian guy did it, and she's going to have him killed! It's my fault!"

"No, it's not," Adam said firmly.

Two had tears in her eyes. "I should have left it alone. But I didn't. I stole it, and now an innocent man is going to die! Because of me!"

Adam went over to her. "If this guy dies, it's on Victoria, not you. Understand? You did great. I mean it. Great. By doing what you did, we're light years ahead of where we were. And we're going to win this battle, okay? And when we do, it will be because of your bravery in getting us the computer."

"But—"

"*She* called for his killing, not you. So stop it."

"I know it's hard, Two, but Adam is right," Gretchen said gently. "This is on Victoria."

Two wiped her nose with the back of her hand. "I hate this."

"I hear you," Adam softly replied. "That said, you have his London address?"

London, England

"I don't like it here," Freddy complained.

"What are you talking about?" Oliver argued. "You eat here every single day."

Freddy studied their outdoor table and started to sway. "I eat at home. Not here."

"Guess what?" Oliver waited. He knew Freddy would eventually look at him. A minute later, Freddy looked at him. "This is London, and we have sunshine today. Actual sunshine. We're sitting outside, enjoying the nice weather. That's one..."

"I like home," Freddy insisted.

"Secondly, I'm starving, and I'm not waiting for food to be delivered. And lastly, you realize what vitamin D is?"

Freddy looked at the tabletop and swayed back and forth, left to right, left to right.

"Vitamin D, Freddy. Talk."

"Vitamin D is a fat-soluble vitamin. It helps with bone and teeth." He tapped an index finger on his front teeth and kept going. "It assists the nervous system, helps with insulin and maybe diabetes. It helps the heart. The body activates vitamin D through two different hydroxylation processes—"

"Okay, okay," Oliver said, cutting him off. "Where does it come from?"

Freddy stared at him. Either confused or annoyed that Oliver didn't know. "Food and the sun."

"Right! The sun! It's a nice day, let's get some sun! Get some vitamin D."

They were interrupted by the server bringing them their lunch. Fish and chips for both. Freddy made a face. "Is this fish?"

Oliver wasn't in the mood. He had heard from his aunt that Freddy was on a new kick—being vegan. Yet when Oliver had ordered his meal, Freddy had been quick to say, "Me too, me too, me too."

Oliver said, "You ordered it. Eat it or don't, I don't really care."

Freddy gingerly picked up a piece of the battered fish and after examining it closely—and somewhat apprehensively—took a small bite.

Oliver hadn't eaten all morning and really was famished. He took a huge bite of his and looked at Freddy. "Good, eh?"

Freddy nodded and eagerly took another bite. "It's good. It's good, it's good, it's good." A bus boy wiping down a nearby table heard Freddy and gave Oliver a smile.

The staff at this small café all knew Freddy since he lived just down the street. They knew that he wasn't autistic, although at first glance, you might think he was based on his repetitive mannerisms. He was actually a high-functioning teenager with Asperger's.

Oliver remembered his aunt's devastation upon learning of Freddy's diagnosis. School had been a nightmare. The kids teasing him. Freddy not testing well, hardly able to write a term paper, and being thwarted in terms of advancement. Yet the kid was super smart. Just super dysfunctional too.

It was Oliver who told his aunt to home school him. She had no clue how to do this, so Oliver set up all the online coursework. He also encouraged Freddy to work on computers in his spare time. He told the kid that there were tons of people that would pay him good money to have their computers repaired, properly installed with new software, and so on. Subsequently, at the tender age of thirteen, he started taking online classes and working on computers.

Oliver's aunt had been dubious. A single mother, she thought she was failing Freddy by not making sure he had a proper education in a school. But in short order, they discovered that Freddy could master any class, any task. Without the pressure of other kids, without the teasing, he was a model student.

At the same time, he soon got a great reputation for computer repair, and he had more work than he needed. It was hardly a surprise that Freddy worked better when he didn't have to go to someone's house. He much preferred that a customer leave their device with him and let him fix it.

He was now seventeen and earning more than his mother. In a few months, he'd take his A levels. Oliver was sure he'd pass with flying colors if he could test at home. However, that wasn't an option, so there was a chance he wouldn't pass. But in the end, it really didn't matter if he passed or not. He was doing just fine.

"Okay," Oliver said. "What did you find out?"

Freddy gave him a puzzled look.

"The Gmail account?"

"Oh, right… Right... It was set up last night—"

"Last night?" Oliver interrupted, clearly astonished.

Freddy ate some chips. With his mouth full, he said, "At 2:49 in the morning, London time."

Oliver knew better than to question how Freddy knew this. He had ways of doing things that probably weren't too legal. "Okay, so they didn't have that email account ready to go?"

"No."

"Anything else you can tell me about that account?" Oliver asked.

With that, Freddy promptly stood up and dug into his front jeans pocket. He tossed a wadded-up piece of paper on the table.

"What's this?" Oliver asked. He carefully uncrumpled the paper. A series of numbers. He looked to Freddy who was stuffing chips in his mouth. "What is this, Freddy?"

"Phone number..." Freddy said.

"Okay... Whose phone number? I'm not following."

"I don't know, don't know, don't know... I didn't see any person's name... No person, no person, no person..."

"Okay, okay," Oliver said calmly. "So, it's a burner?"

"Burner. It's a burner... It's a—"

"Got it." Oliver looked to Freddy. "It's a burner phone number. But help me out here. What exactly does this have—"

"It's the number they used," Freddy said impatiently.

Oliver suddenly got it. "For the verification code."

Freddy nodded. "Google sent the code to *that* number for TB not disease email."

Oliver sat back, marveling at what he had in his hand.

"The Hague," Freddy said, his mouth full again.

"What?"

Freddy reached over and touched the paper, leaving a greasy smudge mark on it. "Phone is from the Netherlands. From The Hague."

"How do—"

"Seventy is the area code for The Hague."

"Ah, right," Oliver said.

"Holland is actually an area made up of two provinces within the Netherlands. A total of twelve provinces make up the Netherlands. People say Holland for all of the Netherlands. Technically, they are mistaken—"

"Okay, okay, enough," Oliver interrupted impatiently. "So just to be clear, the number you found, this number, was used for the Gmail account I gave you? And it is from The Hague."

"All areas have an area code. A prefix for that area," Freddy said by rote. "Seventy is The Hague. The guy who has that phone, he got it in The Hague. I don't know who he is, so I don't know if he lives there. Maybe he was just there, needed a new phone."

"Got it," Oliver said.

"Carrier is Vodafone," Freddy said. "No name, no address for that number."

"Right, right... It's a burner."

Freddy frowned. "No person... No person means they don't want to be found."

Oliver nodded. Freddy was worth his weight in gold. He took out his phone and took a picture of the phone number, then he folded it neatly and put it in his pocket. Finally, he looked to Freddy. "Anything else you can tell me?"

~ ~ ~

Taylor couldn't wait for Oliver to get home so she could learn all about the breach. While it had been a great relief to get his text giving her the correct Manchester United score and to know that she was in the clear, she desperately wanted answers—mainly, how someone was even able to access the Steed account and equally important, how or why they used her name.

All day, she couldn't help but wonder what would have happened if they hadn't outfitted the Steed file with an alarm. Would she be dead by now? She tried to tell herself that there was no way she was ever in danger, but the truth was, she knew in her gut she had escaped by the skin of her teeth.

Ironically, it was the violent deaths of Bart Werner and Michael DeWine that had brought Taylor and Oliver together. Prior to those incidents, she had been working at Red Arrow for over a year. She liked Oliver; he was a good boss, but she never gave him much thought on a personal level since she was dating someone. That all changed when Oliver's buddy stopped by one afternoon to drop off tickets to a Manchester United game, telling Oliver he couldn't go that night. Knowing Taylor was a big fan, Oliver offered her the tickets. Taylor insisted that they go together after making it clear that she was already in a relationship. Oliver had dragged his feet, explaining that he had a lot on his mind and wasn't in the mood to go to the game. However, Taylor prevailed. She had thought attending the game would perk him up, but she couldn't have been more wrong.

Afterward, they went to a nearby pub for a pint. She asked him why he was in the dumps, thinking he had girlfriend problems. Much to her surprise, she learned the details about a Red Arrow employee who had been killed in an explosion in

197

Holland. Oliver kept drinking that night and soon confided that the dead employee had accessed a Red Arrow file that he had no business looking at. Oliver explained how Ethan Redfield wanted that particular file closed to everyone but family. And he wanted to be informed if anyone, anyone at all, ever tried to look at it. So Oliver had told Ethan Redfield about the unauthorized login. He said Redfield had gone bonkers, shouting that DeWine was a "dead man walking."

At the time, Oliver thought Ethan Redfield was just super angry, spouting off. But now DeWine was dead. And Oliver felt such guilt. Taylor tried to reason with him, saying that no way was the death of a Red Arrow employee—who was out of the country at the time—in any way connected to Ethan Redfield. In her mind, there was just no way it was connected. He was at the wrong place at the wrong time. It was as simple as that.

Several weeks later, there was another unauthorized look of the file. Taylor helped Oliver trace the user to Bart Werner, an employee. Together, they gathered the evidence. Oliver didn't want to give the information to Ethan Redfield. He wanted to talk to Bart Werner first, let the man defend himself. But Taylor argued that Werner had hacked into the account and it was Oliver's job to inform Ethan Redfield about the intrusion. If Ethan found out Oliver had taken matters into his own hands, he could be fired. And so Oliver had dutifully informed Ethan Redfield about the breach. After looking at the documents, Ethan asked if anyone else knew. Oliver had lied, saying it was just him. The very next day Bart Werner died in a bizarre attack at the Schiphol International Airport.

This time it was Taylor who shouldered the tremendous guilt—she had convinced Oliver to give Ethan the information on Bart Werner. And then he died under mysterious circumstances. It was at that point that Taylor insisted the file needed a much better protection system. If no one could get in, no one would get killed. It really was that simple.

Together, they devised another level of protection by making sure each family member had to enter another password just for that file. The family might find it annoying, but the worry had been that someone could use a phishing scheme to trick a family member into revealing their Red Arrow password. In this case, even if that happened, it wouldn't allow the attacker to access the Steed account. They also set up an alarm system so Oliver would be immediately notified of any suspicious activity.

She and Oliver discussed the various coincidences—first and foremost that both men had opened the Steed file, secondly that Ethan was made aware of the breaches, and finally, that both men had then been killed. Then there was the fact that DeWine was at a Netherlands café where Bart Werner's cousin worked. A café that got bombed. There was the fact that Bart went to Amsterdam to be with his family. And that he was killed as soon as he had arrived. What were the odds? It was Taylor who suggested that they comb through Bart Werner's office emails. They had ended up working through the night and had found nothing. All of Bart Werner's emails were legitimate Red Arrow business.

Oliver had then taken Taylor with him to meet Freddy. Oliver's young cousin had found a way to look at Bart's personal email account, but it really had nothing of interest. There was one email from another Red Arrow employee, a man named Mac Senton, but even this looked innocent enough.

After that, the two of them had spent a lot of time in her flat discussing the whole thing. They really had no proof that Ethan Redfield had anything to do with DeWine's or Werner's untimely deaths. Then Mac Senton had taken his own life. While in the Netherlands. Another coincidence? They didn't think so, but they really had no idea.

Spending so much time with Oliver, she slowly realized she had feelings for him. She also realized that she had less and less in common with her boyfriend and finally put an end to the relationship. Days later, she and Oliver slept together for the first time. Within a week, he had moved into her flat. And for Taylor, it felt right.

Her cell phone rang and she answered.

"It's Beth," the caller said. "I know you're sick, and I'm really sorry to bother you... Are you okay?"

It took Taylor a minute to remember that she had notified the staff that she had food poisoning and wouldn't be in. "Yeah, I'm okay. Better."

Beth quickly went on, a bit nervous. "I offered to help, I really did. And I'm sorry, I mean, I told her you were out sick, but—"

Taylor didn't need to hear any more. She interrupted Beth. "Look, I'll be in tomorrow, okay?"

Beth hesitated. "She really is insisting on talking to you. Today. Right now. I'm sorry—"

"Who? Who are you talking about?"

"Victoria Tenney."

Chapter Sixteen

London, England

"That's it," Gretchen said, pointing to the two-story deep-blue duplex up ahead. Fortunately, the freestanding building had a short driveway in front with only a small car parked to one side. Plenty of room for their car, which was a huge bit of luck considering there were no empty parking spaces on the street. Adam swung into the driveway.

"Door," Gretchen said, motioning to the first-floor front door that stood partially open.

They both got out and slowly approached. Gretchen instinctively reached for her gun but came up empty. Even though both she and Adam had brought semi-automatics into the country, since they were leaving Elizabeth and Two on their own, it was deemed prudent to make sure they had a firearm. Two hadn't wanted a gun of any kind, but finally agreed Gretchen could leave her 9 mm—as long as it was in a kitchen drawer.

Adam had his gun in hand, pointed at the ground. They took up positions on either side of the open door. Gretchen glanced out at the street. There were some cars passing by, but no pedestrians. She looked to Adam and nodded.

Since he was armed, he went in first. Silently, they covered the first floor. A nicely appointed living room with a flatscreen on one wall. Nothing obviously out of place. Likewise, no sign of disturbance in the dining area, kitchen, or small bathroom. A half-empty coffee cup had been left on a table at the bottom of the stairs. They silently headed upstairs. The first room was an office. Empty and undisturbed. A bathroom. Empty, save a large towel on the tile floor.

"Over here," Adam softly called out.

Gretchen stepped into the master bedroom. The bed was unmade, a scattering of clothes on top. Between the bed and the far wall was a man, sprawled on the floor and conscious, both hands covering his bloody torso. Lots of blood. Probably a stab wound. Two had given them pictures of Charles Adrian Weatherspoon so there was no doubt who the injured man was.

Gretchen quickly pulled out her phone only to hear Adam say firmly, "Hold off."

Adam wedged himself between the wall and the bed, careful not to touch anything. He kneeled down beside Adrian and said, "Adrian, do you know who did this?"

Stepping behind Adam and getting a closer look, Gretchen now knew why Adam didn't want her calling it in—Adrian's eyes were glazed over. He was circling the drain. Adrian seemed to realize she was there and moved his head slightly, looking at her.

Adam shook him by the shoulder. "Do you know who did this?" Adrian turned back to Adam with a blank look. "Victoria Tenney," Adam told him.

His eyes grew wide. He was certainly registering everything Adam was saying.

"You blackmailing her?"

Adrian's face changed. Resolute. Angry.

"No? I'm just trying to figure out what's what, okay?" Nothing. "She paid you lots of money. So I'm thinking you're blackmail her and this is her payback."

Adrian shook his head, his eyes wild.

"Then tell me. Why does she want you dead?" Adam asked.

Adrian tried to speak, but nothing came out. Adam leaned close and waited. Nothing more.

Adam sat back. "Look, I'll tell you the truth, you're not going to make it. Probably clipped the aorta and you're bleeding out inside. We'll call 999. But you're not going to make it."

Adrian started to breathe hard. "I… I tried to make it right…"

Adam leaned close again. "Make what right..? What..?"

"L… Le… Lou… Tet…" Adrian said, out of breath.

Adam glanced at Gretchen then turned back to Adam. "Lou Tet? Who's he?"

"You… you… you… gone…" And that was it. Adrian suddenly stopped breathing, eyes frozen in place.

"Damn it!" Adam thundered, slamming his fist into the bed. "Damn it to hell!"

Gretchen stepped back into the hall, opened her phone, and hit the voice-memo app. "Adrian spoke of trying to make something right, someone named Lou Tet, not sure on spelling or who that is, and then said something about, "You gone..." She clicked it off.

She went back inside the bedroom and found Adam checking Adrian's pockets. But there was nothing.

"We give it five, then we're gone," Gretchen said.

FROG Headquarters, The Hague

Hal popped his head into Marsha's office. "How's it going?"

"We're going to need to set up a conference call with those guys. Fill them in."

Hal glanced at his watch. "They back to base?"

"I haven't checked. Last I heard, there was a bad accident, so they were on secondary roads, but as Adam said, all of England was on the same roads."

"I'll see if they're back and we'll set it up." He left.

Once Adam and Gretchen left Adrian Weatherspoon's home, they had called Marsha asking her to see if there were any cc cameras on Adrian's street, and if so, if there was any footage of them anywhere near Adrian's flat. The system in the UK was painfully slow, but she found that they were indeed on street video and worse, their car was seen coming and going from the driveway. She successfully deleted all footage of their car going back several miles in time. Not for the first time, she wondered how the British police could keep such an easily altered camera system in play. Surely, she wasn't the only one able to simply erase a car or pedestrian from video footage? She then scoured the video for activity before Adam and Gretchen had shown up.

When she called to tell them they were in the clear, Gretchen related that they did a quick search for electronics and had come up empty for a phone, tablet, or computer. However, she had found what she called "a peculiar" USB taped to the underside of a desk drawer. She was anxious for Two to look at the device, but they were trapped in heavy traffic.

Marsha had her send a photo of the device and quickly saw that it was a 2-in-1 micro-USB flash drive, which meant one end was a standard USB size while the other end was quite small, intended to be used with smart phones and tablets. She then asked Gretchen to plug the miniature USB into her iPhone and see what was on the device. It turned out there were just three files. She directed Gretchen to email them to her, and she had all the files within minutes. All while they were stuck in traffic.

Unfortunately, she soon found that all three files were so heavily encrypted that she didn't dare play with them. Instead she passed them off to their in-house encryption engineer who would have to unravel them. Hopefully soon.

Hal popped his head back in. "They're just arriving back at the safe house, said to give them ten minutes."

Surrey, England

"She's more than ready," Adam told Hal and Marsha, their images on display on the TV. They were in the FROG conference room, Marsha with her laptop, notepad, and pen in front of her. "I'm taking her to Heathrow tonight."

"What about her safety?" Hal asked.

"She said she'd take care of it," Adam replied.

"I think she's going to have her sister rent an Airbnb house somewhere in her name, then the family will go there," Gretchen explained. "They'll drive wherever they are going, stay off the grid. She's requesting time off from Goldman due to her ankle. And Adam is right. She misses her family. And it's time for us to get back to normal too."

In other words, Elizabeth was not a part of FROG. Which was why she was sitting outside on the patio and not a part of this conversation while Two, Gretchen, and Adam were all standing within a few feet of the television.

"But we can contact her about the hedge-fund stuff?" Hal asked.

"Oh, yeah. Believe me, she wants to help," Gretchen assured him. "She'll be available."

Hal nodded.

"Okay," Adam said. "Marsha, we're clean from any street cameras?"

"Yes," Marsha told him.

"Thank you for that," Adam said with sincerity.

"So, no laptop, no phone?" Hal asked. "Who doesn't have a phone?"

"Probably taken by the guy who killed him," Adam said.

"Correction," Marsha said. "Looks like it may have been a woman."

"Really?" Hal asked with surprise, turning to Marsha.

Marsha said, "Hold on... I got this off the street cameras, going to put it up now."

In their Surrey safe house, a video took the place of Marsha and Hal on the screen. All three of them moved closer to the TV. Marsha clicked the play button and they saw a pedestrian walking down the street. It wasn't all that clear, just a black and white clip of a person walking.

"Enhancing... look at the pants," Marsha said. "Men don't wear pants like that."

"You do if you're a transgender," Gretchen said sarcastically.

"Let's keep to what we know," Hal said.

"Bell bottoms?" Adam asked. "That's your tell?"

"Look at how much they flare out at the bottom."

"Hold on!" Two called out, stepping closer to the screen. She pointed at the image. "Marsha, can you grab her face?"

"I tried," Marsha said with disappointment. "You know how these CCTVs are."

The face was grainy at best.

"Hair length?" Two asked.

"Just a minute..." Marsha said. They waited, and a different image appeared. It was the backside of the woman. "This is going away from the house. You can see she now has a tote bag. She didn't have any bag on the way to the house."

"So she's carrying a laptop," Gretchen said. "I'll bet you."

"And a phone, no doubt," Hal added.

"Her hair, please?" Two asked impatiently.

Another enhancement, and the video played again, this time in slow motion. You could see long hair blowing in the wind.

Gretchen turned to Two. "What is it?"

"She was at the party," Two said, starring at the image. "I mean, I can't be a hundred percent certain, but there was this woman, total idiot snob. She only wanted vegan foods. She would literally tell me what foods to get her."

"What looks the same?" Adam asked. "What triggered her for you?"

"The bellbottom pants, but they were obnoxiously wide," Two said. "More than just bellbottoms. Almost like she was wearing a wide skirt. But it was pants. Just weird."

"Which this person has," Marsha pointed out. "Extremely wide bellbottoms."

"Age?" Adam asked.

Two hesitated. "Older. Forties, maybe." She didn't see Adam's frown upon hearing her definition of an older person. She went on. "She had long brown hair."

"How long?" Marsha asked. "To her waist? Her bra line? What?"

Two placed her hand against her own back. "Here, maybe."

Gretchen said, "Below the bra line, not down to the waist."

"She was so arrogant!" Two fumed. "I mean, just so demanding."

"You catch a name?" Adam asked.

Two shook her head. "I tried to avoid her, you know? When I brought in another tray of food, I could spot her a mile off and would go the other way."

"Okay..."

"Wait, wait, wait!" Two suddenly said. She hurried back to her computer. "We have Victoria's guest list for the party. It was on her hard drive. Maybe I can find her!"

Just then, a chime sounded. Loud. It echoed at FROG.

"Victoria Tenney's office!" Two said "Everyone quiet..."

London, England

"You're on speaker, I'm ready," Victoria Tenney said over the phone. Ironically, Taylor had Victoria on speakerphone too, but she kept that to herself. Tenney would never know, and she wasn't comfortable talking to any Redfield family member after the breach the night before unless Oliver was with her. Which he now was. They sat at their kitchen table, Oliver with a notepad in front of him.

"Have you tried the Find My app?" Taylor asked.

"What?"

Taylor looked at Oliver and rolled her eyes. "Do you happen to have an Apple iPhone?"

"Yes, of course." Victoria wasn't in a good mood.

"Okay, your laptop is an Apple MacBook Pro, running Monterey. So on your iPhone, you need to open the Find My app." She had to patiently walk Victoria through the steps.

Surrey, England

Adam looked to Two. "Please tell me she won't find the computer."

"It's here anyway, not with you guys," Marsha said. She and Hal were back on the screen looking at them. "And of course not, it's turned off."

"So what's going to happen?" Hal asked.

"It will give the locations of whatever other devices she might have. Her iPhone, her Apple watch if she has one, but not the computer we took," Marsha explained.

"*I* took," Two corrected her. "At great risk, I might add."

"That *Two* took," Marsha said with good cheer. "At great risk."

"Nice of her to use her speakerphone," Gretchen said, now sitting in one of the overstuffed chairs and snacking on a sandwich. "Helps a lot to hear both ends of a conversation."

"I don't see it!" Victoria yelled, her voice blaring over the speaker. "You said this would work!"

London, England

Taylor looked to Oliver, who gave her a goofy look. Taylor wanted to laugh. Instead, she said, "Ma'am, the fact that the Find My app is not showing your computer might mean it was never set up."

"Well, you're the computer person," Victoria said with great disdain. "Turn it back on!"

Taylor looked to Oliver and shook her head. "I can't do that. I'd have to have the device, and I don't."

"I want it back!" Victoria thundered.

"I understand, ma'am," Taylor said calmly. "And we may yet find it. But for now, let's be careful. Let me ask you... When you realized you had lost the computer, did you change any of your usernames or passwords for sites that you frequent?"

"No," Victoria said with great annoyance. "I honestly thought a friend took it. As a joke. But I had an associate go to his flat and check, and it's not mine."

FROG Headquarters, The Hague

"I'll be damned," Marsha said. "She didn't change any of her passwords before now? That's just stupid. You get your laptop back, no harm, no foul. But you don't wait to protect yourself. Stupid woman."

"I would love to have seen her face when she was presented with the wrong computer," Gretchen said from Surrey.

London, England

"Okay," Taylor sighed. "Let's get going. We need to change all your usernames and passwords for your accounts. Let's start with your bank. Do you bank online?"

"Oh God," Victoria moaned. "They've stolen all my money."

"Ma'am, you have to do this now. Go online to your bank using your phone, okay?"

"Well, it's not like I have just *one* bank account," Victoria retorted. "I'm going to have to do this for all *four!*"

Oliver scribbled, Oh the agony of being super rich.

Taylor struggled to keep from laughing, playfully punching Oliver in the arm. Regaining her composure, she said, "Four accounts. Okay, let's start with the one with the most money, how's that?"

FROG Headquarters, The Hague

It was late afternoon when Hal stuck his head in Marsha's office. "Email?"

"Yeah, took her awhile to see it I guess, but she responded."

"You mean she fell for it?" Hal asked.

"Oh, yeah," she replied with satisfaction.

Hal just shook his head. As important as FROG operatives were to their various missions, working behind the scenes and doing the dangerous work, Marsha was truly invaluable. With the entire team listening to Victoria's phone call, they had learned that most of her money was held at the Royal Bank of Scotland. The also knew exactly when she changed the password for her email account. That's when Marsha went to work. Apparently, she had already made a very good copy of the email provider logo using Paint software. With this, she sent Victoria a phishing email that looked like it came from the provider. In the body of the email, it said that in order to confirm that the user of the account did indeed change the account password, the user had to answer the following security questions. Since Marsha had noted the security questions and answers when they first got into the computer, this part was simple. Victoria promptly gave the correct answers, and then Marsha asked for a confirmation of the new password. Victoria emailed the new password, and Marsha quickly responded, saying Victoria could now use her email.

To Marsha, it was a simple day in the office. To Hal, it was quite astonishing. "What's Two doing?" he asked.

"Looking for the bellbottom woman."

"How?"

"Social media." She turned to look at him. "Just need to see if the woman is active in social media and then look for pictures of her. Once we have a name, we can get to work. I took part of the guest list."

"But you didn't actually see her," Hal pointed out.

"No, but I'm looking for the long hair, probably the tendency to wear bellbottom pants. Anyone simply the right age and long hair, I'm forwarding to Two."

"Don't some people have private social media? You can't see their stuff?"

"Nothing is private when it comes to social media," Marsha scoffed.

"People are told their stuff is private if they mark it private," Hal countered.

"Then guess what?" Marsha retorted. "They are as dumb as a box of rocks."

Hal smiled. "Call it a day."

"Yeah. By the way, the three encrypted files from Adrian Weatherspoon's flat? They're proving difficult to break."

"Go home," Hal said. "You have a family, you know."

"I'll be in tomorrow."

"Tomorrow you're off," he reminded her. "Saturday."

"Eddie is taking the kids to his parents."

"Ah," Hal said with understanding. Her in-laws weren't too fond of her for the simple reason that she was American by birth. Nor were they pleased that their grandchildren held dual citizenships: Dutch and American. "Been a long day, go home."

Surrey, England

"Wake up..! Gretchen, wake up..!" Two said in a raised voice. Gretchen moaned.

Two quickly turned on the bedside lamp. Gretchen squinted at her.

"You've got to wake up!"

The urgency in Two's voice was like cold water drenching her face. "What? What's happened?" She sat up and looked at the clock on the nightstand. Just after midnight. "Is it Adam?"

"I found her!" Two said excitedly. When Gretchen just gave her a baffled look, she said, "The woman killer! Bellbottom killer!"

Now Gretchen understood. "Who is she?"

"Come on. I'll show you." With that, Two left the bedroom. "Hurry!" she called out.

Shuffling out to the great room in a pair of sweats a few minutes later, Gretchen saw Two at her usual spot at the kitchen table, working on her laptop. As soon as Two saw Gretchen, she pointed to the TV. Gretchen turned and saw the image of an attractive woman. The image showed her from head to toe with her wide bellbottom pants in plain view. Her very long hair was parted in the middle and cascaded down below her breast line.

"Who is she?"

"Hana Vrba," Two said. She clicked on something. "That photo is from the party. Posted by someone else."

Text from a social media site now appeared. It read: The always lovely Hana Vrba joined the group at VT's. A fun time by all.

Gretchen said, "VT meaning Victoria Tenney."

"Right. But we've got a big problem," Two said. "Look at this. In the comment section, that same person tells us that Hana Vrba is off to New York." Again text appeared. *Redeye to the big apple tomorrow.*

Gretchen looked at Two. "Lots of people go to New York."

"Elizabeth is going to New York! In minutes. On a redeye!" Two said. "It's tomorrow right now!" Two worked the laptop. "It gets worse! Look at this!"

A black and white picture of a young man and a young teen girl. They were staring at the camera, but not smiling. Their clothes were dirty, their faces showing fatigue. Gretchen went closer to the screen. "That her? Pretty young if it is."

"Fourteen," Two said. "A deep-dive name search came up with this. It's in a Bosnian War museum. Picture taken a number of years after the war, when families were chronically split apart, kids left as orphans. It gives her name, but not his. Just says they are siblings."

"Okay…" Gretchen said, turning back to Two, unsure where she was going with this.

"So I ran him through facial recognition."

The screen now showed two faces side-by-side. The young man in the first picture alongside a picture of the same man taken about ten years later. There were identical lines across the faces from the facial recognition software. The resemblance was easy to see.

"Same guy," Gretchen said.

"Goran Petrovic," Two said.

Gretchen whirled around, stunned. "What?"

"They're sister and brother."

Heathrow International Airport, London, England

Elizabeth had checked all her baggage so she just had the single carry-on, her tote bag, which she wore across her body. This way, she could maneuver on crutches and not need wheelchair assistance. She'd taken a wheelchair from the ticket counter to the gate and was now on her own to board the plane. Fortunately, her boarding pass was marked pre-board which would be of great help. When Adam had said goodbye to her at the ticket counter, the flight was twenty-six minutes late. Now, the departure time had been pushed back another forty minutes, much to her annoyance.

Minutes earlier, after exchanging text messages with Gretchen, she had relinquished her prime spot in the boarding area to do a quick look around. She didn't see the woman anywhere in the boarding area for her flight or in the adjacent gate areas. Nothing. Or at least nothing to her novice eye. No one matching the photo Gretchen had sent was anywhere to be seen. She decided to hobble over to the bar and restaurant up ahead. It was where most travelers had taken refuge when the announcement was made that the flight was further delayed.

As she headed toward a small table for two, she couldn't help but wonder if Gretchen was telling her the truth—that the woman was associated with a Middle Eastern terrorist group. The picture Gretchen sent to Elizabeth's phone looked like a model. The stance. The flared, wide bellbottom pants. The long dark hair. The defiant look on her face. Gretchen said she could be wearing pants like that.

Elizabeth pulled out a chair and sat down heavily, relieved to relinquish the heavy tote bag to the chair next to her. She glanced around but didn't see anyone she thought matched the woman in the picture. Her phone chimed. She took it out of the zippered pocket of her tote. It was from her husband, acknowledging her earlier text that the flight was delayed. He sent her a goofy picture of Mia sitting on the kitchen floor, hugging their dog. God, she missed them. It would be so nice to be home. Even if it was just for a day before they headed out. She sent him an emoji of kisses. Something she never did.

A waitress came over, and Elizabeth ordered a glass of chardonnay. As the waitress left, a family with three teens at a nearby table got up and collected their various carry-on bags. After they cleared out, Elizabeth suddenly saw the woman. Sitting at a small table like hers, maybe twenty feet away. She sat by herself, her head down, working her phone. Elizabeth quickly took a couple of pictures and sent them off to Gretchen. The waitress placed the wine in front of her and she took a long drink.

~ ~ ~

Adam wasn't in a great mood. If he only had his passport with him, he would be on the flight. Upon arriving at JFK, he would find a way to grab Hana Vrba and get to the bottom of things. Mainly, was she really Goran Petrovic's sister? If she had indeed taken out Adrian Weatherspoon earlier that day, was she also a professional assassin? Several things told him yes—Adrian's wound indicated the assailant had purposely stabbed him so he would slowly bleed out. He would be incapable of fending for himself and there would be time to question him. Secondly, killing him on the upper floor, the body between the far wall and the bed, meant he certainly wouldn't be spotted by anyone passing by outside, and, truthfully, he really wouldn't be discovered until someone came inside and did a thorough search.

Moreover, if Hana Vrba was a professional assassin, what were the chances she worked alongside her brother? Probably very good since it looked like both worked for the Redfield family. And along those lines, was it a coincidence that she was on the same flight as Elizabeth—a woman her brother had failed to kill? Was she supposed to finish the job? And had her brother possibly been accused of murders that had been done by her hand?

So many questions, yet the way things had worked out, he would never be able to ask her these things face to face. Hence, the anger.

He had found a twenty-four-hour Tesco market and purchased a couple of candy bars, an iced coffee mocha, a package of wet wipes, a large hoodie, and a pair of driving gloves. He paid with cash, making sure he got lots of coins back in change. Two had texted him several places with working payphones. Or so they hoped. His first choice was a few miles away at a BP gas station. There was no real way to know about cameras, but the call had to be made. A few blocks away from his destination, he pulled over and put on the sweatshirt and gloves.

He did a quick drive-by recon and found the area quiet. Lights on at the gas pumps, which were available twenty-four hours a day, but no one currently getting gas, which was good. The adjacent convenience store and garage were closed, a couple of exterior lights on at the buildings but nothing to deter him. The payphone was attached to the far side of the convenience store, no light over it. Good. In case there were cameras recording, he parked well away from the lights and got out of the car, pulling up the hood of his sweatshirt.

At the payphone, he took out his cell phone and found the stopwatch app. Obviously, they'd immediately know where he was calling from, but he wanted to keep it short and sweet. He told himself to speak for no more than a minute. That way, even having his location, he'd be long gone in five-minutes time. He put in his coins and dialed the number for MI6 first. He started the timer while the line was still ringing. Once a live voice answered, he spoke with an American accent. "Listen up. A bomb is going off tomorrow—"

The MI6 person started to interrupt. Adam cut him off. "Shut up and listen, asshole. You're recording this so shut up. A woman named Hana Vrba is flying out tonight on a redeye to New York. She is going to set off a bomb at Piccadilly Circus tomorrow. Lots of tourists. It's a Saturday. She will do it remotely, using her phone once she's in New York. She's stuck at Heathrow right now. Her plane is delayed. Hana Vrba." He then spelled her last name, knowing that in mere seconds, they could find her on the flight manifest. "If you don't get her yourselves, right now, she'll be in the wind. Our FBI is a total joke—"

"Can I have your name, please?" the male voice on the other end interrupted again.

"No, shut up and listen," Adam angrily retorted. "Hana Vrba. She is in the boarding area right now. Besides the bomb, she killed a man today. Last name Weatherspoon, killed at his flat." Adam gave the address. He had no clue if the body had been found yet, but the CCTV footage with Hana Vrba needed to be seen as soon as possible. They wouldn't be able to find a bomb tied to her, but they would find a body and that would hopefully keep her locked up.

He went on. "You need to understand she is the sister of Goran Petrovic—the assassin that you probably know turned up in the Netherlands... She is his sister—"

"Sir, if—"

"Right now, her flight is delayed, so get going. If she is allowed to take off, a lot of people are going to die tomorrow."

Adam hung up as the man was saying something. He hit the stopwatch app at just past a minute. Not perfect, but good enough. He then dialed 999 for emergency services and told the dispatcher everything he told MI6, minus the link between Goran Petrovic and Hana Vrba. That wasn't something the local police needed to concern themselves with.

After he hung up, he pulled several wet wipes from the package and thoroughly cleaned off the handset and the keypad. Even though he was wearing gloves, he didn't want a spec of DNA to be found anywhere. Placing the used wet wipes in one pocket and his phone in the other, he headed for the car, thinking about the chocolate bars and iced coffee awaiting him.

Chapter Seventeen

Heathrow International Airport, London, England

Elizabeth's heart was in her throat. Of all the incredibly bad luck. Her heart beating wildly, she said, "Sorry for the inconvenience."

The woman—some sort of wanted terrorist according to Gretchen—gave a nonchalant hand wave. "Nah. It's fine."

Elizabeth had been sitting comfortably in her first-class aisle seat when the woman showed up standing next to her, wanting access to the window seat. These two seats were in the very first row, offering a spacious two-foot gap between the seats and bulkhead wall. A gap that would allow her to fully extend her casted leg.

With the woman standing next to her, waiting, Elizabeth pulled in her outstretched legs and tamped down her raw fear as the woman moved past and took her seat. The only good thing was that at least in first class there was plenty of space between the two seats. The woman had no sooner gotten seated than the flight attendant asked the woman if she would be okay assisting Elizbeth should there be an emergency. The flight attendant explained that it would be up to the woman to fetch the crutches from the first-class closet and assist Elizabeth to the nearest exit.

The woman had actually paid attention to the instructions and promised to follow them to the letter should an emergency arise. Elizabeth gave the woman a polite nod of thanks. The entire situation was so ironic. A female terrorist, who she had been warned to stay well away from, was now seated next to her and had dutifully pledged to assist her in case of an in-flight emergency. What a joke.

Elizabeth's phone chirped. She kept the phone's screen tilted away from her seat mate. The text was from Gretchen. *Any sightings?*

Elizabeth typed her reply. Sitting next to me in first class.

Please tell me you are joking.

Hardly.

Okay, sit tight.

Sit tight? Did she have a choice?

"Look at this," the female terrorist said.

Elizabeth turned. The woman had rolled up the sleeve of her left arm. A jagged deep scar was visible from the heel of her hand to mid-forearm. Elizabeth looked at her. "That's awful."

"Six surgeries. Six! All so I can move my wrist and fingers." The woman demonstrated that the surgeries had worked, she could flex her wrist in all directions and open and close all her fingers quite adroitly. The woman motioned to Elizabeth's leg. "So I get it. I do."

"Thank you."

"How'd you do it?"

Elizabeth was momentarily taken back. "Oh, car accident." She looked at the woman's long scar. "You?"

"I was tossed off a second-floor balcony." When she saw Elizabeth's jaw drop, she laughed. "True story. Broke several ribs." She lifted her arm. "And this, of course."

"That's terrible," Elizabeth managed to say.

"Hana Vrba?" a man's voice asked. "You need to come with us."

Elizabeth turned, surprised to see a uniformed policeman standing in the aisle. Another policeman, quite a bit beefier, stood right behind the first cop.

The woman narrowed her eyes. "Thanks, but no."

"Ma'am, you have to come with us," the cop said.

"On what grounds?" the woman defiantly asked.

The cop looked to Elizabeth. "Ma'am, I'm going to need you to stand in the aisle."

Elizabeth glanced at the woman next to her. The woman's face had suddenly changed. A mask of pure anger, pure defiance. Her phone in hand, Elizabeth got up as the policeman directed her further down the aisle. However, without her crutches, she had no choice but to hold on to her own seatback. She wasn't going any further, but the policeman didn't seem to care. Nor did he care that several nearby passengers were filming the episode.

"Ms. Vrba, please come with us," the cop repeated.

"You have no authority—"

"Ma'am, please. Let's not make a scene."

"Fuck you. I'm not moving."

He asked her one more time to step out into the aisle. She didn't even respond. With surprising quickness, he stepped in front of Elizabeth's seat and grabbed Hana Vrba by the upper arm. "Come along please."

"Don't touch me!" She half-rose from her seat and violently twisted out of his grasp as if it was child's play.

Surprised, the cop moved forward again, but the terrorist was ready, placing one hand on the armrest and pivoting sharply to kick the man in the face. He cried out and flew backward, cupping his bloody nose in his hands. His partner caught him from falling as passengers started screaming. Once the first cop had his balance, the second cop elbowed his way between the bulkhead and the seats as the enraged woman came after him. But he used his large body to deflect the incoming blows and deftly immobilized her on the floor. Elizabeth watched as he pinned his knee in her back, and quickly handcuffed her as she tried to buck him off.

She saw others filming the show with their phones and quickly joined in. Only for her, the video would go to some very important people.

The hefty cop lifted the woman to her feet and escorted her off the plane as she yelled vulgar cusswords and thrashed about to no effect.

Surrey, England ~ The Next Day

"Good morning," Hal said from the TV screen.

Adam raised his coffee to the screen in mock salute.

Hal and Marsha were sitting at the FROG conference-room table, Marsha busy on her laptop.

"You awake?" Hal asked.

"Getting there." Adam looked at Gretchen sitting in the other overstuffed chair. She too was drinking coffee and trying to wake up. Two was between them on the floor, stretched out on her back, her hands laced behind her head on a pillow, her eyes closed. Hal had been mocking them when he said "Good morning" since it was early afternoon, but in their defense, all three of them had been up most of the night.

"Marsha, what did you find out about Hana Vrba's flight?" Gretchen asked.

Marsha looked up and beamed. "Great news, guys. She booked her flight six weeks ago. Six weeks ago! Elizabeth booked her flight four days ago."

Gretchen gave Adam a devilish grin. "So you're saying there really are coincidences in life."

Adam gave her a playful smile. He was the conspiracy nut in FROG, and he took the ribbing well. "Let's just say that it didn't look like that just a few hours ago. And it's good to know. It means Elizabeth should be in the clear."

"What did you tell her about Hana Vrba?" Hal asked.

"I told her she was a terrorist and to stay well away from her," Gretchen said.

"And then they end up sitting next to each other on the plane," Two jested. "Wonder what the odds are of that happening?"

"You guys saw the video from the arrest, right?" Gretchen asked. "Elizabeth sent that and then all other passenger videos went viral too."

"We got it," Marsha confirmed. "I got into the Met." This basically meant that Marsha had hacked into the British Metropolitan Police system. "They found the body of Charles Adrian Weatherspoon, and, from what I can see, they've found the video of her coming and going."

"And nothing of us?" Adam asked. "Coming and going?"

"I told you that yesterday," Marsha said, clearly annoyed.

"Trust but verify… Trust but verify."

"You're verified, got it?" she retorted.

"His problem is, he doesn't get what we do," said Two, her eyes still closed. "So he needs a little hand holding."

"Hand holding?" Adam asked, looking down at her. "Really?"

"In a good way," she replied, smiling happily, her eyes still closed.

"Anything about the payphone?" Adam asked.

"Crickets," Marsha said.

"Why didn't you use a burner, toss it in some waterway?" Hal asked.

Adam knew what Hal was thinking. If he had used a burner, he could have called from the car, no way he might be on some camera at the gas station using a payphone. He replied, "It was past midnight. No place to buy one, and the call had to be made."

Hal raised his hands in defense. "Just curious."

Two said, "There are cameras on that road, but I corrupted twenty minutes of it—long before he shows up and long after he leaves. If they look, they'll presume the cameras went wobbly. What I don't know is if there are cameras at the gas station, but I can go up there today and take a look around."

"No, no," Hal said. "Leave it... Adam, anyone at the gas station at that time?"

"No one." He looked to Marsha. "What's MI6 doing with the information we gave them, do we know?"

London, England

The original plan—to get lost in the crowds at Piccadilly Circus—was scuttled by police barricades and rumors about a bomb threat. To Oliver's way of thinking, there was no bomb anywhere near the area. No way. It was simply some psycho getting their jollies by shutting down a popular destination for both locals and tourists.

So, like hundreds of others, Oliver and Taylor made their way to Trafalgar Square, which would serve as an alternative hangout. Always popular with those seeking the culture of galleries and museums, it offered plenty of places to grab a bite along with entertainment by way of sidewalk artists and performers. Moreover, the location was often used by protesters busy protesting whatever that day's issue might be. Today, a dozen protesters were advocating for the rights of toads. Yes, toads.

Oliver had purchased the burner phone and SIM card with cash at a flea market, making sure it had a sufficient charge. In his pocket, he had the Netherlands cell number used for the authentication code to set up the Gmail account. For the umpteenth time, Oliver told himself this was a waste of time. Whoever had hacked into the Redfield Steed account was long gone. Their burner phone was probably tossed soon after activating the Gmail account.

However, he couldn't leave it alone. They had used Taylor's name, placing her in mortal danger. They were probably the ones that stole Victoria Tenney's laptop computer. The timing of both made sense. And so, he had purchased his own burner phone to talk to them. Providing they still had their phone and would talk. But he didn't want to communicate with them from their flat. He wanted a very public place just in case these people, whoever they were, had the capability to trace his location. Normally, he would say that capability only rested with America's NSA or England's GCHQ, the Government Communications Headquarters. However, whoever had breached the Redfield system and logged in to the Steed file was good. Very good. So it was best to reach out to them while in a very public place. Hiding in plain sight, as the saying went. Which was why he and Taylor now sat on the front steps of the National Gallery, both tourists and locals alike streaming past.

Taylor tapped his arm and said, "You called it. Look around."

He followed her look. There were quite a few others doing just as they were—sitting on the front steps, most looking at their phones.

Surrey, England

Adam, Gretchen, and Two stood in front of the television screen that now displayed the thread of the entire text message exchange. The group's scheduled teleconference with Hal and Marsha back at FROG Headquarters had been interrupted by the chime of the burner phone. Gretchen found it on the kitchen table, declaring it would be spam and she'd turn it off. Hal reminded her to get rid of it. But when she looked at the screen, she couldn't believe it. She came back into the great room and said, "Text message. It says, *You are evil. You placed Taylor's life in danger with your little stunt.*"

"Who's Taylor?" Hal asked, baffled.

"I used him to get into the Steed account," Marsha said. "Remember? We couldn't get in with Victoria's credentials, so we looked for a tech-support person at Redfield, thinking that might get us in."

"Right, right, right," Hal replied.

"And that Taylor guy, he worked with Victoria Tenney on a computer issue, so we figured he might be high up enough to get us in," Two said.

"Oh, man," Marsha said. "Gretchen, ask if he is okay. Taylor."

"Wait," Two said. "Let me do it on my computer and share it." She was referring to a computer app that allowed her to send and receive text messages on the computer. This way, she could link the text messages in real time to their television and via encryption software to the screen in the conference room. She grabbed her laptop, moved to the sofa, and started working. "Okay, here we go."

Her message appeared on the television. *Is he okay?*

As if you give a shit, came the reply.

Adam frowned. "It was certainly never our intention to cause potential harm to anyone."

"Perfect," Gretchen exclaimed, turning to Two who typed out the message.

Two looked at Adam. "Send?"

"Send it," Adam said.

It was certainly never our intention to cause potential harm to anyone popped up on the screen.

Adam continued. "Add, You should know as well as anyone that enough Redfield employees have died."

The message displayed on the television. They waited in silence for a reply. There was nothing. Hal said, "That's it? He's gone?"

"Someone is typing. I can see it here," Gretchen said, studying the burner.

A new text popped up on the television screen. *Who are you?*

"None of your business," Adam scoffed. "Don't type that... Let's list the names of the dead. I give a name, hit send. I give a name, hit send. That way he'll see a bunch in a list form. Ready?"

"Yep, go," Two replied.

"William DeWine."

They watched as the text appeared. *William DeWine*

"Bart Werner."

Then Bart's name. *Bert Werner*

"Mac Senton."

Mac Senton

London, England

Taylor pivoted the phone in Oliver's hand so she could see it better. They exchanged looks. "Who are these guys?"

Oliver shook his head. He had no idea.

"What if it is Ethan Redfield, playing us?" Taylor asked. He started to type, and she squeezed his hand. He looked at her. "We don't know who these people are! We could be signing our own death warrants!"

"If Ethan knew, we'd be dead by now."

"You don't know that!" Taylor argued.

"Please. We agreed to tell them off, but something's going on, and we need to play along."

Taylor's eyes watered.

Oliver held her look. "Or I'll stop, we'll toss the phone, the SIM card, their phone number, and we go live our lives. But I have a feeling about this."

"A feeling of what?"

"Let's play along. That's all. A few more minutes." He waited, and she finally nodded in agreement.

He started typing.

Surrey, England

Finally, a response came. Mac Senton took his own life. Pedophile. It's public knowledge.

Adam took a deep breath.

Gretchen looked at the texts on the screen. "I say we tell this person we were there, we witnessed the whole thing, Mac was in a corner, and all that."

Hal's voice came over the speaker. "I agree."

"Okay," Adam said, turning to Two. "Don't hit send until I say so."

"Agreed," Two said. "Go."

As Adam spoke, Two typed. She read it back.

"I say we send it," Adam said.

"I agree," Gretchen offered.

"Do it. Send," Hal agreed.

When she hit send from her computer, the text appeared on the television. "Sorry, mate. He was a good man. Trying to get to the bottom of Steed and prevent many, many people from dying in the near future. But the Redfields found out they had a traitor in their midst. He died to save his young daughter.

London, England

Taylor was aghast. "You think it's true?"

"I don't know," Oliver said, quickly typing.

Surrey, England

A new message. A young Dutch girl was kidnapped. Escaped. Read the news.

Adam said, "Type yes, but Mac was told to kill her. He was never a killer. So he drove around in that handicap van—"

"Slow down," Two told him.

Adam continued pacing and dictating the message he wanted sent. Then he abruptly stopped and said, "After that, tell this guy that others have died. Not just Redfield employees."

"Just a minute," she said. "Give me a minute to catch up."

When she'd finished, the text read, Yes, but Mac was told to kill her. He was never a killer. So he drove around in that handicap van keeping her alive. I was there when he died. He got only so far with his look into Steed. He didn't want his daughter to be killed. These guys are capable of it. You know that.

After Adam dictated the next message, it went on: *"There are more deaths. At the café,*

some innocent old ladies. Claire and Arabella Werner—Bart Werner's aunt and cousin.

Then another: More innocent deaths, NOT at the café, are Nancy Ellison, racecar driver, and Hans Wolter in the Netherlands.

The final message read, Check out what I'm telling you. We'll talk again when you know what you're talking about.

London, England

They watched as the older man very carefully put the wand and electric device in their allotted foam cut-out spaces of his carrying case. He then zipped the top closed, took hold of the handle, and gave them a pleasant smile.

"Thanks so much," Oliver said, showing him to the door.

"Peace of mind, I always say. Peace of mind."

"Right." After the man had left, Oliver locked the door and looked to Taylor.

"He's right. About the peace of mind," she said.

He stepped forward and wrapped her in his arms. It had been a long day, and paying the man to be sure there were no bugs in the flat had been worth it. They were in the clear. "We're safe," he told her.

After their text-message exchanges with whoever had hacked Red Arrow Capital, they had both been spooked. They went to a pub that had two computers at the far end of the bar for customer use. One was in use, but Taylor grabbed the other and went to work, only occasionally taking a sip of the chardonnay in front of her. First, she downloaded Tor, a free, open-source software that enables anonymous communication, onto the pub's desktop. It would scramble the pub's IP address so that if her searches did produce red flags somewhere, the pub's location would remain unseen.

Then she searched the name Hans Wolter. There were several men with that name, but only that she could confirm had recently died. That Hans Wolter had been a very wealthy Amsterdam resident who had died from cancer. There was absolutely nothing that she could find linking him to anything even remotely nefarious. There was a chance that he was a client of Red Arrow Capital, but that would be easy enough to find out at the office.

As for Nancy Ellison, she had been a Formula race-car driver who died in a fiery crash during a practice run in Turkey. In digging around, Taylor found images of Mac Senton and Nancy Ellison. A couple, it looked like. Finally, a link to one of their dead employees. They had no idea what it meant, but it was something.

"We're safe," Oliver repeated when they returned from the pub. He pulled back and looked at Taylor. "You okay?"

She gave a sheepish smile.

"We know the house is safe. Talk to me."

"I dunno. I mean, we found whoever was texting us was right. Those people died. An old man in Amsterdam. A race-car driver who probably knew Mac Senton. And more importantly, how do we find the connection?"

"We don't," Oliver said.

"What do you mean?" Taylor frowned.

"Whoever we were talking to, they've done the homework on that. They know the connection. They just wanted *us* to know."

"Know what?" she asked in frustration. "It's not like any of this makes sense."

Oliver considered this. "If I had to guess, it's to say they are the good guys. The Redfield family are the bad guys, not them. They were hacking around, using your name, for a greater good. They said Mac Senton wanted to prevent the death of 'many, many people.'"

She thought on it briefly, then looked up at him. "You really think those others they told us to check out were killed?" she asked. "Murdered?"

"I don't know. It's probably rare, but race-car drivers have been killed. Old men with cancer, guess what? They die. So I don't know. But if they were murdered... This is a lot bigger than we thought. And they told us about it, so we know they are the good guys."

Taylor's eyes suddenly widened with alarm. "They told us because they need inside help. They're going to ask us to help them."

FROG Headquarters, The Hague ~ Two Days Later

Marsha glanced at the clock. Forty minutes until the teleconference. She looked back at her monitor, relieved to have cracked the puzzle. Rising from her chair, she did some stretches. She had been at her desk since seven that morning. Four hours. She suddenly realized that she was famished.

Her great intention of taking advantage of her family's weekend absence by working both Saturday and Sunday at the office had never come to pass. Quite simply, by Sunday morning, fatigue had set in before she could even fix herself breakfast, and she spent most of the day napping on the sofa. She knew quite well from experience that if she didn't listen to her body she would pay a heavy price later.

She had texted Two and told her to take the day off. Whatever they thought they had to do immediately could wait twenty-four hours. But Two had texted back that she wanted to do a deep dive on whoever Taylor B. was at Red Arrow Capital, arguing that they needed to know who they were exchanging texts with—if indeed that was who they were communicating with. Two wanted to get the last name and then find out everything they could on the guy. But Marsha told her to get some rest. Taylor could wait. Two had reluctantly agreed, provided Marsha was really at home relaxing and not on her laptop. Marsha ended up sending a selfie, showing her in her pj's curled up on the sofa with the family cat. So Sunday, most appropriately, became a day of rest for everyone.

Except Gretchen.

When Marsha had arrived at the office early Monday morning, she found a status report from Gretchen. Admitting that curiosity had gotten the better of her, she had driven to the BP gas station to see if there were cameras that might have captured Adam using the payphone. She had found a single camera facing the gas pumps. She had gone inside the convenience store and waited patiently as the Indian proprietor rung up a sale. Once the customer left, she stepped forward and said, "Police," flashing her fake AIVD credentials. When she asked about the camera, she was gruffly informed that she was late to the game—but he would give her the same answer he had given all the other law enforcement people that had descended upon his place. He'd told her if she would like to pay for new camera—one that would actually work—he would be more than happy to install it.

Marsha had smiled to herself.

Surrey, England

"Really? This is important?" Adam grumbled. "Why?" He was standing several feet away from the television, sipping a smoothie that Gretchen had made. Ironically, when she first offered him a glass, he had waved her off, insisting that smoothies weren't his thing. She persuaded him to at least taste it, so he did—and then asked for a full glass.

"Would I be showing it to you if it wasn't important?" Marsha's curt voice came over the television soundbar. "Patience."

When the teleconference had started, Marsha reminded them that the USB Gretchen had found at Adrian Weatherspoon's home contained three encrypted files that had taken a while to decipher. Finally, she had a video for them to watch.

Two sat on the sofa and Gretchen was in the big side chair.

The video began with black people—very dark-skinned—smiling and laughing as they walked toward the camera. Women working a nearby field with what looked like knee-high grass were encouraged to come and they quickly did. Those outside their homes—a woman hanging laundry on a line, two children playing with a soccer ball—stopped what they were doing to join the procession. As they passed more buildings, some brightly painted, more people tagged along. While the surroundings looked bleak, the group was not bleak at all—in fact, they were talking animatedly, happy, speaking in a curious foreign language.

"Translation?" Adam said.

"Working on that," Marsha said. "But this is self-explanatory. Be quiet and watch."

The video showed the group finally stop outside one building, gathering close together and chatting excitedly about something. The people separated so the camera could move in close, focusing on a water spigot attached to the building. The camera pulled back to show a large black man with a bald head and long gray beard standing next to the spigot. He said something, reached down, and turned on the water. There was a moment of silent astonishment before the entire group erupted in joyful screams. Several tentatively came forward, almost afraid. The large man gestured, said something, and several people bravely touched the running water. A few then put their fingers to their mouths, tasting it.

There was a small black girl, wearing a frayed top, who got very close to the spigot, squatting down and studying it. She looked at the gray-bearded man and asked something. He gave a reply, and she carefully put her right hand near the water. She wore a brightly colored pink and white beaded bracelet that contrasted nicely with her dark skin. Finally, she put her entire hand through the running water. Then the other hand. One forearm, then the other. Back and forth, back and forth, one arm, then the other. Suddenly, she was laughing with glee, saying something to the others. She stood, faced the observers, and held up her wet right arm for all to see. As water dripped off her colorful bracelet, she tried to catch the drips in her mouth.

Before long, she got down on her back and let the water spray her face, giggling the whole time. This prompted more kids to descend on the spigot, all of them immersing themselves in the water. There was some commotion, a shout, and the kids immediately stopped playing in the water and obediently stood aside. An old, dark-skinned woman with a lined face and long purple ribbons woven into her long gray hair shuffled forward using a yellow cane. The large bald man gave her a respectful nod, stooped, and turned off the spigot. The old woman asked something. He said something and turned it back on. Now a younger woman came up and helped the old woman step closer. The younger woman then cupped her hands, gathering water and offered it to the woman. The old woman grasped the younger woman's hands and drank the water.

The camera stayed on the two women, their hands meshed together.

The screen went black briefly, and then the video resumed.

The same buildings seen in the earlier, joyous procession. But unlike the first video, in this one, there was no one around. Not a single soul. The place was now deserted. A wind blew the soft dirt into swirls across the area. The camera proceeded past the brightly colored buildings, moving through knee-high grass for quite a distance. Up ahead, a large mound of dirt could be seen. The camera advanced toward it.

Suddenly the earth dropped away, revealing a large, deep pit. Filled with scores of dark-skinned corpses. A mass grave.

The video shifted from one horror scene to another: the large bald man now haphazardly splayed across other bodies, his long gray beard seeming alive and fluttering in the wind. Nearby, the back of a head with long gray hair and intertwined purple ribbons, and like the bald man's beard, a few purple ribbons blew in the wind. A naked woman with a very swollen belly, the last stages of pregnancy, lay amidst the jumble of bodies. A child's arm, frozen in time, a pink and white bracelet on the wrist.

The video ended.

Chapter Eighteen

Surrey, England

At the safe house, the large screen went back to showing a live image of Marsha and Hal. Marsha said, "We've got another video coming."

"Two more," Hal corrected her. "You said there was a total of three."

"This was one and two. Zebra spliced them together." Marsha was referring to a FROG tech who was great at unraveling encrypted text and video. He had gotten the nickname Zebra due to his preference for wearing wide-striped T-shirts. Every single day, without fail.

Two asked, "So, what? Looks like rural Africa, right? They get running water and it kills them? That little girl..." She couldn't finish her thought.

"It is Africa," Marsha said. She looked at Gretchen. "Remember you made a voice memo on your phone, echoing Adrian Weatherspoon's dying words?"

Gretchen remembered. "Yeah. He said, 'You gone,' and a guy named Lou something, I think?"

"Yeah, a Lou Tet," Adam confirmed. "You able to find him?"

"He wasn't talking about a person," Marsha said. "It's a place. Lutete as one word with an E at the end. L-U-T-E-T-E. Lutete."

"Which is where, exactly?" Adam challenged.

"Uganda." Marsha smiled and said the country name slowly. "U... Gan—"

"Oh man," Adam suddenly interrupted, getting it now. "I thought he was saying, 'You gone.' Like I, you, me."

"We missed that completely," Gretchen agreed. "He said the Lou Tet part first, then died saying what we thought were the words, 'You gone.'"

"I only got the location Lutete, Uganda, when I saw these two videos and started working backwards," Marsha admitted. "I

231

thought, why would Adrian have these videos, encrypted and hidden away, unless it had something to do with his company, Al Friqet Industries? A company that specializes in water treatment, right? And lo and behold, they put in the running water—"

"In Lutete?" Gretchen interrupted.

"Actually, no," Marsha said. "Lutete is a fairly big city that already has running water. But Al Friqet Industries put in the water for a small village about twenty miles southeast of Lutete. The African name of the village I can't even begin to pronounce and guess what? It is known as Little Lutete."

"Oh, man," Adam said, shaking his head.

"What?" Hal asked.

Adam grimaced. "To me, I mean, he was dying. So it was like a stutter... L-L, then Lou Tet, two separate words, I thought a man's name."

"But he was trying to say Little Lutete," Gretchen said.

"That's what I'm thinking, yeah," Adam said.

Hal turned to Marsha. "We know what went wrong? Adrian Weatherspoon screw up? He's an engineer—"

"I don't think so," Adam said, looking at Gretchen. "Remember? He wanted to make it right. Those were his words, 'make it right.'" He realized that everyone was baffled. "I kept pushing him about the money from Victoria Tenney. She paid him a big chunk of money, so I was thinking blackmail. I kept pressing him on that. That's when he said he was 'trying to make it right.' Then he gave us the village name."

"So, what did happen exactly?" Two asked. "All those people... I mean..."

"Nothing on the Al Friqet Industries website," Marsha explained. "In fact, you have to dig pretty hard to find out that they even did the water system there. You only find a mention of the village in the local media—the common refrain being that the village was hit by a virus."

"Nothing to do with the water," Two said cynically.

"This video says the two are linked," Hal agreed. "So the question is, was Adrian Weatherspoon killed for this? What he knew about the village? Keep him from talking?"

"It's a lot more than that!" Gretchen said angrily. "He and Victoria Tenney certainly knew each other, had some sort of relationship—"

"I'd argue that they were lovers," Two injected.

Gretchen nodded. "Okay, fine. So the water is put in, people die. You ask me, Steed invested in that company knowing full well about the village. I'll bet you any amount of money that this went according to plan."

"Call Elizabeth," Hal interrupted, looking at Gretchen. "She's in the US somewhere. Wake her up. I want her to tell us who else in the Steed portfolio does water reclamation, water resource projects, hell, water systems of any kind."

Gretchen started for the kitchen where she had left her cell phone charging. But she turned back and pointed her finger toward the TV, at Hal and Marsha. "This was a planned massacre. I'll bet you any amount of money."

"We don't know that!" Hal retorted. "What's your rational basis? There is none. No rational basis—"

"The hell there isn't!" Gretchen retorted. "Mac Senton sent Elizabeth a stick of lipstick that had a USB with the imbedded message that whatever was going on, they are going to create a problem that they have the solution for... What were his words? 'Hatching a plot that they have the solution for, ready to sell.' I remember that part, 'ready to sell.'"

Adam quickly agreed with Gretchen's sentiment. "Water is the essence of life, so somehow, reverse all that and suddenly it takes life. And you have the means to help clean it up."

"We're floating theories," Hal told them. "We need more."

"Okay, fine, we'll go ask this Adrian guy why he had that video on his thumb drive," Gretchen said sarcastically, stomping stomped off toward the kitchen.

"I'm with Gretchen," Adam said. "This was done on purpose. How? I don't know. And unfortunately, Adrian took the answer to his grave. But you ask me, that African village was a trial run."

"Well, they succeeded marvelously," Two said bitterly.

Somewhere in South Carolina, USA

As a general rule, Elizabeth despised Zoom calls. But this wasn't technically a Zoom call—it was something used by the AIVD security agency that was much better than Zoom in terms of picture quality and sound. Most important, Two promised it was very safe. Even if a bad guy knew about the call, they wouldn't be able to hack in.

Just twenty minutes ago, Gretchen had called her, asking if it was possible that the group run something past her. It was urgent. Elizabeth said it wouldn't be a problem. Which was true— England was five hours ahead and everyone in the South Carolina house was just starting to lift their heads and start the day. She had told her husband that she needed to take an important call and locked herself in the tidy office of the Airbnb house, confident that she wouldn't be disturbed.

She could see Hal and Marsha in one frame and Adam, Two, and Gretchen in the other. As soon as everyone was online, she couldn't help but say, "Gretchen said everything's okay, but I have to say, you guys are scaring the crap out of me."

It was Hal who answered. "You're fine. All is good, I promise."

"I'm so afraid we're going to be found," Elizabeth said. "Then you call me, say we need to do this call, and —"

"We need your little gray cells," Adam interrupted. "Your brain cells. Nothing is wrong. As Hal said, you're safe. Hell, we don't even know where you are, right?"

"As if you couldn't find me," she scoffed.

Adam ignored that and said, "Honest, we need your help on something. You have the Steed file in front of you?"

"Yeah, yeah, hold on." Elizabeth opened the hard copy of the file. "What's going on? Is it connected to that woman terrorist who was on my plane?"

"Nope, she's a different kettle of fish and nothing to do with you or this case," Adam explained. "As I think Gretchen told you, we got word that she was on a redeye to New York and found out she was scheduled to be on your flight, so we asked for some assistance. And thank you for that. A huge thank you."

Elizabeth gave a tight smile, still not quite sure what this was all about.

Hal said, "You've spent time going through the companies that this fund has taken positions in, correct?"

"Yes and no," she said, annoyed. "I did just arrive here. I've got kids to deal with. My sister will be here later today, and my husband—"

"Right, right," Hal said. "I thought maybe on the flight—"

"You're kidding, right?" Elizabeth made a face. "The way my flight started, I sort of drank myself silly across the pond."

"Okay, got it." Hal's disappoint was very clear.

"But tell me what's going on."

"We're hoping you can just give us information that might save us quite a few man hours to get on our own."

"Okay..." Elizabeth replied.

"We know there is a company called Al Friqet Industries on the Steed portfolio. They're headquartered in Dubai..."

Elizabeth suddenly got it. Her eyes got big. "That's the company that that man worked for. He was at Victoria Tenney's big party, and she wanted him dead." The others looked uncomfortable, and she quickly went on. "I looked into it when I was with you. We know Steed has a large position in the company."

"Right," Hal said. "We need to know if there are any other companies like that. Specifically, companies that specialize in making safe drinking water? Water treatment companies of any kind?"

Elizabeth shook her head. "I honestly have no clue off the top of my head. I'll have to do some looking. At a quick glance when I was with you guys, I didn't see anything that raised red flags on anything, really."

"Red flags meaning?" Adam asked.

"Wait, come to think of it, one holding did strike me as odd." She quickly started turning pages, searching.

"Odd, how?" Adam impatiently asked.

Elizabeth kept looking through the pages. "Something like a hundred acres in Chile... It's the only thing they have in the portfolio with no earnings. Zilch. I remember thinking, why would Redfield be interested in that?"

"Could just be they got wind someone else wants it, maybe for development? So they're going to flip it?" Hal asked.

Elizabeth frowned. "I don't know. It's odd, that's all I can say. But I'll do some digging and send an email."

"Look," Hal said. "Right now, we want Steed investments in any company, public or private, that specializes in water treatment, wastewater, maybe clean-up of toxic waterways, that kind of thing."

"Yeah, okay..." Elizabeth slowly replied. "Is this what Mac was looking into? Why he died?"

Surrey, England

"I'm sick."

"You're not sick."

"Don't call me a liar!" Freddy complained. "I never lie."

Oliver and Taylor exchanged looks. Freddy had a very valid point. He never lied. He couldn't lie. It was like he had been born with this unique genetic code that didn't allow for telling lies.

Taylor glanced over her shoulder. Freddy was scrunched in the back seat of the Mini Cooper, studying his iPad. Given that he was over six feet in height and the Mini Cooper's back seat was more suitable for a toddler, well, Freddy was uncomfortable to say the least. She and Oliver had already moved their front seats forward, but even so, it was a very tight fit in the back.

She said, "Freddy?" Nothing. He was engrossed in whatever was on his screen. "Freddy!" she repeated, louder.

"Hmm?" Freddy replied, focused on the iPad.

"Freddy! Look at me!" She tapped him on the knee. "Freddy!"

Finally, he looked up. "What?"

"If you're carsick, you have to look around a bit, okay?"

Freddy actually followed her advice and immediately said, "I don't like this place."

Oliver looked at Freddy in the rearview mirror. "What's not to like? It's green and lush."

"We're not in the city. It's icky." He went back to looking at his iPad.

Taylor looked to Oliver and shook her head. Oliver looked in the rearview mirror again. "We on course?"

Nothing from Freddy.

Oliver looked at Taylor with a grin and winked. "We're on track."

"I didn't say that," Freddy whined.

"We're on track," Oliver repeated.

"Yeah, we're on track..." Freddy agreed.

~ ~ ~

"Guys? Guys!" Two said, her eyes glued on her computer.

"What?" Adam asked, standing in the great room. Gretchen had gone on a run, the text messages coming so infrequently that she hardly needed to sit there waiting for the next one. She wanted fresh air and craved some hard running. Adam understood and had told her to go.

"I think we're being tracked."

"What!?" Marsha yelled, her image on the television screen.

"Whoever we've been talking to, they were always in London," Two reminded them. "Moving around, but inside the city limits."

Two was referring to the data she had been gathering from the text-message location tracker app on her laptop. Unlike the last time they had exchanged text messages with whoever was on the other end, this time, they were prepared. Two had downloaded the FROG proprietary location app on her computer. As soon as the first text appeared on the burner—more than two hours ago now—they mirrored the transmission to their own burner number, which immediately unmasked the phone number that had previously shown as "unknown." Two plugged the phone number into the software program and let it go to work. Within minutes, they could pinpoint the phone's exaction location, down to a few inches. The fact that the phone seemed to be randomly moving around London hadn't been a big help.

"Where are they now?" Marsha asked.

"Heading down the A244," Two said.

"They know the location of the safe house?" Hal asked Marsha.

"The fact that it took this long to get this close, I would say doubtful," Marsha replied. "I have a hunch they have the ability to get a good triangulation, but who really knows?" She looked at Adam. "Turn off the phone. Now."

Adam looked to Two. "How far out?"

Two clicked on the program. "Twenty-one clicks. In miles that is—"

"Thirteen miles," Adam replied.

Marsha calmly said, "Just turn it off. Completely off."

"No," Adam countered. He looked at Hal and Marsha on the TV screen. "They want us? Well, guess what? I want them."

"You want who?" Hal replied angrily.

"I think it's that Taylor guy from the IT department," Adam said. "He's pissed we used him to gain access. Maybe he's got a friend, but I don't think this is Redfield and his goons."

"You don't know that!" Hal fumed. "You are making assumptions not based in fact. And if you want to do that, then you need to consider another assumption... For all you know, Redfield and his people found out that guy—Taylor—they found out he breached the Steed file, his body is now floating in the Thames and they've got his phone."

"True..." Adam conceded nonchalantly.

Two said, "Definitely headed our way. Eighteen clicks now..."

"Adam, turn off the damn phone!" Hal demanded "Now!"

"Yeah?" he countered. "And how does that help us?"

"You know how many are coming your way? Do you?" Hal argued. "How heavily armed?"

Two looked at Marsha. "I should have stayed on them. For the last hour, they were in the greater London area... I thought—"

"Stop," Marsha interrupted. "We all presumed they were riding around so *we couldn't pinpoint them*. We didn't flip it around that they may be trying to pin you down."

Adam stepped closer to the television. "I say we string them along. Find out who we're dealing with."

"You seem to be forgetting that you are hanging out there in a safe house. You're hardly armed. What? A couple of guns? Against the unknown. Could be two tech geeks, but it could also be an unknown assailant with an unknown number of weapons. No!"

"I'll get them off this location, if they even have it," Adam argued. He grabbed the burner from the living room table and turned it off. "It's off." He fiddled some more. "SIM card out." He held it up for them to see. "I'll head out. When I find a good place, I'll put it back together and turn it back on."

Hal frowned. The truth was, he was in The Hague and Adam was on site. He couldn't really stop Adam even if he wanted to, and FROG operators were always given a great deal of leeway on decision-making when in the field. Which Adam knew very well, of course. Finally, Hal said, "Find Gretchen and take her with you. You'll need backup."

"You're not leaving me here all alone!" Two argued.

Adam turned and saw the sheer terror on her face, reminding him again how young she was and that she wasn't a field operator. She was a computer tech. He motioned to the laptop. "Can you use that from the car, trace them like you're doing now?"

"Of course." Her tone made it clear that he had asked a stupid question.

Adam said, "Pack up what you need. All electronics. Your passport. Leave your clothes. We're out of here in five."

"God help you you're not walking into a trap," Hal fumed.

~ ~ ~

Taylor pointed ahead. "Pull over."

Oliver turned in his seat and looked at Freddy. "You going to barf?"

"We're too close," Taylor said urgently, studying her cell phone. The burner was at her feet. "Pull over."

"Too close to what?" Oliver asked. As far as he knew, they were on a very narrow two-lane rural road in the middle of nowhere. He had been taking direction from Freddy who hadn't said a word for several miles now.

"I don't like this. None of this." Taylor glanced up. "Pull over."

Oliver could tell by her voice that she was upset, he just had no idea why. He slowed the car and carefully pulled off on the wide dirt shoulder where Taylor had indicated. Off to his left was a large green pasture where quite a few cows were grazing. Double-checking that he was well off the road, he turned off the engine.

Taylor promptly shoved her cell phone toward him. "Look. We're about six miles from that town."

"Oxshott," Freddy piped in from the back seat. "We are close to Oxshott."

Oliver peered at the digital map. A red flag over the village. "Okay, it's Oxshott, like Freddy just said." He looked at her. "So what?"

"Oxshott is the most expensive village in the country," Freddy offered. "Lots of rich people live here. Actors… some footballers…"

"Do you know who lives in Oxshott?" Taylor anxiously asked Oliver.

He shrugged.

"Victoria Tenney," Taylor hissed.

"What?" he said, alarmed.

"We're dangerously close."

"Crap." He turned in his seat, reaching for the iPad. "Freddy, give me that."

FROG Headquarters, The Hague

Hal came back into the conference room, sipping a cold bottle of beer. Marsha saw the green bottle and gave him a nasty look.

"What?" Hal said defensively. "I'm coffee-d out. I'm tea-d out. Okay? And don't tell me to drink water because it's good for me. I divorced my second wife for a reason. It's non-alcoholic." He put the bottle in front of her and pointed to the label. "See? No alcohol." Condensation dripped off the cold glass. Her nasty look remained.

"No liquids near my computers, please," she curtly reminded him.

"Sorry." He took a seat two chairs away from her and glanced at the television screen. It was off. He took another pull from the bottle. Considering it had zero alcohol, it wasn't all that bad.

"They're stopped," Marsha told him.

"Who? Adam and—"

"Taylor," Marsha replied. "If that's who it is."

"So both you and Two are tracking the phone?"

"I don't know what cell reception is like out there. Redundancy is king."

Hal frowned. "They anywhere near the safe house?"

She shook her head. "It had looked like they were headed right there, at least as the crow flies. Then they took another road, off the beaten path as far as I can tell."

"And stopped dead in the water?"

"Yep."

"Doing what?" She gave him a weary look, and he raised his hands in self-defense. "Right. Sorry. Stupid. Thinking gas or food."

Suddenly a loud shrill siren sounded from her laptop, followed by three long beeps. Marsha quickly clicked on something.

"What's—"

"Victoria Tenney's office." Marsha worked the computer keyboard. "We're recording now."

Surrey, England

They had gotten out of the Mini Cooper, if for no other reason than to stretch their legs. Freddy stood by the fence, staring at the cows. As for the livestock, they paid no attention to the people near the road, busy grazing on the grass at their feet. Freddy had admitted that he had never seen a cow before—a real cow like this—and was amazed at their size. Oliver had placed the iPad on the roof of the small car, overlaying the signal of the burner phone they had been exchanging text messages with to the actual address of Victoria Tenney's estate. The two vectors did not line up. In fact, they were miles apart.

He tilted the screen so Taylor could easily see it. "What do you think?"

"What's the distance?" she asked.

Oliver fiddled with the plotting. "A good six or seven miles."

She frowned. "I was so certain…"

"And it's close," Oliver agreed. He sighed. So much they didn't know. He looked at her—her normally gorgeous face now masked with frustration. "Talk to me. Give me your best shot."

She shook her head. "It's so close, I have to think it's someone connected to her. If not her, then the family. At the very, very least, someone at Redfield."

"They've gone silent," he pointed out.

"To entice us in?" Taylor's worry was his worry too.

Oliver shook his head. "No way of knowing, really."

"Hey! Look!" Freddy shouted. He was pointing up the road where six bicyclists were peddling fast down the incline toward them. "Tour de France! Tour de France!" He hurried to the side of the road, waving. "Tour de France!" he shouted. "Go!"

The six cyclists, all wearing bright-colored jerseys, flew past with all but one rider acknowledging Freddy with a head nod or a few fingers raised from the handlebars. And then they were gone.

Oliver looked at Taylor. "I think they turned off their phone. If you want, we can ping them. One message, and we turn our phone off again." He lifted the iPad. "We use this to see if and when they are active, get a reading. What do you say?"

She tilted the screen toward her and bit her lower lip in concentration.

Freddy came up to them. "Do they know they are going to die?" he asked.

Oliver scowled. "What are you talking about? The bicyclists aren't going to die—"

"No!" Freddy pointed to the cows. "Do they know they will die and people will eat them?"

Taylor and Oliver exchanged looks.

Freddy kicked at the soft dirt, looking at the cows. "We're all going to die, every living thing, but do they know that..? Do they know they're going to die?"

~ ~ ~

"Jacob," Victoria acknowledged, turning away from her wide office windows where she had been watching two horses graze on the green grass. How her horses gave her comfort. When this meeting was over, she was taking Oracle, her finest horse, for a long ride. She gave Jacob an obligatory smile. "Thanks for coming. Did you see her?"

Standing on the other side of her massive desk was Jacob Perlman, a man close to seventy now with gray hair and impeccable style and grace. "Yes. As directed, I did meet with her." He put his heavy briefcase on her desk and opened it. "But you need a criminal attorney. I know of a very good one. The very best."

"Oh, please," she whined. "For what? You handle our legal issues. You need to handle this, plain and simple." She was referring to the fact that Jacob was a top business attorney and had been on retainer with Red Arrow Capital for many years.

He didn't reply. Instead, he removed a single business card from the briefcase and placed it on the desk. "His name is Orrin Davenport. He is aware that you might need his services, and he is expecting your call."

"What?" Victoria bitterly retorted. "This is nonsense! No!"

Jacob stood straight. He looked to one of the two plush chairs facing her desk. "May I?"

She gestured with the wave of her hand and pulled out her desk chair and sat down.

Jacob took a seat and sighed. The woman didn't make life easy. "Please understand that your friend—

"She's not a friend," Victoria quickly retorted.

Jacob gave her a long look. "Was Ms. Hana Vrba here the other day? For your party?"

Victoria hesitated. "Yes, fine, but that doesn't mean anything." Victoria realized she was walking a fine line. "Look, I know her; she's an acquaintance. That is not the same as a friend. Just so you know."

"So you asked me to handle a very serious legal matter for an acquaintance? Is that correct?"

Victoria knew better than to answer him directly. Instead, she asked, "I asked you to meet her and get her released. Did you at least get her released?"

"She hasn't been charged. If and when she is charged, bail may be allowed, or it may not, and if not, she will be remanded into custody."

Victoria looked away, annoyed.

"Do you know why she is in police custody?" Jacob pressed her.

Victoria looked up sharply. She didn't like being peppered with questions. She was accustomed to having people jump when she said jump. But the truth was, Jacob had never jumped for her. Not once. She looked at him and said, "She called me asking for help. Saying it was a case of misunderstanding. Mistaken identity, I think was the term she used." He continued to stare at her, making her quite uncomfortable. "That's all I know."

Jacob frowned. "You didn't know that she is being held in connection with the murder of Adrian Weatherspoon?"

Victoria waved this off. "Yes, yes, of course, but—"

"A man, may I remind you, that you were involved with in business as well as personally," Jacob interrupted, his voice firm. "For what? Quite some time as I recall."

Victoria angrily waved away his words. "So what?"

"When I met with Ms. Vrba today, per your instructions, she told me that you need to get her out immediately or—"

"Which is exactly what I asked you to do!" Victoria interrupted angrily.

"I am not finished," Jacob said briskly. "Or she will tell all… About how you instructed her to kill Mr. Weatherspoon."

"What?" Victoria stammered, caught completely off guard. Her heart suddenly started pounding like a hammer in her chest, and she felt her face flush. "Why would I do that? Rubbish! Total rubbish!"

"She recorded your instructions… Given to her over the phone."

Victoria simply stared at Jacob. "No…" she managed to mutter.

Jacob stood. He put a finger on the business card he had laid on the desk and pushed it toward her. "I suggest you call Mr. Davenport right away."

Chapter Nineteen

Surrey, England

"Right in here... Like, right here!" Two said anxiously, going by her laptop resting in her lap as she sat in the back seat.

Adam pulled over.

Upon leaving the safe house, with electronics and everyone's passports in hand, they had called Gretchen to tell her about the change in plan and to ask where they could pick her up. Minutes later, when they stopped for her, she wasn't happy that no one had brought water. Her own bottle was empty. Now riding shotgun, she turned to Two. "If that thing really works to within inches, let's check it out." She got out of the car.

Two walked around with her laptop in front of her as if it were a divining rod. Finally, she stopped. She was now on the other side of the road. Behind her were quite a few cows in a large grass field. "Here."

"Nothing since, right?" Adam asked.

"Nope."

"What are the chances they tossed it?" Gretchen asked. She crossed the road and said to Two, "I mean, the phone. Could it be right there, in the grass somewhere?"

"I don't think so."

"Why not?"

Two looked around thoughtfully. Finally, she said, "Grass is a good five feet away."

"So it was literally right here?" Adam asked, joining them on the shoulder of the road. Looking at the soft dirt, he saw tire tracks.

Marsha had quickly done what they had forgotten to do earlier. On the Red Arrow Capital website, she found a listing of employees, with their job titles. There were two people with the name Taylor—one was Gerald Taylor, an asset manager, and the other was Taylor Brohm, a software engineer. Obviously, Taylor Brohm was their person of interest. Then Marsha crossed referenced Taylor Brohm with England's Driver and Vehicle Licensing Agency. An easy task since they left holes a mile wide in their online registry program. She found that Taylor Brohm was female, age twenty-six, and owned a four-door Mini Cooper. That should have helped them immensely. However, so far they hadn't seen any Mini Coopers, but then, they hadn't been looking for one, either. She'd immediately sent the new information to the team.

"You're standing on it," Two told Adam.

"If we're going to drive around looking for a Mini Cooper, can we find some water?" Gretchen asked.

Something caught Two's eye, and she motioned over Gretchen's shoulder. "Ask nicely. They might share."

Gretchen turned. Three bicyclists were peddling up the grade. She looked at Two. "You're taking after Adam, you know that?"

Two grinned happily.

"Hey, guys, can I ask a question?" Adam said, stepping out onto the road.

"No, no," Gretchen said with great embarrassment, following after him.

Adam glanced back at her with a puzzled look.

The leading cyclist slowed to a stop and looked expectantly at Adam.

"Supposed to meet my cousin here. Had a car problem. Driving a Mini Cooper?"

"Red, right?" the cyclist said, out of breath.

Adam had no way of knowing the car color, but he said enthusiastically, "Yeah, yeah!"

The cyclist turned to the guy coming up behind him. "Red Mini, where'd we see it again?"

"The Fox Trot," said the other, passing them both.

~ ~ ~

Gretchen used her cell phone to guide them to the Fox Trot Inn where they spotted a red four-door Mini Cooper in the car park. During the ride, Marsha had texted each of them two pictures of Taylor Brohm—the first taken from the Red Arrow Capital website and the second from her driver's license. Meanwhile, Two scrolled through the names and images of the Red Arrow Capital IT staff in order to familiarize herself with names and faces should Taylor be with an IT co-worker.

After parking the car, Adam laid out the ground rules. First, Two would stay outside just in case Taylor Brohm showed up and got in her car. But if they spotted her inside and it looked like she wasn't going anywhere, they would tell Two to come in. Otherwise, she was to stay put and watch the Mini Cooper. Second, Adam and only Adam would approach Taylor. Two and Gretchen were to, in his words, "watch and observe. Do not approach." Last, when he left the pub, they were to join him no sooner than ten minutes later. He didn't want Taylor to know he was with them.

"How about you use your phone to tape the conversation?" Two suggested.

Adam clearly hadn't considered this. He glanced at Gretchen who said, "She's right. We can then send it to FROG."

Adam reluctantly nodded in agreement.

"You know how to do it?" Two asked. "Hit the voice memo icon and hit the start button. It's red. Then put the phone to sleep. No one will see the app is still open."

Adam gave her a dirty look. "Think I can do that."

With the ground rules agreed upon, they all got out of the car.

"Give me the keys," Two said, sticking her hand out. When Adam hesitated, she said, "If I stand out here holding my laptop, that might look a bit off, don't you think? And there is no way I'm leaving it the car if you give me the okay to come inside, even if you lock it."

He handed over the keys without a word and promptly walked toward the entrance. Gretchen gave Two a conspiratorial wink and followed after Adam.

Entering the pub, Adam had to adjust his eyes to the dim light. Gretchen came in shortly after and headed straight for the bar where she ordered a beer and a bottled water.

"Bottled?" the bartender scoffed. "Give me an empty bottle, and I'll give you tap water."

"Fine," Gretchen replied.

"Fine meaning you got an empty bottle on you?"

Gretchen wasn't in the mood, but she smiled nevertheless. "Tap is good. I've just been for a run and I'm thirsty, that's all."

With that, the older barkeep gave her a tall glass of water. Her phone chimed. She glanced at it. It was from Adam, to both her and Two: *9 o'clock. Two, come inside. We're good.*

As tempted as she was to look to her left at the nine o'clock position, Gretchen didn't. She drank the water in one long pull, then set the glass on the bar. "Another please."

"How far you run?" the barkeep asked in surprise.

"Not far enough."

Two was at her side, her laptop in its carry bag. "Can we eat?"

"Sure," Gretchen replied. "Let's find a table."

Gretchen led Two to an empty table that would be at the pub's three o'clock. Luckily, only a scattering of tables were taken at this hour, and the three o'clock table gave them a direct view of the nine o'clock table across the wide room. Taylor was not alone. There were two men with her.

"Where's Adam?" Two asked, as she took her seat and placed the laptop case between her feet.

"Gents," Gretchen said. "Allowing us to get a table with a good view, I imagine."

"Why'd he say nine o'clock?" Two asked. "What's that mean?"

Gretchen smiled to herself. "Common orientation. From the starting point, in this case the front door, you look straight ahead, that's twelve o'clock. So standing at the door, to your left..."

Two understood now. She looked across the room, her eyes narrowing. Then she started fiddling with her phone.

"What's up?" Gretchen asked.

Still working her phone, Two said, "See the other guys at that table? One works in IT at Red Arrow. Name is Oliver Gamble. I'm telling Marsha so she can look into him."

"Which one?" Gretchen asked.

"Bright blue, long-sleeve shirt."

"Tell Adam too. Tell him the bright blue shirt."

After sending the text messages, Two noticed paper menus stacked in between the salt and pepper shakers and grabbed one. "Doesn't it bother you?"

"What?" Gretchen asked, also grabbing a menu.

"I don't know. The way he decides things. You could approach the woman too, but he made the rules. He's going to talk to her."

"It's his case."

"What do you mean?" Two asked, puzzled. "We all work together."

"We're independent much of the time. Think back. Who was to meet the mysterious man riding a red bike at an Amsterdam café?"

"Oh," Two said, understanding.

"This was his case to begin with, and it went about as wrong as things can go. I was brought in, but it's still his case. As it should be." She watched as Adam exited the men's room on the far side of the pub opposite them. He had his cell phone in his hand.

The table sat four and Adam pulled out the only available chair, acknowledging Taylor. "Taylor." He sat down and turned to the young man wearing the bright blue shirt. "Oliver."

The group was completely stunned, and it was Oliver who managed to speak first. "Who are you?"

"The guy you're trying to track."

Taylor and Oliver exchanged frightened looks.

"You work for Victoria," Taylor said.

"Hardly," he scoffed just as a waitress arrived with their food. He casually placed his cell phone on the table.

"Vegetarian?" the waitress asked.

The young man to Adam's right raised his hand.

"Meatloaf and mashed?"

Oliver signaled for the plate, and the waitress put down the other two dishes. She looked at Adam. "Eating?"

"Non-alcoholic beer if you have it, and you got fish and chips?"

"We got both."

"Both it is then. Thanks."

The waitress gave a quick nod and left. Adam turned to the vegetarian eater. "You are?"

Freddy glared at him. "You first."

"Fair enough. Charlie."

"Last name?" Freddy demanded.

"Animal proteins are good. Healthy actually," Adam countered. There was something about the young man that seemed off. He wasn't sure what it was.

"Last name?" the young man repeated. "I said last name… Last name… I said last name… I said last name… Last name…"

"Smith," Adam blurted out just to stop the guy from repeating himself endlessly.

The young man frowned. "Smith…" He tilted his head back, looking at the ceiling. "Smith is the most common surname in England and Ireland… In fact, Smith has been the most common surname for centuries throughout the United Kingdom and some commonwealth countries as well." He now looked at Adam. "I don't believe Smith is your true last name."

"I don't believe in eating only vegetables."

"Stop! Please stop," Taylor said. "Both of you." She stared at Adam. After glancing around, she leaned forward and said, "You used my name to hack the account. I could've been killed."

"We discussed this in the text messages," Adam calmly reminded her. "We meant you no harm." She glared at him, and he raised his hands. "Swear to God. You check out the names I gave you?" She continued to glare, so he added harshly, "If I did mean you harm, you would be dead, trust me."

He spoke the words with such certainty that Taylor physically recoiled. She had no rejoinder.

Finally, Oliver said, "That old man, Hans. In Holland. He died of cancer."

"We think so, yes. But truthfully, that one could go either way."

"We?" Taylor asked. "Who is we?"

"Someone in The Hague," the other young man said, his mouth full.

Adam turned sharply, taken by surprise. Thank goodness these guys were amateurs. He just gave an obvious tell. There was no defense for such an error. Golden rule was to never, ever, underestimate anyone. And he had just done that. Studying the young man, he said, "Yes, the phone your tracking is from The Hague. Not bad."

Adam noticed that the vegetarian's eyes lit up as he looked at Oliver with a beaming smile, as if to say, You hear that? I did good. Something off with the guy, definitely, but what? Adam glanced at Oliver and said, "He work for you too? He and Taylor?"

"No," the younger man quickly responded. "I work for myself. And my name is Freddy."

"Okay," Adam replied. "Got it, Freddy."

Freddy stared at him. "You from there? Holland?"

Adam gave him a long look. "Where does it sound like I'm from?"

Freddy's eyes narrowed. "I don't know... Maybe Yorkshire."

Adam was impressed, but he didn't let on.

"City of Leeds..." Freddy said. "City of Hull... City of Wakefield.."

"Freddy, enough," Oliver said with an angry tone. "Eat your lunch. You were hungry, remember?"

Chastised, Freddy picked up a fork and played with his food. Adam thought the man-child was interesting.

Once again, Taylor kept the conversation on track. "Why me? Why use my name?"

"Why not?" Adam retorted since he had no clue why Marsha had chosen the name.

"You're working for her," Taylor said. "This is a test."

"Do you know the name Charles Adrian Weatherspoon?" Adam asked. He got a baffled look in return while Freddy quickly traded his fork for his phone.

"Charles..?" Freddy repeated.

"Adrian... Weatherspoon," Adam told him. He turned to Taylor. "You helped Victoria Tenney when she lost her laptop."

Again, Oliver and Taylor exchanged startled looks. Taylor said, "How did you—"

"You helped her sort out what to do," Adam said, cutting her off. "She stupidly thought you could find it. Track it down. You had to tell her you couldn't, then walk her through changing her passwords on various accounts. First and foremost at her bank."

"Anyone could simply guess that," Oliver argued. "Common sense."

Adam's beer arrived. He took a sip, waiting for the waitress to be out of ear shot. "Maybe. But then, I need to correct my previous statement. It wasn't, as I said, 'her bank.' I should have said banks, plural. What was it? Four of them?"

Taylor and Oliver now looked terrified.

Adam went on. "What you don't know is that she thought Mr. Weatherspoon took her laptop. She had a big party the day before. He was there, an invited guest. She really thought he took it."

"Charles Adrian Weatherspoon was found murdered in his London home two days ago," Freddy announced, reading from his phone.

Adam looked at Freddy. "Yes." He turned back to Taylor, her face now white. "Understand how this works now? One of the Redfields suspects you of anything, you're dead." He lifted his beer glass in a salute. "You're alive. Why? Because I'm not connected to the Redfields... In fact, I want to bring them down."

London, England

It took more patience than Victoria Tenney possessed to sit in the elegant reception area, waiting to be summoned. This wasn't the way things worked in her world. In her privileged universe, when you arrived as expected for an appointment, you were immediately taken to the person you were meeting with. You were never kept waiting. Not for one millisecond. She had half a mind to get up and walk out, but of course, that wasn't an option. It didn't help that her stomach was in knots.

There was only one other person waiting, and it was quite clear that he didn't belong. Perhaps forty years of age with curly hair going gray, he needed a haircut, fresh shave, and better clothes. Just the way he slouched in his seat told her he didn't belong in such a high-end establishment as this, and she couldn't help but wonder why he was here. Perhaps his parents were of means. He certainly wasn't.

When Jacob had left her, she'd found out what she could about Orrin Davenport from the web. Cork, Smith & Knapps was a very well-respected criminal-defense law firm catering to the upper class. They handled everything from money laundering and tax evasion to murder. Davenport had a terrific track record, which, as Ethan had pointed out, was all good and fine, "as long as he makes this go away."

After waiting another eight minutes, she was finally shown into the large corner office of Orrin Davenport. There was a well-appointed seating area off to one side, but the man she had come to see sat behind a massively oversized desk, working on a computer with an equally massive monitor that partially hid him from view. As she got closer, she realized the attorney hardly resembled his picture displayed on the firm's website. In person, Davenport was terribly obese and had aged considerably from whenever the photo had been taken. His chair sat at an angle—the only way he could get close to the desk since he was so rotund.

The receptionist announced her and promptly left, closing the door behind her. As Victoria slowly stepped forward, he finally looked up with a distracted glance and said, "Ah, Ms. Tenney. Have a seat." There were two chairs facing his desk, and she took the nearest one. The desktop held a scattering of papers and a corded black phone with an oversized tilt display.

"Thank you for signing the instruction papers electronically," he said, studying his computer monitor. "Always saves time." No eye contact with the remark, and she immediately thought he was quite uncouth. She waited, glancing around his office. There were no personal photos to be found. Not like most professionals at his level, who would display pictures of themselves with MPs, royalty, or at the very least, their spouse and children. Davenport had nothing on display. But there was a Monet on one wall, so hopefully, the man did have some refinement.

Finally, he pushed away from the desk and looked her over appraisingly. "Jacob speaks highly of you."

"Likewise," she said.

He gave a good belly laugh. "Well, glad that's out of the way." His face turned somber. "You do know that Jacob met with this woman, Hana Vrba, today?"

"Yes, of course."

"I need to know if you want to furnish her with legal counsel. It was my understanding that was why Jacob was to meet with her."

Victoria was thrown temporarily. Ethan had told her to be honest with the barrister. He had to keep her confidences, so be forthright. Taking his advice, she said, "Not if she is going to accuse me of facilitating Adrian's murder."

Davenport leaned back in his chair and nodded thoughtfully, his sagging triple-chin bobbing in rhythm. "If I may offer an opinion…"

Victoria gave a shoulder shrug.

"I suggest you do so. First, she wants to be released from police custody, and if you show good faith by offering to pay her legal fees, then she keeps quiet on whatever she is threatening you with." Victoria was about to speak, but he raised a fat hand. "Whether you did or did not do what she is alleging doesn't matter. If you secure and pay for good legal counsel, hopefully, you at least put off her accusations." Again, Victoria was about to speak, and he raised his hand. "It won't be anyone here. I can set up something outside this office."

"So, give in to blackmail?" she said. "That is your suggestion?"

"If you'd let me finish. As stated, doing this will hopefully keep your name out of any discussions she might have with the police. Plus, as the old saying goes, it is always wise to keep your friends close and your enemies closer."

Victoria gave this some thought. "So you're saying whoever you find to represent her will give us, what? Inside information?"

"Generally speaking, that's the idea." He studied her. "It's worth the expense in my estimation."

"And I get to pay two barrister fees instead of one," Victoria said bitterly.

"It is completely up to you, Ms. Tenney. I'm just offering my advice."

Victoria remained silent. The money wasn't a factor. Her freedom—and certainly keeping her name out of press on such a tantalizing story—were of the upmost importance. "Very well, if you think it best."

He studied her for a moment. "I'm sure Jacob told you I've done criminal law for a good many years. I know the magistrates and the crown prosecutors. I know the senior detectives at the Met and many other detectives in various other jurisdictions. I say this not to boast, but to assure you that my judgment in matters such as this often depends upon what the other side might be willing to share."

Victoria was immediately skeptical. "Or not share."

He smiled and raised an eyebrow. "Well said, and a valid point."

"Well then, I suggest you get started," Victoria said.

"I'm way ahead of you." When she gave him a puzzled look, he said, "As you know, if you read the email, once you signed the e-doc instruction, I had your permission to work on your behalf, and I have made some calls."

Victoria was surprised. She hadn't really read the stupid agreement, just signed electronically in order to get the ball rolling.

Davenport went on. "In this case, there has been what I would call a seismic shift. An earthquake of epic magnitude."

"Which is?" she asked impatiently, not impressed with his metaphors.

"It seems Hana Vrba is a person of interest with MI6."

"MI6?" Victoria repeated with utter astonishment.

"Yes."

She shook her head. "That clearly invalidates your suggestion that I pay Hana's legal fees. She is wanted for much more than a silly murder." She regretted the word "silly" as soon as it was out of her mouth.

But Davenport seemed not to have heard and said, "You will be paying those fees to keep her quiet about even knowing you, let alone throwing you under the bus. And as I said, you are doing it to learn more about what is going on. The fact that this could go to a much higher level makes that all the more important."

Victoria immediately realized that he was right, however, her mind was spinning concerning the involvement of MI6. "I have my friends over there too," Davenport told her. "MI6. I won't reach out until I have your direction, but I'm thinking that MI6 will take precedence. It will be decided in court very soon, I imagine. The government will argue that Hana Vrba has, I don't know… state secrets, foreign secrets, whatever, and they get the first shot at her."

"What happens to Adrian's case? His death?"

"I'm hoping you can tell me." He studied her, a heavy pause. "If you can help MI6 with whatever they might be looking at, I'm sure they will be persuaded to ignore any phone calls between you and Hana Vrba."

She didn't respond, her mind reeling. Davenport leaned forward across his desk with a bit of a grunt and hit a key on his telephone. She could hear a faint buzz.

Almost immediately the office door opened. Victoria turned to see the man from the reception area walk in. She quickly turned back to Davenport who said, "May I introduce Barry Tate. Barry, this is Ms. Victoria Tenney. She would like to hire your services for a friend of hers."

"Acquaintance," Victoria quickly said, correcting him.

Barry gave her a perfunctory nod and took the chair next to her.

"Acquaintance," Davenport repeated. He turned to Victoria. "Barry is quite good. Not as good as I am, but almost." With that, he gave Barry a wink. Turning serious, he said to her, "Your acquaintance will be in good legal hands."

"The very best hands," Barry assured her.

Davenport looked at Barry. "Stella has the particulars."

"Right," he said, standing up. He looked at Victoria. "I prefer cash, ma'am."

"Cash?" Victoria echoed.

"The actual paper money. Cash." He gave her a tight smile. "Might be best to keep your name away from this case." He turned to Davenport. "At least that was my understanding?"

"Yes, yes," Davenport said. "Quite so."

Barry headed for the door, then stopped. "Ms. Tenney?"

She looked at him.

"Prepaid cards are just fine too. If it's easier."

Victoria gave him a baffled look. "Prepaid?"

"Visa? MasterCard?"

Victoria stared at the man, clearly puzzled.

Barry smiled. "It's simple. You go into say a Tesco; they have prepaid credit cards. You put whatever amount you want on that card. Let's say two hundred pounds. You give me the card, okay?"

Victoria continued to look baffled.

"That's it. You just paid me two hundred pounds without writing me a check and creating a paper trail. I'll tell you the truth. Some of my clients prefer to pay this way so that if their spouse looks at their credit-card statement, they just see money spent at a grocery store. Who cares, right?"

With that, he turned to leave before abruptly turning back. "Oh. They'll give you a receipt showing the amount you applied to the card. Be sure to keep that, give it to me along with the card. Just in case there is a screw up and the credit card won't work. I'll need the receipt."

With that, he walked out.

Chapter Twenty

Seated at the head of the conference-room table, Hal looked at Gretchen and then Two, sitting opposite each other. "Good to have you guys back."

"Good to be back," Gretchen replied.

"Me too," Two happily chipped in, scribbling something on a notepaper and handing it to Marsha sitting next to her. She then turned her attention back to her laptop.

Gretchen winked at Hal, who smiled. Technically, the short-term rental agreement on the Surrey house didn't expire for a few more weeks, but since there was nothing more to do from that location, they had come home.

The conference-room door opened, and Adam entered carrying a to-go coffee from the off-site barista cart that he frequented. "Morning," he said.

Hal made a point of checking his watch. "Cutting it close."

Adam frowned and looked back at the office wall that held seven analog clocks displaying the time of day in various cities across the globe. "Got two minutes." He walked around the table and pulled out the chair next to Gretchen and sat down.

"Okay," Marsha said, concentrating on her laptop. "We're live in three, two, one..."

Everyone turned toward the large screen on the far wall. The black screen flickered briefly, and then Elizabeth was looking back at them, papers on the desk before her.

"Morning," Hal said with a smile.

"Little early," Elizabeth responded, holding up a coffee mug. "But this is a double expresso, just to be sure I'm awake and make some sense."

"We appreciate the accommodation."

"Actually, it's best for me at this time. Everyone is sleeping." She now seemed to notice that the group was all in one location and cocked her head. "No more English countryside?"

"Got home late last night," Gretchen said.

Elizabeth seemed to realize nothing more was going to be said. "Good."

"How's the ankle?" Gretchen asked, deftly changing the subject.

"Slowing me down. I have a half a mind to go to a doctor here and beg to have the cast taken off."

"Patience," Adam warned.

Elizabeth actually laughed. "Coming from you? Patience? That's priceless."

"You'd be surprised, but I've been there with war wounds," Adam replied. "I say sit in a nice recliner, enjoy the beauty of wherever you are, and be patient."

"Very well," she said. "I just tend to be impatient by nature."

"Sorry to cut into your time with your family, Elizabeth," Hal said congenially. "We just have a few questions pertaining to the email you sent earlier. In a word—"

"In a word, nothing jumped out at me regarding your quest specifically for water-treatment companies, water-cleanup or water-solution firms," Elizabeth quickly interrupted.

"You say there are some companies covering the issue, but, quote, 'they may be much ado about nothing,' unquote," Hal challenged.

Elizabeth sighed. "Okay, please try to understand. I said that these companies that do water stuff that you're talking about, is 'much ado about nothing' for two reasons. One, the companies do much, much more than just water treatment. Except the Dubai company. That one is solely focused on water treatment, water restoration, that sort of thing. There is no other company like Dubai in the portfolio. And two, it's almost, I don't know, like clean water is an 'in' thing these days."

She shook her head with disgust. "Their board of directors can pat themselves on the back, go to the media and say, yes, we help bring safe water to your neighborhood, stuff like that. But for every firm except for the one in Dubai, the water issue isn't their reason for being. In other words, Steed took positions in publicly held companies that have lots of other services besides water treatment."

"Give us some names," Adam said.

Elizabeth shrugged. "DuPont. They're a good example. Steed took a position in DuPont, but who wouldn't? They're a huge chemical company. They merged with Dow Chemical years back if you recall. If I remember right, it was an all-stock deal. Big, big merger at the time."

"But they do water stuff? DuPont?" Adam persisted.

"Yes, but like I said, if you ask me, some of this is them trying to be, I don't know... be able to say how they're helping the environment. How green they are. Dupont has their fingers in a lot of pies. Water treatment is just one facet of what they do.

"They are big-time innovators in a number of fields. They are working on hybrid electric powertrains for race cars. They make Kevlar for the military and your local police... When it was Dow, they invented Styrofoam that is now used for insulation in all sorts of buildings. They make resins used in just about everything. I could go on and on."

She tapped the papers on the desk. "In that way, Steed investing in DuPont is almost a no-brainer. I mean, tons of people invest in DuPont simply because it is a very diverse company always exploring new technologies. Plus, they do provide a yield, not huge, but you'll get a dividend."

"Okay, that makes sense," Gretchen said as she glanced at a printed page in her hands. "After the much ado about nothing, you said we need to focus on the flip side of the coin, but you didn't elaborate."

Elizabeth grimaced. "Sorry. I was in a rush. We were about to leave for the day." Another sigh. "Here is the way I'm looking at this. On the one hand, you do have companies that, among other things, offer some sort of water cleanup, water restoration. But look at every one of the other investments. That's the other side of the same coin."

Gretchen picked up another paper. "Pepsi, Coca-Cola, Nestle—"

"Exactly!" Elizabeth said excitedly. "See what I mean?"

"In a word, no," Adam said with a frown.

"They're all beverage companies! Not just the Diet Coke you drink, but guess what else they do? Water! Bottled water. Coca-Cola owns Dasani, a huge bottled-water company. Pepsi... They invested in Pepsi, and their bottled-water division is Aquafina. Nestle does chocolate milk, but guess what? They have bottled water, Perrier. Overseas, you have Evian. On and on it goes."

Gretchen sat back. "I saw these investments, and I just thought of them as, you know, the soft drinks."

"Water is a huge business. Worldwide," Elizabeth said. "Go to an airport and see what people buy once they make it through security. Yeah, maybe a plastic bottle of Coke. But most people grab a bottled water. It's a huge industry. Again a no-brainer in terms of investment.

"But it is the flip side of the same coin because if you have water issues, people don't trust their tap water, what are they going to do? Go out and buy a huge package of bottled water. Steed is covering both ends at once."

Hal suddenly tapped his pen on the table quite loudly. This was a sign for the others to hold their thoughts. They didn't need to confirm to a civilian that she was probably spot on. With a smile, he said. "Excellent, Elizabeth. Thank you. One more question, please, and we'll let you go. Last time we talked, you had found that Steed acquired property in Chile that didn't make sense."

"That's right," Elizabeth said. "Diego Properties, located near Antofagasta, if I'm saying it right. It's in northern Chile. I found out Diego Properties has one asset—a gold mine."

"A gold mine?" Hal repeated with surprise.

"Yep. On a ton of acres. But it's out of commission. Has been for the last four years. So tell me, how does that make sense?"

"It doesn't," Adam said.

"My take exactly. And get this... It wasn't even for sale. But they had the cash in hand and bought it—so they have a multi-million-dollar property that has absolutely no return. Zero."

"Development?" Hal queried. "I think that was my thought when we talked before. You said it has a ton of acreage."

"No way," Elizabeth countered. "Not with this piece of property."

"Why not?" Gretchen asked.

"The gold mine was forced to shut down due to arsenic seeping into the nearby waterways."

"Arsenic?" Gretchen repeated.

"Very toxic levels," Elizabeth said. "I called one of our precious-metals experts back in New York. I never knew this, but gold is often found intertwined with arsenic. You have to separate them to keep just the gold. This isn't the first mine to run into this problem. And I'm sure it won't be the last.

"That said, I just don't understand for the life of me why they want it. I'll bet you the environmental cleanup would set you back years. It's a headache."

London, England

To Oliver's way of thinking, he was now entering the dark side. Something he had never done before. He had always had the capability to hack a system; he had just never done it. Even in college at Oxford, he could have changed his grades without a trace. But it wasn't in his DNA to do such a thing. And although it would have been so easy to do today's chore from his office at Red Arrow Capital, he didn't dare, simply because if something went wrong, he didn't need it being traced back anywhere near Red Arrow. After all, three employees had already died attempting to stop whatever was coming, and he didn't need to be the fourth.

Which was why he now sat in a pub on the east side of the city that offered free computer and internet service. While he sipped his morning coffee, waiting for the ancient computer system to get going, he couldn't help but think back that just two days ago, everything had turned on its head. When he, Taylor, and Freddy had hopped into the Mini Cooper that day to track whoever had hacked into the Steed account, they'd no way of knowing how things would turn and what lay ahead. They thought they knew their target and that target's motives. But the sudden appearance of a man calling himself Charlie Smith, a man who knew all he knew and seemed on the right side of things, changed everything. After inviting himself to join them for lunch, he *talked* to them. He answered their questions and kept talking. It all seemed to make sense at the time, and after they had agreed to his terms, he tossed some cash on the table and walked out.

Once back home in London, he and Taylor had gone over the encounter a million times. And each time, they had come to the same conclusion—if Charlie Smith was telling them the truth, they had no choice but to do what they could to help. At least now, they understood why the Steed hedge fund was kept under such tight security—it had been set up to take advantage of some grave event yet to come that would kill possibly hundreds of thousands of people. The investors would be rewarded with even greater wealth than they now possessed because, to use Charlie Smith's words, "The companies tied to the fund will be needed to fix the catastrophic event. In fact, governments will pay top dollar for those companies' services, products, or whatever. To quote Mac Senton, 'you create a problem that you have the solution for.'"

Freddy had immediately said, "Another COVID."

"No," Charlie Smith had said, dismissing the idea. "At least we don't think so."

"But if you have the right medicine to take, you sell it when people are sick and scared of dying, you make money," Freddy had argued.

Smith had agreed, but said, "However, we don't think so. I'm not ruling it out. I'm not ruling it in. We just don't think so at this point."

"So if not a terrible plague what would it be?" Taylor had asked.

"I'll be honest, we don't know yet. But I will say this much— he who controls a country's food supply or water supply controls that country."

"A food shortage," Oliver had suggested. "Mass starvation."

"We can't say for sure. I am being honest."

"Who is we?" Taylor had tried to learn more about their mystery man.

"That's better left unsaid," the man had replied.

When Oliver had accused Charlie Smith of being MI6, he'd gotten a rather curious reply. "No. And don't stress yourself thinking about this, because my friends and I don't really exist. So I'd rather you spend your time helping me stop the impending terrorist attack the likes of which we have never seen before, rather than trying to dissect who I am."

"What exactly do you want from us?" Taylor had asked. "Data from the company?"

"Certainly data on Steed if there are changes," Charlie Smith had clarified.

Taylor and Oliver had exchanged looks. Oliver said, "Those involved, the family members, they can update Steed all on their own. They don't need us."

"Take a look every day, and if something has changed, a new investment has been added—a physical property has been bought or sold—it would be good to know."

"I'm not sure we can do that," Taylor said.

The man calling himself Charlie Smith didn't seem to hear that. "Also, let me know if Clyde Redfield, his son Ethan, or Victoria Tenney leaves the country. Let me know where they are going, their flights, hotels, every detail you can give me."

Taylor and Oliver had exchanged looks again, and Taylor said, "We might be able to do that."

That was when Freddy spoke up. "If you give me those people's cell phones, I can put a tracking app on them that they will never see."

"With what?" Oliver challenged. "What app?"

"It cost me two hundred quid, but I modified it," Freddy had said. "No one will ever see it, I promise."

When Oliver gave him a skeptical look, Freddy had explained that he'd put it on his mother's phone without her knowledge, that he was sure she wasn't being honest with him about her cancer treatments having stopped. He felt bad about challenging Freddy because having to confess what he'd done clearly upset him, and he'd started rocking in his chair and staring at the table.

After a few minutes, Charlie Smith had said, "Okay, inquiring minds want to know Freddy, was your mother done with chemo, like she told you?"

Freddy stared at the table and shook his head no. The three of them exchanged glances. This was news to Oliver, that was for sure. He'd gone on to tell them the exact schedule of her visits and how he knew she simply didn't want him to worry. Didn't want him to know she was going to die.

Oliver had felt so bad. "I didn't know that, Freddy. I really thought she was good."

Taylor had reached across the table and squeezed Freddy's hand. "Let's pray another round gets her well, okay?"

Freddy finally acquiesced with a bob of his head, and with that, the group fell silent. It was Freddy who spoke first, changing the subject back to their common task. His directions explicit, he said to Oliver, "If you give me someone's phone for three minutes, forty-one seconds, I can put the modified app on it. Three minutes, forty-one seconds. I can do it. You'll know where he is in real time forever."

Taylor had pointed out that it would be all but impossible to get the senior Redfield's phone for even twenty seconds. But then suggested maybe they could get Victoria's.

Oliver had explained that they'd need Freddy right there if and when they got a phone. Then he'd thanked Freddy, and said that if they could figure out a way to do it, they would.

With that, Freddy seemed pleased. Realizing Freddy might not realize how serious the situation was and how important secrecy was, he'd said, "And Freddy? Everything we are discussing here can't go anywhere. Nowhere, understand? I swear to you, lives depend upon your silence. So not a word to anyone. Ever, okay?"

Freddy solemnly nodded. Oliver thought he really did get it.

So without Freddy's tracking app, they had only one other option—hacking into the travel agency that all Redfield employees were required to use to book business trips. Fortunately, even though the Redfield family members weren't obligated to use the travel agency, they often did. Probably because that way, the firm was paying their traveling expenses, not them.

Charlie Smith had explained that from that point on, instead of using burner phones to text each other, they would use an encrypted email account. No actual email would be sent or received. Instead, they could draft messages to each other and leave them in the draft folder.

The pub's old computer finally came to life, and Oliver went to work.

FROG Headquarters, The Hague

"I'd like to hear why you just told some young guns at Red Arrow Capital that there is a catastrophic event about to happen. And hey, maybe it has to do with food or water problems." Hal gave Adam a stern look.

Having disconnected from the video call with Elizabeth, it was Gretchen who spoke first. "Remember the parchment paper that Hans Wolter had hidden when he died? It talked of gold. A quote from the Bible."

"That's right!" Marsha said. "Good job!" With a few keystrokes, the translation of the parchment appeared on the screen. "*Surely there is… a place for gold that they could refine.*"

"But the place is defunct, right?" Gretchen asked. "So nothing to refine."

"If it's in the Steed portfolio, it has value," Adam had said. "We just need to find it."

With that, Two, Marsha, and Gretchen had left the room. The idea was to reconvene in an hour when the last video on Adrian Weatherspoon's flash drive would finally be ready for viewing. Apparently, its encryption had been harder to break than the previous two videos. Adam had planned to use the time to walk across the square to get another coffee. Not that he needed the coffee, but he wanted to stretch his legs and get some fresh air. Instead, he had to explain himself to Hal.

"They are civilians and you just spouted off about famine or water problems. And why? It was reckless," Hal argued. "Totally reckless."

"Look, it's done. Did I speak out of turn? I don't know, okay?" Adam said. "I honestly don't know."

"Well, I'm glad Two had you at least record every word of it. I don't need to tell you we are operating blind now. Who is Oliver Gamble? Taylor Brohm? Do we know? Do we *really* know? And what about that younger guy? Freddy what's-his-name?"

"I think he's autistic," Adam said.

"Oh, do you now?" Hal said, with a mocking tone. "Well, good for you. Marsha says it's probably Asperger's." Hal went on, quite angry. "The point is, you told all three of them, three walking time bombs for God's sake, that hundreds of thousands are going to die and maybe it isn't another pandemic, another Chinese virus, maybe this time it is our food or water."

"I said we don't know—"

"No, we don't."

"But there is something going on with water," Adam argued. "We've got the two videos from Weatherspoon about some remote African village getting running water for the first time in history and guess what? The residents do the happy dance, joyful as can be. Then we see those same residents, *those same residents*, dead. You saw what I saw. You know damn well that was a test run."

"So why tell civilians who we haven't vetted in the least?" Hal started to pace. "That was beyond stupid!"

Adam shook his head, suddenly fed up. "I was grasping at straws, I admit, but what the hell! We have nothing right now. Not one thing. Something bad is going to happen. Okay, where? When? Well, we have no clue. What is going to happen, specifically? Sorry, no clue."

"Telling those young people—"

"Was it a risk, yes," Adam admitted, interrupting. "But we need help. And they can give it to us. Hell, if we just get where Victoria Tenney, old man Redfield, or his son Ethan is going, maybe, just maybe, we can be there too, do what FROG is supposed to do, and end the damn thing before it even starts."

Hal shook his head. "You don't get it! What if they make this public? Hmm? Then what? We have worldwide panic!"

Adam actually laughed. "What exactly are they going to make public?"

"What you talked about! Hundreds of thousands dead—"

"Which came from DeWine, by the way, who got himself blown up, so yeah, he was probably on to something—"

"Exactly my point!" Hal thundered.

"What are they going to say?" Adam demanded. "Who told them this? Charlie Smith? Who is he? And how did they find Charlie Smith? Well, he has the burner used to hack their company. That gets out, they're dead. And they know it." In a softer tone, Adam added, "Look, you're right. I don't know these people. But they don't want to die. That I do know."

"I just wish we had discussed it, that's all," Hal said in a resigned tone.

"Not like there was time. And I went with my gut."

Hal looked at him sharply. "Your gut better be right."

~ ~ ~

With the group reassembled in the conference room, they stared at the frozen image of Adrian Weatherspoon looking at them. A play button overlaid part of the image. This was the third and last video on Adrian Weatherspoon's hidden flash drive.

"Time stamp shows he made this the night of Victoria Tenney's party," Marsha told them. "Start time is eighteen-oh-nine."

"He's in his flat," Adam said. "Sitting at his kitchen table."

"I agree, I recognize the print off his left shoulder," Gretchen said.

"Starting…" Marsha said.

Adrian Weatherspoon appeared on the screen and began speaking. "This is an account about what happened in Uganda earlier this year. My name is Charles Adrian Weatherspoon, and I am an executive vice president for Al Friqet Industries, a firm that specializes in water restoration, water treatment, wastewater treatment, and various other water-related services."

There was a pause and then he continued. "Morgan, my immediate superior at AFI, came to me with a dream job about a year ago or so. How would I like to oversee a project where people get clean running water for the first time in their lives?

"I asked where. He said a village called Little Lutete in Uganda. Full disclosure, that isn't the actual name. It's just called Little Lutete since the closest city that Westerners can pronounce is Lutete. Total population of the village was 278 people."

Adrian sighed. "I remember thinking, why Little Lutete? Why this village? I mean this project was estimated to cost millions. For 278 people? Sorry, that doesn't really compute. It's not fiscally responsible.

"The explanation was that it was to be funded by a very wealthy woman. Victoria Tenney. British. She has family money, made gobs more. And her thing was to help this tiny village… So, okay, maybe that makes sense. It's her pet project, and it wasn't like we were going to run out of funding for this thing, so why not, right?

"In short order, we found a place where we could dig a very deep well. More than three-hundred-feet deep. That way we were sure, sure as we could be anyway, that the water table would not go dry. This was two and a half kilometers from the village.

"We worked hand-in-hand with Ugandan officials. We did soil tests like you wouldn't believe. We got all the permits. We didn't cut any corners, I promise you that..."

Another wry smile. "Victoria came to see our progress, and it was the first time I met her... I don't know how it started. She was going to Kenya on a safari. She said I should come. It would just be for five days and I should take a break... I must say, she can be so enchanting. So... I don't know... Wonderful. Giving. Funny... So I went." He gave a sheepish smile with this admission.

"When I got back on site, we had some delays with weather, inspectors, lots of stuff. But that was fine. My time could be my own, and Victoria and I were having fun... I think, in retrospect, I had her on a pedestal. I mean, when you see the women of the village walk nearly a mile to get to the closest water hole, fill up huge jugs with water, and walk the mile back to the village, it gets to you, you know?

"Sometimes, carrying the jugs on their heads. If they were lucky—and I mean really lucky— they had a two-wheel dolly that they could strap the heavy water jug to and push the cart back to the village. Victoria really wanted to help. She wanted to make a difference." Another wry smile. "A lot of people with money like hers would just buy a bunch of two-wheelers and be done with it. But not Victoria. She was going to give them running water, in their own homes."

He suddenly frowned. "Remember that a minute ago, I said we were fully funded, right? But suddenly Victoria Tenney, a woman richer than God Almighty himself, suddenly demands that the villagers help pay. Have some skin in the game, as it were. She had arranged some bank to loan money to make it all happen." He shook his head with disgust. "You have to love the gall of that. Hey, let's help some poor village in Uganda. Start working, and then it's hey, the villagers have to help pay."

Adrian gave a short laugh. "You know what's crazy? When I brought that up to her, she smiled and said, 'The wealthy don't stay wealthy by giving all their money away.' I said it was a bait and switch and you know what? She just laughed.

"Anyway, let me get to the point. Bottom line, in less than six months, we did it. I'll add a video I made the day we literally turned on the water." He smiled. "Such joy. Such fascination. These people, I don't want to use the word primitive, but they were. They had no concept of seeing a spigot, of turning a handle and water is right there. Instantly. Many had never been more than a few miles from the village their whole lives. They had no concept of running water. So when we turned it on, in a word, it blew their minds."

Adrian reached for something off camera. It was a glass of water. He took a long drink. He set it down and wiped his mouth with the back of his hand. "Months passed. I was back in Dubai. Our top brass were happy. We made a good deal of money off the Little Lutete project. I was happy the people had clean drinking water. Don't get me wrong." A grin. "I'm not all that altruistic. While I was thrilled to see what we did for those people, I'm not going to lie. I got a huge bonus, and that made my year, quite frankly. And there was some wink, wink, nod, nod, hey, if Victoria has any other projects…"

Adrian's face changed. "So three months after installation, Morgan came to me… He said he just got word there had been rumors that people in the village were sick. Really sick. A doctor was sent to see what was going on. At that point, I think sixteen had died. Of course, the first thought is Ebola. Then you think, okay, maybe it's malaria or tuberculous or even the black plague. So many worries. The doctor said it was a terrible dysentery. He took blood samples, tests were done, and it was the flu, simple as that.

"But you know what? People kept dying. Scores dead each day. Soon, over a hundred dead. That's more than a third of the villagers. Dead. And you know what's crazy? It was just localized in that village. It didn't spread anywhere. *Anywhere*. Think about that. Now, you can say, well yeah, people stayed away. But I was there all the time for months on end. They have robust trade. People from surrounding areas come and go. This isn't a secluded village. So, if it's a flu, why didn't it land anywhere else? Hmm? So my fear was the water. I wanted to check. To rule it out.

"My boss, Morgan, said I was bonkers. How could it be the water? We had done a zillion tests. It was safe, clean water...

"But I had to know... I jumped on a plane. When I got to Lutete, the closest city, I was stopped right there by government officials. I was a foreigner. I had to leave. I showed them all the paperwork. I said I wanted to make sure it wasn't the water. They thought I was nuts. It was the flu. I begged to test the water... I kept saying, what's the harm? Let me get some water samples. But they had the village in lockdown to stop the spread.

"I spent days arguing with the officials to let me go down there. I said I would sign any waiver they wanted. I called Victoria. So many times I called her. Told her to help me. Begged her to help. I kept telling her we need to be sure."

His face clouded with anger. "No help from her. She gave excuses, but now with 20/20 hindsight, I don't think they were genuine. I'll go so far as to say she knew something. What she knew, I don't know. Just my gut feeling."

He shook his head. "After three days there, I finally got ahold of an inspector who had worked with us. Good guy. I gave him the sterile plastic bottles. Already labeled by color according to where I planned to collect the samples. I begged him to do it. He took my kit and promised he would.

"Two days later, the inspector came back with the samples, and I sent them by FedEx to a lab in Virginia. I didn't want to send them to my own lab, my own company. I didn't want to send them to London. I got the report four days later. I was still in Lutete. Living out of a suitcase, waiting...

"Arsenic. The water—*water we put in*—had six times the lethal dose of arsenic that is usually found in well water. Six times the lethal dose! Those poor souls didn't stand a chance!"

Emotional, Adrian took a beat to compose himself.

"Well, at least the gold mine is explained," Adam said sarcastically.

Adrian drank more water. This time, his hand shook as he set down the glass. "I told the inspector the results, and we went down there on his motorcycle. Snuck in. That's the second video of the village. They were all dead... There wasn't a living soul there..."

Looking straight at the camera, Adrian said, "Six times the amount of arsenic usually found in water is not some strange anomaly in some remote village. No water ever contains that much arsenic. It just doesn't happen in nature. But this did happen. I'd say this was a deliberate poisoning. Why? I don't know. By whom? I don't know. But it was done purposefully…

"There were 278 villagers, remember? There are zero today. Zero… For the record, it took ninety-eight days to…" Overcome with emotion, he couldn't finish his sentence.

Once again, he drank some water, then took in a deep breath, steeled himself, and looked directly at the camera. "Ninety-eight days for total eradication… to kill every living soul in that small village… You'll say I'm a conspiracy nut, but guess what? The inspector who got the water samples? Who saw all the dead as I did? Two days after we came back, he was dead. Hung himself from a tree. His teenage son found him…

"Now, was he suicidal? I don't know. Doesn't seem like the man I knew. But I'll never know, will I? Just so tragic. I think if I hadn't asked him for his help, he'd be alive today… And I wonder about myself. What about me? I'm sort of hoping if Victoria knows something, if she knows the people who did this, I pray that she'll tell whoever it is to leave me untouched."

A sheepish grin. "Got to hope, right?"

His face instantly clouded again. "But you know the saying, *Dead men tell no tales*."

Chapter Twenty-One

Surrey, England

Victoria introduced both attorneys, Orrin Davenport and Barry Tate, to her nephew, Ethan. She shut the office door, which gave its usual protest squeal, and directed the group to the overstuffed chairs close to the fireplace where a gentle fire was warding off the spring chill now that the sun had set.

She watched as Davenport waddled to a chair and slowly lowered himself onto the seat. His girth really was appalling.

Once everyone was settled, Victoria said, "Thank you for accommodating me and meeting here."

"Lovely home," Davenport remarked.

After an awkward silence, she quickly stood up. "Forgive me. Where are my manners? I'm so sorry. Drinks?" She motioned to the nearby mahogany hutch filled with various bottles.

Davenport waved the offer away. Barry took his cue and said, "I'm fine, thanks."

She promptly sat down again, and turned to Davenport. "Where do we stand?"

"As I told you when we met, I have some reliable sources at MI6... Driving down here, I just heard from one source. So bear with me and let me ask. Do you know of Hana Vrba's family, per chance?"

Victoria frowned. "No. I mean I really don't know her all that well as it is."

Davenport looked at Ethan Redfield who shook his head. Davenport then said, "The name Goran Petrovic mean anything?"

Victoria and Ethan exchanged blank looks.

"Petrovic is in the hands of authorities in the Netherlands," Davenport offered.

"The Netherlands?" Ethan repeated, his interest clearly piqued.

"He's been wanted by Interpol for over sixteen years now for murder," Davenport said.

"Who'd he kill?" Barry asked.

"Apparently, a great multitude of people," Davenport replied. "Quite simply, Goran Petrovic is a hired assassin. Or at least that is what the Dutch authorities say."

"Why are we talking about him?" Ethan asked, confused.

"He and Hana Vrba are siblings," Davenport said. "From Serbia, originally."

"Serbia? That's news to me," Victoria frowned. "I always thought she was from here. Isn't she a UK citizen?"

"No. Which means she is now being held on immigration charges too." He frowned. "Whether that is completely legitimate or perhaps a good excuse, I don't know. But it does allow the authorities to hold her for a period of time. However, I'm told there is CC footage of her going to and from Mr. Weatherspoon's residence very near the estimated time of death. So there is that."

"Bail?" Ethan asked.

"There's the question as to who gets custody of Ms. Vrba first, if you will. Our friends at Scotland Yard desperately want her for Weatherspoon's murder. MI6 wants to question her on what she knows on her brother's activities, and now there are rumblings that the International Court in The Hague wants her for the same reason."

"The International Court?" Barry asked, surprised. "I can't imagine the mess we could get into if this becomes a three-way tug-of-war."

"Okay, bottom line?" Ethan asked impatiently. "How do we make sure my aunt's good name is not dragged through the mud?" He gestured toward Victoria. "I think she made it clear, she hardly knows the woman. This is simple blackmail to get my aunt to pay your fees."

"Barry and I haven't as yet shared information," said Davenport. "It's been quite a hectic day." He looked to Barry. "You saw her this morning. If you would be so good as to fill us in."

"We met for nearly an hour." Barry turned to Victoria. "She says to tell you she is grateful for your help."

"So nice to know," Ethan said sarcastically.

Barry went on. "Ms. Vrba has been informed of the situation with MI6, and under no circumstances does she want to be, to use her term, 'tortured by MI6 agents trying to frame her for things she didn't do.'"

"Be wonderful to know what's really going on there," Davenport mused.

"I can tell you this, she greatly fears MI6," Barry said. "Why, I don't know. I tried to get her to talk about that, but she shut down. My concern is that she will do or say anything if it could help stave off our foreign-intelligence guys from getting ahold of her."

Victoria looked at him. "You mean she is going to lie and tell the police I told her to kill Adrian."

Barry grimaced. "Concerning that, she says she has the conversation saved digitally on the cloud."

"Rubbish," Ethan scoffed.

"She also says no one can access it. Only her," Barry added. "I asked to hear the tape, and she laughed and said no way. It's her 'get of jail free card' and she is saving it for the trial."

"What? By throwing my aunt under the bus?" Ethan said angrily.

"I made it clear that it won't work," Barry reassured them. He looked at Victoria. "Let's just say she tries to pin the Weatherspoon murder on you and she gets a lighter sentence. She is simply postponing the inevitable. MI6 will grab her as soon as the Weatherspoon murder trial is finished."

Davenport studied the younger solicitor. "So what, pray tell, did you advise this woman to do exactly?"

"That she cooperates with MI6. She obviously has something to hide and they know she does, so toss them a bone with the agreement that they get the Weatherspoon charges to disappear. It wouldn't be the first time something like that has happened."

"But if she is as fearful of MI6 as you say, she will feel backed into a corner," Davenport reasoned.

"In my experience, animals backed into a corner will fight to the death," Ethan stated.

"Agreed," Barry said.

"The scandal this will cause..." Victoria said quietly.

Barry looked at her. "Ma'am, she might never go on trial for Weatherspoon. First things first. Tomorrow at two p.m., she has to appear in court. MI6 and Scotland Yard will duke it out."

"You'll be there?" Ethan asked.

"Of course," Barry replied.

"What are the odds?" Victoria asked. "That MI6 wins tomorrow?"

Davenport frowned. "Let's just say if I were a betting man, I'd put my money on the foreign-intelligence service. If this woman thinks she has leverage due to a supposed conversation with you, it is a moot point. This is a jurisdictional hearing, plain and simple. The fact that she's not a legal citizen works against her. And quite frankly, in my experience, if MI6 wants you, no matter who you are, your wealth, your family title, your landed-gentry status, what have you, it won't matter. They will get you."

There was a long silence.

"What court is it?" Ethan asked. "Tomorrow?"

FROG Headquarters, The Hague

"When did this happen?" Gretchen asked, after reading the transcript.

"Last night," Two replied, wheeling her office chair around so she was facing Gretchen. "Time stamp is at the bottom. Tiny font, I admit."

Gretchen saw it. "Okay, just past eight last night."

"Victoria and her nephew met with her attorneys last night, then the two of them talked among themselves after the attorneys left," Two said.

Gretchen nodded. "Not much we didn't know in terms of Hana Vrba. Heck, Adam was the one to tip off MI6 about her in the first place with that phone call. So hardly a surprise that MI6 wants to get their hands on her."

"The new stuff is about Clyde Redfield."

"I see that. He's pretty sick," Gretchen said as Marsha came into the IT office.

"Who?" Marsha asked.

"Clyde Redfield."

"We knew about the cancer surgery," Marsha said. "But we had no idea that he's been battling stage-four liver cancer."

Gretchen glanced at the transcript. "Ethan Redfield says his father has two months. Victoria asks about speeding things up so that Clyde will be well enough to see the fruits of their efforts."

"And he says no, they are set for two weeks, and his dad will make that for sure," Two said.

Gretchen shook her head in frustration. "We have two weeks, but we still know next to nothing in terms of where, when, and how… Frustrating."

The entrance door chimed. They all turned. It was Hal. Gretchen turned to Two.

"Where's Adam?"

Marsha glanced at a wall clock. "Should have landed an hour ago."

"Where?" Gretchen asked in surprise.

"London." Marsha motioned to the transcript. "As soon as he saw that about the court hearing today, he wanted to be there."

"Is it open to the public?"

"Not sure." Marsha replied. "He took an ID that has him as a staffer at the International Court."

"You're kidding."

"I think it's a long shot, but he wants to talk to Hana Vrba to see if she knows about the impending water problem."

"You mean when a zillion people die from arsenic water poisoning?" Gretchen asked sarcastically.

"That would be it. The two-week deadline has everyone freaked out," Marsha said.

"Think they'll hit here?" Two asked. "The Hague?"

London, England

Adam sat in the windowless security office in the courthouse basement parking garage, looking at the flatscreen TV mounted on the opposite wall. A split-screen view of the feeds from the various CCTV cameras throughout the building. By habit and training, he had scoped out the entire office. The bullpen where he now sat held three desks, all currently unoccupied. There was a separate supervisor's office with a glass window facing the bullpen. Beyond that were a bathroom and a locker-room changing area.

The underground parking garage was exclusively reserved for those with courthouse business, and an RFID personnel badge was required for entry into the security office. A nearby stairwell and elevator led to the courthouse above. Once brought to the basement office by a police officer manning the court's front entrance, Adam had introduced himself to the security officer on duty, a man named Ryder. The man was older, probably counting the days until he could collect his pension. He wore the standard uniform of black trousers, a white shirt, and black clip-on tie. Similar to law enforcement everywhere in the UK, he carried a baton, but no sidearm.

Adam had offered his International Court credentials and explained that a female murder suspect named Hana Vrba was scheduled to appear before the court within the hour with regard to a jurisdictional matter. He went on to explain that the IC just needed a few minutes of Ms. Vrba's time—preferably before her court appearance, and yes, of course, her solicitor could be present. He had said it really was a matter of great urgency and many lives were at stake. When the man had given him a dubious look, Adam implored Ryder to call the IC home office in The Hague and verify what he was saying.

This, of course, was a gamble. A huge gamble. He didn't really exist at the IC, so there was no authorization for him to do anything at all, let alone talk to Hana Vrba. However, Adam knew human nature. And generally speaking, when you encouraged a person of some authority, in this case a courthouse security officer, to call someone with greater authority, the IC, they would rarely pursue the matter. Usually, for the simple reason that they didn't want to bring attention to themselves for questioning that greater authority.

Ryder had taken Adam's ID and gone into the supervisor's office, closing the door behind him. Sitting in a chair in the bullpen, Adam could see Ryder as he stood behind the desk talking on a landline telephone and staring at Adam. If Ryder found out his ID was bogus, all bets were off. In fact, he risked immediate arrest. He knew Marsha was going to try to create an ID by infiltrating the IC system, but she couldn't promise him she would be able to get in. "They've massively improved their firewall recently," she'd told him. He met the Ryder's eyes through the glass, reminding himself not to look away first. In psychological terms, it gave him more gravitas if he won the staring contest. In other words, *I'm important, I will stare you down until I get what I want.* More simply, it was a game of chicken, and he found his heart beating a little faster than normal as he continued to meet the man's gaze. Finally, the security officer looked away, giving Adam a somewhat childish victory.

His phone chimed and he took it out of his pocket. A text from Marsha. *You're covered for 24 hours. Don't push it.* He smiled to himself and texted her back. *Understood. I would demand a raise if I were you. You really are the best.* He sent it off.

He looked up to see Ryder emerge from the inner office. He stood as Ryder approached and handed him back his ID. "They are on the way."

"ETA?" Adam asked.

"Ten minutes."

"Once she is here, I get three minutes," Adam confirmed.

"That I can't promise," Ryder said. "Her attorney is upstairs and I asked that he come down."

Just then, the same police officer who brought Adam downstairs came in with a middle-aged man with curly hair and wearing what appeared to be a new suit. The man looked from Ryder to Adam and said, "I'm Ms. Vrba's solicitor. Barry Tate."

Adam stepped forward and offered his hand. "Adamander Vorst, IC," Adam said using the name on his ID. "The International Court of Justice wants just a few minutes of your client's time today."

Barry looked around. "Can we talk somewhere private?"

Ryder gestured toward the inner office. Adam led the way and shut the door behind them as Barry turned and asked, "What the hell is this?"

"She may have pertinent information that can help save lives."

"What's in it for her?" Barry asked.

"Goodwill?" Adam offered.

"Right, that will do wonders," Barry scoffed.

"It really is a delicate issue. But I assure you, lives are at stake."

"Dutch lives, I take it," Barry said.

"Actually, all of Europe, the US, Asia, and Australia." Barry seemed surprised, and Adam added, "All I ask for is three minutes."

"What's in it for her?" Barry repeated.

"I don't know," Adam replied. "Maybe the conversation with Victoria Tenney is allowed to see the light of day."

Barry stared, aghast. He opened his mouth to speak and closed it again.

"Oh, wait. Wait, wait, wait," Adam said. "I got mixed up. You *don't* want that tape to see the light of day. It's so confusing." He gave a shoulder roll. "How about it goes away? Forever. That work for you?"

Barry again started to say something and held back. Finally, he asked, "Is that possible?"

"Three minutes," Adam repeated.

Barry shook his head. "She insists that she is the only one that can access the recording. I doubt you can—"

"In a word?" Adam hotly interrupted. "She's in the big leagues now, and in the big leagues, all files, digital, paper, whatever, are accessible by the people who know how to get them." He waited. "Three minutes."

Barry studied Adam. "And it goes away?"

"It goes away," Adam promised.

Barry finally agreed. "Three minutes."

"Alone. I suggest you use the restroom."

"What?" Barry argued, surprised. "No. No way."

"Then Victoria's voice ordering Adrian Weatherspoon's death gets heard by the world."

Barry stared. "No! Look—"

"Stay in the bathroom, or Victoria is going to have to answer a lot of questions she'd rather avoid," Adam told him firmly. "Got it?"

Before Barry could answer, there was a knock on the door, and Ryder opened it and stuck his head in. "Three minutes out."

Adam looked to Barry for an answer, and the solicitor gave a slight nod.

Adam then did his best to get an idea of the parking garage layout. He didn't have time to check it out on foot, but Ryder had explained that the parking structure only allowed for one-way traffic flow. From the street, vehicles drove down the entrance ramp to the first parking level area where the security offices were located. Arrows on the concrete floor guided drivers to circle counterclockwise, or head down to the lower level for additional parking. When leaving the structure, vehicles were directed to the one-way exit ramp to the street.

Satisfied he had a good idea of how things worked, Adam stood with Ryder just outside the security office. It was at this location where detainees were escorted from a vehicle to the stairs leading to the courthouse above. Adam made it clear his three minutes started once he was alone with the prisoner inside the security office. Ryder had simply ignored Adam's demands. Adam glanced around looking for Barry—the solicitor was near the security-office door that led to the garage, busy texting someone. Adam had to think he was telling Davenport what was going on.

The quiet of the garage was suddenly broken by the sound of two loud police motorcycles. Adam looked up the vehicle ramp to see the motorcycles' intense blinking strobe lights advancing toward them. A Ford police-transportation van, complete with more strobe lights, came next, followed by two more police motorcycles bringing up the rear. The procession seemed almost orchestrated, the van slowing to a crawl and stopping right where Ryder said it would. All the vehicles kept their engines running, but the noise from the motorcycles was especially irritating in the enclosed concrete structure.

Ryder placed a hand on Adam's arm and moved him back. They backed up a good fifteen feet. Once they were out of the way, the driver got out and went around to the rear of the vehicle. Adam moved so he could see better. The driver opened both rear doors, and an armed policewoman hopped out. She deftly unfolded a metal step bar at the bumper and disappeared back inside the van. A minute later, Hana Vrba appeared, wearing a prison jumpsuit, her hands cuffed in front of her. The policewoman took hold of Hana's upper arm and guided her down the steps to the garage floor.

Laying eyes on the woman for the first time, Adam thought she looked hard. MI6 was not going to have an easy time breaking her. His mind scrambled on how best to get something out of her in just three minutes time. Suddenly there was a muffled shot and the policewoman silently crumbled to the ground, leaving the prisoner completely exposed. Another muffled shot blew a hole in Hana Vrba's head. She was dead before she hit the concrete floor as frantic shouts erupted from all directions.

Adam took cover behind the van and instinctively reached for his handgun. But he wasn't carrying. Then there were two loud pops followed by a hissing sound. He immediately recognized the telltale signs of a smoke grenade, and the area was instantly covered with thick, red smoke obscuring their vision and rendering any pursuit useless.

An instant later, Adam thought he heard a motorcycle come to life in the distance. He blindly ran in that direction, his eyes stinging from the smoke bomb. When he emerged on the other side of the smokey haze, he saw two men on a motorcycle speed around the far end of the structure. He turned and screamed for the cops to cover the structure's exit.

But he knew it would be too late and doubled over, coughing.

The Hague, Holland

Marsha handed Two a shawl to ward off the cool night air, and the younger woman wrapped it around her shoulders. They sat alone on the apartment's wide patio overlooking the city lights. "Sorry to barge in like this," Two said.

"As I recall, you rang the bell, so that's hardly barging in."

"You know what I mean." Two could see the kids through the large windows. One was on a laptop, the other was doing schoolwork with a textbook and note papers close at hand. She looked back at Marsha.

The patio door slid open and Nathan, Marsha's husband, peeked his head out. "Tea?"

"Oh, no thank you," Two said.

He looked at Marsha. She shook her head. "Thanks."

Nathan smiled and closed the slider.

Marsha waited, but Two was simply staring at the view, seemingly lost in thought. "Spill it."

Two turned, surprised. Finally she said, "I'm not sure you'll tell me anyway."

"Tell you what?"

"What really happened today in London." Two said.

"What do you mean?" Marsha replied, genuinely puzzled.

"It was Adam, right? Adam did this."

"What?" Marsha asked, aghast. "No. Why would you—"

"Because it's what we do!" Two interrupted heatedly. Through the glass, she saw the older kid look up. In a quiet voice, she said, "It's FROG. This is what FROG does."

"No, it's not."

"It is. And I get it. We cut off the head of the snake before it can strike and—"

"Hana Vrba wasn't the head of anything. She wasn't a catastrophic risk to a nation state or humanity. Those are the FROG guidelines for termination." Marsha turned to glance back inside. No one was nearby. She turned back to Two. "If anything, we'd love to know what she knew about the Redfields and what they're planning. That's why Adam went over there. To see what he could find out. It was a long shot, but worth a try." When Two didn't say anything, Marsha added, "We would have loved to have her *alive*. Not dead."

Two frowned. "It's an odd coincidence, you have to admit. I mean, Adam suddenly goes to London, and Hana Vrba is shot dead. Right there. At the courthouse."

"We *lose* with her death. FROG loses. There is no gain." She waited a bit and added, "So ask yourself, who gains from this?"

Two hesitated and then looked at Marsha. "Victoria Tenney since she put the hit out on Adrian Weatherspoon."

"Exactly. And who had the means to bomb a café in Amsterdam?"

"Ethan Redfield, it looks like."

"And to kill Bart Werner as soon as he stepped off a plane? To make sure Mac Senton would kill himself rather than risk telling what he knew and having his daughter die?"

Two slowly nodded.

Marsha went on, "This is big. Big as it gets. And we have two weeks to stop it. Fourteen days to stop who knows how many water plants around the world from being polluted. How do we do that? I don't know. I honestly don't. But there is one FROG option, if necessary. If it will stop it."

Two looked at her.

"You need to think of it this way," Marsha went on. "If Clyde Redfield, Victoria Tenney, and Ethan Redfield are the ones to turn the lights out on the world, wouldn't the world be safer if we turned the lights out on them first?"

"Yeah."

"Big time yeah." Marsha took a deep breath.

The slider opened again. It was Nathan. "Supper's on."

Two slowly got up, lost in thought. She looked at Marsha, "Thank you. Sorry to interrupt your evening."

"Hey, you're not leaving," Nathan said. "The kids want to know what it's like to work with Mom. They've never met someone from work before. We're having frikkadel. American style." It was a skinless, deep-fried sausage, often accompanied by a curry sauce, served in long, warm buns, like an American hotdog.

Marsha winked at Two. "Nathan makes the best frikkadel in the world."

"Table's set. C'mon." When Two remained frozen in place, he clapped his hands. "Let's go. My cooking waits for no man... Or woman."

Two glanced at Marsha, unsure.

Marsha smiled. "Please join us. I mean it."

Two smiled, happily surprised.

Nathan had gone back inside as the two women headed toward the slider. "A word of advice?" Marsha said quietly. When Two gave her a questioning look, she said, "If you want to keep your job, tell them I'm awesome at work."

Two laughed.

London, England

Oliver was more nervous than he'd like to admit as he approached Ethan Redfield's private office on the eighth floor. The day before, Oliver had purchased a tablet and set up a VPN solely to infiltrate the travel agency to see if any Redfields had travel plans and to check the draft folder in the encrypted email.

So far, nothing. The routine came to be that he would check at lunch and dinner, outside the office.

Just a few hours ago, he and Taylor had been enjoying a nice dinner at an Indian restaurant near their home, which was the last time he'd checked the travel agency records and the email drafts folder. Still nothing. It was at that instant that Ethan Redfield had called asking him to come to the office around nine that night. Needless to say, the call had ruined their evening, with Taylor insisting that the night meeting meant only one thing—that Ethan Redfield knew of his treachery and Oliver would soon be dead.

Taylor had gone on and on about it. After her second glass of wine, she finally said that if Ethan Redfield suggested they go for a ride, meaning Redfield was going to kill him and dump his body somewhere, Oliver just needed to explain that he had a severe case of the trots. Taylor had laughed. "You really think he is going to have you ride in his beautiful Maserati if you've got the shits?"

"You need to stop watching so many police dramas," Oliver told her. "My life is not in danger."

"Right. So why the meeting tonight? Not six in the evening, but nine at night. A little late, don't you think? And what for? He didn't tell you." When Oliver didn't say anything, she went on. "That ever happen before? Last minute like this? Be honest."

"No."

"He finds out we're on the other side, we're done for," Taylor had said.

He had gotten up from the table and leaned down to kiss her. "I'm coming home tonight in one piece." He gestured to the tablet sitting on the table. "You haven't done today's Wordle. Do that, and don't worry about me, okay?"

She had given him a tight smile, but there were tears in her eyes. He had left while he still had the courage.

He found Ethan Redfield's office door closed, which surprised him. There was hardly anyone was in the building, so why keep it closed? Oliver stepped up to the door, took a deep breath, and knocked.

"Come!" a voice called out from within.

Ethan Redfield was sitting behind his massive desk, working on his laptop. A tumbler of whiskey was close at hand. He looked up. "Good, you're here."

Oliver felt his mouth go dry and slowly approached the desk.

"I bought a portable Wi-Fi router, and, of course, it says it's easy to hook up, but I've come to discover that the word 'easy' when it comes to phones or computers only works if you're five years old." He had a silly grin on his face, and Oliver briefly wondered how many drinks Ethan had consumed. If he wasn't drunk, he was definitely headed that way.

When Oliver didn't respond, Ethan quickly added, "Sorry, sorry. I didn't mean *you* were five years old. It just seems like kids, they can do this stuff with ease. I'm failing miserably tonight. So I just need you to hook it up. Walk me through what to do when I get there, and I can't find a hotspot. Last time the internet was so spotty down there it drove me bonkers."

Oliver nodded and moved around the desk. It took Ethan a moment to realize that he would have to relinquish the chair, and he got up quickly, not completely steady on his feet.

Oliver sat down, opened the router, and immediately saw the problem. He glanced at Ethan. "Where you headed off to?"

Chapter Twenty-Two

Antofagasta, Chile ~ 48 Hours Later

Maximo was like a fly on the wall, seeing everything that was going on in the spacious office below while remaining completely unnoticed behind the air-vent grate. What he saw horrified him. His father was on the floor, his back against the opposite wall, his face bloody, his left arm limp, the lower part of the arm twisted at an obscene angle, his hand lying palm-up on the floor, also in an unnatural position. The two gringos Maximo had seen earlier were on either side of his father. The older one was now sitting on the seat of his handicap walker. The younger man spoke in a raised voice in English to his father, calling him by his given name, Tomás. The gringo kept demanding something, but Maximo couldn't make it out. Suddenly the man stepped forward and kicked his father in the ribs, eliciting a moan. Another kick, this time to the twisted left arm. His father screamed in agony and fell over on his side, and Maximo felt his bladder release. Twelve years old, and he had just wet his pants.

With silent tears streaming down his face, Maximo would swear that his father saw him peering down at him through the grate. He would also swear that his father shook his head no. He watched as his father's eyes closed and his body went limp. Only then did Maximo move.

It had just been six weeks ago that Maximo had found this airflow shaft, crawling through the ventilation duct until he came to the end—at his father's office. At the time, his father had been sitting at the old metal desk, talking on the phone. Only after he hung up did Maximo speak. His father had whirled around, seeking his son. Finally, Maximo laughed and said, "Up here, Papa. Up here."

His father had been astonished, coming around the desk and staring up nearly twelve feet to see his son's face behind the wide-open grate flaps. When his father asked how he came to be there,

Maximo told him that he had been playing on the side of a nearby mound of dirt—truthfully, he had been scrounging around in the hopes of finding some gold nuggets—when he spotted the metal ladder attached to the side of the building that led to a large access screen. Curious, he had gone up the ladder, unlatched the screen cover, and crawled all the way to the end. He was hopeful it would open to some hidden cache of gold. Instead, it had simply led to his father's office.

His father told him it was dangerous and to get out. He had gotten out and decided not to venture back. There was no gold to be discovered, and as his father explained, it was simply an air-circulation shaft for the building. He hadn't gone in again until his father had been gone for well over an hour for what was supposed to be a twenty-minute meeting.

The nighttime meeting had been requested at the last minute, and Maximo had only been allowed to accompany his father by reminding him how he had gotten straight A's on his last report card. Plus, there was no school tomorrow, so why couldn't he go for a ride? Not surprisingly, his father had given in. Ever since his mother had died, Maximo and his father spent as much time together as possible.

Upon arriving at the old mine, his father had told him to stay in the truck. This was a meeting with the new owner of the mine, and he didn't want Maximo running around making a nuisance of himself. Maximo promised to stay in the truck.

He had seen the owner arrive in a Land Rover. He knew cars, and he knew the man must have money because only the wealthy drove Land Rovers. Stretching out across the truck's bench seat, he peeked through the driver's window to watch. A gringo got out of the driver's seat and opened the rear hatch. He took something large out of the back, closed the hatch and then went to the passenger door. With the passenger door open and the car's overhead light on, Maximo saw that the driver had removed a handicap walker from the back of the SUV. He unfolded it and helped an older man get out. When he shut the passenger door, it had gone dark again.

~ ~ ~

Adam drove the small VW SUV as Gretchen used the GPS on her cell phone to guide them to their destination. It was just after ten at night local time, and they had both used the flight time to catch up on some much-needed sleep since the past thirty-six hours had been a whirlwind of activity.

It had begun when Adam had seen Oliver's email in the draft folder several hours after Oliver had posted it. It read:

Saw E tonight to help him set up a wireless router for a trip he is taking. The following is taken from our conversation tonight. He had been drinking quite a bit. I can't substantiate what was said via any records, etc. It is just from our conversation.

He is taking his dying father to Antofagasta, Chile, since his father 'had always wanted to see the place.' (I Googled city name by how it sounded phonetically. I think this is correct, but again, this was a conversation, and he wasn't completely sober). They are going by private jet due his father's rapid decline from cancer and the need to keep him as comfortable as possible. Clyde Redfield's personal nurse will be accompanying them.

No clue on the name of the private-plane company being used.

Nor any confirmation on where the plane will be departing from or the exact time. 'Tomorrow evening' was all E said at 2200.

No clue regarding hotel accommodations or the like once in Chile.

He plans to stay in Chile anywhere from three to seven days.

Hope this helps.

Adam had read the email several times before he replied by creating a new draft email that said, *Very well done. Thank you for the information. Please update as needed and stay safe.* He had then called Hal, waking him in the dead of the night.

Hal had given everyone instructions to be at the FROG office by seven in the morning. The first priority was to arrange private air travel for Adam and Gretchen to Antofagasta. Two and Marsha had tried to uncover the Redfields' air-travel details, but they had come up empty. Two had found that the Redfields were taking a very large suite at the Hilton. She booked adjoining rooms for Adam and Gretchen on the ground floor of the same hotel, knowing full well that FROG operators always took the ground floor for a quick exit should the need arise. No elevator waits or dashing down flights of stairs. She also arranged an all-wheel SUV to be available upon landing.

Hal's job was to arrange armed backup for his two-member team. After exhausting all the resources he had in the neighboring countries that would allow for a quick infiltration of backup, he was left with picking and choosing mercenaries. Adam had vetoed that idea. He didn't know the men, didn't trust them, and didn't want them. He and Gretchen would go alone, with no backup. There were some arguments about this, but Adam prevailed.

What he did want was a good interpreter since neither he nor Gretchen was fluent in the local Chilean Spanish dialect, and they didn't want any communication errors. Using the ruse that they were coming down there as Interpol agents, Hal finally got someone from the Chilean Department of Justice to find an interpreter.

A few hours before flight time, Two had given them five different burner phones ready for use in Chile. Hal had unlocked the armaments vault, and Gretchen and Adam selected their weapons of choice. For Gretchen, an eight-inch combat knife and two semi-automatic Glock pistols, one quite slender and lightweight for her ankle-holster backup. Adam chose Sig Sauer guns and two knives. They also took lightweight semi-automatic rifles, plenty of ammunition, night-vision goggles, Kevlar vests, and lightweight rappelling rope should they need it. A tactical-trauma kit contained tourniquets, morphine, QuikClot gear, surgical gauze, and tape.

Their fifteen-hour flight was courtesy of Monarch Air Group, which catered to wealthy individuals who could afford the convenience of private air charter. Their Interpol IDs explained the tactical-gun-carry cases that were stored safely in the luggage hold. Adam had been a bit concerned that the crew might talk about their law-enforcement passengers once they were on the ground during their layover, but there was nothing he could do about it, so he let it go.

"We're on it," Gretchen told him.

Adam slowed and moved off to the right although there was hardly any traffic. They found the property parallel to the highway secured by a heavy-duty chain-link fence. There were the usual "No Trespassing" signs posted in both Spanish and English. A metal swing gate stood at the mine's entrance. As the headlights hit the gate, they saw that it was partially open. Gretchen hopped out, her right hand ready to draw her gun if need be. She pushed the gate fully open and closed it after Adam had pulled through. Getting back in, she said, "Well, I guess it's safe to say we're not alone."

"Nope." With that, Adam shut off the headlights so they wouldn't be an obvious target to anyone inside the property. Gretchen reached down at her feet for a pair of night-vision goggles and handed them to Adam.

~ ~ ~

Maximo scurried backward through the air shaft, his heart in his throat. He imagined the younger man knew he was there and had seen the whole thing and was simply waiting for him to exit the shaft; and then he'd be dead, just like his father. But Maximo had no choice; there was only the one way out. And he desperately wanted out. Finally, he reached the opened screen. He peeked out, making sure he didn't see anything in the dark shadows. He tried to listen for noises, but his heart was hammering so hard it echoed in his ears. Finally, he turned around and silently went down the ladder.

Once on the ground, he carefully ventured around the side of the building. The office lights were still on inside, but there was no activity outside. His father's truck and the Land Rover were still there. It was as if nothing had changed since he had gone into the air shaft. Except the entire world had changed during those few minutes. His world, anyway.

He was desperately thirsty and thought of grabbing his bottled water from the truck cab. But he knew that if he opened the truck's door, the overhead light would come on. He wished his father had left the keys with him. Though he was much too young to have had any formal driving lessons yet, but he was tall for his age and his father had let him drive around the vast mine acreage from time to time, so he had the basics down. He could have at least made it to the main road. Asked for help. However, as was his father's habit, he had pocketed the keys when he exited the truck, telling Maximo to remain there.

~ ~ ~

"How far?"

Gretchen enlarged the route-guidance map with her fingers. "About a hundred yards."

Adam grunted and pulled the small SUV off the main road they'd been following. The landscape was dotted with large boulders, but none large enough to conceal the car, so he simply pulled way off the road. So many parts of an operation were luck. If they were lucky, no one would come in and see the vehicle. If they weren't lucky…

At the back of the vehicle, they geared up with the Kevlar vests, their knives, and added firepower and ammunition. No longer needing to look at her phone, Gretchen now put on a pair of night-vision goggles.

They had a good idea of what lay ahead since Marsha had come through with interesting articles about the mine. The first one was from *National Geographic Magazine,* and it had featured fifteen-pages of both color and stark black-and-white photos of the mine. At the time of publication in 1986, the Diego mine was a thriving, industrious place with a large processing plant, heavy dump trucks, bulldozers and excavators moving about, and hundreds of miners in hard hats tackling the arduous work.

More recent articles depicted the mine as a shell of its former self. As the years went on with the mine producing less and less gold, the various buildings and main plant fell into various states of disrepair. An earthquake just over two years ago leveled every single building on the site except for the main office building—the single-story standalone structure built of slump stone had sustained only modest damage. This generated conspiracy theories that it had been purposely built much stronger than the other buildings since it was home to "the important people running the mine." In other words, the miners could be sacrificed.

However, a subsequent newspaper article debunked such talk as "nonsense," pointing out that you could walk down any street in the world after a severe earthquake and find one structure had completely collapsed while the neighboring structure sustained only negligible damage. The author pointed out the many scientific factors that determined a building's fate during an earthquake, including exactly how strongly and deeply the earth moved underneath the structure.

For Adam and Gretchen, all this meant was that if there were people in the mine at this time of night, most likely they were in the office.

~ ~ ~

Maximo could hear his father charging up the grade right beside him, cheering him on. "You got it! Fast now! Fast! Go, go, go!" His head cleared, and he realized this wasn't another regional school track meet—this was life or death. He was sorely tempted to look over his shoulder to see if the Land Rover was coming up behind him, but again, he could hear his father's voice. "Don't look back! You got this! Go, go, go!"

He was wondering how long it would take to find someone on the highway who would be willing to pull over and help when he suddenly ran straight into a brick wall. He was lifted off his feet and taken to the ground in one fell swoop. He landed on his back with an audible "Oooof," and suddenly he realized he couldn't breathe. Panic set in. Why couldn't he breathe? Something was on top of him. He looked up and saw a large monster staring down at him with an angular metal face and that was it. His heart stopped.

~ ~ ~

"It's just a kid!" Gretchen said. She ripped off her goggles and cradled the teen. She glanced up at Adam. "You scared the crap out of him! Take them off or move off!"

Instead of doing either, Adam proceeded to pat down the teen. Finding nothing, he elected to move off.

The boy came around and Gretchen told him, "You're going to be okay... You're okay... *Está bien.*" Her Spanish was limited to yes, thank you, and it's okay. Pathetic, really.

The boy strained to move but couldn't. She knew he'd had the wind knocked out of him. She also knew it hurt like hell, and when you couldn't breathe, panic ensued. Coupling that with seeing Adam in the night-vision goggles staring down at him, the poor boy was terrified.

"Speak English?" Gretchen asked. Nothing but frantic eyes looking about. "*Está bien... Está bien...*" His eyes met her. "I know it hurts, I know. But you've got to sit up, buddy. C'mon... Sit up." She got an arm under him and, with some effort, got him to a sitting position. He gasped for air. She got in front of him.

"Breathe deep, through your mouth." She took her own deep breaths, and he followed her direction. "That's it. Keep doing that. Deep breathes. *Está bien.*"

She looked around but couldn't see Adam. She didn't want to scare the kid by putting her goggles on, so she simply said in a normal voice, "Sitrep."

Adam was off to her left. "All quiet. Two cars down there. Office, I presume. Lights are on."

The boy whirled around, looking for the voice as Gretchen said, "It's okay. *Está bien, está bien...* You're okay. *Está bien, si?* Sorry about the tackle, but I promise you're fine, okay?"

The boy continued to look around for the unseen voice.

"It's okay," she repeated. "No one's going to hurt you." She waited, then smiled, grabbed her goggles, and carefully, slowly, put them on her head. Then she took them off and helped the boy slip them on his head. He looked around with complete wonder. She gently pulled them off, and he blinked his eyes rapidly. "That's how we saw you and you didn't see us, okay?"

Nothing. The boy was still traumatized. "Deep breaths. Keep breathing deep, okay?"

This time, she didn't have to take deep breaths to show him, he followed her verbal instruction. This meant he understood English.

"What's your name?" Gretchen asked. Nothing. He was too busy looking around, probably wondering where Adam was. She took his hand to get his attention and said, "I'm Greta." She released his hand and pointed to her chest. "Greta." She pointed at his chest.

"Maximo," the boy said quietly.

Finally, an answer. "Okay, good. Maximo. Sorry about the tackle, okay? My friend was worried you were a bad guy."

Suddenly the boy started crying.

~ ~ ~

Gretchen could hear the voices now. She kept going, methodically crawling ahead, the night-vision goggles a godsend in the dark air shaft. She wore a communications earpiece so she could hear Adam, but obviously, she didn't dare speak for fear that whoever was in the office would hear her. However, she could tap the tail end of the earpiece so that Adam would hear a click sound.

One click acknowledged that she heard whatever Adam might be saying to her. Otherwise, she was to give two clicks to confirm she had eyes on the office. After waiting ten seconds, she would give a click for each tango. Maximo had said there were just two men, but they couldn't rely on that. Meanwhile, Adam had taken cover outside the office.

Right now, she prayed her instinct that Maximo could be trusted had been correct. When he had started sobbing, Gretchen had moved to sit right beside him, wrapping him in her arms and talking soothingly. Finally, he had wiped his nose with the back of his hand and told her that his father had been killed by two gringos. He wasn't sure why, but one gringo kept asking his father something and kicking him. That started a fresh set of tears.

It took a good five minutes to get a layout of the situation. She and Adam had moved away from the boy to discuss how to proceed. Adam wanted to bound and gag the kid so they would be free to operate. She didn't like that one bit.

"You got a better idea?" Adam had asked impatiently.

Truthfully, she didn't. She also knew telling Adam the kid had been traumatized enough was not an answer. Finally, she had said, "He stays here and tells us if we have company coming."

"Right, right, we'll make him operational. That works for me," Adam replied sarcastically. "Can't believe I didn't think of that myself."

"We're going in blind," she had argued. "Maybe it's just the two Redfields, but who knows?" When Maximo described the men in the mine office as white, with one being an older man appearing quite frail and using a handicap walker, they presumed Clyde and Ethan Redfield were on site." She went on. "For all we know, more people are coming, and we have nothing. No backup, nothing. At least have him keep an eye out."

Finally, they had compromised. Maximo would be hog-tied, with only one arm free, and positioned behind a large boulder. He would have sight of the road but be far enough away that no one would be able to spot him. Adam primed one of their burner phones with both his and Gretchen's phone numbers and a text message ready to go that read, *STOP*, in all caps. Maximo understood he was only to wake up the phone and send the message if a vehicle approached from the highway. Then he was to toss it as far as he could. The kid actually argued he could toss it very far if he wasn't tied up. Gretchen explained if more guys showed up, Maximo's best option for survival would be that he was captured and tied up.

"You were too heavy-handed!" a man's voice. Angry.

"And where did I get that from, dear Pops?" another voice. Ethan Redfield talking to his father.

"Hand me some files, I can at least be useful."

"This is stupid. We talk to the seller. He knows where to find it."

The light at the end of the air shaft got brighter. The voices were clear as day. She pulled down the night-vision goggles, took her handgun from her holster, and continued to creep forward. She needed to have eyes on but stay far enough away that they wouldn't see her face if they happened to look up.

A short time later, she was close enough. The office was as Maximo had described—with one metal desk, a chair, filing cabinets, and a landline phone. She saw a large man on the floor, one arm splayed at an awkward angle. Maximo's father. She recognized Ethan Redfield from photos. He was going through a large filing cabinet. His father sat on the seat of the handicap walker, looking through pages on his lap.

She tapped the earpiece twice. She had eyes on. After ten seconds, she gave two distinct clicks. There were two of them. Adam gave a one-click response. He understood.

Just then, there was a loud moan. Her heart jumped as she saw Maximo's father move slightly. Another moan. He was alive!

"Get on him! Find out where it is!" the elder man yelled.

Ethan lunged for the desk and then she saw it. A handgun.

Another moan from Maximo's father. With great effort, he used his good arm to push himself up to a sitting position, his back against the wall. Breathing hard, he found himself face to face with Ethan, the gun in his face. "Where do we find it?" Ethan demanded.

Gasping for breath, the man finally replied. "I don't know, I told you…"

"Where!" he yelled. "Where is it!"

Maximo's father shook his head, the move barely discernable.

Ethan stiffened, clearly enraged. "I swear to God, I'll kill you! Where do we find it?"

The injured Chilean stared up at Ethan and defiantly said, "I don't know."

"Your choice," Ethan said. "A bullet in the head and you die, or a bullet in the knee and you live... Tell me!"

"I don't know..."

"Not the answer I wanted..."

The battered man replied by spitting blood toward Ethan.

~ ~ ~

Hunkered down outside under cover, Adam heard two shots. Boom, boom! Loud. "Sitrep! Sitrep..!" he hissed. The waiting nearly killed him. "Gretchen, talk to me. Sitrep!"

It seemed to take forever, and then he heard her voice. "Ethan Redfield is down. Repeat, Ethan Redfield is down. His father has a body shot. Repeat, father has a body shot. I'll wait for you to secure the scene. Safe to enter. Repeat, safe to enter."

Within seconds, Adam burst in, two hands on his weapon, surveying the scene. Ethan was face down on the floor, blood pooling around his head. As Gretchen had said, Clyde Redfield was on the floor with a shot to the abdomen. Adam secured Ethan's gun. The severely injured Chilean looked at Adam with great bewilderment.

"Who are you?" he asked in English.

"Maximo sent us," Adam replied.

Chapter Twenty-Three

Amsterdam, the Netherlands ~ 78 Hours Later

Justine Wolter was now in a small, private room in the ICU ward, hooked up to all sorts of electronic devices monitoring her vitals. A single chair was nearby for a visitor. Just the day before, she had finally felt pretty good. The flu symptoms of severe stomach pain, nausea, and vomiting had finally abated thanks to an IV drip of anti-nausea medication primarily used for cancer patients undergoing chemotherapy treatment. But later that night, the skin lesions appeared and her heart went into atrial fibrillation. She was finally stabilized and moved to an intensive care unit. When she woke, she asked for Vicar Werner. Her stubborn father might not have wanted to receive the prayers of healing and be anointed with holy oil as he left this world, but she certainly did. And she knew she was dying.

It was some hours later that she awoke to find the vicar standing at her bedside. He wore a bright ankle-length tunic with the traditional white collar at his throat. He lovingly took her hand, and relief flooded through her. "I'm dying," she managed to say.

"Perhaps we best leave that to God, eh?" the vicar replied, with a wink and a smile. Turning serious, he added, "Many have this. I was laid up with this too. It is awful."

Justine frowned. "You're better."

"Thanks to the Lord, yes."

Just then, a doctor came in, concentrating on a chart in his hands so intensely that he didn't even see the vicar until he nearly ran into him. He immediately apologized. "Sorry. I didn't mean to interrupt."

Justine said to the doctor, "He's been our family vicar all my life. I asked him to come. To administer the anointing for the sick." She looked at the vicar with tears in her eyes.

"We have some preliminary good news," the doctor said. He looked at Justine. "We now know that the water in some parts of the city has been contaminated with high levels of arsenic."

"Arsenic?" the vicar repeated, stunned.

"That's the word. The authorities are trying to locate the source." He looked to Justine. "And your symptoms correspond with arsenic poisoning. A nurse will be in shortly to draw blood and collect a urine sample. From that, we'll know if you have been exposed, and if so, what your levels are."

"Is it treatable?" Justine asked.

He smiled. "Yes. We'll be more aggressive with IV fluids and see what else is needed when we get the results of your lab work. And of course, we will be containing your exposure. That's the key, obviously."

"But I haven't had water here, not that I remember," Justine said.

He smiled. "I was just looking at your chart. You have been drinking quite a bit of tea. Which is good, we want you hydrated, but—"

"Tea is made with water, and the water is tainted," the vicar interrupted.

"Exactly," the doctor said, looking at the vicar. He turned back to Justine. "From now on, only water from sealed bottles will be used for everything, drinking, cooking, everything. That goes for everyone. City-wide." He smiled again. "Let's get the lab work done and see where you are. But I'm quite optimistic."

At that point, the vicar collapsed into the nearby chair. The doctor hurried over. "Are you okay, Father?"

The vicar looked up at him, stunned. "I was telling Justine that I had this too. I was so sick. I thought it was a flu."

"You obviously didn't succumb, that's the main thing," the doctor said.

"No, you don't understand. I stopped drinking tea and coffee, even regular water. I drank only Gatorade. I still am. It's the only thing that makes me feel better."

FROG Headquarters, The Hague

In his heart and his head, Hal knew he had done everything possible and he had to be satisfied with that. It hadn't been easy to sound the alarm since FROG didn't technically exist. However, they had gotten word out to those that count, including the Prime Minister's office, the Ministry of Health, and something called the Freshwater Management Council, that the water supply in Amsterdam had been tainted with arsenic.

This was all done with Marsha's magic—she had set it up so it looked like the tip had come from the US State Department in conjunction with the CIA. Bogus emails ending in state.gov and cia.gov gave the impression that it was legit, as did phone numbers with the area code and prefix for those agencies, which were all linked back to FROG. Hal, Two, and Marsha had handled the various phone calls from Dutch authorities attempting to confirm the tip.

However, getting them to act on the tip was like trying to turn the Titanic on a dime. It simply wasn't going to happen. And the Dutch government proved to be like any other western government—cumbersome and slow to react. At one point, Hal thought that if the authorities didn't get on the ball, FROG would have to give attribution to a known terror group. The media would gobble that up and spit it back out ten times over. However, that would open a can of worms that he'd rather not open.

On one phone call, Two, using a perfect American accent, bellowed at the person from the Netherlands Ministry of Health that if he didn't believe her, he needed to have the water companies test for arsenic and then put immediate water treatment methods in place. This included ion exchange, reverse osmosis, ultra-filtration, and so on. After that, he needed to find the terrorists that poisoned the water, and he could start by turning over to law enforcement all water-company employment records and security camera feeds from the various water pumps and water-treatment centers. The Dutchman suddenly told her that Holland did not take direction from Americans, and he had hung up.

Twenty-four hours later, things finally started to move when a senator in the upper house of the legislature held a press conference in The Hague to announce that Amsterdam residents might be experiencing "spells of illness" due to "a water issue." When reporters pressed for more answers, he admitted the water "may have been compromised." The politician didn't say how, or with what, but he urged people to thoroughly boil all water before use. Watching the press conference on the television in the conference room, Hal went ballistic, screaming at the politician that the people were being poisoned! And boiling water would not remove the poison—in fact, arsenic concentrations could increase after water loss due to evaporation.

Immediately after that, the truth came out about arsenic poisoning and people were directed to avoid all tap water. The military was set to deliver pallets of bottled water throughout the city, while officials treated the water supply to get it back to safe levels. Finally, since doctors now knew the cause of the illness, they were able to successfully treat the sick.

Sitting alone in the conference room, Hal played the two videos again. The first was filmed by Gretchen using her iPhone as she questioned Clyde Redfield. The elderly man was flat on his back, his blood-soaked hands pressing on the abdominal gunshot wound. He said, "You can't kill us all. Many more will carry on after me… You can't stop this."

Gretchen replied, "I live in the here and now. And right here, right now, you have failed. So guess what? That means you don't get to kill off half the planet after all. How about that?"

Nothing. Redfield simply glared.

Gretchen added, "You've probably heard the saying, *The best-laid plans of mice and men often go awry*."

"Not so," Redfield retorted, blood appearing on his lips. Internal bleeding. He didn't have long.

"Yeah, it is so," Gretchen smugly told him.

He struggled to catch his breath. "Amsterdam…"

Taken by surprise, Gretchen tentatively asked, "What about Amsterdam?"

"You tell me… Many are sick… It will only get worse."

"I don't believe you," she replied.

"Testing for COVID… Always COVID… No one thinks of the water."

Gretchen shook her head, defiant. "That won't work. The idea is to hit as many cities as possible all at once. Authorities see arsenic in the water in one place, and they'll be looking for it everywhere."

A resigned smile, more blood on his lips. "As you say, of mice and men. We needed better men. They didn't listen. Acted a bit too soon. But it's okay. Justine will die. That is good..."

Puzzled, Gretchen asked, "Justine..?"

"Hans betrayed me. I didn't get to kill him. Cancer did that... But his daughter? She may be dead now... She is in the hospital... You can check... Diepenbrockbuurt..."

Adam's voice. "Hans Wolter's neighborhood."

The video focus changed to Adam. He was wearing sterile medical gloves and tending to the injured Chilean, the man's son at his side. Adam was looking at the camera. "Hans Wolter lived in Diepenbrockbuurt."

"Yes..." Clyde said. The video went back to Redfield, his eyes closed. "First water pump station was for Diepenbrockbuurt..."

"Hans wanted his money out," Gretchen said. "He didn't think it was a good idea to kill millions of people."

"Better population planning is a necessity," Clyde said, his voice weakening. "We have to do it..."

"Hans didn't think so." Nothing. "You know what Hans called you? He had a name for you."

Clyde opened his eyes, obviously curious.

"The Joker. You're a joke."

Clyde's face changed. Angry. "He didn't see. He should have seen..."

"What city is next?" Gretchen asked. Nothing. Louder now. "Clyde? What city is next?"

With that, Clyde Redfield stopped breathing.

Hal changed to the next video. As it started, Adam was administering an IV. He turned to the teen boy. "Max, stand up and hold this for me. Keep it high."

Maximo did as he was told. Gretchen spoke next. "Maximo, three minutes of questions for your father, then we go to the hospital. But this is important. I need your father to explain. If he doesn't understand, you answer for him in English, okay?"

"Yes," Maximo replied. "My English is better."

"Ha!" the father teased, clearly in a weakened condition.

Adam turned to the camera. "Applied a QuikClot to what looks like a knife wound in the ribs. Left shoulder separated, broken elbow, shattered wrist. Got a compression bandage there. Low-dose morphine. Three minutes, starting now."

Gretchen began. "Why did they beat you up? They were asking where it is? What is it they wanted?"

The man looked at her. "The dust…"

"Dust?"

He turned to his son and went back and forth in their native tongue. Finally, the boy said, "Arsenic Trioxide?" He looked chagrined. . "I don't know…"

"It's okay," Gretchen told him. "Just translate as needed."

The father said, "It's a dust. Fine dust, *si*?"

"Yes," Gretchen said. "You hid it?"

"No. No, no." He closed his eyes and went on, "It is in very heavy concrete containers. Underground. I no move. No move if I want to. Too heavy. No one move."

"Okay, so where is it?"

He opened his eyes. "Underground. Shaft thirty-three. Underground," he said. "Where it has been for years."

Gretchen frowned. She motioned to the bodies. "They asked you and you said you didn't know. Why?"

He sighed. "Men came here. A month ago, *si*? I was told, let them in, show them where the dust is."

"Who told you to show them?" Adam asked.

The man pointed at Ethan's body. "He told me. He own it now. I think, yes, all good, maybe it taken away so mine can work again, no?"

"He was here?" Adam asked.

"No, no. He tell me on phone. He not here. Tonight? I meet him for first time."

"Okay, the men that came here for the arsenic dust, go back to that," Adam said.

"The men, they wear…" He looked to Maximo. Some back in forth between them.

"Protective suits," Maximo explained. "White body suits. Gloves, helmet, air tank, like you wear swimming underwater."

"Hazmat suit," Gretchen interpreted.

The boy shook his head. It wasn't a term he knew.

"Go on," Gretchen said to the father. "You showed them where it was."

"*Si, si*. They take quite a bit. I don't know how much. But one man. He from here. He tell me the men are going to poison people. I say, here? In Chile? He say, no. Europe. He is scared. He asks if the owner knows." Another gesture toward Ethan's body. "I say, I don't know."

"What happened next?" Gretchen asked.

"I didn't know what to think. What to do." He glanced at the body. "But the owner, he pay me to oversee the mine. I come, once, maybe twice a week. Make sure nothing going on. I tell him, I say, I think the men that took it are bad men, so I moved it to a different place, to make it safe. It was…" More back and forth with Maximo.

"A test," Maximo explained. "My father says he didn't know if the owner was a good man or a bad man."

"Okay, then what?" Gretchen asked. "What did he say when you said you moved it?"

"On phone, he ask, is it still at the mine? I say *si*, it is at the mine. But those men might come back, I think to poison people, so it is moved now. They can't find it."

"And obviously he believed you," Adam said.

"*Si.*"

"What happened tonight?"

"We meet for the first time. I…" He looked to Maximo and they talked.

Maximo then translated. "He thought maybe the owner would be pleased he protected the arsenic from bad people. He was hoping he would get a reward. More money."

"Instead, you got beaten up," Gretchen said. "I can't believe you didn't cave…" She saw his puzzled look. "You didn't tell him the truth."

The father and son talked. Finally Maximo said, "My father asked why he care so much about the arsenic. He got mad." The boy motioned to the desk. "He took a letter opener and threaten Papa… He got very mad and stabbed my father. He tell Papa to tell him or he will kill him…"

The father nodded in agreement. "He was going to kill me if I lie or if I say the truth. I know what is right and wrong. I did what was right…I just wish I had left Maximo home… He beat me, and I pray… Not for me…I pray for Maximo…I pray to God they wouldn't find my son… That my son would live…"

Overcome with emotion, Maximo crumbled to the floor and held on to his father. The video ended with a closeup of father and son clinging to each other.

London, England ~ Five Days Later

Oliver knew who Eve Mendenhall was of course, but he had never met her. Nor had he ever been in her spacious office. Standing before her massive desk, he couldn't help but look around, admiring the beautiful furniture, the plush carpet under his feet, and the large paintings on the walls, each one probably worth more than he could even fathom. If nothing else, the office was certainly appropriate for the president and chief operating officer of Red Arrow Capital.

She finished writing something and looked up at him. "We've never met, but I assure you, I'm well aware of what your engineering team does for this firm."

Oliver thought she looked older than he had been expecting. In her mid-sixties, at least. He knew she had been with the firm since the beginning, so it made sense that she was older.

Eve Mendenhall put down her pen and sat back in her chair. "A formal announcement will be forthcoming…" She gestured to the paper in front of her. "You're a computer guy, but I prefer writing by hand. Old school, I guess you would say."

Oliver smiled. "I understand."

She sighed. "I prefer you don't share this right now, as I say, a formal announcement will be made… I'm afraid both Clyde and Ethan Redfield have recently been killed."

Whatever Oliver had been expecting today's meeting to be about, this was not it. He felt his legs go weak.

"They had gone to Chile…" She picked up another piece of paper and read from it. "Antofagasta, Chile."

A wave of nausea rolled over Oliver. "Wh-wh-what happened?"

"Carjacking." She saw his face pale and gestured to a chair in front of her. "Sit. Please... Are you okay?"

"No, I mean, yes..." Oliver managed to sit down, grateful to get off his feet. "Just... Shocking, I guess." His mind raced. All he could think was that he had told Charlie Smith where the Redfields were going, and now they had been killed. No doubt by Charlie Smith. But at the same time, their blood was on his hands too.

Eve Mendenhall went on. "As I say, keep this to yourself for now. My understanding is that it took the local police a few days to simply identify the bodies. There were no IDs on their remains. But we do have confirmation now."

Oliver managed to nod.

Eve Mendenhall continued. "But I wanted to talk to you because we need to secure Ethan's office email account. No doubt there will be very sensitive information on it that we must protect." When Oliver just numbly stared at her, she added, "My job is to protect this firm."

"Of course," Oliver managed to say, his mind reeling in a thousand different directions.

She continued. "Can you do that? Secure Ethan's email account?"

"We can shut it down."

"No, no. No, I thought of that. But he had his own set of clients, worldwide. We need to keep it active, at least for the next month or so, so we don't miss something from some client, a vendor, what have you."

Oliver considered her request. "I can add a layer of authentication. In this case, we can add your cell phone number. Someone tries to get into his email, an authentication code will be sent to your phone. The person would then need that code to get into the email." He suddenly realized this wouldn't be enough. Charlie Smith had hacked the Steed account. He could no doubt get around a phone verification link. Oliver said, "It would be best however if we also have a second password built in. To do that, you will need to create a password that only you will know... No one, but you." Only this way could Oliver be reasonably sure that Charlie Smith couldn't hack into the account.

She gave this some thought and finally said, "I see. Well, I'll leave it to you then."

Knowing he had been dismissed, Oliver started to rise. Then he sank back in the chair. "And Clyde Redfield, ma'am? He had an in-house email account too."

The look on her face showed that question had clearly caught her unaware. "Yes, yes, of course... So sad... He had been quite ill lately. I don't think he used it very much. But you're correct, of course. We need to lock down his email account too." She gave him a curious look. "You sure you're okay?"

Surrey, England

"Okay, okay, enough," Adam said in surrender. He moved off the road and walked through green landscape. Gretchen followed. They were both wearing athletic running gear with belts for their water bottles and Lycra armbands on their upper arms that held their cell phones. Finally, Adam stopped and put his hands on his knees. "I'm getting old."

"True," she replied. "Still, use it or lose it."

Adam looked up at her and rolled his eyes before plopping down right where he stood. "Distance?"

She fiddled with her watch. "Five miles. Almost. But we'll call it five."

Another roll of the eyes. "Thank you." He stretched out on his back, exhausted.

"You said you wanted to be in better shape. I'm just doing what I normally do. If you can't keep up, no worries on my part." As she settled in next to him, her phone rang. She took it off her armband. "Two."

"Speaker," Adam instructed.

"Maybe this is private," Gretchen retorted. But she put it on speaker. "We're both here. What's up?"

"Just giving you a Chilean update. First, their military has now officially taken over the gold mine," Two said. "They're keeping things quiet, but it has to leak. The mine was shut down due to arsenic, and the world knows about Amsterdam—there are over six hundred dead now, mostly the elderly and people with compromised health. I think word will leak."

"Not necessarily," Adam countered, propping himself up on his elbows. "You could argue that they're being proactive. Making sure the arsenic is under lock and key."

"Yeah, okay, I can see that," Two replied. "Next, Tomás has been upgraded from critical to stable."

"B.S. I had him stable all the way," Adam argued.

After recording the man's testimony, Gretchen had uploaded the videos to Marsha and Hal. Meanwhile, Adam had taken possession of Clyde's and Ethan's wallets and cell phones as well as Ethan's laptop which was found in the Land Rover. Adam had also grabbed the car-rental agreement from the glove box since it contained Ethan Redfield's name. His thinking had been to delay the identification of the bodies for as long as possible.

Adam and Gretchen had then loaded Tomás into the cab of his truck, positioning him on the passenger side of the bench seat. His son climbed in next to him and Gretchen got behind the wheel. Adam followed in the rented SUV, using his cell phone with end-to-end encryption to talk to Hal. His biggest concern was getting out of the country. They didn't need to be answering a ton of questions from Chilean authorities. He said they would get rid of Gretchen's pistol and magazine in two different drops so there wouldn't be any physical evidence linking them to the deaths of Ethan and Clyde Redfield.

As it turned out, Marsha could only get them on a NetJets private charter leaving out of Valparaiso. They would have to drive all night. But that was fine with Adam—it put more distance between them and the gold mine. The flight was going direct to London, and that was also fine with Adam. They could hunker down in the Surrey safe house and figure out what to do about Victoria Tenney. Their main worry was that she would finish what her brother and nephew had started.

The long drive to Valparaiso had allowed them to decompress. Gretchen admitted that she had had no idea that Maximo's father was alive until he struggled to sit up. She just couldn't let Ethan Redfield kill the man, so she had acted. As for Clyde, she hit him in the torso in the hopes that they could possibly question him. Adam would have preferred to also have a chance to question Ethan, but it was what it was. If he had been in the air shaft, he may have done the same thing. Or maybe not. He really didn't know.

Driving to the hospital, Maximo had asked many questions, presuming that Gretchen and Adam were US Army soldiers. So Gretchen had explained that she and Adam worked for Interpol, and then she went on to describe what Interpol was all about.

"Do me a favor," Gretchen had told him. "Be sure to tell the police about the arsenic. We need the mine secured. For all we know, bad guys are coming to get more arsenic, okay?"

"You're not staying?" he had asked, surprised.

"No," Gretchen had said. She knew the boy was upset and gave him a smile. "You'll be fine. Trust me."

Less than two hundred yards from the hospital, Gretchen had pulled over. The emergency-room entrance was clearly indicated with a bright red arrow. "Max, I need you to drive from here, okay?"

The boy had been surprised, but he bravely agreed. Acting older than his years, he had said, "I don't care who you work for. You saved my father's life. I will tell them that you are Interpol if that's what's best."

She had been caught by surprise and managed to smile. "That's the truth, so yes, that's what's best."

She and Adam had watched as Maximo drove the truck to the emergency entrance. He had dashed inside, and moments later, a team of nurses and doctors extracted Tomás from the truck.

Later, they'd found an all-night FedEx office in Valparaiso and sent off the cell phones and laptop.

"Well, whatever," Two said. "He's stable. Next, the police have gone public with the deaths of Ethan and Clyde Redfield, saying it was a carjacking. Took place in town, nothing to do with the mine."

Adam chuckled. "Smart."

"No doubt MI6 is in full agreement," Gretchen added. "They don't want the deaths in Amsterdam attributed to a couple of crazed Brits who bought the mine for its arsenic. Cover it all up as best you can and hold your breath."

"Now, the best news," Two said with some excitement. "Ready?"

"Go for it," Gretchen told her.

"We got everything off Ethan Redfield's computer. And guess what? It looks like the first batch of arsenic, all of it, was used in Amsterdam."

Adam sat up straight. "That's huge! That means Victoria can't do anything. She has no arsenic."

"That's what we're thinking," Two agreed. "But, if you remember, we used Ethan Redfield's phone to tell his troops to stand down and await further instructions so—"

"They'll go to ground when they hear that Ethan Redfield is dead," Adam interrupted.

"Right," Two said.

"Getting a lead on who they are?" Gretchen asked.

"No clue, all burner phones. But Marsha says they got paid somehow, so we have to follow the money. It's a long shot, but maybe we can get a few. Hal says it will be the State Department alerting whoever the local authorities are to deal with them."

With that, they heard Two talking to someone else. Then Marsha came on the line. "Guys?"

"Yep," Adam said. "We're both here."

"Okay," Marsha replied. "Heads up. Oliver just sent a draft email. He says the deaths of Ethan Redfield and his father are on you, and he thinks you're the scum of the earth and on and on."

"Aw, geez," Gretchen sighed.

"He thought he was giving you their itinerary so you could stop them from whatever they were going to do. Not kill them," Marsha said.

"Draft a new email," Adam said. He looked at his watch. "Tell him we'll meet at the same place as before at 1500, today."

"What?" Gretchen retorted.

Adam looked at her. "He's feeling guilty, and I get that. But he needs to grow up and understand the real world."

"Just let him go," Marsha advised.

"Why?" Adam replied. "Because he's served his purpose?"

"In a word, yes."

"Tell him to meet me at the same place. He'll know it. 1500, today."

"He could show up with the police," Two said.

"And what? Implicate himself in the deaths? I don't think so. That's why he's wound up to begin with. Let me talk to him."

"What are you going to say?" Gretchen asked.

~ ~ ~

"What do you want me to say?" Victoria looked from Davenport to Barry and back to Davenport. "I had nothing to do with her death."

The three were sitting outside on the expansive west terrace overlooking the wide grass that seemed to go on forever. Five horses were grazing in the distance. Drinks had been served, and the sun was actually shining for a change, making it seem like the perfect day, although it was far from that.

"As I mentioned on the phone, this is a courtesy call," Davenport said. "Better here than some MI6 office somewhere."

"This is stupid," Victoria bitterly complained. "I didn't tell Hana Vrba to kill Adrian, and I didn't tell some hitman to kill Hana Vrba. This is utter nonsense!"

"Someone very much wanted Hana Vrba dead," Barry said, speaking for the first time. "I was there. No doubt it was a professional hit."

She glared at the man. "And what? I orchestrated it?"

"They're going to say you had motive."

"That's insane... Just insane...To think..." Victoria ran out of words.

Davenport gave Barry a nasty look. "Enough. We're here to see what they have to say, not speculate." He turned to Victoria. "We've got two battlefronts going. One, the police. Right now I don't think they are so concerned with who might have killed Adrian Weatherspoon. They can peg that on Vrba. What they do want to know, however, is who took her out. If nothing else, one of their own was hit. Fortunately, she was wearing a bulletproof vest and she is fine. But it looks bad, if you will."

Victoria turned to him, suddenly furious. "Oh, I see. So, the police couldn't protect someone they arrested, and it looks bad. Read my lips: I had nothing to do with it."

"The other front is MI6," Davenport calmly told her. "Let's put both to rest today, and we're done. Agreed?"

Just then, they were interrupted by Victoria's housemaid opening a French door. "Ma'am. A Miss Paige Willoughby is here."

Still furious, Victoria stood and presented an amiable face, knowing she had to put her best foot forward. "Please have her join us out here."

Her housemaid promptly returned with a woman who appeared to be in her mid-forties with long blonde hair. She wore black slacks, a black shirt, and a tan blazer with tan boots. She carried a file folder in one hand. Davenport and Barry politely rose from their chairs and introductions were made.

After declining any refreshment, the woman sat down and turned her attention to Victoria. "You have my condolences, ma'am."

"Thank you," Victoria replied.

"You've lost a dear friend—"

"A mere acquaintance if you are referring to Hana Vrba," Davenport injected.

The woman looked at him but didn't say anything. Again to Victoria, she added, "And now your brother and nephew."

Victoria nodded. She truly was heartsick about Clyde's and Ethan's deaths, so she didn't need any role playing for that. "All for a car. A stupid, stupid car."

The woman opened her file. "That's the cover story, yes."

Victoria stared, dumbfounded, as Davenport said, "What are you saying? Who's cover story?"

"Done by mutual agreement, if you will," she told Davenport. "The Chilean authorities didn't want the world knowing that the arsenic poisoning the fine people of Amsterdam came from their country." She let the words hang in the air, watching Victoria. "Nor do we want the world to know that the arsenic poisoning the fine people of Amsterdam was from a gold mine owned by one of Britain's wealthiest families."

Victoria and Davenport exchanged looks. But he was at a loss to assist her since this was all news to him.

The woman looked only at Victoria. "What can you tell me about the Diego Gold Mine? Parent company was Diego Properties."

Victoria's heart raced. "I don't understand."

"Your brother and his son were killed at the gold mine seven nights ago, late at night."

"It was a carjacking—"

"They purchased the gold mine through a hedge fund they managed," the woman went on. She looked at a paper in the file. "They purchased large stakes in an interesting array of companies. Mostly firms that handle water treatment, in terms of water-treatment chemicals, water-treatment equipment, basically anything to help purify tainted water." She looked up at Victoria who was now white as a sheet. Referring to the paper, she said, "Other companies they took large positions in included companies like Coca-Cola. Companies with their own water-bottling plants."

Davenport said, "I don't understand what this has to do with—"

"Please," the woman said sternly, cutting him off and giving him a warning look. Davenport stopped, and she turned her attention back to Victoria. "Tell me about this fund. Seems rather focused on water, wouldn't you say? Treating water, providing bottled water to customers…Water, water, water."

"I… I don't really know. I don't pay attention to investments," Victoria managed to reply, her mouth suddenly dry.

"And then you have the gold mine. A gold mine that had produced less and less gold over the years until it got in trouble when arsenic runoff began polluting the water table. And people in a nearby village became quite ill. Later, an earthquake essentially leveled all the buildings except one. The one where your brother and nephew were found murdered."

"What is the point of this?" Davenport boldly asked, finding his voice. "Ms. Tenney is in mourning. This meeting today was simply to get clarification on some things and—"

"And that's exactly what I'm trying to do, get some clarification," she shot back at Davenport. Looking at Victoria, she said, "You do follow, don't you? Your family gets an investor group together, they take huge stakes in various water-treatment and bottled-water companies, and then you buy a gold mine—"

"*I* didn't purchase anything," Victoria rebutted. "*I* don't pay attention to the investment side of things. I told you that." She turned her attention to the horses in the pasture.

"Well, you can see our concern. We have arsenic coming from a gold mine you own, poisoning and killing hundreds—"

"You don't know that!" Davenport thundered. "That's speculation!"

"And we see you and your investors are well positioned to benefit from that poisoning," the MI6 woman continued, ignoring Davenport's outburst. Victoria continued to gaze out on the horse pasture. "Really, all very clever when you think about it. People get ill, everyone thinks COVID. Or a new variety of COVID. They think flu. No one thinks about the water supply. No one. Total genius, really." She waited a beat and then said, "Tell me about Uganda..."

Victoria's head suddenly whirled around, and she stared at the woman.

The woman went on. "You found a small African village in the middle of nowhere in need of running water. And you arranged for them to get it... This was your pet project. And then, what? Six months later, the entire village was dead... Every single person... Two hundred and seventy-eight people, dead. From what? Arsenic." She now looked at a piece of paper from the file. "In fact, the arsenic found in their water was six times the safe level. Six times the proper level."

Victoria sat very still. She could feel everyone's eyes on her. And she had no words of defense. Nothing at all.

The woman went on. "Okay, we'll back up. Who put in that running water? A company headquartered in Dubai called Al-Friqet Industries, or just AFI. And who oversaw the water installation for AFI? A man named Charles Adrian Weatherspoon. A man who had a long-running affair with you. A man who was murdered not too long ago. By a woman, Hana Vrba, who told the police that you told her to do it... And now, she herself is conveniently dead.

"But you know what isn't so convenient? Mr. Weatherspoon created a video in which he describes everything. He wanted it on record. And we now have it."

Chapter Twenty-Four

Surrey, England

Once again, there were only a few customers dining at the Fox Trot Inn in mid-afternoon. Adam had chosen the same table they had first found Oliver and his friends. There was a quasi-psychological reason for this—studies have shown that when a person repeatedly sat at the same restaurant table or the same seat on a public bus or in the same seat in a classroom, they felt a great deal more comfortable within that environment. Adam had wanted Taylor Brohm and Oliver Gamble to feel comfortable.

But of course, they weren't. They were both stiff as a board.

Taylor gestured to Adam's iPhone on the table, face down and secretly recording the conversation. "You get to keep your phone?"

"My meeting, my rules," Adam told her. Hal had vehemently argued against the meeting, but Adam was determined to have it, so he had agreed to Hal's safety measures. First, both Taylor and Oliver—and Freddy if he came along—had to be checked for wires. Second, Gretchen would hold their phones, car keys, wallet and purse at a nearby table. Third, Adam would record the conversation.

When Oliver and Taylor had arrived and approached the table, Adam had stood and explained that they would have to be checked for wires. When Oliver balked, Adam had sat back down. "Then go back to London. We're done."

Finally, Oliver and Taylor had given in. Gretchen took Taylor to the ladies' room and made sure she had no wire or weapon. Adam did the same with Oliver. Then Gretchen had gathered up their personal items and left them alone. She now sat across the room, nursing a lemonade and keeping an eye on them.

Oliver glared at Adam. "I think you are a despicable man. You killed two people in cold blood. You could have just told the police. You didn't need to kill them."

Adam looked at Oliver. "My meeting, my rules, okay?"

"You're despicable!" Oliver repeated.

Adam waited a bit. "Done?"

"I know what you want," Oliver said. "You want Ethan's and Clyde's email information. I'm supposed to give it to you. But I can't. It's been locked up tight."

"We don't need it," Adam calmly replied. "But thanks for thinking of us."

Taken by surprise, Oliver asked, "What do you mean, you don't need it?"

"My rules means that I have the floor. You listen and then you can call me names. Or I leave right now. It's up to you," Adam said.

Oliver and Taylor exchanged looks. Finally, Oliver gave a slight nod in agreement. Behind Oliver, an older woman came in and took a seat. She reached into her tote bag and removed a bottled water, placing it on the table. Fortunately, she was too far away to hear anything being said at their table.

"So, first thing you need to know is that Clyde Redfield was nuts about overpopulation. He talked freely about the fact that overpopulation was going to do us all in, ruin the planet and so on. Years ago, he started a group called the Sustainable Growth Syndicate to advocate for population control. He and other liked-minded wealthy people put a lot of money into his global initiative." Adam said. "Google it. I'm not making this up."

"So what?" Oliver said angrily.

"So, if that's your mindset, it's helpful to have a catastrophic event that kills lots of people and maybe you get the world population down to wherever you think it should be in your sick little head. Nuclear war will do the trick, but if you don't have access to said weapon, it's kind of hard to pull the trigger." Adam removed a small piece of paper from his breast pocket. He put it on the table in front of Oliver.

A waitress appeared and Adam said, "Non-alcoholic beer." He looked at the others, but they declined. The waitress left.

"What's this?" Oliver asked, unfolding the paper.

"You need to look at the Steed holdings. Lots of companies that do water treatment, help in terms of cleaning up dirty drinking water, and lots of companies that produce bottled water." He nodded behind Oliver. "Lady that just came in, no doubt eating something from here, but look at that. She brought her own water..."

They both turned and looked. The woman was oblivious to their stares.

Adam went on. "She is frightened now, given the news about Amsterdam, so she brings her own bottled water. Think she did that just a few weeks ago? I doubt it. So who benefits? The companies that produce bottled water. The age-old rule, follow the money."

Adam pointed to the paper. "Steed has holdings in those companies. Why? Because they wanted to create a disaster—in this case, water poisoning on a massive, worldwide scale—and then have a solution too. Introducing high levels of arsenic into municipal water supplies is the liquid solution to overpopulation, and investing millions of dollars in firms that do water cleanup, water treatment, and produce bottled water is the financial solution. A nice win-win scenario."

"Why was Amsterdam the target?" Taylor inquired. "I would think they would hit New York City. San Francisco. London."

"You remember the names I gave you?" Adam asked. "One was Hans Wolter."

"Died of cancer, I checked," Oliver argued.

"Yes, but his daughter lives in the neighborhood first hit with the arsenic. She was in critical condition for a while. And I can tell you that Clyde Redfield pulled the trigger on her neighborhood early because he wanted her to be one of the first to die."

"Why?" Taylor asked, puzzled.

"He thought he had an ally in Hans Wolter. A man who understood the world-population problem. He was one of the first investors in Steed. You can look. But then, he learned what was really going on. He found out that Redfield was going to create some sort of catastrophe and lots of people would die. He wanted out. Clyde wouldn't let him out.

"So Hans talked to Bart Werner, his vicar's nephew, who worked at Red Arrow. Bart started to do some digging. He brought in his friend William DeWine who tried to warn authorities. Although he was killed in the café bombing, I'm not sure how much he knew. The water and arsenic? I don't think he knew quite that much. But he knew who was behind the coming disaster. All the investors wanted stringent world-population control. He did know that much. We're guessing Bart wanted government oversight on the fund so their plan could be stopped."

The waitress brought Adam his beer and he took a long sip.

"We will probably never know what happened, but Ethan Redfield found out about DeWine. He personally took the backpack to the café and blew it up."

Oliver and Taylor exchanged looks.

"Meanwhile, Bart was building a chart of who was who with the investors. As you know, not anyone could look at the Steed files. Who the investors were, what they were investing in. But there was chatter within the company among different brokers, and he was tracking it as best he could. And he befriended Clyde's sister, Victoria Tenney. She liked younger attractive men and he fit the bill.

"Again, we don't know everything, although at the time of his death, he had befriended Mac Senton, his half-brother, and they worked on figuring it out. They must have had enough of the pieces of the puzzle that Mac Senton decided to go all in. He befriended Clyde Redfield, posing as a nutcase on world population. He managed to convince Clyde to allow him a leave of absence while he helped orchestrate the plan."

"And he died," Taylor said quietly.

"Clyde or Ethan, I happen to think Ethan, didn't trust him. He knew that Mac's one weakness was his young daughter. He made sure Mac knew that if he talked, his daughter would be killed. So Mac took himself out of the picture rather than be put in that position."

Again, Adam pointed toward the paper. "See Diego Gold Mine? A defunct gold mine, not producing gold anymore and Ethan scoops it up. Why? Because the gold mine got in trouble for arsenic runoff in the waterways. Arsenic is often found in gold, and you have to strip it away to have the gold. You can Google this too. It's a common problem for gold mines. So Diego no longer had gold, but it had arsenic."

Studying the paper, Oliver suddenly looked up, stunned. "The gold mine is in Antofagasta, Chile."

Startled, Taylor grabbed the paper to see for herself.

"But Clyde and Ethan ran into a problem trying to reduce the planet's population," Adam told them. "A man who works at the mine, he found out that the arsenic being removed was for nefarious reasons. To hurt people in Europe. So he told Ethan that he moved the arsenic, for safe keeping. He thought the new owner of the mine would be happy. Keep things safe. He didn't know who Ethan really was."

"That's why Ethan went down there?" Oliver asked.

"And he ran into trouble."

Oliver glared. "You. You killed him."

"Actually, no, I didn't." He put up his right hand. "Swear to God. But if you ask me if it bothers me that Ethan and Clyde Redfield were stopped before they could poison half the world—poison innocent men, women, and children in Europe, America, Australia, Indonesia, and so on... Does it bother me that they were killed? Truthfully, no."

There was silence for some time. Then Taylor pointed to a line of text on the paper. "What's this? I can't pronounce it. In Uganda?"

"That you can Google too. A tiny village got running water for the first time ever. It was put in by Adrian Weatherspoon's firm—"

"The man who stole Victoria Tenney's laptop," Oliver said, cutting him off.

"No, no," Adam corrected. "She *thought* he stole it. So yeah, she had him killed."

"By a woman from Serbia," Taylor said. "And then she was killed at a courthouse in London."

"Very good," Adam commended her. "So back to Weatherspoon... I should say, he was a good guy, just for the record. He put in the water system for a small village in Uganda, having no idea that it was a test run for how much arsenic to use. The villagers—to a man—died from water poisoning.

"Two hundred and seventy-eight villagers in central Uganda. Dead from arsenic water poisoning. Last I checked, nearly eight hundred in Amsterdam have died. And that was *with* the authorities learning pretty quickly about what was wrong and addressing the problem. Imagine if it had taken them longer to figure out it was a tainted water supply... Remember, you can't taste it; you can't smell it. It's really the most perfect chemical weapon.

"Imagine if Clyde hadn't been so eager to kill off Hans Wolter's daughter... Imagine the entire world experiencing massive arsenic poisoning all at the same time. Or within weeks of each other... Imagine how many dead then... Imagine if one man in Chile hadn't tried to hide where the arsenic was... And imagine if you hadn't been brave enough to tell us where Ethan and Clyde were going... It's estimated that hundreds of thousands, probably millions, would be dead or dying right now."

With tears in her eyes, Taylor reached for Oliver's hand and squeezed it. Adam pushed back his chair and stood. Gretchen immediately came over with their personal effects.

Adam took one last sip of beer and looked to Oliver. "Turn over the paper, and you'll see a number. It just goes to voicemail, but here's the thing... Freddy sort of intrigues me. What he says he can do with someone's phone. If he ever wants to discuss a new job, tell him to leave a message."

FROG Headquarters, The Hague

Hal stood at the head of the conference table, watching the American news channel C-SPAN2 on the large television. The door opened and Marsha came in, carrying her laptop. She glanced at the screen. A large bald man was sitting behind a table and speaking into a microphone.

"What's this?" Marsha asked.

"CIA director testifying before the US Senate." When Marsha frowned, clearly confused, he added, "Appropriations time. In a nutshell, the CIA is giving all the reasons they need more money."

She finally got it and grinned. "Let me guess. They miraculously uncovered the plot to poison the drinking water of the people in Amsterdam. A plot that could have gone worldwide. They can't discuss how they learned anything, that's top secret, but needless to say, they should be rewarded with lots and lots of funding."

"You got it." He looked back at the television and shook his head. "Hypocritical jackals."

"We didn't have much of a choice, you know," Marsha reminded him. "The scope of this was just huge. We needed a very large spy apparatus to take the credit. Besides, we did share. MI6 got the Adrian Weatherspoon videos, so we spread the wealth a bit." When he didn't respond, she added, "We did discuss it."

"I know, I know." Hal bitterly gestured toward the television. "He sits there testifying under oath, and he has no idea how the largest case in a decade just landed in his lap, yet he'll sure sit there and take all the credit he can. That's what kills me. They all lie so easily."

"Think he'll get more than sixty million, US?" Marsha asked.

He turned with surprise and then smiled. "Point taken." Having Ethan Redfield's laptop and phone well before anyone knew the man was dead, she'd moved all his cash—more than sixty million—through various banks until it ended up with FROG, nice and clean. A huge windfall that would sustain FROG for a very long time.

"Just be glad you don't have to answer to politicians like that," Marsha said. "Elizabeth contacted us. Wants to talk to you. Video if we can."

Hal agreed. "Can't be any worse than watching this crap."

Three minutes later, the image of the CIA director was replaced by Elizabeth. She smiled. "Hi there."

"How are you?" Hal asked.

Elizabeth came right to the point. "Well, you'll tell me it's none of my business, but... What happened in Amsterdam? That was what Steed was all about wasn't it?"

"I wouldn't say no to that line of thinking," Hal hedged.

"I saw that Clyde and Ethan Redfield were killed in a carjacking."

"That's right."

She looked a bit awkward. "In Chile, in the same city where that gold mine is located. I mean, that's not a coincidence, right?"

Hal sighed. "I really wouldn't be able to say."

Elizabeth gave a tight smile.. She undoubtedly knew how this game was played. After some hesitation, she said, "So if they were in charge of Steed and they're dead... Does that mean I'm safe? I mean, really safe?"

"I'd say so, yes," Hal responded encouragingly, silently rebuking himself that he hadn't thought to reach out to her. Instead, she had called him. Still, at least she was getting good news.

"And that man who hurt me, the man who shattered my ankle—"

"His days of hurting people are over, be assured of that," Hal interrupted.

Elizabeth pressed on. "What about Victoria Tenney? We know she wanted Adrian Weatherspoon dead... And she got her way... She might want me dead."

"That was personal. She thought Weatherspoon stole her laptop, so she got her revenge. The brains of the business side of things, the ones that hired the man who came after you? As you know, they're both dead."

Another long pause. "So I'm safe? Honest? I'm safe?"

"You're safe," Hal assured her.

Tears of relief suddenly streamed down her face. "You know what's funny? I'm a New Yorker through and through. And now? I mean, I told my husband, what if we just stay here? Not in this Airbnb, obviously. But someplace like this? Might be healthier for all of us, and the kids like it. Going outside. Not out on a high-rise balcony with so much plexiglass that they'll never fall, but just outside. Play outside. In the fresh air. Run around and be kids, you know?"

"What's Goldman going to say?" Hal asked.

"If I get the work done and use video calls like this, they're okay with it."

"Sounds like a plan, Elizabeth. A good plan."

She wiped a tear and smiled. "You do have to give me some credit for one thing, you know."

"Yeah? What's that?"

"I said it was the flip side of the same coin. Steed has made good money from this. I don't know if you've been paying attention, but Dupont is helping with the cleanup and they're up more than nineteen percent. An astonishing amount. Unheard of. And all the companies that manufacture bottled water? They're up through the roof. People all over the world are suddenly buying a ton of bottled water. Hoarding bottled water. Even here, in the US. My husband, he can't buy enough bottled water. So I did call it."

"You did indeed. You did indeed," Hal said with a generous smile. Then he grew solemn. "Elizabeth, truly you were a huge help. So thank you."

She nodded. "You guys saved my life, so the thanks goes both ways, believe me." She started to tear up again. Thanks for talking to me. I just wanted to know that I'm safe. Finally."

"You are. So enjoy your family and live a good life."

She was smiling and crying at the same time when they disconnected.

Surrey, England

"We could be here all night," Gretchen complained.

"You're hungry," Adam said.

Gretchen lowered her binoculars. "Am not."

"We have pretzels and whatever those nuts are that you bought," Adam reminded her.

"Almonds. They're called almonds."

"Well, eat a few, and you'll feel better."

"I'm not hungry," Gretchen argued.

"You are always snippy when you're hungry."

Gretchen mumbled something under her breath and kept watching. A few minutes later, she realized he was right. She was hungry. How could he read her so well? She grabbed the bag of almonds from the back seat, opened the bag, and popped a few in her mouth.

Their rental car was off of the street by a good ten yards and under a large tree. Gretchen put the bag of almonds on the hood of the car and propped herself against the driver's door, resting her elbows on the car roof. Stakeouts, no matter how they appeared in the movies, were a terrible bore. Although, she had to admit that the view of the manor was actually breathtaking. The sun had just started to set, and a few lights could be seen on inside. Unfortunately for them, the garages were on the other side of the house, closer to the barn, so they wouldn't see anyone leaving until they got past the west side of the manor, leaving them with little prep time.

But there hadn't been much of an alternative. A few hours ago, Marsha had sent over a recording picked up on the microphone in Victoria's office. Unfortunately, Victoria had been talking to someone on the phone, so they only got her side of the conversation, and even that seemed to cut in and out. The bits they had for sure were, "Thames Ditton, houseboat, freighter and tonight."

Victoria Tenney was going to make a run for it. Unfortunately, no matter how many times Marsha played it back and enhanced the audio, nothing else gave them solid footing upon which to act, hence, they had no choice but to wait at the end of her long drive. "Don't let her leave home, don't pass let her pass GO, and don't let her collect two hundred dollars," Adam had quipped.

Headlights appeared around the edge of the manor. "Notify Two," Adam told her.

Victoria's thoughts had been a million miles away when she finally noticed that a vehicle was blocking the end of the drive and stomped on the brakes, bringing her full-size Volvo sport utility to an abrupt stop. A woman wearing a ballcap had the car's bonnet up and gave her a sheepish wave. Victoria cursed under her breath and lowered her window. The woman hurried over. "So, so sorry," she said. "Going out, are you?"

Victoria had to hold her tongue. "If you can just move your car please."

"Oh, if I could, yeah, but that's just it! Bloody car just stopped dead." A cockney accent. The woman was working-class, no doubt. She gestured toward the broken-down vehicle. "Just died on me, it did."

Victoria couldn't care less about the damn car. "Look—" she started.

Suddenly the woman held a gun to her head. "Put it in park."

Victoria froze.

"Now! Put it in park!" the woman demanded, the Cockney accent gone.

Victoria did as she was told.

"Not so hard, was it?" the woman said as she reached inside and pressed the button to unlock the doors. In one fluid movement, the woman opened the door and reached across her, knocking the rearview off kilter and grabbing her cell phone from the console.

"Hey!" Victoria protested as the rear door opened and someone slid in behind her. She started to reach for her seat belt when suddenly something was drawn across her throat, pulling her firmly back against the car's headrest. The seat belt forgotten, she desperately tried to grasp whatever was across her throat. It wasn't sharp, like a knife. It was something soft and slippery. Fabric? Whatever it was, it was holding her head tight against the headrest.

"Stop! Please stop!" she managed to say as panic set in. She instinctively looked into the rearview mirror to see who was behind her, but it only showed the passenger footwell. "I have money!"

As the restraint slowly tightened across her throat, she tried to pull it off, but the woman standing at her door seized one wrist, then the other, and her hands were swiftly locked in plastic restraints before she even realized what was happening. The woman was quite strong and forced Victoria's arms down to her lap where she looped another plastic restraint around the bottom of the steering wheel. Her heart raced as she realized that between the seat belt, her neck pinned to the headrest and her hands tied, she was powerless to do anything.

Then she remembered—her phone! Did the woman toss it? Turn it off? If not, the car was still running, so it would still be connected to the Bluetooth! All she had to do was hit the call button on the steering wheel and say *Call 999*. Help would come.

Victoria casually rested her hands on the bottom of the steering wheel. She found the call button near her left hand and pressed it. On the dash, she saw the green phone button activated. She quickly yelled, "Call—!!!"

Adam instantly covered Victoria Tenney's mouth with his hand. He kept his hand firmly over her mouth for a good minute. Too hard, he knew. But he was angry. That had been close. Too damn close. Gretchen quickly turned off the car's ignition, disconnecting the Bluetooth. They exchanged looks. They had been over every angle. Or so they had thought. He finally removed his hand, wiping his palm on the plush leather upholstery.

"A few questions," he told Victoria. "Then you can go."

"I don't talk to—"

Adam tightened the silk scarf, cutting off her airway. She started to cough. He leaned forward. "Easy or hard. It's up to you. Easy is a few minutes' time, you talk to us, you can go, got it?"

Victoria nodded and he released the tension, easing the pain on her throat. He knew she desperately wanted to touch her throat, an instinctive reaction, but her hands were bound to the steering wheel. Gretchen was now standing near the road, checking both directions.

"Tell me about the bombing at an Israeli café. The Kadi Café."

Victoria's mind scrambled. What kind of question was that? And more important, who were these people?

Her first thought was that they knew that she was linked to the fiasco in Amsterdam and had come for revenge. Then, when she realized they were professionals, she thought they were hired by Ethan and wanted their money. But asking about the Kadi Café?

The woman was now watching the road. Were more people coming? Were they going to kill her? Or was the woman worried about a passerby? She could have told the woman it was a waste of time to think someone would come along. There was only one home past hers on this road and the owners were never there, preferring to stay in Winnipeg. Heaven knows why.

Suddenly the clamp on her throat tightened again. She struggled to free her hands, but she was helplessly tied.

"Easy or hard, easy or hard," the man whispered in her ear. "Your choice." The tension eased. "Kadi Café?"

She closed her eyes. "It was Clyde. All Clyde. Stupid, but he was angry."

"Go on," the man said.

"He wanted revenge. Clyde did. A man named Eli Yanni. He screwed Clyde over in a deal. Don't ask what, I don't know. I swear."

"Eli Yanni own the café?"

"No, no. He went there. Every single morning. Got his coffee and pastry. I guess you could set a clock by him. Eight-ten. Every morning. Same café. Same time, to the minute."

"Nothing more than that? No politics?"

"I don't think so. I think it was some financial scheme."

"What financial scheme?" the man asked.

"I don't know. Easy money for Clyde, but the man didn't have it. Or said the deal fell apart. I don't know."

"The C-4?"

She tried to shake her head but couldn't. "I don't know what you're talking about." She saw the woman put an earbud in her ear. She was making a phone call.

"Explosive," the man said. "C-4 is a powerful explosive. It was going to be used to blow up the Israeli café."

Now she got it. "Army. US Army. Don't ask, I don't know. Ethan knew some man who worked at an airbase… I think in Germany. He could skim off some from time to time."

"American?"

"I presume. He's on that base. Has access."

"Ethan took more than he gave Hamas for the bombing that didn't happen. More than he needed to blow up the café in Amsterdam, more than he needed to blow up his cowboy hat. Where's the rest?"

Victoria's heart pounded. Who was this man? He knew everything. How could that be? Unnerved, she replied honestly. "I swear, I don't know."

The man quickly went on. "How did the bombing get leaked? Authorities stopped it from a tip. A leak on your end. Who leaked it?"

"Ethan. Always Ethan. He drinks…" Victoria sighed. "He *did* drink."

"What's next? Amsterdam is done. What cities get the arsenic?"

"I don't…" He pulled the restraint so tight, she thought she was going to choke to death.

"Easy or hard," the man said, his hot breath on her neck. "Tell me the truth. What cities are next?"

"None," she managed to say. "They used the first batch on Amsterdam. Ethan went to get more, but…" her voice trailed off.

"But he died."

"Who did he hire for the operation?" the man asked.

"I don't know. I swear to you."

Adam believed her. He saw that Gretchen was coming back. Their eyes met and he nodded. He was done questioning her for the time being. With the driver's door still open, Gretchen came up and placed Victoria's cell phone near her bound hands. "Unlock it."

Victoria just glared. Gretchen swiped the phone. "It wants your fingerprint. Do it right or I'll break each one until this unlocks."

Victoria gave in and placed her left thumb on the phone. It unlocked and Gretchen said, "Which one? Royal Bank of Scotland?"

"What are you doing?" Victoria nervously asked.

"Moving some money around," Adam told her. He could see her visibly stiffen. She wasn't happy. "You know what kind of people I hate? I hate anyone who would wipe out an entire African village."

"That wasn't me," Victoria nervously said.

"Yes it was."

"It was Adrian Weatherspoon."

"Really?" Adam asked. "Then why did you kill him?"

She stiffened as Gretchen came back. "Here's the deal," Gretchen said. "You're going to give me the username and password for—"

"I don't have it, not off the top of my head," Victoria said.

Adam tightened the scarf as hard as he could. She gagged, her arms desperately trying to move, her legs kicking in the footwell.

"Time," Gretchen told him. When he didn't relent, she repeated, "Time. Now."

Adam finally released the pressure. Victoria gasped, taking deep breaths. He leaned forward again. "Easy or hard, it's up to you... Got it?"

She promptly bobbed her head.

"Login for Royal Bank of Scotland," Gretchen said.

Victoria grudgingly gave it up, and Gretchen repeated it to Two at FROG Headquarters.

"Password?" Gretchen asked.

Again, Victoria gave it up. It took just seconds, and there was an audible ding on Victoria's phone.

"Got it," Gretchen said, stepping away from the vehicle as she rattled off the six-digit verification code. So far, so good. They had known that logging into the bank account with an unknown IP address would trigger the verification authorization on her phone. Although they could have avoided that step by using Victoria's phone to look at the bank account, Hal wanted FROG to do it if possible. Adam had a hunch they were going to keep it open for a while. See all her transactions, copy much of it, and then start moving money around.

"You know why we wanted that bank?" Adam whispered in her ear.

She could feel the man's hot breath on her neck again. "Because that's the bank where you put Adrian Weatherspoon's money. Remember? You wrote him a check, he deposited it electronically, but then you had Ethan move it back to your bank the next day."

Her mind raced. How did this man know so much.

He went on. "So now, we're putting it back where it belongs... Know why? Because he had a niece. Did you know that? I kind of think she should inherit all his assets. Including the assets you so greedily stole... Stealing isn't nice, wouldn't you agree?"

She didn't dare answer the man.

"Tell me about Nancy Ellison."

Victoria couldn't help but flinch.

"Truth, or I can strangle you," he said. "I don't really care which way this goes."

"She was dating a man from Red Arrow," Victoria quickly told him. "He left Red Arrow to help Clyde when the cancer became too onerous. Not in the office, per se, but..."

"The arsenic and all that," the man said knowingly.

"Yes. He was helping Clyde and Ethan."

"So he dated a race-car driver. Why kill her?"

"Clyde didn't like loose ends."

"And she was talking to Interpol."

She flinched again, instinctively looking to the rearview mirror, but she couldn't see the man.

"Talk to me!" the man said, suddenly angry.

"Yes, she was being questioned by Interpol."

"So you had her killed."

Victoria didn't answer. Suddenly the restraint tightened across her neck.

"Talk to me…"

She gasped for breath for what seemed like an eternity. Finally, the pressure eased.

"Talk to me…" the man repeated.

Finding it hard to breathe, she said, "Her manager called me… I told Clyde what was going on…That Interpol was talking to her about Mac…. He told Ethan to get rid of her."

Epilogue

The Hague, Holland ~ Three Weeks Later

Returning from the restroom, Adam stopped at a nearby table to retrieve his half-filled non-alcoholic beer and take in the scene. It was chaos, but a nice chaos. It had been a long time since he had been a part of such a thing. He watched as Marsha and Nathan's two children, along with Two, sprawled themselves on the Twister mat in a variety of awkward positions. Adam had a rudimentary grasp of the game—the spinner would land on one of four colors that denoted a specific hand or foot and the players had to try to position themselves on the correct color spot without getting too tangled up and falling down. Marsha's husband was having fun slowly calling out the next combination.

"Yellow... Right..." Nathan slowly read off.

"Say it!" his daughter screamed, laughing as she held an ungainly position.

"Call it, Papa!" said the boy.

"Yellow right foot!" Nathan quickly announced.

The three players scrambled to find a yellow spot for their right foot. Two barely got her foot where it needed to be, but she had to contort herself into a pretzel to keep it there. Meanwhile, the boy was leaning against her in order to maintain his balance, making Two laugh hysterically.

Nearby, Hal and Marsha were at a game table, setting up a Monopoly board—a game Adam couldn't remember the last time he played... As a kid, perhaps? There was already quite a bit of cash in an empty wine glass for the winner.

The entire evening had been Two's idea. She felt that they deserved a fun night out. Marsha knew of this place—a rather large restaurant just outside of town, with several small cottages available for private celebrations such as birthdays, family reunions, bridal showers, and the like. A waitstaff from the restaurant served dinner and drinks, and after that, you could have your own private party, shooting pool, playing Ping Pong, or playing one of the many board games available. One of the kids had found the Twister game on a shelf, and that was all they needed.

"You're next," Gretchen told him.

He turned, surprised to see her there. He really had been lost in the moment. "Might be dangerous. I might pull something."

"I thought I had gotten you into shape," she teased. She studied him. "This was a good idea, you have to admit."

"Terrific," Adam agreed. "Just terrific."

Technically, it went against whatever might have been drawn up decades ago in the FROG operations manual. Back then, the worry was that if operators socialized, they might become lax. As decades passed, such stringent rules were bent bit by bit. The comradery among operators proved to be a value, not a hindrance. But usually, such social events simply meant a nice supper out. Nothing that included spouses and children. And nothing quite as entertaining as this.

"Red... Left... Foot!" Nathan called out.

The players scrambled, with Two reaching so far with her left foot that she went down in a heap, laughing with joy.

"Two remaining players," Nathan announced. "Hold your position...I will spin..."

"Hurry!" the girl said anxiously, giggling.

"We deserve this," Gretchen told him. "It breaks all the old rules, but this time, we deserve to have some joy for a change."

"No arguments here," he said taking a sip of his beer.

After they had successfully gotten into Victoria Tenney's bank account, and she had answered all of Adam's questions, he had silently slipped from the back seat and planted a tracker under the rear of her car. He had then gone back to the rental car. Gretchen had patiently waited as he lowered the bonnet and had driven off. Only then did she remove the scarf that bound Victoria's neck to the headrest and cut off the plastic restraints. Victoria rubbed her wrists. To give themselves time for a good head start, Gretchen had lobbed Victoria's cell phone into the car's cargo area and tossed the car keys further up the driveway. Victoria had watched all this without saying a word. Not one word.

"We're done, Ms. Tenney," Gretchen told her and then casually jogged away.

Minutes later, she caught up with Adam. As soon as she hopped into the car, she heard Two's voice on Adam's speakerphone. "Not moving..."

"She has to retrieve her cell phone and the keys. Give her a minute," Gretchen had said. Adam drove within the speed limit, keeping his eye on the rearview mirror. "Then again, she just might decide to stay home. I would."

"She's making her run," Adam assured them. He glanced at Gretchen. "How far you toss the keys?"

"Thirty yards, max," she said defensively. "They're in plain sight."

"Okay, vehicle is moving," Two told them. "Vehicle is moving."

Once again, they had handed MI6 a nicely wrapped package as agents were waiting for Victoria when she drove to the village of Thames Ditton where a houseboat had been waiting for her. She was immediately taken into custody. In her small suitcase, they found a valid Canadian passport. The woman was resourceful, no doubt about that.

Snooping on their internal communications, Marsha later learned that even though the spy agency had Adrian Weatherspoon's videos implicating Victoria Tenney for the poisoning of a rural African village—one of the first gift's FROG had sent their way—politics had raised its ugly head. The agency had done their due diligence by sending an MI6 agent to interview Victoria at her home and with her attorneys present. After that, any thought of taking it to the next level was put on hold. In a nutshell, Victoria Tenney had close ties to several high-level MPs, and MI6 didn't want to upset the applecart by having the politicians screaming mad. Angry politicians weren't good for business.

It really was that simple.

Finally, it was decided that Victoria should at least relinquish her passport. Which she did. Thus, the matter could be tabled for a bit while everyone thought how best to handle things.

But once FROG overheard her part of a conversation about leaving the country from Thames Ditton, they had forced MI6's hand by spilling the beans. The truth was, MI6 knew they had been completely in the dark until the "CIA" had shared information, so they really couldn't ignore the tip about her unauthorized departure. If nothing else, they needed to be seen as cooperating with their closest ally.

And so they had agents on the scene at Thames Ditton ready to pounce. Adam and Gretchen had watched from their parked car, relishing the sight of Victoria Tenney in handcuffs.

Marsha had found other communications that revealed that the MI6 brass wanted to keep all things Redfield (and that included all things Victoria Tenney) under wraps. It was just a week later that the media reported that Victoria Tenney had gone to a clinic in Switzerland for rest under a doctor's supervision after the horrific killings of her brother and nephew in Chile. In truth, she was still in London under lock and key, and with any luck, singing like a canary in the hope that she would actually end up at a clinic in Switzerland rather than a prison cell. But time would tell on that.

"Blue, we have blue…" Nathan slowly revealed.

"Papa!" the boy urged, laughing.

"Blue, right hand," Nathan swiftly announced, and the kids twisted to find the right color.

Gretchen's cell phone chimed. She looked at it and said, "Cousins coming for a visit." She started to text a reply.

Just beyond the game of Twister, Adam saw William DeWine, Bart Werner, and Mac Senton gathered together and laughing. Each of the three men held a beer bottle and all were clearly enjoying the festivities. Mac suddenly looked right at him from across the room. Their eyes locked, and Mac raised his beer in a silent toast.

Adam raised his beer in return. "Cheers, mate," he said under his breath. "We got the bastards. Thanks to you…. So, well done, boys… Well done…"

"What?" Gretchen asked, distracted as she slipped the phone in her pocket. "What was that?"

But Adam didn't respond. She could see he seemed to be engrossed in the Twister game, but it was over now.

"Adam?" Gretchen said. "Ready?"

Finally, he turned and gave her a baffled look.

She cast a glance across the room.

Adam followed her look. Everyone was now gathered around the game table, and Marsha was laughing and beckoning them on. Her kids were animated, hanging all over her, probably telling her about the Twister game.

"Let's go," Gretchen said.

Adam looked back past the abandoned Twister game.

The dead men were gone.

If you'd like to check out another team of operatives, try M.H. Sargent's nine-book CIA MP-5 series listed below.

Seven Days From Sunday, Book One
The Shot To Die For, Book Two
Operation Spider Web, Book Three
The Yemen Connection, Book Four
Alliance of Evil, Book Five
The Birdwatchers, Book Six
A Containable Incident, Book Seven
Ghost Gathering, Book Eight
The Rapier, Book Nine

Also by M.H. Sargent:
Toward Night's End

M.H. Sargent would love to hear your
comments on this book.
You can write to the author at mh.sargent@hotmail.com

Made in the USA
Monee, IL
28 January 2024

52529622R00193